D1742627

# FAR REMOVED

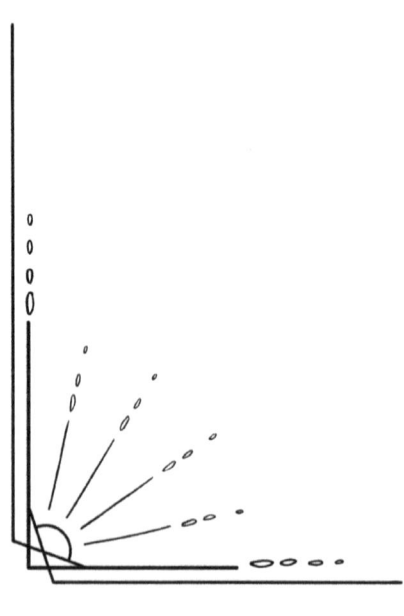

# FAR REMOVED

## BOOK I IN THE APIDECCA DUOLOGY

# C B LANSDELL

COE
BOOKS

*Far Removed: Book 1 of the Apidecca Duology*

To request permissions, please visit the contact page of the publisher's website: https://cblansdell.com/contact/

First Printing 2023 / Printed and bound on demand internationally

Hardcover ISBN: 978-0-6397-7039-0

Paperback ISBN: 978-0-6397-7040-6

Ebook ISBN: 978-0-6397-7041-3

Editor: Jonathan Oliver

Proofreader: Laura Soppelsa

Typesetter: Phillip Gessert

Cover and Interior illustrations: Coe B Lansdell

# CONTENTS

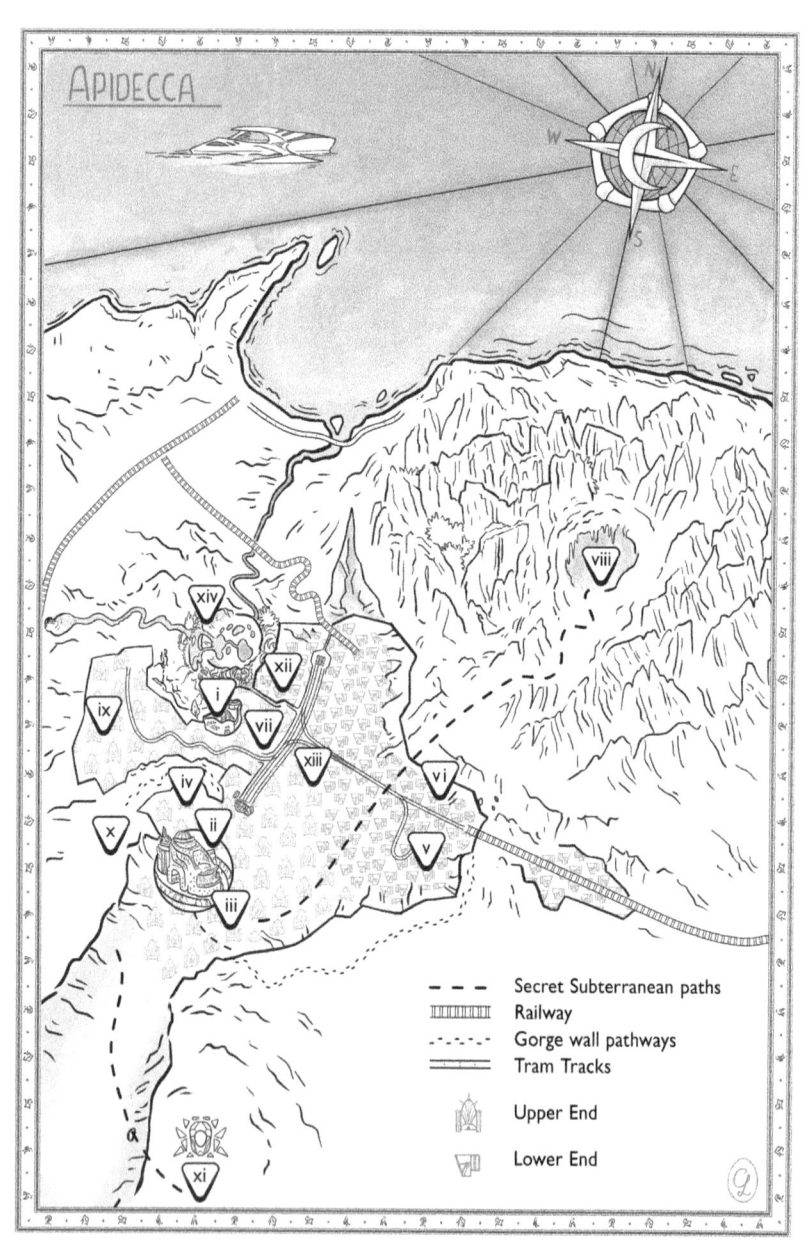

APIDECCA

Secret Subterranean paths
Railway
Gorge wall pathways
Tram Tracks

Upper End

Lower End

*Map Key:*

i. Emisrian College
ii. Assembly Chambers
iii. Servants' Quarters
iv. Ancient stairway
v. Gilstren
vi. Industrial District
vii. Traditional Quarter
viii. Large Coastal Cavern
ix. Lepotra District
x. Villas of the Erudean Pentarchy
xi. Possible Road to the Guild
xii. Dolna District
xiii. Light-phase Market
xiv. Crater Gardens

*Knyadrea, a large moon, does not rotate on its own axis but is tidally locked to the planet around which it orbits. It is for this reason that early knyads named the planet Axis. The chemical composition of Axis's atmosphere renders it unable to support complex life as its moons do. Further out in orbit is Dryadene, Axis's second moon.*

*Units of time mentioned throughout this book include segments, phases and revolutions. More information on this subject can be found in the appendix at the end.*

## 1st KNYADREAN REVOLUTION

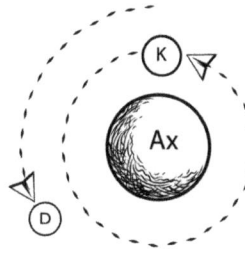

## 2nd KNYADREAN REVOLUTION

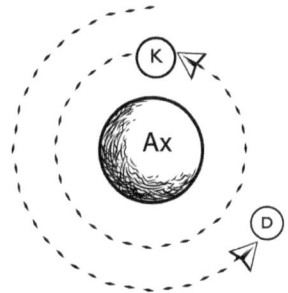

## 3rd KNYADREAN REVOLUTION
## 1st DRYADENEAN REVOLUTION

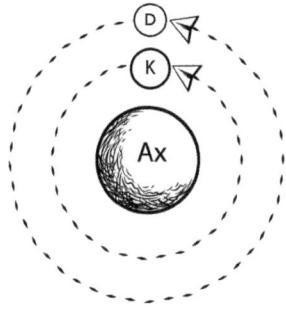

KEY:
K: Knyadrea
Ax: Axis
D: Dryadene

*Knyadrea and Dryadene have an orbital resonance of 1:3. For every revolution around Axis that Knyadrea completes, Dryadene completes ⅓ of a revolution.*

## Content Advisory

This book contains science fiction and horror literary conventions. Sensitive readers might find some descriptions of visuals and events disturbing. A detailed list of warnings can be found after the link:

https://cblansdell.com/books/content-warning/

To Paul, a calming influence, ecology consultant and fine brother.

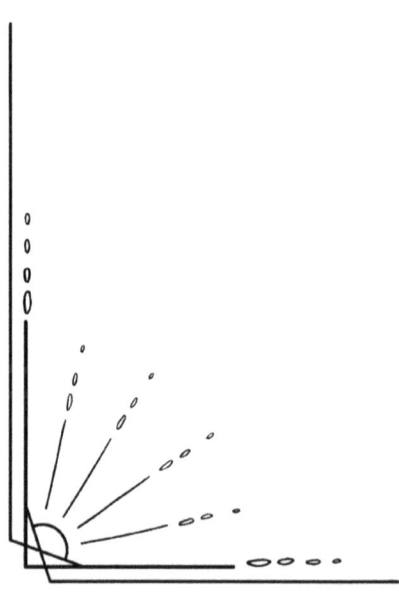

# CHAPTER 1

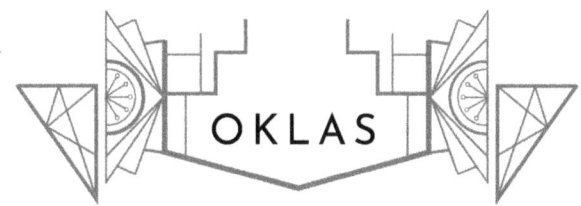

# OKLAS

S TRIDING DOWN A corridor, Oklas loosened his cravat, hissing
through his teeth as it began to unravel. Behind him, his aide—a pied
knyad in a crisp white shirt—fretted as they entered the Flintspark Auditorium from the back. Tall oval windows perforated the wall in two undulating rows; sunlight dazzled through the glass but did not slant into the
building. The sun would shine at a direct angle for at least another segment.

'Allow me, kyr,' said Domaćin, reaching for the pale yellow cravat.
'If you wish to make a favourable impression on Minister Rhestat, you
should appeal to her appreciation for military precision.'

Minister Rhestat was Oklas's visiting lecturer that segment. Her
sonorous voice carried backstage, where Oklas and Domaćin waited.
Oklas had spent much of his segere sprinting from one side of the sprawling college grounds to the other and had arrived at the lecture hall with
just enough time to smarten his rumpled clothes. The light coat he wore
was an enduring favourite. Zig-zagging pleats agitated the fabric of the
upper arms, and it featured a pleasing array of white-gold studs and buckles at the front.

As Domaćin folded Oklas's cravat, he asked, 'Shall I schedule a formal
meeting with the minister when you both return to the General Assembly?'

'No, thank you, Domaćin. I only need to catch her for a quick discussion about a private matter.'

'Very good, kyr.' Domaćin was privy to many details of Oklas's personal life. So much so that Oklas often depended on his involvement in it. But this was different. Some information would only endanger his staff. Oklas had tried to explain this to his aide, and Domaćin had politely silenced him, insisting that everyone was permitted to keep some secrets.

Domaćin stepped back to appraise his technique. His complexion was dark but a white patch stretched over his left eyelid. 'Hold still,' he instructed, narrowing his pale eye. From his mitter, Domaćin displayed a live hologram of Oklas's head. It could just be the hologram but Oklas's skin glowed a healthy shade of blue. He resisted the urge to tousle his stiff tendrils, knowing how hard his aide had worked to tame them.

'Thank you, Domaćin,' he said, 'you've been indispensable these past few phases.'

Almost imperceptibly, Domaćin's posture eased. 'While the change of scenery has been refreshing, I'll confess I am looking forward to working exclusively from your office in the Assembly Chambers once more.'

Oklas supposed he had rather disrupted his aide's routines. After the inquiry into the Emisrian College, a few of his administrative staff members resigned. While Oklas searched for suitable replacements, Domaćin had come from the General Assembly to help him run the college.

'I will have a basket of baked goods sent to your desk at the Chambers,' promised Oklas. 'Are you going back there now?'

'Yes. And might I remind you of your presentation in Apex Hall at fourth-median? I advise that you leave here half an hour ahead of time.' Domaćin was all too familiar with Oklas's tendency to neglect taking travel time into account. Traffic was usually light, but the college stood a fair distance from the Assembly Chambers.

'Don't worry,' replied Oklas, 'I won't forget it. Enjoy your median break.'

With that, Domaćin bobbed his head in a bow and left.

Moving to the folding screens at the wings, Oklas looked to the stage where Dy Erla stood with her back to him. He could make out the golden geometric symbols of her clan, Rhestatyn, along the hem of her deep indigo robes. Her tone of voice carried a weightiness that only decades of experience could bestow.

'In Rhestatyn, there are records of resyn's use at the height of our civilisation. It enhanced the adaptability of knyad bodies. Some could breathe underwater past early youth. Others enjoyed,'—creases around Dy Erla's eyes betrayed a wry smile—'or rather came to endure, increased longevity. As our resyn supplies dwindled, many blamed Adecai for withdrawing Aer gift, abandoning us.' She suspended the possibility in a moment of silence.

'Today, we mainly speak of resyn when referring to clean energy. Though, owing to its scarcity, it is seldom used to power standard technologies. Some of the engineers among you may have the privilege of refining resyn. And a gifted few can still tap into its mystical properties. To use it well is to catch a glimpse of concentrated creative power. Adecai has intervened at key moments in the past, recently enough for certain elders to remember. As long as tidelings are harvested from our waters, I believe we will be entrusted with the resources to meet our needs.'

Dy Erla swept an elegant arm in an arch, motioning from one side of the room to the other. 'I suspect the director has bribed you to appear so attentive,' she said, her blue sleeve surging like a wave. There was a murmur of laughter, and she continued, 'I am grateful for even the impression of a rapt audience. You are released.'

Eddying footsteps sounded below. Rather than retreating backstage, Dy Erla descended the stairs at the front of the platform. Oklas pushed aside the collapsible screen and trailed her. A group of students engaged in a lively discussion cut across his path. From the snatches he overheard, they were going over the titles of books Dy Erla had referenced. Upon noticing the director, they greeted him enthusiastically and drew aside to let him pass.

Many of them were under twenty, only a little younger than he had been when he'd founded the college fourteen years prior. Initially, Oklas had worn more formal suits to distinguish himself from the first intake of students and enhance his perceived credibility. But as he grew more comfortable in his leadership roles, he began to enjoy his clothing's capacity for expression. He couldn't quite pass for a juvenile anymore. Fine lines gathered under his eyes; just a few years ago, they evened out when he wasn't smiling.

The Flintspark Auditorium was all winding walls and curved, artfully-lit balconies. Rounded corners and contours defined classical Apideccan architecture. The architect, Viraj Balint, had adhered to these parameters while imbuing the college buildings with a timeless quality. Oklas had watched the Emisrian College of Innovation grow from the earliest sketched drafts to on-site visits during its construction.

It was an impulsive move, founding a college at the start of his political career while still grieving the loss of his mentor. Oklas had only completed his studies at the Engineering Consortium a year before Emis's death; he had not even had the chance to specialise in his field. But if he had paused to think about what he was doing, the college may have never come about. The place kept Emis's memory alive. Oklas hoped the brazen old knyad would have approved of it.

It did not take him long to spot Dy Erla near one of the exits. Today she wore—slanted firmly over her bound tendrils—a brimless, straight-edged hat. Dy Erla's outfits weren't complete without headwear in a complementary colour, though she avoided anything showy. She already stood out in a crowd, towering over most knyads.

Upon noticing Oklas, her eyes widened. 'Hello Director Sayve. What are you doing here?'

Oklas broke into a jog and drew alongside her. 'Listening to your lecture, of course,' he said breathlessly. 'Moving words as always, Minister. You have such a rallying presence; who could doubt your war record?'

'Pray I will never have to conscript your charges,' said Dy Erla, her brittle smile cracking. The lines on her marbled indigo and brown cheeks echoed those around her mouth. 'You asked me to speak as the Minister of Collective Heritage, not as a retired soldier.'

Oklas had to lengthen his strides to keep up with her. 'It's hugely encouraging for the students when someone like you makes time for them.'

'I think it important that the youth know their worth.' She gave a furtive bow and whispered, 'Still, they looked as relieved as expected when it was over.'

Oklas pulled his grimace into a smile. 'Wisdom is often lost on juveniles.'

'It's understandable,' she remarked coolly, 'I am the last hurdle between them and a stretch of recreation.'

'Your stories, our cultural tenants, are part of what inspired me to build this place,' he told her as they started down a stairway at the back of the auditorium foyer. 'That's a credit to you.'

'Oh, please. You find inspiration at every turn. You brought all this about, Oklas, through sheer blarne-headed determination. Now here you are, fourteen years later.' She gestured at the brilliant white oval window set in a thick wall on her left. The building was specially adapted to insulate against the extreme heat and cold of the light and dark phases. Oklas squinted and the light subsided, revealing the buildings adjoining the college.

Dy Erla gave a dry laugh. 'I'm surprised the General Assembly hasn't closed this place over some of your more subversive ideas, let alone allow you to continue serving as a minister.'

'And yet you still associate with me,' replied Oklas with what he hoped was his most incandescent smile. 'Admit it, Dy, you love to ruffle them as much as I do.'

'Perhaps, but we must respect the limits of their tolerance,' said Dy Erla and Oklas understood she was not speaking only of the General Assembly. 'Even knyads of our stratum are not untouchable. You need to be more careful.'

'No laws have been broken here,' he said, batting away the notion as if it was buzzing in front of his face. 'I've just taken liberties interpreting some of them.'

They reached the bottom of the stairway. It opened onto a mossy, partially-shaded quadrant with a canal running through the centre. It was empty save for a few students in the distance, and the pair halted on the bridge. Oklas spread his hands against the warm brickwork of the low wall, leaning forwards.

Dy Erla kept her eyes fixed on the whitewashed building opposite them. 'And what "liberties" are you taking here, at the college?' she asked.

Oklas answered her in a low voice. 'I hope to show people what we can accomplish when we do away with social stratification. Knyads harvested from Praemor clans have no more potential than those of a lower stratum. All that separates us from them is access to an education.'

Dy Erla angled her head in a tawny stare. 'The sacred texts described the virtues of the early clans rather than prescribing a rigid hierarchy for all time—Uin Adca showed us that much—but even two centuries later, many fight his interpretation.' She shook her head. 'I also long for change but act too rashly and...you must not underestimate the lengths the Pentarchy will go to strike you down. Please consider my warning, if not for yourself, then for the sake of your students.'

Oklas looked away from Dy Erla. Below them came the clear, bubbling sound of the stream. 'I do consider them. This college is for people the system leaves behind.'

The creases on either side of Dy Erla's mouth lifted, softening her expression. 'The Erudean Pentarchy cannot stop you from providing the lower strata with grants but, Oklas, they have put obstacles in your way since you started. You offer your students a lot of hope, but how many have found employment after graduating?'

Oklas could depend on Dy Erla for objective counsel, even if it was sometimes hard to take. He liked to forget the restrictions Apidecca imposed on unclassified and Orta knyads. He shifted his weight from one leg to the other. 'Many find employment abroad, in cities of the Orta Stratum. And the Praemor are always quick to take on our resyn engineers.'

'Only because they don't have enough local engineers to meet the demand.' Dy Erla folded her robes over her arms. 'The Assembly also opened resyncraft to anyone with an aptitude for it.'

Oklas sighed. 'Not everyone is an engineer or resyncrafter. What about those streamed into menial work and told it is what Adecai designed them for?'

Dy Erla started down the path again. 'All knyads possess an inherent dignity, which cannot be lessened by what they do for a living.' Such a remark, made by another upper-stratum knyad, could sound like an excuse for inaction. But in her years of service to her clan and its neighbours, Dy Erla had voluntarily come under authority and endured hardship. As if reading Oklas's thoughts, she continued, 'I understand you want them to find satisfaction in careers of their choosing.'

Oklas beamed at her. 'We'd benefit from mixing things up. For centuries our rulers have been selected from the same five clans. It's getting stale. The Pentarchic cities are not even the best in Knyadrea anymore.'

'Adecai help you if you challenge the Eruds on their divine right to rule.' Dy Erla shook her sleeve, and something glistened with reflected light at her wrist. She checked the time on her mitter. 'Well, I'm glad to have spent the segere at your fine institution.'

'Have I introduced you to the new archivist, Antolat?' asked Oklas suddenly. 'He has proposed a couple of systems to organise our records; the one I had left behind he termed "confounding". I've been happily banned from his office ever since.' He indicated one of the smaller buildings on the left.

'Oklas, you're stalling.'

'He shares your passion for antiquities. You'll like him.'

Dy Erla strode towards a gleaming archway that marked the end of the college grounds. 'I'm sure I will encounter him next term. Now I must go. There's the meeting at the Assembly Chambers at fourth-median.'

Oklas ran ahead and blocked Dy Erla from progressing beyond the archway. 'I know, I have to be there too—I'm presenting today,' he said, facing her. 'I was waiting for a quiet moment so we could discuss something of a sensitive nature.'

'We've discussed social and educational reform. Is that not sensitive enough?'

'If you have even half an hour,' he said with an imploring tweak of his brow. He could rely on his pretty sky-blue eyes to get around her.

Dy Erla sighed and cast him a withering look. 'Couldn't we have spoken in the privacy of your office?'

Oklas laughed. He could trust Dy Erla with his secrets more than he could himself. 'Have you seen my office? Open plan, people come and go like it's the High Street.' He liked it that way, but it wouldn't serve for today.

'Come on,' relented Dy Erla, gesturing towards a giant cútalpur tree just outside the grounds.

The heat was as intense as it had been four hours prior, when Oklas had arrived at the college. Oklas and Dy Erla stopped under the tree. Its furry silver leaves fanned out in a vast, bristly canopy. Oklas removed his coat and hung it carefully from a branch. He liked the contrast of the pale blue fabric against his dark slate complexion, but it dirtied with ease. He sat on a raised root in a patch of shade which spread over the ground like a stain.

Dy Erla flipped her robe to the front and lowered herself next to him. 'It'll be cool and dark in Rhestatyn today,' she observed. 'I used to do reconnaissance under the lake when it iced over—even that is preferable to this humidity.' She winced at the light poking through the leaves. Oklas found he could not recall the sun's position in Dras Sayve at this time of revolution. Perhaps it had been too long since he last visited his home clan.

'I won't keep you out here long,' he said, glancing sideways. 'You remember Keanon, my uh...contact?'

Dy Erla pinched her hooded eyes shut. 'Oklas, you're not still dallying with the Ardedrian Front, are you?'

'They're the closest thing we have to political opposition.'

'Which is why the Pentarchy prefers to regard them as insurgents.'

'I've been helping Keanon with a few projects,' said Oklas, and Dy Erla's expression turned wary. He raised his hands, palms outward. 'I haven't joined the Ardedrians but am I so wrong to acknowledge them, to support their cause?'

Dy Erla rubbed her temple. 'You act against the establishment to which you belong. Some would call it treason.' She must have read the disappointment on his face because she continued more gently, 'But, as always, anything you share is safe with me.'

'Keanon reached out to me with news about a student.' Oklas's mouth suddenly felt dry. 'She was meant to hear your lecture today. Illanu Mahnaz is one of the best in her program, but I'm afraid I won't see her graduate. It has become too dangerous for her to return to the college.'

Dy Erla frowned but made no response.

Oklas got up and started pacing slowly, his arms folded across his chest. 'I know that look: You're wondering how I created this problem.'

'Those are your words, not mine,' she said, bobbing her head.

'I wish I could say for sure that it hadn't anything to do with me. But I may have encouraged her—unintentionally—to go somewhere she shouldn't have.' He sighed and looked from Dy Erla to the distant city cascading down the gorge. 'There's a warrant for her arrest. The Eruds want to make an example of her, intimidate the other students.'

'What do you need from me?'

'Your friend, the guide, to smuggle Illanu out of the city.'

Dy Erla bit her lip. Oklas knew it was a lot to ask. She would much rather put herself at risk than send another into danger.

'The Ardedrians have come up with a plan,' he explained. 'I'll tell you the details on the way to the Chambers.'

# CHAPTER 2

## PRISMER

SUNLIGHT POURED FROM an aperture in the domed ceiling of Apex Hall, turning flecks of dust white as they drifted to the floor. The Deputy Minister of Research and Development stood at the podium. Sketchy silver patterns straddled the black and white panels of his waistcoat. But in most respects, his formalwear was surprisingly conventional today. Even his muted blue tendrils were smoothed back from his face.

Concealed a level below the stalls opposite the stage was a projection booth. There, a masked knyad signalled the last hologram in the presentation sequence—a capture of Knyadrea from space. It was unlike anything the projectionist had ever seen. She lost herself in the moon's curving horizon and jagged coastlines.

Onstage, Minister Sayve began fielding questions. From a far corner of the stalls, someone asked about the lifespan of his satellite.

Sayve made his reply. 'With the inclusion of onboard propulsion, this prototype has a lower orbital decay rate than previous—'

The rest became background noise as Prismer went over the next presentation scheduled. It was not as if she was missing much. Ambassadors and ministers would make their objections known, talking over one another like attention-starved tidelings.

Minister Sayve had designed a satellite to speed up the rate of communication between partner colleges on either side of the moon. Several wealthy clans had launched satellites in centuries past, but Sayve had significantly improved upon existing designs. Minister Dhara of Education had collaborated with him on the project. Few other departments had been as forthcoming in offering him their support. Minister Cantuce expressed doubts about the security of Sayve's new communication channel. It was to be expected as Cantuce worked closely with the Erudean Pentarchy in promoting line-of-sight propagation. The Pentarchy contained the spread of information across the moon, claiming it preserved the cultural tenants of different clans. Of course, restrictions only made such subjects more appealing to Minister Sayve.

'Consider this,' he said, holding his palms out. 'If a single satellite improves the communication between even two education centres, we could more quickly solve the problems Knyadrea faces.' He dropped his hands. Though he kept his demeanour casual, his fingers tapped restlessly against the side of the podium. The sound echoed faintly through the announcer. 'Knyads with different perspectives would be able to build on one another's research. We may see them use raw materials in ways we haven't considered, or even discover alternative energy sources.'

Prismer's cheeks twitched in an imperceptible smirk. The young minister always did like to end his presentations on an expansive note.

He left the stage via a stairway at the side and passed through a spotlight on his way across the arena floor. It highlighted his broad forehead and cheeks. The striking planes of his face softened around his tapered jawline and small chin.

Rather than making his way back to the stalls, Sayve stopped at the projection booth. He leaned over the side, close enough that Prismer could see the blue of his eyes—bright as the aperture in the ceiling against his dark skin. 'Thanks for pulling it all together so seamlessly at short notice,' he said with a disarming smile.

Prismer's speech synthesiser started up with a stutter. 'I-it ... ' She drew herself up. There was no need to fall apart over charm and a pleasing bone structure. 'It wasn't ideal,' she admitted, 'but I am glad it got their attention. Your work deserves more recognition.'

'Projectionist.' An amplified voice interrupted them. Minister Albryn had activated his announcer. He stood at the podium with his arms folded. 'Next graphic, you vacant.'

The heat caught behind Prismer's mask intensified.

Sayve stepped back, shooting Albryn a look of distaste. 'I'm holding her up. Give us a moment, will you?' he shouted. He leaned back into the booth and grinned. 'I'll organise my next presentation ahead of time—make your life easier.'

Prismer patted her headscarf as he left, then loaded Albryn's presentation onto the display system. Sayve made the same promise at every meeting. But time and again, he rushed in ill-prepared and she forgave him.

To Prismer's relief, Minister Albryn's presentation was the last of the median. He brought up the difficulties in maintaining infrastructure and the shortage of skilled labourers. Maybe the Praemor would soon have no choice but to train knyads of the lower strata. Albryn delivered a report rather than a proposition, and there was no need for comments. The meeting ended with a low rumble as knyads got to their feet.

Members of the General Assembly thronged around Minister Sayve before he could reach the aisle. Wearing a faraway expression, he briefly engaged with a few of those trailing him.

Ministers and ambassadors dispersed through the exits above Prismer as she copied the data from the meeting onto the General Assembly casting network. She folded the control panel and stacked her trolley with the large holographic projectors and casting equipment. She would leave Fenett, the young technician on duty, to return the sound cones and spotlights to storage.

Wheeling the loaded trolley around, she staggered to avoid colliding with a statuesque figure in blue.

'Sorry, Prismer. Did I alarm you?' asked Dy Erla, placing a large, steadying hand on her shoulder.

'No-no. It's not your fault'—Prismer tapped the eyehole rim of her mask—'I didn't look where I was going.' Her mask limited her peripheral vision—maybe it was time she made a new one, with a lens extending across her face in a band. She pulled the scrunched maroon fabric of her uniform under her belt and looked up at Dy Erla. 'Is there anything I can do for you, Minister?'

'I know you need to leave the floor soon. May I speak with you in private, later?' asked Dy Erla.

'Of course,' said Prismer, holding one gloved hand in the other. 'I should be finished by second-segeind.'

'I will come to you,' said Dy Erla, bowing her head.

Prismer returned the bow, bending at the waist.

Restrictions on fuel-reliant forms of transport encouraged many to live close to their workplaces. But few could say they lived under the legislative core of Knyadrea. The ancient network of cavernous rooms, bedecked in glass and ceramics, was carved into solid rock. Prismer made her home at the very base of the Assembly Chambers.

Above ground were the lavish properties of the Lepotra District. These belonged to politicians, members of the peerage, or wildly successful merchants—knyads of the Pentarchic and Praemor strata.

The staff quarters, built over natural caves, occupied the subterranean levels of the Chambers. The Assembly steward, Ognitta Balint, stayed in the largest insula. When Prismer first arrived at the Chambers, she had been given a loft room with a street-level window. She missed the light, warm space—but not the jealousy of her neighbours. Many had worked at the Assembly Chambers longer than her, but her stratum had afforded her the coveted insula.

Much had changed since then. Her mask, rather than some meagre Orta privileges, now set Prismer apart from the other staff. They mostly left her alone, and she liked it that way. Continuing down the corridors, Prismer made her way to the smallest of the insulae. It was separated from the others by a storeroom. She suspected her insula had once been part of the storeroom: a bricked wall divided them. The walls were dry now, but moss grew from the grout of the flagstone floor. A canal steered rainfall away from the staff quarters, but dankness often permeated the depths of the Assembly Chambers.

Prismer unlocked the door and leaned her shoulder against the chipped wood to push it open. She entered, careful not to trip over the potted herbs she had left in a blurry rectangle of natural light on the floor. A row of windowpanes lay atop the outer wall. They opened onto the base of a rocky moat that clung to the ramparts of the Assembly Chambers. Prismer had worried heavy rains would flood her insula but the water never came over the glass. Drainage points in the moat channelled it deep into underground canals.

She pulled off her black gloves by the fingers, revealing scaly, marble-green skin. Speckles marked her hands like impurities in rock. Her thick dewclaws were growing in a curve—she would soon have to file them down. Prismer folded the gloves and put them away. There was no time to change from her uniform. She brushed dust and lint from the beige band on her upper arm. It had been revolutions since she last hosted a visitor. The landscape of herbs, books, and tools piled on furniture had become so familiar that she could reach for the reed pen on the third shelf of her overflowing bookcase without looking.

Wedged between the other objects were small, abstract sculptures. They were plain, crudely-hewn things, wholly unlike the monuments she had dreamed of creating when she arrived here sixteen years ago. Sometimes she barely recognised the juvenile she had been then.

Those she served had pared down her expectations. It was almost a mercy. She had always asked too much of herself. Still, there was danger in allowing her world to become ever smaller. Gradually, even simple tasks like leaving the house to buy food became challenging. To combat this, she took long walks down quieter paths around the city. Over time she amassed an intimate knowledge of Apidecca's secret places. She did not fear coming to harm travelling alone. Her safety didn't matter as much as it once had. She thought back to dark segeinds spent with her harvest-mates around a bonfire, watching Elder Pelle add kindling to it. By segere, only a cold, ashy pit remained. More than extending her life, Prismer had to keep the dull embers of it aglow.

Her craft took up whatever time remained at the end of each segment. She had already placed too much on the altar of her feckless ambitions. But if she never created anything again, she would lose the surest part of herself. With only her misshapen fingers to hold her tools, Prismer struggled to replicate the fine detailing of her earlier sculptures, and yet she enjoyed working on the new ones. It eased the loneliness that sometimes threatened on quiet segeinds.

'I don't know why I bother,' she muttered as she attempted to clear a path to the seating area so Dy Erla could enter without knocking into obstacles. Prismer no longer sold her work, but her room was too small to keep everything. When she finished her moving sculptures, she added them to the hundreds of kites above Oeillade Street. Knyads strung up the kites and wind instruments in honour of Adecai. Maybe if she contributed enough, the knyad god would overlook all that was wrong with her.

The rest of the clutter in her tiny insula was too functional to discard.

*Or too valuable*, thought Prismer as she carefully picked up a frame, forgotten on the floor behind three metal pots of assorted herbs. She brushed some of the dust from the mounting board. Two of the three cut-out panels displayed printed captures of smiling juveniles in groups or pairs. The bottom panel was empty—she would look for that capture later. She put the frame back on the shelf, face down.

She had to make some attempt at hospitality. Dy Erla deserved her best more than any of the other ministers. Though Prismer's old friend had seen her at her worst, this mess might yet chase her away.

There was a knock at the door, firm and brief. Prismer tossed a sheet over some unfinished sculptures leaning against the wall, then crossed the floor.

She took a deep breath and opened the door. 'Minister,' she said, inclining her head.

'Just "Dy" please, Prismer,' insisted Dy Erla as she stooped to cross the threshold. 'This is your home. There's no need for titles.'

'I will get there,' replied Prismer, closing the door behind her. 'I'm a-acclimatising.'

Dy Erla linked arms with her in greeting. 'I don't believe I've seen that scarf on you before. It suits you.'

'Thanks,' said Prismer, pinching the knot of ash and maroon patterned fabric at the side of her head. 'It's even in regulation colours.' She held out her arms to model her uniform. The high-necked garment draped loosely from her shoulders, covering her arms to the wrists. Its bottom hem and the shafts of her boots obscured the length of her black trousers.

Dy Erla settled on her preferred dracca accent chair and removed her hat. She politely overlooked the tatty furniture, tools, and assorted projects surrounding her. Her gaze landed on the open folder of abstract botanical sketches lying on the table. She had long encouraged Prismer to return to her creative pursuits, even buying her first attempt at a moving sculpture: Three spiny brimmers made of ribbed xylemfibre segments with inset shells for scales. At the time, Prismer believed Dy Erla had bought the clumsily-constructed sculpture out of sympathy, but the minister continued to express a fondness for it. Dy Erla turned to look at the covered sculptures leaning against the wall. The sheet had slid from the one closest to her. 'Is this new?' she asked.

The sculpture depicted a dancer with aer arms outspread and aer back arched. A solid base held the figure upright. Using castingware, Prismer had molded the form as a hologram and grown aer from xylemfibre. Around the figure were thin panels arranged in rows—forming sliding compound wings.

'*The Herald*? I started aer over a year ago, but ae still doesn't ride the winds.' Prismer walked to the sculpture and gently turned the gears at the figure's back. An unfurling motion carried a third of the way down the wings. Then something clicked, and the gears jammed. Prismer gestured towards the panels, which overlapped at odd angles. 'I can't have positioned the pivot points correctly. I don't know what I was thinking, making something so intricate. It will take an engineer to fix this. I was going to put aer in Oeillade street, but maybe ae should remain a static sculpture.'

'Is *The Herald* from one of your visions?' asked Dy Erla, watching her closely. She always looked for a prophetic interpretation of vivid dreams. It made Prismer feel like a fraud; the future was a myriad of changing pathways and she could make no sense of them. But she no longer insisted the folklore she revisited lacked symbolic significance.

'Ae is an impression...of the northeast wind,' said Prismer.

Dy Erla nodded. 'A good omen.'

People believed the spirits of the air could bring abundance or destruction. Their alignment was traditionally associated with wind direction. The northeast wind often brought life-giving rains to Apidecca at the start of the dark phases. Prismer found herself courting light and life in her work—the darkness came too close to the corruption written in her flesh.

Concern touched Dy Erla's smile and her eyes narrowed. 'I believe I owe you some instalments on the engraved plaques. Would you prefer food or transport tokens?'

'A box of redlint tea would be more than enough,' replied Prismer, perching on the arm of a two-seater bench. She had made the xylemfibre plaques as gifts for the minister to present to visiting diplomats last year. Dy Erla always found such inventive ways of repaying her. Prismer doubted she had accurately converted all these little gestures into the equivalent value in substants. 'You've probably covered their worth several times over.'

'Don't be ridiculous,' said Dy Erla, raising her chin regally, 'the value would have increased over time.'

'If you say so.'

Dy Erla's eyes stayed on Prismer. In a too-casual tone, she said, 'I haven't seen you above ground recently. Is everything alright?'

'You know I like to avoid the crowds.'

'There is more to it than that.'

Closing the folder of sketches resting on the table, Prismer sighed. 'I appreciate the concern, Dy. But I keep my head down and do my job—avoid places where I'm not welcome. No one troubles me.'

'That's somewhat reassuring,' said Dy Erla, her expression sceptical. 'One hears stories, you know. About the harassment of *maskads*.'

'The life of a maskad isn't...it's not a constant struggle,' said Prismer, fiddling with an empty reed pen. 'It depends on how you choose to live it.'

The embers within her grew a little colder. It did not matter—she had never been the type to burn brightly. She thought Dy Erla might press her for more, but the minister closed her mouth in a line.

Prismer left the bench and slipped behind the counter island to search her cupboard for something to offer her guest. 'I would like to see more of the rising and setting segments. Or a good, clear dark phase.' Colourful skies and brilliant stars crossed her mind as she spoke. Prismer caught herself staring vacantly into the cupboard and withdrew an unopened russet bottle from the shelf. 'Do you still take Wodenn Bitters in your cordials?' she asked.

'Yes,' replied Dy Erla. 'But do come and join me in a drink. Otherwise, it feels like I am being waited upon.'

'I won't subject you to watching me ingest anything.'

'At least relax a little. You're still wearing your mask.'

Prismer's stomach tensed. It had been some revolutions since Dy Erla had seen her unmasked. It was taboo that the minister, a whole knyad, should look upon Prismer's scumbled form. But Prismer would not remind her of this and invite pity.

'I sometimes forget I am wearing it,' she said, consciously lowering her shoulders. Disconcerting heat rose again to Prismer's neck as she unbuckled and removed her mask, setting it on the counter. Two breathing slits in either of her cheeks expanded to inhale the cool air, like gills filtering water. At least the deep red of her optic pattern, with its edges diffused into her speckled skin, would disguise her blushing. Blinking in the light, Prismer felt the protective red membrane expand over the gaping black pupil at the centre of her face. Her hand brushed the rubbery flat surface above her chin, where she still sometimes expected to feel a nose or mouth. She had no teeth, but flat plates met beneath her skin when she closed her jaw.

Dy Erla reacted to her friend's appearance as if Prismer were an ordinary knyad who had just removed a hat or a display visor. She did not scare easily, and that had earned her Prismer's trust.

Using a dropper, Prismer mixed the bitters into Dy Erla's ginger-pear cordial. The vapours reached her gills, and she coughed. Bitters were too strong for her liking. She only bought them for the minister's occasional visits.

'I spoke to Driminn from Maskad Support,' said Dy Erla. 'The group meets in the backroom of Kaldrend's workshop now. He mentioned you haven't been to a meeting in the last eight revolutions.'

So that was why Dy Erla had come to see her. Prismer's self-consciousness gave way to irritation. She willed the grousing vocalisations below her speech synthesiser into a chiding reply: 'Oh, Dy.'

'He was only asking after you.'

Prismer handed the drink to her. 'I gave him and Taber my reasons for leaving—they couldn't have been listening.'

Accepting the glass of bitters, Dy Erla tilted her head to one side. 'So why *did* you stop going?'

Prismer made an irritable clicking noise. It was tempting to vent at Dy Erla, the only one who would tolerate her impertinence. But that would be unfair. She sighed through the slits in her cheeks. 'The purpose of the group is to help new maskads adjust. It was about time I moved on.'

'Come now, Prismer,' said Dy Erla, 'they did more than counsel you. They offered you companionship.'

'We really weren't that close.' Prismer picked up her mask and traced the thin grey lines engraved in the off-white base.

Dy Erla sipped her drink. 'So what are you doing with the extra time? Devoting yourself to your work?'

A hollow laugh escaped Prismer. 'You sound like the other maskads now.' She lowered herself onto the bench opposite Dy Erla and placed her mask on the table between them. 'I'm working less, actually. I stopped taking orders for masks, couldn't keep up with the demand.'

'When we last spoke, you said you found it fulfilling.'

It was true. Crafting masks for her scumbled contemporaries had given Prismer a sense of purpose. It had been her contribution to the group—a service offered freely to those grieving the loss of their faces. Sometimes it was too much for her.

'Isn't it best to stop while I still feel that way?' She chanced a sideways glance at Dy Erla.

A tangle of amusement and sympathy played upon the minister's features. 'You're right, of course. I apologise, Prismer.' She leaned forwards, resting a hand on her knee. 'I suppose you must find me interfering?'

'In the best way,' said Prismer, putting her hand to her chest. 'You don't give up on people easily—it's why you're here now.'

Dy Erla looked up at her, her amber eyes meeting Prismer's cycloptic stare. 'I just want to know you will have friends to check in on you when I'm gone.'

The idea of outliving Dy Erla seemed wrong. The Rhestian minister was like a great tree, a constant fixture as generations of knyads rose and fell around her. But Prismer could not expect her to remain here forever. Apidecca had no hold on Dy Erla.

'You should retire, travel where you like,' said Prismer. 'I can manage well enough on my own.'

'I know you can,' said Dy Erla sadly. 'That's what worries me. You subsist admirably. But with the support of a community, you could do so much more.'

Prismer folded her sleeves into her palms. 'At Maskad Support, they try so hard to be cheerful. They fill their lives with distractions to forget their losses. I can't play pretend, Dy. There is no comfort I can offer them.'

Dy Erla quirked her brow at Prismer. 'You could stand to pad your truths a little. But for all our imperfections, we do need one another.'

'Out there, I can't be anything but a maskad,' said Prismer, gesturing to the window, then touching her face. 'Here, I am just an employee. There is some peace in accepting that and moving on.'

'I know you, Prismer. You will never be content down here. You still miss the sky—still look for beauty in your surroundings.' Dy Erla gestured towards the peaks and slopes of sheets concealing unfinished sculptures.

Prismer did not need a surplus of acquaintances strewing the outskirts of her life, but she was grateful for someone who could change the current of her thoughts. Someone who could go for revolutions without seeing her and remain her friend.

Dy Erla downed the last of her bitters. 'Come, walk with me. I want to take you somewhere where you can feel the sunlight.'

# CHAPTER 3

## PRISMER

S INCE HER SCUMBLING, Prismer had not visited Dy Erla's home in the Lepotra District. Even at work, she kept their interactions brief. But it was different in the cosmopolitan High Street. While uncommon, it was not scandalous for such different knyads to keep company.

The top of the High Street was a short walk from the Assembly Chambers. Running northeast, it passed through a deep, shaded gorge. Gaps between the overhanging rocks lit the floor with patches of sunshine. An easterly wind whipped through the eolian caves, humming shrilly. Because of this, the exposed parts of the Traditional Quarter and Upper End were widely known as the Whistling Gallery.

Regular commuters jostled up and down walkways to reach their homes. The warm phase had also drawn many visitors below ground that segeind. They marvelled at the stark sandstone forms carved by the elements. While the wind made walking outdoors uncomfortable, it also cooled the area and improved the air quality. Prismer saw no other maskads in the crowd—it was unsafe for them to linger in the Upper End. Walking with determination helped to throw off enforcers. Better to look like a worker running an errand than a beggar.

She and Dy Erla travelled only a short distance down the High Street before veering southwest, towards the older buildings of the Traditional Quarter. After reaching a quieter path, they started up a stairway carved into the rock face. The stairway opened onto a series of sacred grottos where the ancients had carved ornate symbols into the walls, displaying their devotion to Adecai. Prismer looked between pillars at the city on her right to avoid the probing eyes of the enforcers they passed.

The Whiteledge Division stationed enforcers outside Apidecca's grander buildings and heritage sites. The division was named for the whitewashed sandstone-brick buildings in the area. In their powder-grey uniforms, the enforcers almost blended into the stairway wall. Their varying skin tones, and the umber and white trim on their sleeves, gave them away. Those conscripted into the enforcer ranks were powerfully built knyads. Prismer suppressed the urge to shrink against the pillars. Even maskads were allowed to visit places of spiritual significance. And she had no intention of vandalising the rock reliefs. She looked at the minister, who seemed to belong here, among the arcane. The arched bridge of Dy Erla's nose lent her the profile of a classical statue.

'I showed you this place sixteen years ago,' remarked Dy Erla, hardly aware of the enforcers on her left. 'Do you remember what we discussed?'

'No,' replied Prismer, adjusting the strap of her mask to stop it from pulling on her headscarf. 'I was new to the city. There was too much to take in.'

'You had started working at the General Assembly a revolution prior,' said Dy Erla as they left the sentries and grottos behind. 'You were considering returning to your clan after suffering a bout of homesickness.'

Prismer recalled that segment. 'You asked me if I could be content in Inclatia, after what I'd seen here.'

'I did.' Dy Erla sighed, looking back down at the steep path they had climbed. 'I'm sorry. Given how things turned out, it seems I advised you wrongly.'

'I wanted a reason to stay,' said Prismer with a shrug. Her choices and the consequences were hers alone.

They walked in the shade, but the air was warm and sticky. Prismer's breathing became laboured. She wasn't used to being out in the heat; even with air filters, the mask smothered her. Dy Erla politely followed, matching her pace without comment.

The tunnels Prismer and Dy Erla walked eventually opened at the surface. The stairways were built up in places where they had worn smooth. These routes were better maintained than others in the city. The tunnels beneath the Assembly Chambers had been out of use for centuries. Prismer took a turn to the right and came upon a spacious lookout.

The sandy walls were striated with layers of rock in coral pink and orange. The cave wall split into a wide natural window, revealing a portion of the city beyond as it climbed to the surface. Tildransia vines grew from cracks in the outer wall. Their pronged blue leaves rustled in the breeze. Prismer pulled her journal from her sling bag as they came to a halt.

'Is this still the Traditional Quarter?' asked Dy Erla, searching for landmarks among the buildings below.

'This is the area bordering Lepotra. I believe the closest of the old buildings is'—Prismer squinted through the lenses of her mask – 'there, see the turf roof?'

'The Mimadri Centre?' said Dy Erla, surprised. From above, the gardens of the cultural centre looked like a bouquet. Black creepers with pale yellow flowers spilt over the sides of the building. 'I seldom come this far up the path from the grottos. I'm impressed at how many of these obscure routes you've committed to memory.'

'I'm not the only one who knows about them,' said Prismer, comparing her page of measurements with her scaled drawing of the ruins beneath the Chambers. 'These paths tend to be quiet.' She balanced the reed pen between her fingers, adding contoured strokes to suggest a path heading north. The lines began to blur. Her eye refused to focus on close detail today. She held the page at a distance to examine it.

'You mentioned you were charting new tunnels when I last visited,' recalled Dy Erla, marvelling at the black tracks on the paper. 'Perhaps you've found your calling as a cartographer?'

'Don't say that where the Assembly can hear,' said Prismer, returning to her map. 'It's just a hobby.'

'You undervalue the knowledge and skills you've acquired. Remember the time you helped my guest home after curfew, using your hidden tunnels?'

'The delegate from Neem? She's not making a habit of staying out late, is she?' asked Prismer with a laugh beneath the rasp of her synth-speech.

'No, thankfully.' Dy Erla gave a rueful smile. 'But that brings me to something I had hoped to discuss with you today. Would you mind deactivating your mitter?' Prismer's hand stilled above the page. Dy Erla pressed on. 'What I am about to share is...it's highly confidential and, quite honestly, more than I am comfortable asking of you.'

Prismer set the sketch pad and pen down on a ledge. Her mitter was dormant, but she detached the whole unit, including the thermoelectric charger, from her skin. 'You never ask for anything, Dy,' she said, folding her hands in her lap. 'This is for someone else, isn't it?'

Dy Erla lowered her voice just above a whisper. 'A contact of mine has been providing the Ardedrian Front with resources. They are an opposition group to watch. Ae tells me key members are leaving Apidecca. They plan to regroup elsewhere and organise their efforts. However, it is not the leaders who require a guide, but a vulnerable recruit.'

Of Prismer's many questions, the first one she could articulate was, 'Vulnerable, how?'

'She is a juvenile from an unclassified clan and a student at the College of Innovation. She was identified as an agitator after evading arrest at a rally. The Ardedrians hope to evacuate her during the next dark phase.'

'If the Ardedrians are sending members offshore, why can't they help?' asked Prismer incredulously.

'The evacuation routes they take to the sea are too physically challenging for her. I assume they travel along the cliffs. This knyad's legs are malformed. She can walk with some support, but she won't make the journey without special accommodations. An easier, hidden route to the sea is required.'

Prismer looked purposefully from the window to the whitewashed turrets beyond. They jutted from the sea of buildings like waves crashing against rocks. She stroked the front of her mask, her blunted claws tapping the cold suggestion of lips.

Dy Erla laid a hand on Prismer's shoulder. 'I don't expect an answer today. Take some time to think it over.'

'I wouldn't call this an *easy* route,' said Prismer abruptly, 'but with some light scrambling, the juvenile should manage a descent through the caverns beneath the Razor Forest. We could afford to take it more slowly there.'

Dy Erla gaped at her.

It was an outlandish expedition, requiring the sort of recklessness that used to fitfully take hold of Prismer in her youth. Her rational mind baulked at being any part of it. If anything could reignite her resolve, it was this.

'I want to say "no".' Prismer met Dy Erla's exacting gaze. 'But if I choose not to help where I can, won't that make me the empty husk people believe maskads to be?'

'Don't say that,' whispered Dy Erla, closing her eyes. 'Your answer has no bearing on our friendship. It is not wrong of you to consider the risks.'

'But I now know about that juvenile. If something were to happen—'

'Should you take on the mission, I will think you as imprudent as the one who approached me with this request.'

Synth-speech stabilised the quaver in Prismer's voice. 'Then I suppose that makes me imprudent.'

'But right-hearted,' said Dy Erla with a sigh.

The muscles at the back of Prismer's jaw tugged as if to smirk. 'You mentioned that controversial school. Said the person who put you up to this is a colleague—'

'Don't make me name him. I've already shared more than you need to know.'

'Is it your young friend who spoke at Apex Hall today?'

'You're actually around the same age.'

'Minister Sayve is quite the overachiever, isn't he?' remarked Prismer under her breath. 'Not bad-looking either.'

'He likes to be thought of as "dashing".'

Prismer huffed. 'I'd hold that against him if he weren't so obscenely likeable.'

Dy Erla stared into the distance. 'I'm trying and failing to keep him in line.'

'Don't bother—he makes the meetings more interesting,' said Prismer. Judging by the sly curve of Dy Erla's mouth, Prismer suspected that her friend was not fully committed to curbing Sayve's defiant streak.

Dy Erla rested a hand on the sandy window ledge. 'He wants to pay you for your assistance. Or for forgetting his request—should you refuse it.'

'You told him, of course, that I can't accept his substants?'

'I explained your situation.'

The assembly closely monitored Prismer's transactions. Maskads could not own property or investments. While she could accept gifts, a considerable deposit into her account would attract attention. Her sentence began with the consignment to life behind a mask, but there were many aspects of scumbling that people never saw.

'I wouldn't want to be paid for this sort of thing, anyway—it's not right,' said Prismer coolly. The hum of activity around the city below had quietened. It was well into the segeind with only an hour until curfew; the sun still baked the outer wall of the caves. Recalling some news of a recent altercation between enforcers and rioters, Prismer asked, 'This student, she isn't a radical, is she?'

'No,' Dy Erla assured her. 'Though Sayve's students tend to be politically curious. He treats them all equally within the college, but he must prepare them for the world outside. For their own benefit, he must educate them about the realities of social stratification.'

Prismer could not comment on what Sayve ought to have done differently. She merely observed the world he and Dy Erla inhabited. She sat upright, then asked, 'What else should I know?'

'The student is around seventeen years old and goes by the name Illanu. I have a means for you to contact her. Once you reach open water, the Ardedrians will see her the rest of the way.' Dy Erla took Prismer by the wrist. 'There may be enforcers patrolling the coast. Should you get caught, you could lose your job.'

Though she was still warm from the climb through the humid tunnels, a shiver prickled Prismer's back. 'Illanu could lose even more.'

Dy Erla's stare pierced Prismer's mask. 'I would understand if you decide it's too dangerous. We may yet find another way.'

Prismer snickered. Dy Erla reminded her of a mother prede, fussing over her chick one moment and coaxing her over a cliff edge the next. 'It makes sense that Minister Sayve is involved in all this, but you...?' Prismer trailed off, tilting her head.

'I felt the need to intervene this time,' said Dy Erla. 'It is dangerous when rulers come to fear the people they serve.' She turned her back on the window ledge and headed into the shade. 'I also realise that these are my convictions, yet you are taking all the risks.'

Prismer shrugged. 'I have to defy the Assembly once in a while, so I know I still have it in me. But I won't do this for every waif with a sad story,' she said, slashing at the air demonstratively. 'I'm no wellspring of the heart, more like a...stagnant puddle.'

The reproving look on Dy Erla's face was held valiantly in place for a few seconds before she let out the full-bodied laugh Prismer longed to hear. A dull sound pulsated in Prismer's ears—she too was laughing. They had both quietened when a shadow crossed Dy Erla's features. 'Something wrong?' asked Prismer, looking over to her friend.

'I hope you do not take my silence in session for standing in agreement with the Assembly on all matters.' Dy Erla folded her robes over her arms and glanced at Prismer from the side. 'I would understand, of course, if you did.'

Though their different strata generated distance between them, Dy Erla had always been kind to Prismer. She had taught her to temper her blunt observations—in a highly political work environment, Prismer could have done with that lesson sooner. She drew alongside the minister. 'You helped me through the most difficult times, Dy. I know why you can't openly defend me, and I don't expect you to.'

'Practising self-restraint should not serve as a disguise for apathy,' said Dy Erla, leaning heavily against the stony wall. Dusty sand clung to the hem of her robes. 'Ghastly procedure, scumbling. And yet, it has been with us as long as resyn has been in use.'

Prismer hugged her arms against her body. Dy Erla had the vigour of a young knyad, but Prismer sometimes sensed in her a weariness. It was not set in the lines of her skin but deeper still, in the drumming of her great heart. The minister did not needlessly augment her body to keep up with changing trends, although she could afford cybernetics and resyn-craft. Prismer respected her for that and much more. 'You take on everyone's troubles,' she said, placing a hand on Dy Erla's broad shoulder. 'I can feel the weight of the moon, right here.'

Dy Erla smiled and crossed her arm over her chest to squeeze Prismer's hand. 'I have a communicator for you. It is one of Minister Sayve's designs.'

She checked the passage behind the cave wall for passersby and offered Prismer something resembling a pebble.

The metal object felt smooth and warm in Prismer's palm. It was more solid than the bracelet-like mitters, but it still had the insubstantial quality of city technology.

'Oklas calls them *towayes*,' said Dy Erla, rolling her eyes.

'Two-way communications?' ventured Prismer, her fingers investigating the innocuous grey object. Something resembling a touchpad with unfamiliar orange symbols slid out from the side of the device. Prismer could not tell what she had done to prompt the action. Despite its initial sensitivity, the towaye failed to respond to the few operating gestures she tried on it. She missed the rustic technology of her home clan: the push-back of struck keys or the grinding twist of a dial. Prismer clicked her gills in frustration and held out the device. 'Does the interface have to be so counterintuitive?' she asked.

'Oklas can be unnecessarily creative,' said Dy Erla, taking the towaye, 'but in this case, he has a good reason for it.' She swiped along the top of the touchpad in a downturned crescent to open the device menu. 'I believe the arrangements he wrote into these are derived from obsolete casting languages. This renders towayes incompatible with mainstream technologies, enhancing the security of Ardedrian communication channels.'

Prismer nodded. It made sense that the Ardedrians wouldn't use mitters in plots against the Pentarchy. Not when Minister Cantuce's department controlled their production.

Prismer familiarised herself with the four unusual gestures used on the towaye in different combinations. Once she could operate the device without difficulty, she agreed to hold onto it.

'The city's communication towers don't facilitate these signals,' said Dy Erla. 'Sayve has provided the Ardedrians with a private network.'

Prismer's synth-speech crackled in surprise. 'Not the satellite that Sayve spoke of today, surely?' Dy Erla waved for her to quieten, and Prismer added in a lower tone, 'He's even bolder than I thought.'

'He is reckless, spurred on with each obstacle he overcomes. But I fear ...'—she shook her head—'... nevermind, the less we discuss it, the better.'

Prismer gave a hoarse laugh. 'If he's left the shallows, surely we have too?'

Dy Erla's amber eyes creased at the corners as she considered Prismer. 'There is so much more I want to tell you about things I have planned. Things that go beyond Apidecca's politics.'

Prismer raised her chin inquiringly.

'Later, perhaps. You have enough to contend with for now.' Dy Erla reactivated her mitter, and shining numerals emanated from the device.

'Best we both head home,' said Prismer, realising she would have to hurry back ahead of curfew. The two continued up the tunnel, parting before the stairway that opened onto the Lepotra District at the surface.

# CHAPTER 4

## OKLAS

A DUSTY PINK sky signalled the arrival of an enduring sunset. Apidecca would not enter the night for at least another segment. Dim lanterns fluttered in rows above the streets of Gilstren. The pavement was rapidly emptying. From windows came snatches of conversation, strains of music and the savoury aromas of food cooking. Up ahead, near the edge of the district, appeared a hostel. Above its two floors of brick was a wooden gambrel roof. A narrow alley separated the hostel from the next building. Behind a waste skip was the entrance to the basement. Double doors jutted out from the floor at an angle.

Oklas clicked his key into the slots of an intricate lock. Then he grasped the handles and hauled the doors open, swinging them outwards. The people in the basement fell silent—or perhaps they had been quiet even before his arrival. From the top steps, he glimpsed the lower half of a wiry knyad; her hand was on the pistol holster at her thigh. A canid looked up from the bottom of the stairway, her nose twitching. She did not warble an alert.

Oklas shut out the warm easterly breeze and locked the door behind him. He skipped the rest of the way down the wooden stairway, his drumming footsteps echoing off the sandstone-clad walls. It was cool inside and surprisingly airy for an underground venue. He lifted the visor of his helmet to see the faces of the four Ardedrian Front members awaiting him. He had met each of them at least once and knew a couple of them well.

'Director Sayve.'

'Keanon,' Oklas wheezed as the large, dusky knyad swept him up in a powerful embrace. Keanon sported the unusual brindle markings of knyads from Clan Caswor and the Iridium Gulf beyond. The striated patches extended up his muscular arms, which he exposed on all but the coldest segments.

Satisfied with her master's acceptance of the newcomer, Nesta—the canid—nudged Oklas's hand. He dug his fingers into the downy undercoat around her neck.

'We worried you had lost your way,' said Keanon, his white teeth gleaming in a smile.

'Unbelievable'—Oklas drew back from him in mock offence—'that you think so little of my navigation skills. I'm the one who suggested we meet here.'

'You barely got in before curfew.'

'I made it, didn't I?' said Oklas, presenting himself with outspread hands. He removed the helmet and ran his fingers through his feathery tendrils; they had grown to their full extent, covering his ears and brushing his neck.

He looked around the room. Crates, chairs, and foodstuffs piled in corners diminished the spaciousness of the basement. A washroom cubicle, three bunk beds in an alcove, and a table at the centre of the room provided some semblance of accommodation. The only indoor access to the hostel above was a metal ladder on the other side of the room, leading to a hatch in the ceiling.

A smooth-voiced knyad asked, 'Did you drive here?'

Oklas faced Tanuk—the speaker—a pale knyad nearly two decades his senior. The rigid fabric of Tanuk's jacket raised his narrow frame, disguising the bend in his spine.

'I left the bike at the tram station and walked,' replied Oklas.

'You could be mistaken for a maskad in that,' said Tanuk, his black eyes on the helmet in Oklas's hand.

Keanon rubbed his chin. 'I don't think so. Even if he was, it shouldn't draw attention. Maskads aren't an unusual sight in an Orta District.'

Oklas placed the helmet on a stack of chairs and pulled off the shapeless coat he wore over his clothes. 'It's not a look that'll do me any favours, but it helps to go unrecognised.'

'I don't know many maskads who wear fancy dewthread shirts under their coats,' said Yvere, the knyad with the holster. She sat at the table and kept her back to Oklas. Stray crimson tendril braids obscured her face; the rest were bound in an impressive topknot.

'I believe the garments maskads wear are called *fulvers*,' he corrected her. 'I bought this at Tramways Square. I think it looks respectably shabby.' He swayed with the coat at his front like a limp dancing partner. The others laughed. From the side, Oklas thought he saw even Yvere's mouth sharpen into a smile as she gutted her weapons. Before her, fulmenum cells and stun pistol cartridges lay strewn over the table. A comfortable, mauve-skinned knyad sat opposite Yvere, sorting the old cartridges from the new. Oklas had met her before but could not remember her name. He suspected she was the Ardedrian agent who ran a few safehouses and now harboured Illanu.

Keanon leaned towards Oklas's ear and, adopting a more sombre tone, asked, 'You did check you weren't being followed here, didn't you?'

Oklas heaved a sigh. 'You still need to ask after how many of these secret meetings?'

'I don't mean to doubt you, only the knyad who showed me in here was...very attentive.'

Oklas chuckled. He expected no less from the hostel owner. 'It is his business to be hospitable.' Keanon and his comrades had been on the run for so long that they could not accept acts of kindness for what they were. The thought saddened Oklas. At least he could offer them some comfort—if only for one segeind. 'I've known Selim for years,' he continued. 'He often caters for my private functions. Some of my students even stay here outside term time.'

'I still say we'd be safer somewhere more densely populated,' said Yvere as she reassembled a pistol.

Oklas shook his head. 'The High Street is too central. If the enforcers aren't patrolling Praemor residences, they're at the Lower End doubling down on raids. Gilstren slips their notice.'

'There's more to the Lower End than the properties along the High Street,' said Yvere, her topknot exaggerating the turn of her head.

'This venue will suffice,' said Keanon, who seemed eager to get on with the proceedings. 'I was relieved to see that there is an escape route—just in case.'

Oklas followed Keanon's gaze to an opening in the gutter at the base of the wall. It led to stormwater channels. Wading waist-deep through the canal would be quite an adventure, but Oklas preferred the prospect of a cosy segeind spent with friends. 'You can rest easy. There are no prying strangers above us,' he assured the group. 'I reserved all the rooms for my students and the college staff. They're celebrating the end of term.'

The safehouse agent looked up at him. 'Do they know you're here with us?'

'No,' he answered.

'With the security issues settled, can we move this along?' asked Yvere as she packed away her gear.

Keanon looked from Tanuk to Oklas and clapped his hands. 'Let's join Hidreth and Yvere at the table, shall we?'

*Hidreth.* So that was her name. Oklas made a point of remembering her: safehouse agent, kindly face, mauve skin.

Yvere drew out her chair, wordlessly motioning for Oklas to take her place between Tanuk and Keanon. She stretched and perched on a small ladder next to Hidreth.

Up close, Oklas noticed that what he thought was a table was actually an oblong structure made of several barrels bound together. A jug of water and five mismatched tumblers weighed down a cloth. Spots of charging-cell acid stained the coarse material.

'Thank you for offering to meet with us in person, Oklas,' said Keanon, inclining his head towards him. 'You must be eager to discuss the evacuation. Know that we share your concern for your student. Hidreth can attest that Illanu has already become a valued member of our team.'

Oklas nodded. 'Thank you. I'll try not to send others your way.'

'You can leave the recruitment to us,' said Tanuk. 'You've already lent our cause considerable support. I understand you have launched a second satellite for the Ardedrian Front?'

'I have.' Oklas spread his hands flat on the table. 'Our first will soon burn on re-entry. The latest satellite is already propagating signals, so you shouldn't experience any disruption to your networks. It's better than the last—I've found a way to provide the active transponder with a continuous power supply.'

Rapid footfalls thudded against the basement ceiling. The music volume intensified. Above the beat came the familiar voices of the Emisrian's livelier students. Oklas brushed specks of fallen debris from his shirt, laughing awkwardly.

'Since the launch of the first satellite,' said Tanuk, his reedy voice straining above the clamour, 'the Ardedrian Front's reach has grown exponentially, especially in more remote areas.'

Opposite Oklas, Hidreth raised her eyebrows and let out an impressed murmur.

He grinned.

'Don't be smug about it, Sayve,' snapped Yvere, raising her chin at him. She turned to Tanuk. 'Is there any other news of our kith abroad? Hidreth and I haven't left Apidecca in revolutions.'

'I am getting there,' said Tanuk, an impatient edge in his voice. A few strands of his silver tendrils had escaped their neat fastenings. 'It has worked to our advantage that the Pentarchy and the General Assembly underestimate less-developed clans. Many knyads outside cities lack mitters, so the authorities do not monitor communications as carefully as they do here. We have been able to distribute towayes to our members in Orta clans and among the uncategorised. This new satellite should establish our presence across the moon.'

Oklas leaned back, keeping a foot on the ground as he rocked on the rear legs of his chair. 'When the Ardedrian Front secures Apidecca, we can launch all the satellites we want.'

Tanuk gave him a cautious half-smile. 'Should the Ardedrian Front come into power, our priority would be to access existing communication networks.'

'Oklas,' interjected Hidreth, 'I hope you don't mind my asking, but have there been any inquiries into your spending? These projects are expensive, and you are a high-profile figure.'

Oklas grounded his chair and pushed his tendrils from his face. 'I haven't gone out of my way to keep the first satellite a secret from the Assembly. Some ministers dismissed the experiment as indulgent; most don't take me seriously, which is advantageous.' He looked to the far wall and smiled. 'Though it'd be brilliant if I could convince the Pentarchy to fund schemes against them.'

Hidreth returned his smile but her brow knitted in concern. 'And if the authorities established a link between the satellites and the Ardedrians, would that not implicate you?'

'Should they learn that insurgent groups have been exploiting them, I wouldn't necessarily be to blame.' Oklas leaned back, watching passing shadows block the gaps between the floorboards above. 'With your sophisticated casters and spies,'— he glanced at Yvere, who stood propped against the ladder—'the Ardedrians could feasibly access the signals without my involvement.'

'And you wonder why the Assembly doesn't support your projects,' said Keanon, pouring himself a tumbler of water. 'Careful you don't unsettle them too much, or they will regulate communication tech even further.'

Oklas shrugged. 'You'll outmanoeuvre them before that happens.'

'Adecai willing,' muttered Keanon.

Yvere rummaged through her duffel bag. 'On a related topic, I have something for you to fix.' With a metallic clatter, she dropped a box in front of him.

Inside were dented oval casings. Oklas also glimpsed wires, photovoltaic plates and fulmenum cells among the loose parts. 'I know you like cooking in your downtime, but you realise this is a communicator, not a pestle?'

Yvere rolled her eyes. 'We destroy them at the slightest chance of capture. There are some salvageable parts in there. I reckon that'll keep you occupied for a while.'

'You must have the components of at least six devices in here,' said Oklas. 'If I take them apart, I may be able to reassemble one or two, depending on the damage.'

Keanon swigged his water. 'Don't spend too much time on these older models. Our engineers are producing more.'

'It's no trouble. I have all segeind.'

'Unfortunately, we do go through them rather quickly,' continued Keanon. 'Keeping the towayes out of the enforcers' hands protects the integrity of our network, not to mention you.'

There was little danger of casters tracing the towayes back to Oklas. But he understood Keanon would not want his network compromised. 'If your goal was destroying these, you could have done a better job. They will be fiddly but not impossible to repair.'

'That's why we held onto them,' said Yvere, crossing her arms. 'They are only partially wrecked. It seemed a shame to waste them.'

'Toolbox, please,' Oklas beckoned with an open palm.

Yvere handed him a surprisingly light metal box. Oklas slid open the latch and withdrew a soldering iron.

Yvere watched him, resting her hand on the top rail of his chair. 'You're a skimmer, Sayve—dabbling in politics, astrodynamics, and who knows what else.'

She spoke plainly—as if stating the city lay in a gorge. Oklas faced her, awaiting her upcoming snide remark.

'Ever think about returning to your origins as an inventor?' she asked.

It was a fair question. Oklas picked up an undamaged circuit board. 'That would depend,' he mused, 'on the environment, on opportunities for exposure to new ideas. I can't stay holed up in a laboratory all the time.'

'So you entered politics for the entertainment value?' asked Keanon.

Hidreth suppressed a giggle.

'The comedy has deteriorated, I can tell you that much,' said Oklas.

Hidreth looked over her shoulder to Yvere. 'You want him to join the Ardedrian Front as an engineer so you can boss him around more often.'

'I doubt he'd take to roughing it,' said Yvere, placing her hands on her hips and inspecting her boots. 'But Oklas is decent with ideas. Maybe he does his best thinking from his gilded turret in Lepotra.'

His mouth twitched. '"Decent with ideas." Such flattery, Yvere.'

She waved him off. 'Forget it.'

Oklas relished the small victory. Teasing Yvere was the highlight of these meetings. Before segere, he might even see her dark skin flush the red of her tendrils. It would be worth the blows she would likely throw his way—Yvere did not turn bashful, she fumed. 'Honestly, though,' he said, reaching for the soldering iron, 'I need an incentive to actualise my ideas. If my inventions don't make a difference in people's lives, what's the point?'

Keanon folded his large arms on the table. 'Maybe it is time you joined us.'

Oklas grimaced. 'I could have done with a coup today—it would have livened things up at the Chambers. Kemia runs our department admirably but the Eruds block all meaningful progress.' He wiped away the excess solder dribbling from a wire pressed against the circuit board.

Hidreth sighed and said in an ironic tone, 'Only our theocratic elect have the divine wisdom to vet important decisions.'

'They may as well do away with their ministers for the meagre powers they grant us.' Oklas's free hand curled into a fist. He would not even be at this meeting were his leaders more open to change. He glimpsed Hidreth opposite him, the warmth in her round face undiminished despite his irritable demeanour. Embarrassed, he straightened his fingers and arranged his features into an amiable expression.

She gave a sympathetic smile. 'You've made a difference in at least one young knyad's life, *baca*.'

*Baca*. Oklas had not heard that term of endearment in a while, but it was oddly comforting. He couldn't remember if it meant "little bead" or something else. It came from an old dialect. 'There is something I've been meaning to ask about the rally that segeind,' he said, setting aside the towaye parts. 'It wasn't started by the Ardedrians, was it?'

'No,' said Keanon, his expression grim. 'We used to stage peaceful protests in cities across the moon, you remember?'

'Of course.' Still new to Apidecca, Oklas had met Keanon at one such protest.

'Then the Assembly started to come down harder on us.' Keanon's gravelly voice wavered. 'Enforcers rounded us up and sent many of our members away to serve their sentences in labour communes.'

Criminals had to earn their food and shelter—able bodies could farm, mine and generate energy. Living conditions in labour communes were often poor. Oklas would sooner storm the Pentarchy's throne room than see someone in his care sent to one. He flicked his wrist, releasing some of the tension in his limbs. 'Did you find out who was behind it?'

Yvere answered, 'A group of recently-discharged enforcers started the riot. Can't be sure of their motives yet.'

Oklas smirked. 'How embarrassing for the Eruds.'

The Erudean Pentarchy's rule depended on the loyalty and efficacy of their enforcer divisions. Some enforcers rapidly rose through the ranks, and their excellence was greatly rewarded. But competition for the Eruds' favour was fierce. Clearly, some resentment was harboured by those who could not outmatch their contemporaries.

'The rioters claimed to have our endorsement, which lent them support,' said Keanon, frowning. 'Many smaller factions share in our frustration. But they do not bind themselves to our codes of conduct. We have become synonymous with rebellion; it's one of the disadvantages of being so widely known. People get hurt in our name.'

'I'm just glad Illanu wasn't,' said Oklas. He picked up the broken towaye again, clicking his tongue as he ran his fingers distractedly over the circuit board in its ill-fitting casing. 'The students enrolled at the Emisrian are bold and curious; I want to foster those qualities in them. But I can't let something like this happen again.'

The knot between Keanon's eyebrows slackened. 'It was one of Yvere's informants who smuggled Illanu out safely.'

'Thank you,' Oklas said to Yvere. He wondered whether the earnestness in his voice surprised her as much as it did him. She closed her eyes and gave a swift nod.

Tanuk regarded Oklas. 'You mentioned in your last transmission that you have outsourced a guide to take Illanu to the harbour?'

'Yes,' replied Oklas, lightly planishing out dents in the metal casing. 'She's a reticent type. Would you believe she works at the Assembly?'

Tanuk's bearing turned cagey. Oklas held up a hand in concession. 'I know how that sounds—'

'I must ensure the safety of my crew, Oklas.'

'And I am entrusting my student to her. She has no reason to harbour loyalty to the Pentarchy. She is a maskad, you know how they treat her kind.'

Oklas's elaboration did little to reassure Tanuk. 'How much has the guide been told?'

'Only her part in the mission,' came Keanon's steady voice. 'The director and I have discussed the involvement of non-members at length. I can vouch for her.'

'Very well,' said Tanuk, inclining his head at Keanon. 'For my part, I've arranged Kelvan as a skipper. He'll take over from the guide at the harbour.'

'He won't be able to pilot a watercraft near the docks unnoticed,' interjected Yvere, 'not even in the dark.'

Tanuk arched his slender fingers. 'Kelvan will meet them underwater and lead Illanu to the watercraft. His crew will wait for him a league offshore. They shouldn't need to surface for air in the half-hour it will take to reach the vessel.'

'We still have some segments to finalise the details,' said Keanon, placing both hands on the table as he got to his feet. Nesta got up from the floor with a yawn and drew alongside her handler. 'Since we are spending the rest of curfew here, we can afford to adjourn now.'

Yvere followed Keanon to the other side of the room. Hidreth held out a flute glass to Oklas. He reached for the nearby jug to fill it. 'You know,' he said, 'if you'd told me you only had water, I'd have brought us something more interesting.'

Yvere looked at him from over her shoulder, tossing the loose tendrils framing her face. 'We need to stay clear-headed while in the city. Not everyone here can handle their bira as well as I can.'

Oklas placed a hand on his chest; the affronted pose stood at odds with the smile on his face. 'I only want to share some indulgences with you besides the pleasure of my company.'

Keanon chuckled. 'Yvere has made us nohdrut dumplings. You've never tasted better.'

'I got the ingredients from the High Street at great personal risk,' said Yvere, waving a knife at them.

Above, the music had quieted. Other voices and noises rose louder from surrounding buildings.

Yvere pulled her stray tendrils back into the elegant bundle on her head. 'The neighbourhood is getting merry. It's not even phase-end.'

'They don't need a holiday to celebrate when the sky is this festive,' said Hidreth as she got up to help Keanon and Yvere unpack.

Tanuk scraped his chair to the side, so he and Oklas faced each other. 'I visited the Dras Channel once,' he said. 'I found the cultural emphasis on innovation and the sciences most impressive.'

Oklas thrust his shoulders back appreciatively. 'I believe Dras Sayve's technology could catch up to where Rhestatyn's was in its prime, with a little more access to resyn.'

'Resyn is quite the commodity everywhere. Perhaps you can win us more recruits from your clan?'

'An invitation to dissension,' Oklas considered aloud. 'Not the easiest subject to bring up during my short visits to the Academy. Still, you never know when an opportunity will present itself.' He had to feign the optimism in his voice. Sadly, many of his people were motivated by resource management rather than social concerns. Dras Sayve was a self-sufficient clan, owing nothing to the rest of the moon.

Tanuk's dark eyes narrowed inquiringly. 'And what brought you to the sacred city? Apidecca's rulers are enamoured with the glories of the past and their own importance. That doesn't exactly align with your interests.'

'Yes, Apidecca is steeped in creeds and traditions, but the resyn imported here is relatively inexpensive. And below the surface is something peculiar, wild even.' Oklas breathed in the musty air, surrendering to the enchantment. 'It's not a phenomenon most Drassian knyads would understand. They hold in esteem that which can be measured.'

Keanon returned to the table, balancing a packed meal in each hand. A third he deftly secured between his shoulder and chin. At the scent of the food, Nesta sprang up on cleft hooves. Yvere dropped the cutlery set on the table. Oklas assisted in distributing the food parcels, each wrapped in edible laminiri fronds.

Keanon beckoned for the others to join him at the table. 'Come. Let us ask for Adecai's blessing on this feast.'

'And on the chef,' added Hidreth.

'She won't let us forget.' Oklas chuckled, narrowly dodging a playful punch from Yvere.

# CHAPTER 5

## PRISMER

NEON LIGHTS IMMERSED crowds of pedestrians in garish turquoise, then red as they trundled through the darkness. Something solid struck Prismer's shoulder. The burly, loping knyad who had collided with her shot her a glare as ae forged ahead. She reached for her upper arm, rubbing away the dull ache. Inhaling deeply through the filters at the sides of her mask, she went over the plan again, careful not to vocalise it with her synthesiser. Breaking it into manageable fragments helped tie her to the present—an ongoing challenge. A part of Prismer was already going over three potential routes home from the site where the underwater caverns met the harbour. Loosening the high neckline of her fulver, she continued towards the Lower End.

She had left her mitter at home. Allegedly, the devices didn't track knyads' movements, but she had always been suspicious of them.

The Ardedrian Front had requested Prismer's name and description; it was more than she was comfortable sharing. Now she was carrying their illegal technology. She had arranged a meeting point with this "Illanu" earlier but had to bring the towaye along in case they got separated on their way to the sea. Her ungloved hand went to the pebble-shaped device in her pocket.

The signs and flashing lights diminished as Prismer wound her way down the backstreets. The inhabitants of the Lower End used energy more sparingly; solar cells would have to hold out for another phase before the sun returned, and the prevailing wind did not generate much power. Her sight adjusted to the gentler light cast by the stars and Knyadrea's neighbouring moon of Dryadene, its brightest phase on the wane. Densely packed buildings protruded from the rock walls, seemingly growing over one another like overlapping layers of bark on a trunk. Windows pitted the structures at random and narrow doorways lay squashed between dilapidated shops. The frontages were also at odds with one another. One was dark and plain, the next painted with sinuous patterns in colours that would be vivid in daylight. The chaos was strangely entrancing.

It was mad of her to agree to this task but on she trudged, motivated by something she could not name. She wasn't doing this to please Dy Erla. Prismer was well-practised in declining unfavourable propositions, even from those she cared for. Something else was at play here. The walls of her home had whispered nothing new for some time. Perhaps she needed this. She could pick apart what it all meant later.

Upon reaching a charging-cell supply shop, Prismer halted at the right of the entrance, as agreed. Illanu did not know the area well, so Prismer had made a special effort to arrive early and identify the juvenile. Meeting in such a public area was risky, but the crowds were a necessary cover. At least maskads were less likely to be arrested for loitering at the Lower End.

To avoid confusion, Prismer had dressed as distinctively as she could. She usually went for segments wearing her Assembly uniforms on rotation. The rest of her wardrobe was limited to loose-fitting practical wear. The long-sleeved fulver she now wore was charcoal grey with several pockets and a swirling, embroidered pattern—her crude attempt at disguising a stubborn stain. Much like the other garments she wore in public, it covered every deget of her scaly skin.

While waiting, Prismer watched the passing pedestrians, looking for someone matching Illanu's description. Even with her cycloptic eye hidden, people had a way of noticing when she looked too intently at them. She changed tactic, scanning their lapels for the glassfolia brooch Illanu said she would wear.

A maskad walked past, gesturing from the eyehole of aer mask to Prismer's. Prismer silently mirrored the greeting. Though she did not know the other maskad well, she recognised aer from the support group. Aer custom mask, trimmed with niddarwood, was not one of Prismer's designs. Ae was the third maskad Prismer had seen that segeind; whole knyads greatly outnumbered their scumbled counterparts.

Across the street, haulers loaded a wagon. Two bulky aftills waited amenably at the front. Prismer had never seen anything like them in Inclatia. She remembered finding the burden-bearers alarming, with their armoured hides and manifold horns spread wide, like uprooted trees. But she had grown used to them and had once ventured close enough to notice their gentle blue eyes. Far be it for her to judge by appearances. Every so often, one of the aftills would turn his great head to the pavement and flick his ear, his wickers quivering. Prismer thought she saw a figure dart behind one of the beasts. Eventually the wagon pulled away, revealing a lanky young knyad with short dark tendrils and straw-coloured skin. Ae was a juvenile—too tall for Illanu and able-bodied. Ae stared in her direction for a moment before backing into a nearby shop selling dried foods.

It was getting late now. Prismer's chest tightened, and a chill nipped at her fingertips. She stuffed her hands into her pockets, her vestigial thumb brushing against the towaye. It was not safe to ask Illanu for her location here. 'Deliver her to me, please,' she murmured at the lowest frequency. She was insolent to think she could appeal to Adecai. Prismer no longer shared in Aer likeness: their connection was severed. Though, if she was honest, she had distanced herself from the Creator even before her scumbling. She would take what shreds of consideration she could get.

The young knyad who had been watching Prismer left the shop and walked purposefully towards her. She faced the stranger head-on, and ae began to fidget, aer wide-set eyes avoiding the mask. Ae was around twenty, maybe younger, and of a reedy build that leaned towards andrid, though she could not say how ae might identify. 'Are you Prismer?' ae asked suspiciously.

'That would depend.'

'On what?'

'On the manner of business you have with her,' replied Prismer curtly.

Suddenly a petite, hooded knyad shuffled between them. 'Let's not get confrontational, Rosh,' ae scolded the lanky juvenile, 'we have the right person.'

'Illanu Mahnaz?' guessed Prismer, noticing the brooch pinned to her blouse. It was a compound leaf made of crystal and framed in silver.

'Yes,' she answered, looking up at Prismer with round, grey eyes. Under the hood, she wore her pale pink tendrils in a short, choppy style. A crutch supported her slight frame, and she had a watertight rucksack slung over her shoulder. Prismer looked from Illanu to her tall companion. 'You didn't say someone else was joining you.'

'This is my friend, Rosh,' said Illanu. 'He only wants to see me off. I told him he couldn't come, but he's been very stubborn about this.'

'You shouldn't have to do this alone. Someone from the safehouse should have come with you,' Rosh told her. His gawky demeanour somewhat undermined the hardness he was trying to project. Coercing his tender features into a look of determination, he fixed his hazel eyes on the gaps of Prismer's mask.

Prismer exhaled through the slits in her clenched jaw. 'Come then, both of you,' she instructed, waving them along as she strode back up the street. The change of plans vexed her, but arguing about it here would only attract onlookers.

She led them down narrow streets, heading southeast towards the Industrial Park and the hidden tunnels in the side of the gorge. Several steps behind her, Rosh and Illanu chatted. Their words were indistinct, but she soon became familiar with the melodic interplay between Rosh's nasal drawl and Illanu's breathless expounding. To Prismer's relief, the enforcers' presence was weak away from the High Street. They had congregated around the Traditional Quarter, as predicted. It was the segeind of the glamorous Praemor Induction Ball—the culmination of a phaselong conference known as the Charter's Exchange. Inventors and clan delegates travelled to Apidecca from across Knyadrea, which would surely warrant extra security. In recent segments, Prismer had set up equipment in the smaller auditoriums before being rushed out of sight. Many of the visitors facilitated their own presentations, which freed up her time at work. It was just as well; she had thought of little besides this mission for segments. And it gave her time to plan her route.

A sheer rock wall stretched from the edge of the Industrial Park, over the tram tracks, and on to Gilstren. An unassuming doorway cut in the sandstone marked the tunnel entrance.

'I need you two to quieten for a while. With more of us in the tunnels, it'll be harder to go unnoticed,' said Prismer jerking her chin at Rosh.

'Really? One more person going up there will make a difference?' he said sarcastically.

Prismer squared her shoulders. 'I have planned this carefully, and I don't like surprises. So forgive me if I am not overjoyed about minding a fugitive and her mouthy cohort for the segeind.' She took in a steadying breath, her frustration subsiding. 'Since you're here, you can help Illanu cover more ground.'

'What I don't like is the Ardedrian Front sending us a criminal for a guide,' muttered Rosh.

Prismer rounded on him. 'Isn't Illanu here the one trying to escape the law?' She kept her voice even, aided by the synthesiser's brief lag in forming her words.

The soft cleft in Rosh's chin puckered. 'It's not the same.'

'You can't know that,' said Illanu, placing a hand on her hip.

'She's a maskad, Ilu. They can't be trusted.'

'People say the same about our stratum,' she countered, frowning. 'Maybe I don't know anything about Prismer,'—she closed her eyes, took a deep breath and opened them again—'but I trust the people who selected her as a guide. If you keep questioning their judgement on this, I will go on without you.'

'I'm only trying to—'

'I mean it,' she said, holding Rosh's gaze.

He slumped in reluctant acceptance.

A peculiar certainty struck Prismer like a sudden change in wind direction: she had to make a success of this mission. Illanu deserved this chance.

'Alright.' Rosh turned back to Prismer with open palms. 'Sorry, I'm just on edge.'

'You're not the only one,' said Prismer mildly. She could not quite muster an apologetic tone. 'The route we are taking will lead us closer to the city centre before we move further away. Be careful what you say. We won't be alone in there.'

They entered the network of tunnels and started up an embankment at a gradual incline. Other tunnels intersected with theirs, drawing together, then diverting like the wiring in storage under Apex Hall. Glass panels of cultivated algae dimly lit their path at intervals a few steps apart. At each intersection, Prismer read the differing patterns and hues of the algae for directions. They passed only one other knyad, bent with age and slumped against the wall opposite a cave overlooking the city. Prismer placed a subst token in aer open palm as they passed. It was an act of appease-ment rather than kindness; a little generosity helped to secure a home-less knyad's silence on one's comings and goings. Eventually, the incline plateaued. Prismer turned to Illanu, who had managed to trail her closely. 'We are going to leave the public corridors,' whispered Prismer as she started down the jagged steps of another footpath.

The luminous panels of algae did not continue this far. The group was in near-complete darkness, save for the pale light of Prismer's torch.

'I can't see anything. Where are we now?' asked Rosh at the back of the line.

'Around Gilstren. We're entering the Assembly Chambers through the staff quarters,' replied Prismer, running her fingers along the walls to feel her way down the tunnel.

'What?'

'I told you we were heading to the city centre. Our route to the sea starts in my insula. Don't worry—my co-workers seldom go to the place where this trail ends.'

Rosh cast an incredulous look from Prismer to Illanu. 'You didn't say she worked at the Assembly.'

'If she were a criminal, they wouldn't have employed her, would they?'

'No, they would rather protect the public from dangerous radicals like you.'

Prismer glanced over her shoulder to see Illanu give him an affection-ate nudge. Both juveniles laughed.

A water channel trickled on their left, and the trail became less clear.

A bump against her back caused Prismer to overbalance. She struck her elbow against the wall and stopped her tumble.

'Sorry,' hissed Illanu, 'I got too close.' She offered Prismer a hand up. 'It's just, um ... You don't need to slow down for me.'

'I'm not.'

'It must be hard to see from behind a mask, especially in the dark.'

'It serves its purpose, and I can see well enough.' That was not entirely true; the imperfectly designed eyeholes of the mask obscured her periph-eral vision. But Prismer's mask was the face she presented to the world, and she would not readily replace it.

Illanu bit her lip. 'You're welcome to take it off if it makes you more comfortable.'

'I will manage. We will all be more comfortable if I keep it on for as long as possible.'

Rosh helped Illanu over a few rocks strewn across the path. 'You haven't seen a maskad's face before, have you?' he asked her.

'And you have?'

'No. We aren't allowed to, are we?' He looked to Prismer at the front of the line. 'It's why they make you wear that.'

Prismer gave a dry laugh. 'I could be arrested for unmasking in public, but I don't think there are any consequences for knyads who choose to see me in private.'

'I prefer the urban legends about maskads over the folktales,' mused Rosh. 'Gudro at work says they wear masks because they lost their faces to resyncrafters.'

'Let's not talk about that now,' said Illanu through clenched teeth. 'Besides, you shouldn't believe everything Gudro says. He thinks the General Assembly uses the Lower End soup kitchen to poison unclassifieds.'

Rosh lowered his voice to a conspiratorial tone. 'It's not as if there are more plausible explanations for the maskad curse, and resyncrafter sects do exist.'

Prismer walked more briskly, staring purposefully ahead. There came a light tap on her shoulder.

'Sorry. That was rude of us,' said Illanu. 'Are you all right?'

Unsure what to do with the juvenile's apology, the only response Prismer could manage was, 'I'm fine.' And she was, as far as she could tell. The background noise of Rosh and Illanu's speculation had actually helped keep her mind from leaping too many steps ahead. Now the only sound came from their boots clicking against the wet floor.

Prismer led them the rest of the way down the dank, informal trail in loaded silence. Eventually they came upon a fissure in the wall and she turned off her torch. The churning of a waterfall echoed from the other side. They had reached the canal at the far end of the staff quarters' main corridor.

'Stay here. I'm going to see if the corridor is clear,' said Prismer.

'You live down here?' asked Illanu in a pitying tone, looking at the damp cave.

'It's drier on the other side. Just stay put.'

In the warm phases, the other workers sometimes gathered around the canal. There was nowhere dry to sit, and they seldom lingered. Some of the more curious knyads had entered the fissure, thinking it a narrow cave. But, to Prismer's knowledge, none of them had explored the trail far enough to realise it eventually joined with the Industrial Park tunnels. Prismer walked to her door and unlocked it, before heading back into the depths.

She had almost reached her unlocked insula, with the juveniles in tow, when—further up the corridor—the storeroom door flew open. She signalled for Rosh and Illanu to hit the ground. From the storeroom swayed a slim knyad. It was Tolka, a new cleaner and Prismer's neighbour. She must have been fixing the light panel that had gone out. Prismer padded into the dim light of the torch bracket outside her home, reaching for her door handle and trying not to look at Tolka.

'Grike—Prismer!' shrieked Tolka with a jolt. 'You rattled me. What are you doing skulking in the dark like that?'

Prismer held her hands up, protesting innocence. 'It wouldn't work if I tried it on purpose.'

'Unlike Fenett,' said Tolka. 'The little flot is always sneaking up on me.'

The young technician delighted in pulling pranks on his co-workers. He was often on duty with Prismer, but she was not his preferred target. Even when he succeeded in shocking her, he found her slight twitches and strangled gasps underwhelming.

'He knows he can get a rise out of you,' said Prismer, angling her body to hide the juveniles in the shadows.

Tolka huffed. 'Surely there are better places to go for a walk than the canal? It's chilly down there.'

'I don't mind it.' Prismer opened her door the rest of the way. She took a tentative step forward, hoping to end the conversation and send Tolka back to her insula.

Tolka frowned at her, perplexed. 'Alright,' she said, turning aside. 'Good segeind, Prismer.'

'Good segeind.'

Tolka disappeared around the bend, and the jangling of her keys in the door lock echoed down the corridor. The juveniles got up and followed Prismer into her insula. Street lights glinted through the moat-level windows, and a green glow emanated from a shallow algae panel in the ceiling. Prismer flicked a switch in the wall, lighting two torches in brackets on either side of the living room. The space was less cluttered than when Dy Erla had visited; Prismer had carefully packaged and stored away her large moving sculptures. But her potted herbs and tiered drying rack remained in place. She noticed Illanu staring at a small, alabaster sculpture on the bookshelf. It stood no higher than one alkar, roughly the length of her forearm.

Illanu looked up at her. 'It's beautiful. Almost like an arching vine, or a wave.'

Prismer's face flushed under the mask.

'Wait, you made this?' asked Illanu, noticing the rasp and file tools lying next to the sculpture. 'You're very talented.'

Though she was less than half the size of Dy Erla, Illanu affected the same affirming tone as the minister. The sentiment was a little patronising, but not unwelcome.

'Thanks,' said Prismer stiffly, leading them to the back room. Her laundered fulvers and uniforms lay in a rumpled pile on her bed, along with things she wore only in the privacy of her room: garments with short sleeves or low necklines.

Prismer removed her boots and slipped off her headscarf from under the straps of her mask. Their journey would end in a long swim, and she did not want to carry anything non-essential. She kept her fulver on over her aquaskin. It would be cold in the caverns. Rosh stood close behind her—she could feel his stare at the back of her tendril-bare head. Her companions may not have seen her face, but even the sparse scales dusting her scalp held clues as to what she was. Scumbling had made Prismer stand out more than she would have ever dared.

On the floor was a medium-sized sling bag packed with the tools she would need. She flicked her torch on again. Pushing aside a wooden panel she had painted to match the blue walls of her room, she revealed a hole in the brick wall, just big enough to crawl through—her secret tunnel. She beckoned the juveniles over. 'Come, this is where we start.'

# CHAPTER 6

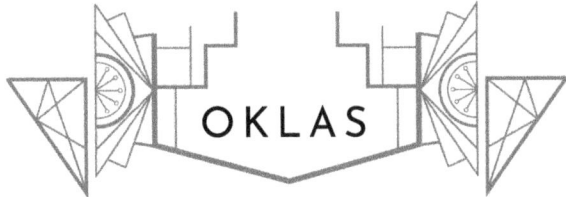

## OKLAS

THE MIMIDRI CULTURAL Centre was once the residence of Apidec-can-harvested peers and Eruds. Though Apidecca was a Pentarchic clan—one of the first five known harvesting sites—their indigenous population gradually declined. Later generations of Apideccans agreed to bequeath the clan estate to the Erudean Pentarchy.

Oklas had only ever known Mimidri as a venue for special functions; the last native Apideccan had passed away before he had taken his first shaky steps on land. The glass and white stone facade of the villa soared above him as he approached it on his scrambler. The estate sprawled over the border that separated the Traditional Quarter from the Lepotra District. It was positioned high enough up the side of the gorge that rays of moonlight washed over its shell-like turrets. Oklas braked and gently squeezed the clutch, letting the light vehicle glide in a semi-circle in front of the estate before he parked it at one of the empty charging bays. It seemed none of the other guests shared his preference for this kind of transport. He removed his helmet and locked it to the frame of his scrambler.

Disinclined to go home and change, he arrived dressed in his formalwear. Domaćin had arranged for the suit's delivery to the Chambers. A knyad of discerning tastes, Domaćin knew Oklas's measurements and colouring better than anyone. The slim-fitting dark jacket Oklas wore had a sheen that oscillated between teal and blue, as his eyes did. Geometric embroidery adorned his pale waistcoat. He'd secured his sleeves with his favourite cufflinks—white gold bases with stones the colour of seafoam. They were a gift from Emis, and wearing them had always brought Oklas luck.

Oklas ran his fingers through his flattened tendrils, restoring their volume, then swept them to one side in a deep parting. The look brought some balance to his features; the tendrils covered his broad forehead and strengthened the appearance of his pointed chin. If he straightened his nose and added a few degets to his height, he might even pass for handsome. Tomorrow he would want something else. Dissatisfaction, it seemed, was common to all knyads. But Oklas trusted in the form he had settled on as a tideling, and he knew how to emphasise his good features. With any luck, his helmet-mussed tendrils would look like a style choice.

Oklas entered the artfully-lit foyer and joined a short queue. At the front desk stood a young enforcer from the Whiteledge Division, checking the guest list. His skin was dark and variegated, and he sported the unadorned sandy-coloured uniform of a junior officer. There was something familiar about his open face and cheerful demeanour, pleasant qualities uncommon among enforcers. Oklas had encountered him at another function, though he did not know the officer by name.

'Minister Sayve, here already.' said the officer, raising his eyebrows. 'Not that you aren't usually—'

'Alarmingly punctual?' said Oklas brightly. 'I thought I could use an extra hour. I only have this segeind, and there are many conversations to be had here.'

The young knyad smiled as he scanned the list. 'A phase of conferences and still so much to talk about?'

'Always.'

'I don't even know how to greet the guests,' confessed the officer quietly, marking Oklas's attendance. 'How do you think of what to say?'

'I understand your dilemma. With so many possibilities, it can be hard to pick a starting point.' Oklas plucked at the air as if selecting one of the ideas floating before him. 'We could, for example, examine the motto of your division.'

'"Preserve our foundations...and advance"?'

'What does that adage mean to you?'

The officer blinked hard and turned back to his list. 'That...that you need something solid to stand on, something to inform where you are going.'

'Can you preserve anything without adding something new to it?' prompted Oklas. 'Something to honour the original intent behind a tradition, rather than the tradition itself?'

Behind him, another guest cleared aer throat.

The officer lowered his gaze. 'I had better not hold up the queue, Minister,' he said politely, motioning for Oklas to present his mitter for scanning.

Oklas complied, and his mitter recorded the security tag. 'Thank you,' he said with a remorseful smile. Perhaps this was not the place to challenge the young knyad's views. 'Do enjoy your segeind—try and make a game of this.'

Beyond the foyer lay the entrance hall with grand stairways winding up four floors on either side. A bridge, supported by pillars, joined the stairways on the third floor. Along its length were balconies overlooking the entrance hall and the ballroom on the other side. The interior glimmered with strings of warm lights which multiplied in mirrors at the upper levels. Crystal decorations sent jagged reflections scattering up the walls, and flecks of quartz blinked, star-like, from the pillars. Long tables, covered in cobweb-fine gossamer, crossed the entrance hall in rows.

The General Assembly had redecorated the gathering areas; they were no doubt aiming for "understated elegance". Oklas found these parts of the historical building coldly impersonal. He preferred the rooms that retained their original character, the lived-in spaces with wonderfully tatty furniture and painted portraits.

It really was early—less than half of the expected guests had arrived. *Better to be here than wading through a bureaucratic mire back at the office,* thought Oklas. He must have spent the whole median reading amendments to the regulation of solar cell charging facilities. He could sign them off tomorrow.

Delegations from technologically progressive clans had spent the past phase in Apidecca for the Charter's Exchange. It was one of the busiest events of the year for Oklas's department. Over several segments, innovators of every kind presented their research at the Assembly Chambers. The phase culminated in the Praemor Induction Ball that segeind.

It was up to Oklas and the other ministers to welcome esteemed guests and potential investors. Among those expected were several peers. All Praemor clans belonged to the peerage. Knyads harvested under special tidal conditions were named "heir presumptive", but only one among them could hold the title of Clan Peer at a time. Peers managed large estates and, most importantly, selected ambassadors to stay in Apidecca and liaise with the Erudean Pentarchy. The same influential people came here each year, idling in echo chambers of accord.

Only breakthroughs in research garnered Orta delegates their invitations. Oklas found them easy to identify in the crowd. Many dressed more formally and less fashionably than their Praemor counterparts. Too alert to fully embrace the festivities, they lined the walls, anxiously gripping the glass stems of their drinks. By the end of the Induction Ball, one Orta clan would attain Praemor status and all the social and economic benefits that came with it. Such high stakes did little to put the delegates at ease.

Oklas took a tray from the table and started offering appetisers to the more subdued knyads. After introducing himself, he gathered those with complementary interests and set up a few flourishing conversational ecosystems. From there, he gleaned details of the exhibits he had missed: a new tidal energy converter supplemented Dalga's power during the long nights; the Sikrans had discovered a novel way of filtering micro-polymatter from large bodies of water, using a residue from resyn processing; and Verci had drastically improved the energy efficiency of their waste management system.

Where there was emerging talent, there were also bands of opportunists. Oklas noticed a group of Praemor shipping merchants vying for the custom of a timid-looking Orta inventor. Ae appeared reluctant to engage with them, but it was only a matter of time before their pushiness wore aer down.

Oklas drew alongside the inventor. 'Are you trading with the East?' he asked.

'Yes,' ae replied, 'I supply components to the wind farms at Fentu Brise.'

'You struck me as a purveyor of lightweight goods,' said Oklas thoughtfully. 'Now, I am sure these reputable knyads do a marvellous job of transporting grains or silica by the tonne.' He gave the merchants an ironic bow before returning to the inventor. 'But someone in your position ought to investigate alternatives. May I introduce you to a contact of mine at the next table?'

'Sayve is a politician in need of the odd courier service,' scoffed a stout merchant in a modish black jacket, 'he knows nothing of trade. You need to plan for the expansion of your business.'

Oklas ignored the merchant. 'Diabra,' he called out to his contact, waving her over. He leaned towards the inventor. 'My "courier" owns a commercial flotilla. She often works with small and medium enterprises. The larger container vessels hug the Nebbian coast to reach the Pale Sea, but she takes a more direct route there.'

A merchant wearing a cape over aer dress said, 'There is no alternative trade route. Knyadrea's greatest landmasses lie to the south. Sailing around the Nebbian continent is your only option if you want to trade with clans on the other side.'

'Maybe this courier's vessel can cut through the mainland?' suggested another merchant.

A new, emphatic voice sounded. 'I don't need to when there is already a canal to the Pale Sea.' Diabra rounded the corner of the table, her unbuttoned red coat flaring behind her.

'Surely you don't mean the Atkeis Canal?' The first merchant laughed and turned to the inventor. 'This charlatan will only strand your cargo on the sandbanks.'

Diabra strode up to aer. 'The open ocean may be the only option for your hulking vessels,' she said, 'but my watercraft are built for darting between the sandbanks. Going through the canal makes for a fast, fuel-efficient passage.'

After basking in the heat generated between the debating parties, Oklas moved on, satisfied that even if the inventor did not use Diabra's services, ae had a chance of sneaking away from the merchants.

A quintet of musicians tuned instruments on the border of the entrance hall and the ballroom. Oklas recognised the plucked zither and a Sikran horn, but the other instruments were a mystery to him. The presence of a soundcasting booth to the side suggested the music would grow louder and more energetic as the segeind progressed.

One of the musicians began to play, and knyads made their way through the pillars in pairs. They wore billowing gowns, cloaks, or streamlined suits in the colours and cuts favoured by their respective clans. A few began to dance, and the melody swelled as the other musicians joined the first. They played a piece in the style of the Southwestern clans.

Someone prodded Oklas on the shoulder. It was Minister Kemia. Though neatly dressed in a dark brown suit, she seemed out of place here, among things that sparkled. Her green-tinged skin had taken on an ashen hue, and her short tendrils stuck out at odd angles. She looked up at him with sunken eyes.

'Oklas, are you staying here until after curfew?'

'I plan on exploiting our exemption from it to the full, Minister,' he replied, a smile tugging at his mouth.

'Oh, would you please stand in for me?' she asked, visibly relieved and a little desperate. 'It has been a taxing phase, and I could do with turning in early.'

'Of course.'

Minister Kemia's expression lifted in gratitude. 'Field any questions, though I doubt anyone will want to talk business tonight. Enjoy yourself.' She gave a curt nod and scuttled away.

Oklas strayed towards the drinks table and helped himself to a small glass of Mindalill wine from a silver tray. The fleeting interactions of the early segeind had warmed his wits. He sipped the earthy, aromatic liquid, priming himself for more stimulating conversations.

❖═◦◉◦═❖

A short while later and Oklas was draining his second glass. Perhaps he was taking things faster than was wise for a formal occasion, but the frequent gulps excused him from having to speak. A musty intellectual from Dras Nauka had cornered him. Maroe always clung to knyads he knew at these events, usually those from the Dras Channel. His ill-fitting suit could have passed for sleepwear, and it lent him the appearance of a recently-moulted crustacean.

'The snowfall is heavier on Dras Sayve but you also have clearer light phases,' said Maroe, his high voice strangely suited to his spongey form. 'You're lucky to have such a climate. Cold fronts don't clip your part of the channel as often as they do ours.'

'I don't know about that. When I last checked, the outlook was over-cast,' muttered Oklas. There were two hundred better conversations to be had here—he had to extricate himself from this one. Maroe could also do with meeting people from other clans.

Suddenly, from among those clustered near the foyer, an intriguing knyad emerged. Between her exotic striped skin and her glittering cultural attire, Peer Kelabek was easily recognisable. Like a ray of sunlight breaking through a thick forest canopy. She had only recently assumed the title of Clan Peer but was fast becoming known for her charm and exquisite taste. The gown she wore that segeind was a little lighter than her warm brown skin, transitioning from copper to pink as she moved.

The peer and her envoys passed the banquet table. Maroe's mouth continued to move, but the sounds he made washed over Oklas. Peer Kelabek's tendrils were the warm hue of coral. She wore them looped through a burnished-metal headdress and plaited down her back. She was heading towards the ballroom. Oklas had to follow her.

'Agh,' he interrupted Maroe with a groan, wincing and shifting from one leg to the other. 'I've been standing too long. Do you also get leg spasms?'

'No, strangely enough. But my neck and back are another matter.'

'I had better go and stretch it out on the dancefloor.'

Maroe took a step back, tightly gripping the stem of his glass. 'I'm staying here. I don't care for dancing.'

Oklas had been counting on that. A dance with Maroe would be a terrible way to spend the segeind. Walking between the pillars that separated the ballroom from the entrance hall, Oklas looked for Peer Kelabek in the crowd. He spied her chatting with her envoys and watching the dancers with interest. Her high heels and elaborate tendrilstyle elevated her above the crowd.

Oklas swooped before her, keeping a respectable distance. 'Would you like to show them up?' he asked, offering her his hand. 'I'm volunteering to sway around the room with you and send them scattering.'

'This segeind is getting interesting,' she said, smiling at him but keeping her arms at her sides. She mouthed to her companions, 'What do you think?'

One of her envoys, a knyad with striped skin matching the translucent blue of aer cloak, gave the peer a playful push. Peer Kelabek took Oklas's hand and stepped forwards. 'Very well. I will put you through your paces.' The fragrance she wore was at once floral and peppery.

As he walked arm-in-arm with the peer, Oklas met the envious gazes of knyads at the sidelines with a smug smile. It was hardly his fault if they had failed to approach her. Peer Kelabek was captivating from afar, even more so up close. Her cheeks were dewy and her nose sloped to a neat, rounded tip. Around her striped neck and shoulders, her brown skin took on an almost purple hue.

'So what is the name of my dashing companion?' she asked.

*Dashing.* Oklas tried to downplay his delight at that. The dancers parted in a path as he led her near the centre of the ballroom. 'Let's maintain the mystery,' he said as they came to a halt. 'When you return home, you can tell everyone about the enchanted segeind you spent dancing with a dashing stranger.'

'I'm going to take a guess.' She pouted in mock concentration. 'Minister Sayve, of the Research Department.'

He laughed nervously. 'You can call me Oklas.'

'And I am Ailynn Nal Kelabek,' she said, drawing up with regal grace before adding offhandedly, 'I had a feeling you would be the first to ask for a dance.'

'How did you know it was me?'

'I had your roguish reputation to go on,' she said evenly, before breaking into a full-lipped smile. 'And we have a mutual friend, Geshan Sprijin. He said if I wanted a good time, I should look out for you.'

Oklas huffed a laugh.

Kelabek continued, 'It was your ambassador, Osura Sav, who pointed you out to me.'

'And warned you of my roguishness?'

'Something to that effect.'

Oklas scrunched his eyes closed. 'I'd trust Geshan's judgement over hers.'

'Why?'

'Osura is somewhat biased against me. I may have unintentionally caused her some embarrassment over the years. Shortly after I joined the Assembly, she abbreviated her clan name to "Sav".' Oklas cleared his throat and pulled at his collar. 'Rather decent of her. I now have the name "Sayve" all to myse—'

He inhaled sharply. Kelabek had taken his hand in hers; the other she rested on his shoulder. They were dancing. Her gaze travelled over his face.

'Geshan failed to describe the thick barbs of your eyebrows.' She lightly brushed his upper cheek, her thumb following the slant of his eye. 'What resyncrafter worked this magic?'

'Adecai naturally endowed me with them.'

'I confess I'm a little envious.'

'Don't be. You had the greater choice of prospective dance partners.' He whirled her around to show her the onlookers standing in front of the pillars. 'When I saw your glittering tendrils from across the room, I knew I had to act quickly.'

She touched her headdress. 'They're not a natural asset. There's an excellent filament studio just northwest of Apidecca. They stock the best hand-spun fibres on the moon.'

Oklas knew it was unlikely that anyone's tendrils could grow to such a length naturally. But the delicate extensions were so seamlessly woven into the peer's tendril vanes that he could not tell where the transition began. 'The artistry behind them only makes them more impressive. It shouldn't matter whether or not they have grown from your head.'

'Oh, but it does,' she said, her eyes widening. 'With enough substants, you can modify anything. But people are still drawn to innate qualities. Beauty should always seem effortless.' She gently pressed his shoulder, steering him in line with the other dancers. 'I like how you wear your tendrils—less stiff and formal than everyone else's.'

Oklas ruffled the tufts at the front of his head. 'The riding helmet helped achieve the look.'

Kelabek laughed; the throaty, musical sound filled Oklas's chest with sunbeams. He momentarily lost his bearings and bumped into someone behind him. Apologising, he adjusted his footing. Kelabek cupped her hand over her mouth, but he saw the smile reaching her eyes.

She composed herself and said, 'I thought you had pale blue fibres woven here.' From behind his ear, she stroked loose his longer tendrils. 'Gorgeous. Your tendril shafts are dark, but the tips are so light.'

He shrugged off the compliment. 'I thought they might be sun-bleached, but I don't spend nearly enough time outdoors for that to be the case. It's just how they grow.'

'How unusual.' Ailynn Kelabek's lips curved upwards. 'Then again, so much about you is.'

'Why, thank you.'

The tempo of the music slowed, and so did their dance. Peer Kelabek kept Oklas from going against the flow of dancers as they progressed around the room, and he mirrored her steady grace as best he could.

'The music, I recognise the tune,' said Oklas. 'Is it "Crystal Tides"? No? "Seaglass"?' He tipped his head back and sighed. He had heard it played on the ocean liners Emis had taken him on during his studies. 'The style is Southwestern. Is it Kelabekian?'

The peer watched him with a bemused expression. 'The composer is a knyad named Ritim Yaprak. She is a Southwesterner; her clan is some leagues from ours. This piece is called "Mirror Pool".'

'I knew it had something to do with a reflective substance.'

'We do play it to death.'

'I'm not yet tired of it.'

'I wish I could hear it afresh.' Kelabek leaned to the side of Oklas's face and whispered, 'Perhaps you can share your experience of it?' The layers of her floral fragrance unravelled, revealing base notes of incense and sandalwood.

Oklas rocked back and forth as he thought aloud. 'Listening to it makes me think of the Sayvian coast. When the sun is low, the light ricochets off the glass fronts of the buildings. It looks like they are beaming spotlights into the fog.'

'How poetic. Do you miss it? Dras Sayve?'

'I miss skating on the frozen lakes. The coniferous forests and the noodle broths. But I've spent most of my life away from the Dras Channel. Apidecca is my home.'

He leaned into the high notes of a string instrument, letting them stream through his limbs, guiding first his movements, then hers.

She laughed. 'I have danced since I left the water, but never quite like this.'

'Is that a compliment?' asked Oklas, raising an eyebrow.

'I meant it's refreshing not knowing what to expect. Are you self-taught?'

'I had a few dance lessons as part of my schooling. I remember some of the steps, not necessarily in the correct order.'

Kelabek closed her eyes, grounding herself in the rich timbre of the horn as it played. The music did not move her as it did him. Instead, she forged into it.

'My feet can't quite match the agility of my mind,' said Oklas, exaggerating a shrug. 'Mostly, I just run my mouth off. I think we both know who is really leading this dance.' He gave her a knowing look.

Kelabek caught herself steering him and looked at the floor, embarrassed.

'Someone has to,' he added reassuringly. 'I prefer it this way.' For once, Oklas found he had nothing more to say. He was content to bask in her radiance.

'I am surprised at how few peers were at the Charter's Exchange,' remarked Kelabek. 'Your ambassador said Peer Sayve was unable to make it this year. I had hoped to meet him.'

'He wasn't here last year either. Not every peer shares your interest in developments outside aer clan.'

'Seems like a waste of an opportunity. There is valuable information to be gathered.'

Oklas nodded. 'Have you always been a patron of the sciences?'

'Yes. I had to be here in person. I like to understand what I am supporting and how it measures up to the research of others.'

'Did Clan Kelabek exhibit anything?'

'We did. There is much volcanic activity along the Kelabekian coast, and we want to tap into this resource. Our scientists are in the process of developing safe ways of recharging resyn crystals with geothermal energy.'

'That is an ingenious use of your environment.'

'It is still hypothetical at this stage, but we prepared a scientific model to outline our expectations. Did you see it?'

'Unfortunately not. Only Minister Kemia attended this year. She felt I could better use my time elsewhere. I was only overdue on two reports. And my presence at the Engineering Consortium's meeting about resyn shortages was unnecessary.' He ran his fingers through his tendrils, grimacing. 'I won't bore you with the details. We also have our share of excitement at the Assembly. Each segment is different from the last.'

'Kemia mentioned you have set up sustained long-range communication between two colleges. I'd like to hear more about that.' Kelabek advanced on him, sending his feet skimming back.

Oklas's chest fluttered. 'Ah, the sinkhole of my favourite subject. It's better if we don't go there.'

'Why is that?' she asked, her lovely neck sloping to one side.

Oklas looked to the ceiling and back to her. 'Because it will take up the rest of the segeind, and I would rather hear what you have to say.'

'You think I can unlock the mysteries of knyadkind?'

'We can start there,' said Oklas, beaming. 'Are we merely an anomaly? Does some as-yet-undiscovered natural process cause us to develop from simple marine polyps? Or is it supernatural intervention?'

'So you are saying that, in another life, I could have been a coral colony?'

'A bright coral with fanned branches.'

'It could be boring, staying in one place your whole life.'

'Maybe not. You could digest your neighbours and spread your glorious self over their remains.'

She wrinkled her nose. 'When you think about all this, where does it lead?'

'To anything but a conclusion,' said Oklas with a grin. 'But in the process, I discover things I wasn't even looking for.' He looked upwards, grasping for something else. 'What is...your most treasured possession?'

'Why? Are you in the market for valuable Kelabekian antiques?'

'I was thinking of something special to you personally.'

The peer's amethyst eyes became unfocused. She came to a standstill, staring at something past Oklas's shoulder.

He followed her gaze and the warmth drained from his cheeks. The other knyads at the edge of the room drew apart to allow a spectral figure onto the dancefloor.

Peer Kelabek dipped into a reverent curtsey as Erud Teprill approached them.

A brief delay, and Oklas bowed deeply.

In her pleated, shell-white robes, Teprill resembled the stone pillars behind her.

'Good segeind, Peer Kelabek,' said the Erud with practised sincerity. 'I trust you have experienced Apideccan hospitality at its finest?' Her glance flitted towards Oklas, but not so briefly that he did not notice the simmering contempt in her orange eyes.

The peer maintained her poise as she answered Teprill, 'I have been well-catered throughout my stay. Minister Sayve has made my last segeind here most ... invigorating.'

'Entertainment is his primary contribution here,' said Teprill with a thin smile. 'I need to have a word with the deputy minister—when you finish with him, of course.'

The Erud slowly turned from them, watching Oklas through the corner of her eye with the unspoken expectation that he would not keep her waiting. Whatever Teprill had to say, it likely came not only from her but the whole of the Pentarchy, for she was the elected speaker. Oklas's mind raced, searching for something that might warrant their attention; if experience was anything to go on, it was not to commend him.

Then he was hit with a sickening realisation: this was the segeind of Illanu's escape. Had she been apprehended? His panic must have shown because Peer Kelabek lingered at his side.

'Are you alright, Oklas?' she asked, placing a hand on his shoulder.

He smoothed his features into a carefree guise. 'I will be fine. Thank you for the dance, Ailynn.'

She nodded with a slight frown. 'The treasure you asked about—I have a collection of alabaster balm jars. Perhaps I can show the display to you one segment?' She squeezed his hand and pulled away. He reluctantly unfurled his fingers from hers.

The Erud unblinkingly angled her head at Oklas and walked away, knowing he would follow.

# CHAPTER 7

## PRISMER

T HE LIGHT OF Prismer's torch fell over reflective specks in the walls. Above ground, curfew had not yet begun; the sense of urgency that had earlier plagued her began to ease. Flaked pale patches with teal rims—some fungus she could not identify—appeared on the ceiling. There was nothing on it in her books. She resolved to look it up in the public library on her mitter when this was over.

A pained grunt came from behind, followed by hissed curses. Rosh had walked into a rock protruding from the ceiling—he was the only one tall enough to clip it. Illanu had been managing better than expected, but she relied more heavily on her crutch as they made a steep descent.

'It'll get easier soon,' Prismer assured her, anticipating the gradient levelling.

'It's not a problem,' said Illanu airily. The tunnel was too narrow for them to walk side by side, but she followed Prismer closely, leaning to the left so they could see each other. 'Are these natural caves?'

'Some are.' Prismer ran her hand over the carved sandstone wall. 'Though possibly deepened or extended.'

'Back there, near your home, were those bricks and pillars ruins?'

'There was once a vast basin of resyn down here,' said Prismer, brightening. 'The ruins we passed are all that remain of the infrastructure built around it. As the resyn level receded, the Assembly Chambers expanded. They must have built the staff quarters over the tunnel entrance.'

'Are you sure the structure is stable? We aren't even wearing helmets,' said Rosh, drawing alongside them as the tunnel widened.

Prismer shone her torch from the ceiling to the smooth floor. 'I haven't seen rockfalls here. These pathways are over a thousand years old and still intact.' Her explanation brought little relief to Rosh's doubtful expression.

'Back at the ruins, I recognised a hard coral motif on the scattered bricks,' said Illanu, her movements growing more fluid. 'I saw that symbol in a book I read on Apidecca's Late Waxing Era. But there was no mention of anything important down here.' She paused, looking into the gloom at the way they had come, then back to Prismer. 'Where did you study this?'

'Nowhere. There are few written records about this place. I'm just well-positioned to explore the area.'

'Now you've done it,' Rosh told Prismer with a smirk. 'She'll interrogate you for the rest of the segeind.'

Illanu tucked a wispy tendril behind her ear, her smile innocuous. 'Classical Knowledge was my favourite supplementary.'

Prismer seized the opportunity to deflect some attention. 'What were you studying at the college?' she asked, having some idea of the answer.

'Inter-clan relations. I wanted to become a diplomat—help clans of different strata better cooperate.'

'It must be difficult for you, setting aside your plans.'

The torch lit the edge of Illanu's cheek in a crescent, veiling the other half of her face in shadow. 'Leaving my friends behind may be harder still,' she said, reaching for Rosh's hand.

'I'll catch up with you before long.' He curled his long fingers over her palm.

'And this is what you want now—to join the Ardedrians?' asked Prismer, a trace of scepticism in her modulated voice.

'As if she has a choice,' said Rosh darkly.

Illanu's brow pinched in a faint frown. 'The more I learned, the more I realised the Assembly would never accept someone like me into their ranks. Even Director Sayve's influence there is limited—and he's Praemor.'

Prismer thought of the minister's many rejected proposals. The Pentarchy only valued his contributions to projects headed by others. He liaised with the Engineering Consortium and had advised Kemia during the recent tramline upgrade, but these were not where his passions lay.

Initially, Prismer had enjoyed watching the Assembly prune away Sayve's entitlement. No one had a right to rise to prominence as quickly as he had. But even after his youthful conceit had lessened and he conformed to their ways, they did not stop cutting. They wanted only his bare intellect at their disposal.

The company arrived at a gaping cavern, large as a buried temple. Its top reached the surface, and the ceiling shone as if a galaxy lay embedded in the rock.

Illanu gasped. 'I've never seen algae glowing like that.'

The group took a few awed steps into the clearing. They tilted their heads back, basking in the light of the rare phenomenon above.

'It could be bacteria on the rock surface,' said Rosh. He turned from Illanu to Prismer. 'Couldn't we have climbed up to the ceiling from outside and lowered Ilu down here?'

'You'd need a different guide to scale the Razor Forest.'

'A forest?' asked Illanu.

'Made of carbonate rock,' elaborated Prismer, looking up at the moonlight pouring through gaps in the rock. 'The ridges are sharp, and as tall as trees.'

'The Razor Forest ends in cliffs that go down to the sea,' said Rosh. 'We must be close, surely?'

Prismer planted her torch at the centre of a looming karst stone, one of several eerie forms at floor level. The light threw the flinty recesses into sharp relief, making an abstract sentinel of it. 'We are closer to the coast than the city,' she agreed, 'but the next part of the journey will be riskier. If you want to rest, now is the time.'

Illanu and Rosh eagerly collapsed on something resembling a smooth, curved bench. Illanu put her crutch to one side and stretched her too-thin legs before her. A spring bubbled at the base of a nearby wall. Rosh filled his water bottle, then offered it to Illanu.

'Thank you,' she said, accepting it. 'How long have we been walking for?'

Rosh checked the timepiece he wore in place of his mitter. 'About four hours. It's after sixth-segeind.'

Illanu grinned. 'Look at us, out during curfew. We really are rebels now.'

'We are making good time,' said Prismer, still standing, 'but let's keep the break under an hour.'

Illanu looked up at her. 'I want you to know how grateful I am to you for doing this,' she said, searching Prismer's mask. 'Before the segeind is over, I'd like to get to know you better.'

Prismer angled her head at the juvenile. 'You want to know about scumbling?'

'What?'

'My "curse".'

'Uh, I didn't mean...only, it must be a sensitive subject.'

Prismer let out a humming sort of laugh. 'Don't be coy. Most are at least a little curious.' She interlaced her bony fingers, allowing the juveniles to see her ungloved hands.

'What happened to your skin, your face?' asked Rosh, staring.

Illanu's gaze flicked to the side, and she elbowed him in the ribs.

'What? She told us not to be coy,' he reminded her. 'The superstitions are entertaining but they don't answer my questions. I'm tired of being told the masks mark criminals or people infected with some incurable disease. Prismer lives with this "scumbling". I want to hear what she has to say.'

Prismer tilted her head thoughtfully, considering what she ought to share. 'It's a resyncrafting technique.'

'I knew it,' whispered Rosh.

'There are knyads out there who can rewrite your being. I don't remember much of the process.' She cradled her arms against her chest. 'I still have something of a face, if you can call it that. I can breathe. And see.'

Illanu winced, brushing her fingers against her cheek. 'Did it hurt?'

'Not as much as you might expect.' The dripping of water echoed through the cavern. Prismer looked at her hands. 'For some phases afterwards, there is a tingling. You feel it in the places that have changed the most.'

Rosh hunched forwards. 'The Assembly tries to keep this quiet, but most have heard the stories about a sect of resyncrafters experimenting on people. The Pentarchy provide them with a secret base,' he said. 'Is that where they sent you?'

'I don't know if it's the same place.'

'But it's in the city?'

'Possibly on the outskirts, deep underground.'

'Wait,' said Illanu, stepping between them. 'Resyncrafters have the power to adapt bodies for the better, to heal. Why recruit them to disfigure people?'

The trickling of the spring seemed to grow louder. Then Rosh spoke. 'Maybe no one can perform miracles with resyn? From what I see, this "rare gift" only causes harm.'

Illanu shook her head and turned to Prismer. 'There must be some decent resyncrafters, or a mender who could restore you?'

'No,' replied Prismer. 'Resyn can stimulate a transformation, but it is difficult to control, near impossible to reverse.' She couldn't remember where she had heard that. She wondered whether the resyncrafter working on her had mentioned it, and the skin at the nape of her neck prickled.

'I see this sort of thing at the clinic,' said Rosh. 'It takes no skill to tear ligaments or break bones. But even the best menders and surgeons can't heal every injury completely or prevent scarring.'

'Rosh is training to be a biomechanist,' explained Illanu, patting him on the back.

'I make prostheses, cybernetic implants, that sort of thing. That's when even the surgeons can't help.' He snorted a laugh. 'So, Prismer...why *did* they scumble you? Was it something you did?'

'You're not still accusing her of being a criminal,' protested Illanu.

'He isn't wrong to think that way,' said Prismer, looking above Rosh to the starry ceiling. 'This is not my first time crossing the Assembly.'

Ignoring Illanu's disapproving look, Rosh persisted. 'I met someone who had served six revolutions in a labour commune. Enforcers caught aer trading in medicinal herbs without certification. It was hard labour, but they didn't scumble aer.'

'I don't think the severity of the crime has much to do with scumbling,' said Prismer, settling on the floor a few paces away from Rosh and Illanu. 'Most of us are released after the procedure, though many lose their jobs. It's different for each maskad.'

Illanu held Prismer's gaze, silently goading her into sharing more.

Prismer exhaled through the filters in her mask and cocked her head to one side. 'I will tell you what I did and why—if you really want to hear it.'

Rosh nodded. 'We do.'

'Please,' added Illanu.

Maybe Prismer missed Maskad Support more than she knew because her words flowed with surprising ease. 'I came to Apidecca from a lower Orta clan to start a job arranged by the Assembly. For years I had sent through applications, trying to get here. I had only seen captures of the city, but I knew I had to walk among the ancient buildings and learn the secrets of the knyads behind them. When I found out I would be accommodated under the Assembly Chambers'—beneath her mask, the corners of her gills tautened in a mouthless smile—'I can't describe the joy I felt.'

The wistfulness sealed within Prismer shone from Illanu's face. At that moment, some invisible thread connected them. Prismer continued, 'But it wasn't enough to admire the place. Generations of knyads had left their mark on the city, and I wanted to stay and do the same. I suppose I was not unlike you,'—she looked pointedly at Illanu—'ambitious, more gullible perhaps. I started studying bridging courses to fill the gaps in my education.'

As she spoke, exquisite designs, framed by the black eyehole rims of her mask, filled her view. 'You may have heard of the Pentarchic Institute of Developers. Their artisans come to restore embellishments around the Chambers. Sometimes they even create something new. They have a workshop on one of the higher floors of the Assembly. I used to watch them through the windows whenever I passed by.'

The images began to fade, and Prismer looked down at her clasped hands. With the blunted claws of her right hand, she stroked open the left. 'The beauty of the buildings brought me to Apidecca, but the power here took hold of me. I devised a way to get my share in it.' The devastating obsession overcame her afresh, sharpening her tone of voice. 'Spatial planners have such an influence over people's lives. They create centres and peripheries. They can complement social stratification—or nullify it. That was to be my profession. Years after my death, knyads would continue to move along the routes I had laid out. I would not be forgotten.'

Illanu stared uncomprehendingly at her, their connection frayed. Prismer looked away. Had she shared too much? No, she decided. Her young charge needed to see her as she really was. 'I couldn't afford to enter the Spatial Planning program, nor were my abilities so exceptional that I could attract sponsorship. I used what skill I had to earn another income.'

'The sculptures in your room,' said Illanu, her eyes widening in realisation, 'you sold them?'

'Visitors to the Assembly commissioned me, usually to mimic popular styles of sculpture. I was versatile, and my rates were relatively low.' She leaned back, gliding her rough fingers over the cool floor. 'Around that time, I started borrowing materials from the workshop to practice or to supplement my supplies. Carving stone is expensive, and my patrons were seldom willing to part with any substants upfront.'

'Didn't the artisans notice the materials disappearing?' asked Rosh.

'No one would miss twenty minahs of clay lifted over a few segments or a block of alabaster from a large consignment. I kept this up for revolutions.' Her laugh sounded bitter even to her own ears. 'I knew it wasn't right. I thought if I showed initiative, if they saw what I could make, they might look past my stratum. I would be accepted.'

Rosh watched her with a frown. 'But they eventually caught you stealing.'

Prismer nodded. 'As careful as I was, I still had to move the things I took between the workshop and the staff quarters. I didn't want to see the risk.' Shimmering droplets skipped from the spring, their cheerfulness contrasting starkly with her dredged memories. 'I won't go into it all, but the Assembly enforcers arrested me and searched my rooms. I was scumbled not long after that.'

Prismer hesitated, waiting for them to interrupt her, but they did not. She swallowed hard. 'They made an example of me. I am a warning to the Chambers' staff.' Shifting uncomfortably, she tapped the cheek of her mask. 'If there is something common to all maskads, it is this: each of us has undermined the order of things. Our leaders quietly turn us into outcasts before we can influence others.' She rose to fetch her bag. 'Now, you had better eat. It's still two leagues to the sea, and there won't be time for another stop.'

'Are you alright?' asked Illanu, watching Prismer shakily sling the bag over her shoulder.

'Just scouting ahead.' She turned from them too swiftly and staggered. Rosh got to his feet. She raised her hand to keep him from following her. 'I-I need some time to myself.' He assessed her stance. When he seemed sure she was well, he returned to Illanu's side.

The floor became like a dense sea, swelling and dipping under Prismer's feet. She took several more faltering steps away from the young knyads. The cavern began to close in on her. Bleak algae panels replaced shafts of moonlight, and the karst stones and stalagmites turned into the walls of her holding cell. Here, the memory she had tried to suppress fully resurfaced. Her breaths came rapidly and her chest felt tight. She needed to press on, but not like this. When an unwelcome vision came upon her, the quickest way to regain her wits was to step into it.

Prismer had been restrained in her seat ahead of the Erud's arrival. Armed enforcers waited on the other side of the holding cell door. She had never seen an Erud up close, though she had worked for them these past two years. The thought of confessing her wrongdoings to such an important visitor made her stomach churn. Even as she relived this moment, Prismer stood outside her younger self. She couldn't remember what she had looked like. Only some of her features came into focus: her long nose and high forehead, marble-green braids a shade darker than her skin. The Erud, with her wide, painted mouth, was easier to recall. She was a sturdy, gaudily attractive knyad of around sixty years—an arresting presence in the small room. Despite her relaxed demeanour, a throbbing current emanated from Erud Aurel, like the warning of a cruttlefiend about to lash out with a stinging spur.

She pushed a stack of pages towards Prismer with a heavily decorated hand. The rows of thick rings she wore made her fingers appear stubby. The deep purple gems embedded in the metal were almost as dark as her richly layered robes. 'Is this yours?' she asked throatily.

Prismer accepted the pages. Even the crisp texture of paper beneath her fingertips failed to calm her. On the front page was written, in a curling script, "Application for Apprenticeship". Next to the pages lay an empty envelope with a broken wax seal, bearing an emblem of coral sprigs and the rising sun. It was from the Pentarchic Institute of Developers.

'It is, Your Grace,' answered Prismer. Her voice was as low then as it was now, but the words rolled over her tongue with a raw cadence that synth-speech could not recreate.

The Erud gave a pitying quirk of her brow and folded her hands at her front. 'And the stolen materials? I presume they generated you the substants required to pay for this?'

In truth, Prismer had not saved even half of what she needed for her first year of study. 'I shouldn't have taken anything,' she blurted out, 'but I was going to reimburse—'

'I'm going to stop you there, sundew. I've heard this story before, dressed up in different excuses.' Though firm, Erud Aurel let none of her staged warmth subside. She held up the papers and continued, her mirth building. 'You thought this was your ticket to a Praemor lifestyle?'

Prismer gaped at her, but thought the better of speaking immediately.

Erud Aurel winked. 'It is not uncommon for juveniles coming to this city to develop a taste for grandeur.'

'It was never about wealth,' said Prismer earnestly. 'I only wanted to learn how to create the sort of wonders I see in the Chambers.'

'What a martyr for the arts you are,' said the Erud with a hearty laugh. 'You serve the greatest establishment in all of Knyadrea. If that doesn't give you a sense of significance, I don't know what can. It's a pity that you should gamble it all away for something that was already far beyond your reach.'

Aurel met Prismer's look of surprise with a simper. 'Yes, I have seen your portfolio. The sketches of your city plans are charmingly naive, like the castles that tidelings build in the sand. Even if you were Praemor, you would not meet the Institute's standards. We identify promising students during their tideling years. By your age, the other applicants would have studied under mentors around Knyadrea and gained specialised knowledge.'

It was as if Aurel had struck her across the face. Prismer gripped the table in front of her and looked away from the Erud. Her red eyes, dark as berry cordial, brimmed with tears.

'You don't seem like a troublemaker,' said Erud Aurel. 'Perhaps someone misled you into making the wrong choices? Had you set your sights on more realistic goals, you could have assisted our artisans in the workshop.' Aurel turned from the table and started to pace back and forth behind Prismer's chair. 'What we cannot overlook, sadly, are the crimes you committed against your employers.'

'I never meant for—' Prismer's voice came out in a whisper, and she found she could say no more. Her head hung low, and her braids fell about her face.

'People are not judged by their intentions, sundew.' A gravity entered Erud Aurel's voice. 'The fact is you are a thief running a side job on the

Chambers' grounds. Do you know how many knyads with clean records would gladly take your position at the Assembly?'

'I wronged the Erudean Pentarchy...and the General Assembly.' Prismer's voice cracked, and hot tears tracked her face. 'I c-can't expect to keep my job, but please, where will I serve my sentence?' The words had barely left her mouth when she feared she had overstepped a boundary. People did not demand answers, however politely, from the Eruds. But Prismer was tired and desperate for this ordeal to end. She had spent two segments alone in the dark, anticipating retribution. No labour commune could be worse than that.

'Such contrition,' the Erud soothed, sliding back into her more kindly manner. 'As it happens, I hold sway in the Erudean Pentarchy. When we agree on the terms, we will convince the Assembly to let you stay on.'

'Thank you, Your Grace,' said Prismer cautiously as she wiped her face on her sleeve.

Erud Aurel gave a broad smile that did not cooperate with her features in anything close to compassion. 'I am not without mercy. After the guild processes you, it will be difficult for you to find employment elsewhere.' Before leaving, Erud Aurel lifted Prismer's chin and looked at her appraisingly, her chunky jewellery digging into Prismer's skin.

'Some of the others had more to lose,' she commented, more to herself than Prismer. She stroked a long braid back from Prismer's shoulder. 'Still, a shame.'

It could not have prepared Prismer for what would follow: being dragged out into startling daylight and stashed in a casket-like vehicle. Her grim journey ended in a starkly lit theatre clad in cold black tiles—the place of her unmaking.

A flash of awareness struck the scene. This was not happening now. Prismer could not afford to inhabit this illusion any longer. The theatre lights flickered as she willed the memory into dissolving at the edges, sinking it into the depths of her mind. The cave wall was dank and cold against her back– she bolted upright.

Pulling down her mask, Prismer rubbed the skin around her eye and temples. She retrieved a nutrient pack from her bag and used her thick nails to tear it open. Feeling for the beaked opening at the base of her throat, she tipped her head back and, squeezing the pack, siphoned the gel down her oesophagus. She gagged and got to her feet. Snatches of

Illanu and Rosh's conversation echoed from the other side of the wall. Prismer started back, confident in her preparations if nothing else. She had to concentrate on what awaited them at the coast.

# CHAPTER 8

## OKLAS

TRAILING ERUD TEPRILL, Oklas started up the stairway to the north wing, his apprehension growing with each step he took. Two Furtim enforcers occupied the space between him and Teprill—he would have thought nothing of this were they not leading him away from the safety of onlookers.

He recognised the enforcer at his right by her protruding chin. Furto Seron was more than Teprill's bodyguard—she was her confidant. Like the other members of her division, she wore a plain uniform that seemed to melt her edges. Combined with holographic technology, the reflective fabric mimicked the hues and patterns of the surrounding environment. She wore her tendrils cropped to their spiny bases—only a deget long, they bristled in agitation as she caught him looking her way.

The Furtim Division was unlike any other. They did not answer to the Board of Generals as other enforcers did, and they forsook their clan names, pledging their allegiance to the Eruds alone. They took their directives from no one outside of the Pentarchy.

While strong, Seron was not the most physically imposing of the enforcers. It took more than sheer bulk to be selected by the Eruds for special operations. Oklas's cold shirt stuck to his skin. He folded his hands behind his back. He hoped Seron was only accompanying her master as additional security tonight. He would hate to be targeted by her.

The Erudean Pentarchy did not want to give the impression that the Assembly could summon them collectively. Teprill was their lone representative at the Induction Ball. Given a choice of Eruds to meet, Oklas would have sooner picked Erud Quental—someone argumentative but easy to misdirect. Teprill was Oklas's senior by only a few years, but he knew better than to underestimate her. She ceaselessly stored impressions of those in her company, making them known when they were most damaging. Protocol required Oklas to follow several paces behind her, allowing him to avoid the white heat of her gaze a little longer and brace himself for what was to come.

Even after a decade in politics, he struggled to keep currents of emotion from flickering across his face. Setting off such signals had never been more dangerous. They communicated everything he could not say, and Teprill would be watching for them. Oklas had to bury his concerns about the cliffside escape, deep enough that even she couldn't detect them.

On the third floor, Teprill left the stairway. She walked a short distance down the corridor and passed through a pair of open doors. Oklas followed her into a study. It was one of his favourite pleasingly-cluttered rooms here, and he resented her all the more for souring his impression of it.

The Erud stopped in front of the floor-length windows overlooking the city. Oklas held back, alongside the Furtim, and waited. Teprill turned from the window and lowered herself onto a solid chair of dark wood, making a throne of it. She placed her hands on the interlocking triangles of the armrests and sat straight-backed, her delicate chin raised. The glow of the city lights hardened the edges of her silhouette, heightening her otherworldly splendour.

'Thank you, Furto Seron, Furto Durus,' she said, nodding to each enforcer in turn. 'You may wait at the door.'

Seron sneered at Oklas as she passed him, disappointed perhaps that it was all she could do to intimidate him. He held back a smirk. Did she take him for a threat to her precious master? He did not hear the doors close. She and Durus would likely remain within earshot.

'Come closer, Sayve,' said Teprill listlessly. 'I'd rather not go hoarse calling to you from across the room.'

Oklas obeyed, inwardly debating when to stop walking. It had been years since he had been granted an audience with the Pentarchy. Without the courtiers flapping about and relaying instructions, he did not know where to put himself. Opposite Teprill were several mismatched chairs, low-set and shabbier than hers. Oklas drew alongside one of these and stopped several alkar from Teprill, far enough that he did not look down on her while standing. He lowered his shoulders and dropped his hands to his sides. If he were really in trouble, Teprill would have left him to the Furtim rather than pull him aside for a private conversation—not that this was much better.

She looked around the room, the dim lights of girandoles highlighting the cut-crystal planes of her thin face. 'The venue is looking tired,' she remarked.

Her sovereignty was no less apparent here than in the Throne Room above the Assembly Chambers. She still had not invited Oklas to take a seat. The Eruds were revered from afar and pandered to in public. But Teprill relished cornering her subjects in more intimate settings, where she could flex the full extent of her control over them. Oklas consciously unclenched his jaw.

Seemingly preoccupied with the curtains at her side, Teprill asked, 'On which of this year's Orta clans would you bestow Praemor status?'

Oklas doubted she would give any weight to his opinion, but he could play along. 'Sikra and Etmek's work comes to mind. Then there's Dalga, another worthy contender.' He crossed his arms to keep himself from fidgeting. 'Of course, I can only comment on the fraction of them I learned of this segeind.'

She did not comment on his choices, but turned from the curtains to face him. 'And which of the Praemor clans would you demote to the Orta?'

Demote. The word rang in Oklas's ears. He opened his mouth and, unable to summon a sound, closed it again.

Unsurprised by his reaction, Teprill continued, 'For the sake of discretion, we do not broadcast demotions. People prefer to hear about the newly-inducted Praemor clans, but the reality is that Knyadrea can only sustain so many of these.' She tapped the arm of her chair. 'So I ask you again, who is not proving their worth?'

'I-I would need more information to make such a suggestion, especially given I didn't attend the exhib—'

'And yet you knew enough to put forward names for promotion.' Her voice turned icy.

Oklas lowered his gaze. To speak while incensed would be disastrous.

He let some searing moments pass before replying, 'In that instance, the clan only had something to gain, Your Grace.'

'What's this?' She performed an airy laugh. 'Could it be that my position is not so enviable? I thought you would know by now that leadership imposes difficult choices on us.'

Oklas raised his head. 'I do not claim to know better than our Erud elect,' he said, his eyes meeting hers, 'but what necessitates these demotions?'

Teprill gestured towards the chair nearest to Oklas. He sat down, leaning forwards slightly.

'Oklas, you know as well as I that the current of power moves between disparities,' said Teprill. 'It's what drives the innovation you crave. You cannot moderate it.'

Emboldened by his convictions and the lingering effects of the swiftly-downed Mindalill wine, Oklas pressed on. 'Surely we have enough to take some chances on those with potential, regardless of stratum or the performance of their clans?'

Erud Teprill folded her hands in her lap. 'What you propose is merely a variation of our current system, only more complicated in that it elevates individuals rather than entire clans over one another. Stratification honours the design set out by the Initiator.'

*The Initiator* was a vague term used by the Erudean Pentarchy in recent decades. It described anything from Adecai, the most widely-recognised of knyadkind's purported creators, to some mysterious force beyond the waves. The Pentarchy undermined the worship of a supreme being to consolidate their power, but they did not renounce Adecai. Not when they could tweak doctrines to portray themselves as Knyadrea's divinely appointed rulers.

Oklas let the muscles of his face relax into a neutral expression and asked, 'What does this design look like in practice?'

Teprill's lips threaded into a smile. 'Take our Orta farmers, attuned to the seasonal shifts of their respective regions. Many of those same farmers fall ill when they move to the cities, a sign perhaps that they are departing from their course. Even while they were polyps at sea, their stratum was already predetermined. The same is true of all of us. What reason is there for us to evolve into complex organisms if not to perform specific functions within a system? The younger clans emerged to serve our growing civilisations. You and I, as Praemor knyads, are designed to orchestrate the whole. It is a great honour, but it won't always earn you popularity.'

Oklas drew in a deep breath to keep himself from speaking. He designed his inventions for specific purposes, but knyads were not machines. They operated within a beautifully complex system. They could change themselves and their environments. Oklas put no faith in the Pentarchy, but he did believe in a higher intelligence as the source of all life. Someone who had created beings with unique abilities and yearnings would not intend for them to be limited. But to explain this to a knyad so entrenched in her dogmas would be a waste of time.

Something shifted in Teprill's demeanour, and the knuckles of her spindly fingers whitened. 'Dissenters are sowing confusion among the lower strata. Some would have them covet the breadth of choice available to the Praemor.' She turned the full intensity of her gaze onto Oklas. 'They see only the benefits of power, not the sacrifices it demands. It is possible to educate the unclassified, and they may even learn to imitate those of a higher stratum, but they will never have the favour of the Initiator. Tragically, they will waste their lives striving for what was never theirs to attain.'

Her venomous reference to the Emisrian College's applicants struck Oklas. He bit his tongue.

When the Erud was sure he would not take the bait, she continued, 'Teaching a knyad to resist aer function is to rob aer of peace. I think you and I agree that peace is what we want most for knyadkind.'

Oklas nodded stiffly. 'It is something I actively secure for those under my protection.'

Teprill smoothed her long pleated skirts over her knees. 'Your commitment to your students is admirable, but I wonder, does it take precedence over your commitment to your government?'

'Your Grace?'

'Growing up in a Pentarchic clan, I learned there is no higher calling than to serve Knyadrea as an Erud. In the same way, you cannot hope to achieve a role greater than that of a minister in the General Assembly. I am only concerned that your college is a distraction.'

Oklas frowned. 'It is a distraction that connects me to the knyads I serve.'

'And I am sure they are most appreciative,' said Teprill lightly. 'But you have assumed many roles: engineer, educator, and deputy minister. Some members of the Assembly feel you are struggling to strike a balance between these. If you cannot choose between your competing interests, others may have to decide for you.'

'I am not alone in this, Your Grace. A great many ministers are involved in projects outside of their portfolios.'

'And yet dissent does not fester within their organisations.' She looked past him to the Furtim watching from the doorway.

Oklas straightened. 'The General Assembly has vetted my staff.'

'And what about your students? Was the juvenile from Maha so carefully screened?'

Oklas's hands went cold, and he became aware of the ache behind his temples. 'Illanu?'

'I presume you have not heard from her since the rally? Or found further evidence of insurgent activity within the Emisrian College?'

He blinked, clearing his throat. 'Regrettably, I have no new information to offer.' He allowed some honesty to shine through his words.

The Erud searched his face for something more. Oklas's mouth tightened. Teprill got up and strayed over to the bay window. 'Someone has been sheltering her,' she said, a curious hush in her voice. She let the silence that followed give weight to her observation as she looked at the city below. 'Our enforcers are searching for insurgents. I fear there is more rot in this city than we first thought. But the gap between their evacuation and our pursuit closes with each raid. Earlier this segment the Industrial Division found—'

Oklas's throat tightened in a silent gasp.

Teprill's head snapped back to him. 'A hastily abandoned warehouse in Dolna,' she finished. Her narrow nostrils flared, making her even more reminiscent of a serpent on a scent trail. Slowly, she walked towards Oklas. 'You are no longer so new to the Assembly that we can dismiss your repeated misdemeanours as mere oversights. But you needn't suffer any repercussions. If you find you have news to share, I trust you will bring it to us timeously?' She stopped in front of him and tipped her head to one side.

He exhaled. 'Of course.'

Teprill's shrewd smile hardened her features. 'Good,' she said, returning to her chair. 'Minister Cantuce told me about your experimental transmissions with the Drassian Academy. Perhaps it would be beneficial for you to collaborate with her department in future?'

Oklas restored his casual smile and forced his hands open. 'My dabbling in communications has run its course. Minister Cantuce made it clear that satellite technology is better left unexplored.' He needed the Pentarchy to have a superficial awareness of his projects, to diminish the impression that he was hiding anything from them. But only a short while ago they had been indifferent to his satellite. Where had this newfound interest come from?

'Certainly, its implementation should not accelerate unchecked,' said Teprill. 'But Cantuce and I concluded that some Praemor cities might benefit from faster communication—from your research.'

'That's...thrilling news.' Oklas pressed his hands together, attempting to reframe his sudden release of nervous energy as excitement.

'Obviously, any networks set up would have to be secured. We can't have any knyad with a mitter accessing them.'

Oklas pushed away thoughts of the Eruds seizing his technology and misusing it.

'If you think it is something you would like to pursue,' Teprill continued, 'I can even arrange for your transfer to Communications.'

Oklas shifted uncomfortably in his seat, pulling at his jacket. 'I might not be the best fit for such a specialised field. Kemia would be the first to tell you I generate far more ideas than I can realistically execute.'

'Exactly. The focus of the Research Department is broad, nearly directionless. You are attending to short-term problems as they arise. Under Minister Cantuce's guidance, you could refine your concepts and effect lasting change.'

So the Eruds wanted him working exclusively on what they deemed useful, supervised by a minister loyal to them.

'Thank you, but I believe I am where I belong.'

Something horrid churned beneath Teprill's coldly beautiful exterior, like a shadow under the surface of still water. 'You soon will be,' she said, leaning back in her ugly chair. 'Everything can be perfectly appreciated when it is in its proper place, even hedonism.' She called to her Furtim and turned back to Oklas. 'You should return to the party. Your antics amuse our guests.'

*Better you take me for a fool than a threat*, he thought. Now, if only Teprill would hurry up and release him.

'Kelabek has another year to improve their contributions,' she said disinterestedly. 'Perhaps you could charm the delegates from Behrantz next? It may lessen the blow when we relegate them to Orta in the segere.'

# CHAPTER 9

## PRISMER

Prismer, Illanu, and Rosh continued northwest, making a gradual descent. The stalagmites were thick but spaced in such a way that Illanu had no difficulty weaving between them. The weak light of the night sky occasionally splintered the ceiling, but the underground temple shrunk as they progressed, breaking into smaller cavities that bubbled through the rock.

The two juveniles did not ask Prismer where she had gone or what had happened back at the stopover, for which she was grateful. Her recount of the lead-up to her scumbling had, however, sparked an uncomfortable discussion between them.

'If studying above your stratum were illegal, they would have to arrest half of the Consortium trainees,' said Rosh, squeezing his half-eaten nectarpod.

'Your field is stratum-exempt,' countered Illanu. 'It's different at the Emisrian. What if I've put the other students in danger?'

Rosh popped the rest of his nectarpod into his mouth and shrugged. 'Your college director has kept them safe so far. At worst, the authorities will send you back to Maha. No one is going to scumble you.'

'It won't. Happen. To me,' interjected Prismer, slowly forming each word. 'I was certain of it too.' She returned the volume of the synthesiser at her throat to its usual setting. Her natural voice had always been too easy for others to talk over, and she found the option of amplifying it useful.

'Enforcers started that riot,' claimed Rosh. 'Ilu is taking the fall for it, but she's done nothing wrong. There are witnesses to prove it.'

'The courts handle ordinary transgressions. Given a fair trial, Illanu might be acquitted. But I understand her case has reached the notice of the Pentarchy, and they do not need to justify their verdicts.'

Illanu rubbed the arm she used to lean on her crutch. 'Hidreth, the knyad at the safehouse, said something similar. I can't stay here.'

Prismer watched the two juveniles wrestle with their concerns. 'It is better if we don't dwell on what might happen to Illanu should she be captured.'

'She won't be on my watch,' said Rosh, drawing alongside Illanu. 'Not that you seem to care—this is just a job, isn't it?'

Prismer snickered. 'You assume I am making a profit from this arrangement?'

Illanu did not denounce Rosh's accusations this time. She stood aside, allowing him and Prismer to voice what was brewing between them.

Rosh adjusted the satchel of Illanu's rucksack at his shoulder, while the thumb of his other hand stuck out from his pocket. 'So you're not a mercenary. Not an Ardedrian sympathiser. You work for the people hunting Ilu but you're helping her evade arrest. Tell me, Prismer, why are you doing this?' There was a note of challenge in his voice, but no scorn.

Prismer held his gaze. 'Let's focus on getting "our" friend out to sea, shall we?' she said, slanting her torch beam towards the tunnel before them and turning to leave.

Illanu walked past Rosh and joined Prismer, wearing a small smile.

The stalagmites gradually disappeared from the floor, and a crisp, salty scent entered the air. The group traced the progress of a freshwater stream as it carved its way between rocks towards the sea. Their sodden boots surged through ankle-deep water which gathered momentum on its way down. Illanu's pace slowed as Rosh and Prismer helped her over rocky obstructions along the river bed. Karst stones still loomed in corners, their shadows moving with the torchlight. More than once, the illusion of dark figures surrounding them was too real, and at the front of the line, Prismer jumped.

'You gave me a start that time,' said Illanu with a nervous laugh.

'Sorry,' said Prismer, pulling her gaze away from the shadowy corner. 'I keep expecting...'

Though the air was still, a sound akin to wind sweeping through the High Street reverberated in the distance. Something slick glistened on the rocks.

Prismer ran a scaled hand along the wall. It came away wet. 'Seawater,' she murmured, stepping forwards. 'We must quieten.'

Illanu frowned. 'What do you mean? Is someone here?'

'I came this way a few segments ago to see where the Aquatic Division begin their patrols,' said Prismer in a hushed tone. 'There weren't any enforcers on this side then, but we can't become complacent. Porous borders attract their attention.' No one outside knew these flooded tunnels eventually connected with the base of the Assembly Chambers, but Prismer doubted she was the first to explore the tubular vents in the cliffside. Many ended in air pockets—suitable hiding places for smugglers to secret hauls in transit.

'Oh look,' cried Illanu. Prismer and Rosh both jolted.

'Sorry. I only meant there is a pool of water down there.' She pointed at a hole in the floor.

Prismer recognised this part of the tunnel, though she had been swimming when she was last here. They climbed through the hole and skidded down a slope to a tidal pool.

Rosh looked back at the way they came. 'Is that the high tide line up there?'

'Yes. It's receding now,' said Prismer. Since Apidecca faced away from the planet they orbited, the seas on this side of the moon were relatively shallow. However, Knyadrea and Dryadene's orbital resonance was such that, during a period of three Knyadrean revolutions, the moons drew close twice.

Every revolution, sea levels on Knyadrea's far side steadily rose and fell by hundreds of alkar. It was something Prismer had to consider when charting their route. The tunnels looked different from the way they did when she last scouted the area underwater. Around her were glistening rocks, worn smooth. The waves gently lapped at the sides of the tunnel, occasionally ebbing from the wall with a wet *thunk*.

Illanu peered into the black water. 'When we come out on the other side, will we be close to the meeting place?'

'We should be. I have tried to veer right where possible,' replied Prismer, handing her torch to Illanu. 'I think it best if I go ahead to find Kelvan.'

'We should keep in contact over the towayes,' said Illanu.

Prismer withdrew her towaye from her pocket. 'I'm not sure how well the signals will travel underwater. But I will keep it on.' She removed the fulver and pants she wore over her aquaskin suit and utility belt. The lightweight garments were easy to pack away. From her bag, Prismer withdrew a coil of thin cord. She unwound a section and handed the end to Illanu.

The juvenile accepted it and asked, 'What must I do with this?'

'Secure it to something. This pool is one of several openings to the sea. Marking the route will help me find my way back to you.'

'What if we lose contact?' asked Rosh. 'How long should we wait for you?'

Still hunched over her bag, Prismer looked up at him. 'Give it an hour before following me. But don't turn back, or you'll get lost in the caverns.'

'Kelvan said he would stay close to the seafloor on the eastern side,' Illanu reminded her.

Prismer crouched beside the heaving pool and swung her legs over the edge. The bracing water slid over her scaly feet, then her calves. She waded deeper. When the water reached the aquaskin at her thighs, she kicked back, plunging her shoulders below the surface. Prismer relished the cold embrace of the sea. There were precious few deep pools in the city.

Every knyad felt the pull to the ocean from which they were all harvested. It stirred in Prismer the recklessness needed for the next stage of the journey. She held her sling bag above the water and opened it again. There was one last thing she had to put away.

'I hope you don't startle easily,' she warned, unbuckling the straps at the back of her head. She would prefer it if they never saw her face, but it would be impractical to wear the mask while swimming. To experience their ease around her for this short time had been a gift, and now she had to let it go.

Prismer tipped the mask forwards into her cupped hand and drank in the cold air; unfiltered by mesh, it tasted strongly of salt and seafronds. Her heartbeat lashed against her ribs and she quickly stashed away the mask with the rest of her gear, daring an upwards glance at Illanu and Rosh.

They stood over her, frozen in place. Rosh's wideset eyes travelled over the alien anatomy of her face until he sensed her watching him, perhaps by the movement of her optic pattern. His eyes closed tight, as if stung by the briny air, and he turned aside, pressing his long fingers against his lips. Illanu's expression was hardly more readable than Prismer's mask. Sinking to her knees, she removed her brooch.

'Here,' she said, holding the brooch out to Prismer. 'I told Kelvan to look for it.'

Prismer swam up to Illanu and allowed her to pin it to the aquaskin.

Illanu drew back. 'The knyads at the safe house prayed over it for me. It'll give you protection.'

'I will look after it,' said Prismer, placing a rough hand over the brooch.

'Prismer,' called Rosh. He was looking at her again. 'Turn back if it gets risky.'

She nodded, and he pressed his lips into a tight smile.

With the cord in her hand, Prismer widened her gills in a deep breath and submerged.

Though she referred to her breathing slits as "gills", the only advantage they offered underwater was sealing more tightly than nostrils, preventing accidental gulps of seawater. The air she breathed still flowed to her lungs and, like any whole knyad, she would have to make it last down here. Surrounded by darkness and the sound of water rushing over her ears, she became keenly aware of the intermittent throbbing of her slowed heart rate.

Her thoughts strayed over to the juveniles. She didn't know what reaction she had expected from them. Until now, Dy Erla was the only whole knyad to have seen her unmasked, and propriety kept the minister from divulging what she truly thought of Prismer's appearance. Though they had no reason to spare her feelings, the juveniles had not cursed or jeered at her; it was almost disappointing. She knew too well how she would have reacted to seeing even a concealed maskad when she was their age.

She tethered a section of the cord to a jagged shard of rock, leaving a marker on her way to the open ocean. Unimpeded by the mask, her large eye came into its own here. Growing along the walls was a wild variant of the algae that knyads cultivated in light panels. By its faint glow, Prismer could see few colours, but the outlines of her underwater landscape were clear enough to navigate. While she would always maintain that no good came from scumbling, she conceded that her vision in the dark was better now than when she saw with two eyes.

She withdrew the towaye from a pocket in her utility belt and stroked the faint golden symbols of the keypad to signal Illanu. A strained gurgle rang out. It couldn't have broken, surely? Sayve would have made the thing waterproof. 'Is anyone there?' she asked, her synth-speech sounding at a frequency that carried underwater.

'Prismer?' came Illanu's voice over the towaye. The transmission was scratchy at this depth.

'Just checking the connectivity.'

'We can hear you.'

'Good. There are some splits in the tunnel. The last turn I took only led to a sealed cave, but the current feels stronger here. I may have found the right vent. If all goes well, I will come back to you. If not—at least you will have a trail to follow.'

Both juveniles murmured something in an assenting tone and ended the transmission.

It was not long before she reached the final junction in the vent. Tiny beads and flat fragments glinted under the warm light of the towaye, remnants of a time before the use of polymatter became severely restricted. The debris scattered with mesmerising grace. She took its presence as a sign that she was getting close to the ocean. Prismer felt the push and pull of the current more strongly now. Rocks jutting from above and below narrowed her path. She tucked in her elbows and clawed through the small space. A dim blue circle appeared at the end of the vent—a porthole to the moonlit sea.

Her feet gently touched down on the floor. She held the towaye to her throat to give another update. 'I see the exit. I'm just going to look—'

Prismer struck the power button of the device—switching it off. A blinding light had penetrated the murky water, pouring across the floor, over the swaying litter. Faster than she could think, Prismer propelled herself to the ceiling and crawled upside down, her body hugging the crags. The light slowly crept from one side of the exit to the other before blinking from view.

Prismer suppressed a hiss of pain. Her gills tasted iron in the water, and she looked down to see the sharp rock that had grazed her arm. A wisp of near-black blood hovered above the shallow wound before diluting. Stored oxygen saturated knyads' dark muscles, but her supply would not last if her pulse continued at this panicked pace.

Taking a calming breath wasn't possible here, so she closed the optic pattern over her eye and willed her limbs to still. The adrenaline burst subsided until she could hear the roiling tide over the quietening beats of her heart. Buoyed by the current, she clung like a whelk to the ceiling. Eventually, her grip began to slacken. Numbness spread up her left arm, where an old injury had weakened her.

Cautiously, she pulled herself along the ceiling to the place where the torch beam had appeared only minutes ago. In the distance, a figure swam slowly west towards the docks. The light underside of the aquaskin ae wore camouflaged aer against the ripples of moonlight above. The Aquatic Division was scanning the cliffside tonight.

From her hideout, Prismer could hear the swish of displaced water and the bleeping of an incoming call on the enforcer's mitter. Aer reply was indistinct. Prismer remained still. The enforcer was far from her now, but sounds travelled further underwater than they did on land; if she swam too vigorously, ae would hear her strokes. She floated back into the vent and secured the end of the cord around a rock, deep enough that successive searchlights would not fix upon it.

Only when the enforcer's torch appeared as a pinprick of white in the distance did Prismer swim from the exit. What had brought patrols this far east of the docks?

It did not matter. She shakily grabbed a few shells and the broken holdfasts of marine plants and placed them at the front of her vent in an arrangement she would recognise on the way back. Slinking through tunnels could only take her so far. She had to head into open water if she hoped to find Kelvan.

# CHAPTER 10

## OKLAS

H IS GAIT DRAINED of vitality, Oklas reached the bottom of the
stairway. He had agreed to nothing, and revealed nothing about
the Ardedrians. So why did it feel like a stone had dropped into the pit of
his stomach? He would soon hear from the Pentarchy again, of that much
he was sure. But he could not worry about that now. Teprill's overconfi-
dence suggested she knew nothing of the escape plan at the coast—for
now, at least—though Oklas could not say what she had gleaned from
him during the interrogation.

He was back in the entrance hall. The fragile glass decorations had
taken on an ominous quality. Cold and sharp, they looked like they would
shatter at the slightest touch. The shadows cast by the artificial lights
seemed to have deepened, and the white furnishings appeared as desolate
as bleached shells.

He sped past the delegation from Behrantz. They mingled and
laughed, happily unaware of the devastating news they would have to
bear to their people upon their return home. It had never occurred to
Oklas that a Praemor clan could lose their status. But it stood to reason
that if the stratum kept expanding, it would gradually lose its exclusivity.
With bitter certainty, he knew the Pentarchic clans would be immune
to the threat of demotion, regardless of how little they contributed. The
Eruds looked after their own, carefully curating the uneven distribution
of resources.

Oklas passed through the pillars without a clear idea of where he was going. He only knew he had to keep moving. Tracking the performance of his clan in recent years, he noted Dras Sayve was likely safe. They were an established clan, wealthy and inventive. The relief came with a wave of self-disgust. He was no more deserving of prosperity than anyone else. There were no borders in the open ocean. His life could have been very different had the currents carried him to another coastline. He had to use his good fortune to change all that.

Through the corner of his eye, he thought he saw the glint of a copper gown. *Ailynn?* He whipped around. The guest—another knyad with black tendrils—looked at him, confused.

Teprill's warning came to Oklas: *Kelabek has another year to improve their contributions.* The Erud knew he had enjoyed the company of Ailynn Kelabek early that segeind; it could be that she was lying, taking pleasure in making him worry. But what if there were some truth in her statement? Were Ailynn and her delegation still at the party? Oklas checked the time on his mitter. It was still early, but all the promise of the segeind had waned, and a desperate weariness washed over him. It was so tempting to escape this farce and forget in sleep all he had learned. But he couldn't leave now. Not until he had found a way to contact Ailynn. He could offer her clan assistance, prepare them for review the following year.

The guests, once so intriguing in their colourful garments, swept past him in a nauseating blur as he scanned the entrance hall, then the outskirts of the ballroom. Some called his name, and he slowed just enough to wave or smile vaguely in reply, hoping to see Ailynn shining out from among them. A breeze from the terrace doors at the back of the ballroom chilled Oklas's neck. Perhaps the Kelabekian delegation was outside? He marched out onto the patio.

A stairway ran against Mimidri's outer wall; it led to the rooftop gardens. The gate would be locked for the dark segeind. There did not appear to be any knyads in the courtyard, but Oklas continued to walk its length. The flagstone path ended in a purling fountain and a secluded alcove. Lush trees and black bushes, the sort that only grew on the temperate shelves of the gorge, surrounded the alcove. They thrived in the garden, where they received angled sunlight and shelter from extreme cold. Clouds passed, revealing a bright blue disc in the sky. Dryadene cast writhing shadows on the ground.

Oklas's sleeve flapped at his wrist, brushing his hand. He cursed, wheeling around to look at the floor. One of his cufflinks was missing. He retraced his steps outside, hoping to find it glittering on the flagstones. But it wasn't there. Nor was it next to the fountain. There was a chance it could have fallen to the ballroom floor. Or on the stairway...or in Teprill's meeting room.

Oklas groaned and headed back to the doors. He hesitated at the threshold. If he returned, he would have to put on a show again: dancing, feigning interest, joking. He slumped against the wall.

'Looking for something?'

The resonant voice did not belong to Ailynn, but Oklas sprang up at the sound. Dy Erla stood over him, gallant in her suit and ceremonial robes. She smiled, a knowing look in her warm eyes.

'Thank Adecai, a friendly face.' Oklas launched into a hug. As always, the Rhestian minister took it with dignity.

'It's good to see you, Oklas,' she said, drawing back to grip his forearm in a more customary greeting. 'I am afraid that Peer Kelabek had to leave early.'

'Oh,' he said, unable to conceal the disappointment in his voice. He plunged his hands into his pockets and watched the eddying shapes of dancers beyond the doors. 'I suppose she needs the time to prepare for her departure tomorrow.'

'You just missed her. She was dancing with a couple of the other attendees.' Taking pity on him, Dy Erla added, 'Though their encounters with her were rather more brief than yours.'

'You were watching us?'

'I like to pay attention to people's comings and goings,' said Dy Erla, mischief lining her smile. 'Curfew has only just begun. You could engage in another dalliance before the segere.'

Oklas gave a dry laugh and turned from the ballroom, resting his elbow on the balustrade top rail. 'I'm not sure I am in the mood for it.'

Dy Erla's forehead wrinkled. 'Was the meeting with Teprill that grave?'

'I've lost my cufflink,' said Oklas bitterly, showing her his loose sleeve. 'As for the Eruds...well, you know how they are. They like to feel the weight of my chains in their hands. With every tug, they reassure themselves that they are in control.' He looked to the northern walls of the gorge that led to the sea.

Dy Erla's expression became troubled. Was she also thinking about the cliffside escape? Even in the quiet courtyard, it would be dangerous to mention Illanu by name.

'There was no mention of activity out there,' he told her quietly, trying to muster a smile.

'The tide is still very high; it should offer them some cover.' Pressing her lips into a line, Dy Erla looked from the coast to the moon. 'I never used to see Dryadene this clearly back on Rhestatyn.'

'It still has nothing on Axis viewed from your side,' said Oklas, following her conversational turnaround. He recalled standing on the deck of an ocean liner for hours, watching the orange sky gradually fade to blue as the vessel followed the curve of Knyadrea. 'I first saw the full face of the planet on a trip to Rhestatyn. I never dreamed it could take up so much of the sky. It was like daylight in the middle of a dark phase.'

'I thought you would have seen the planet's edge from the Dras Channel?'

'Maybe north of Dras Sayve,' allowed Oklas. 'If you look to the horizon, you sometimes see a glow reflected off the clouds—like a blue sunrise.'

'We are always enchanted by what is out of reach.' Dy Erla ran her hand over a frieze on the garden wall. 'Maybe that is why my people were eager to fly to Dryadene. The cousin moon is a mystery to those of us living planet-side.'

'Think of the propulsion it must have taken for a shuttle like the *Rhydenfarer* to leave the atmosphere,' said Oklas breathlessly, gesturing up at the moon. 'What a feat of engineering it must have been. And how did those early explorers even land on Dryadene?'

'If a return journey were possible, they could have taught us much,' said Dy Erla. 'They found life—that much is certain.'

'Do you believe transmissions of their findings are still locked away in Rhestatyn?'

'I would like to think so. It was a special time in our history. I remember watching the *Rhydenfarer* disappearing into the sky.'

Oklas let out a doubtful laugh. 'Dy, the *Rhydenfarer* launched almost three centuries ago.'

She nodded. 'I was a tideling at the time of the expedition.'

The longevity of certain Rhestians was well known, but such a lifespan was exceptional. If Dy Erla was from a preternaturally advanced generation, Oklas had been squandering their time together. His satellites did not come close to classical Rhestian technology at its height.

He leaned against the garden wall, splaying his hands over the cold stone. 'I sometimes feel trapped,' he confessed, 'not just in Apidecca, but on this moon. Until we can replicate the anomaly that creates knyad life, we can never venture too far. No colony on Dryadene or any other world can last generations.'

Dy Erla smoothed her robes, lifting the hem away from the dried leaves that clung to it. 'I wouldn't be so sure of that. Even life here is a miracle. If it is Adecai's will for us to venture further, Ae will show us the way.'

Oklas smiled and looked up at the stars, which appeared faint in the moonlight. 'It must have been exciting to live in a time of expansion, so many possibilities opening before you.'

'It was, but the vigour of youth also coloured my experience of it.'

'You still have plenty of vigour. Maybe some Rhestian foresight is what Apidecca needs?'

'Rhestatyn still prospers, but we have sacrificed much of our knowledge, our culture, for short-term gains. I am a relic of another age.'

'From before the Proliferation War?' prompted Oklas. 'I believe Rhestatyn had many military successes.'

'And many losses.' Dy Erla stared past the flagstone floor. 'Better knyads than I perished long before they reached the one hundred and twenty years allotted to most. I cannot say why Adecai allows me to persist.'

'I'm glad Ae does.' Oklas gave her an affectionate prod with his elbow. 'Did you see it coming, the war?'

'Are you looking for signs of another?'

'Well, yes, and Teprill wasted the better part of my segment with propaganda. I need to counter it with some historical truth.'

Dy Erla looked over the wall at the black-leaved bushes. 'There were inequalities, discontent, just as there is today. Around the time of my harvesting, many tidelings were appearing on new shorelines. The Praemor clans absorbed those found closest to them. Of course, the Pentarchic clans took in no one but the outsiders they enlisted as servants. Our cities quickly grew, and people became reluctant to welcome immigrant tidelings. I recall my elders saying I should be proud to be a "true" Rhestian.'

The synthesised music from the ballroom throbbed distantly. Her expression turned reflective. 'Our peers decided to identify harvest sites and develop them into new clans.'

This period of history Oklas remembered from his foundational lessons. Many Praemor clans, including Dras Sayve, had played a part in founding clans abroad; it was from these dependencies that the Orta and the unclassified strata grew.

Dy Erla continued, 'The Orta provided us with natural resources and skilled workers. We developed a sense of ownership over the territories we considered valuable. More than one Praemor clan had invested in each of them, and disputes arose. Many wanted to expand their borders, to create formal colonies. There was a strong recruitment drive for young knyads to serve in Rhestatyn's military. I was among the first to sign up.'

'And you served for the full duration of the war?' asked Oklas.

'Yes. Although I spent the later part of it stationed at a garrison in Fentu Brise.'

'People must have started questioning the point of it all after a couple of decades.'

'Things changed after worldwide tideling populations began to decline,' said Dy Erla, bending to Oklas's level. 'The waste of life was not worth diminishing gains. Dependencies became less attractive.'

'And the unclassifieds were left behind.'

Dy Erla shook her head. 'We also let down the Orta when we withdrew from them too quickly. They needed time to adjust.' She straightened and walked away from the wall. 'I was told we were fighting to keep our dependencies, clans like Fentu Brise or Inclatia, from being exploited by others. But it was never about what Rhestatyn could offer them.'

'Inclatia,' said Oklas, his fingers covering his mouth and chin, 'isn't that where the projectionist is from?'

'Yes,' replied Dy Erla, her eyes growing distant. 'When I met Prismer, she had not yet been in Apidecca a revolution. She leaned into every affirming word like a dry vine revived by the mists. Though a quick learner, she wasn't accustomed to receiving praise. I'm ashamed to admit that I initially befriended her out of guilt; I wanted to make up for Rhestatyn's failure of Inclatia.' The corners of her mouth creased. 'But something stronger than guilt has forged our friendship over the years. I have gained much from knowing her.'

Oklas looked away from Dy Erla as a guilt of his own caught in his chest. He cared for Illanu, of course, but she was one of many students under his protection. He didn't know her like Dy knew Prismer. 'I'm sorry for involving her in this,' he said. 'I didn't realise you were that close.'

Dy Erla placed a hand on his shoulder. 'Most approach Prismer only with orders. You presented her with an opportunity and she took it willingly. I do worry for her, but I have to respect her choice.' She turned from him and stepped into the rectangle of golden light shining from the doorway. From inside the building, the music quietened and voices sounded.

'It looks like the Induction Ceremony will be starting shortly,' said Dy Erla as she made to leave. 'I will see you inside?'

'I'll catch up.'

Oklas needed a moment to sort through his thoughts alone, but it was not what he wanted. A rekindled desire for company pulled at his chest. He looked once more to the north of the gorge before following Dy Erla.

# CHAPTER 11

## PRISMER

WITH HER FINGERS pressed together into fin-like shapes, Prismer crawled her way through the current. The water was colder here than in the cliff vents, but she was moving swiftly enough to keep the chill from seeping beneath her skin. Her sling bag caused some drag, but the water reduced its heft on her shoulder. There had been no high winds for segments, and the sea was calm. A shoal of tiny pokmati appeared at Prismer's side. Some brushed their tentacles against her skin as she swam, and she twisted her neck to look at them. They stared back at her with glassy, cycloptic eyes—an imitation of her own in miniature. The pokmati closest to Prismer shifted the colour and texture of his skin to match the pale green speckles of her arms. He was using her for shelter. Laughing at the little shapeshifter, she recalled her tideling years when her features and markings had also changed with dizzying regularity.

Ahead all was clear, but Prismer continuously glanced over her shoulder to watch for approaching patrols. Dots of light alerted her to more enforcers coming from the docks. By their movements, it seemed the lights did not enter any of the vents in the cliffside. Had some earlier activity spurred the Aquatic Division into searching the coast more thoroughly, or was this a routine patrol?

There was no sign of Kelvan, but Prismer did not expect him to linger here. He would be waiting for her further east. If only she could swim faster and reach him sooner. She had not lived at the coast for many years now, had not laboured at sea as she had back on Inclatia. Her swimming muscles were out of condition.

A shadow fell over the seafloor and she looked up. The water above her stretched higher than some of the buildings in the city. Licks of moonlight curled at the surface. The streamlined silhouettes of ships sliced through the waves. Knowing she could not surface here only made her crave air more. A stitch pierced her side, and her emptying lungs started to burn. But she had once remained submerged for an hour on a single breath –– she could manage a little longer.

Prismer hovered a few alkar above the sand, following the boundary of the sheer rock wall at her right. It was unsafe to venture too far from the cliffs and seafrond-covered bedrocks. Not only did they help maintain her sense of direction in the depths, but they also sheltered her from view.

She felt for the towaye in the pocket of her utility belt. An irrational part of her insisted the important device was liable to disappear at any moment, but her fingers found its pebble shape. She needed to warn Illanu and Rosh of the patrols outside their hideout. But first, she had to find the skipper.

On the towaye, Prismer could make out the time displayed in faint digits. Though the journey had taken longer than anticipated, she was still well within the estimated arrival period. But where was Kelvan? She should have found him by now—she was far enough from the docks.

The parts of the mission within her control were nearing an end, and the contingency plans she had concocted would not work here. Prismer was now operating as part of a team. She had to trust the Ardedrians to send their contact as agreed.

'Kelvan!' she called out, her synthesiser boosting the sound through the water.

No reply.

She could survive down here for another half-hour. But it was her mind, more than the oxygen levels in her stinging muscles, that would determine how much longer she could remain submerged. Her resolve was slipping. The begging of her lungs overwhelmed her thoughts.

Prismer called out for the skipper again, her arms and legs treading water as she spun around. The enforcers were sure to discover the juveniles at the poolside. Should she turn back? Even if she safely slipped Illanu past the patrols, where would they go if no one had come for the young fugitive?

Something struck Prismer on the shoulder. Too surprised to synthesise a sound, she opened her gills in a gasp and choked on a trickle of salty water. Bubbles clouded her vision. A flailing hand tried to grip her arm, but she dodged it and whirled around. Her body slammed into something hard. Her attacker, now behind her, had pinned her against a boulder. Ae clapped aer hand over the place where ae expected Prismer's mouth to be. Upon feeling only the flat front of her face, ae recoiled.

Prismer turned around, her eye refocusing. Opposite her hovered a knyad, well-muscled and slightly larger than her. The knyad's skin bore striated markings commonly found on those harvested around the Partesian Coast. Notably, ae did not wear enforcer camo but a simple, dark aquaskin. Aer gaze travelled from Prismer's scumbled face to the brooch pinned on her aquaskin.

Prismer found her voice and asked, 'Are you the skipper?'

The knyad nodded, considering her. 'And you—you're the guide.' He spoke Elementary, rather than the land-based Collective. While Prismer understood the underwater dialect, the synthesiser at her throat emitted only Collective vocalisations.

She introduced herself. 'I'm Prismer.'

'Kelvan,' he said, linking his forearm with hers in greeting. 'So, where's Ilu?'

'Hiding in the cliffs. I'm scouting ahead of her.' Hand signals clarified the smaller range of sounds in Elementary.

Kelvan opened his palms apologetically. 'I reacted too quickly back there. Did I hurt you?'

'I'm fine,' said Prismer rubbing her arm.

'Sorry. I wouldn't want you thinking I attacked you because of––' Kelvan bit his lip. 'What I mean is, I'm used to maskads. We actually have a few in the Ardedrian Front. I mistook you for an enforcer.'

Was he worried she might think him prejudiced? Prismer wondered at the strangeness of these Ardedrians. 'The Aquatic Division was active back there,' she said, indicating the way she had come.

'That's just it,' said Kelvan, relieved. 'The water's murky. I couldn't be sure what I was seeing.' Arms outstretched, he floated back into the current. 'I've been waiting down here for two hours. We arrived in the harbour earlier than expected.'

'You must have surfaced in that time,' said Prismer, looking up at the heaving blue ceiling. 'I need to breathe—urgently.'

'I have a safe place for that.' He motioned for her to follow him. 'We can talk more there.'

With a kick to the boulder, she propelled after him. He led her to the opening of another vent. Its jagged sides were closer together than those further west, and she swam the first few alkar of the narrow gap with her shoulders perpendicular to the floor. Just as she started to panic in the tight space, the walls parted.

Prismer had never explored the vent network on this side of the cliffs, but she doubted they would link up with the pool where the juveniles waited half a league away.

'The cave isn't far,' said Kelvan, noticing her lagging behind him.

The vent curved upwards, and dancing green lines shimmered from a corner—an air pocket. Kelvan broke the surface of the water above her. With a burst of speed she followed, her lungs now aching for the air within her reach.

Prismer's gills gaped, and she felt her chest rise. She and Kelvan were in a small cave, not high enough to stand in. Rays of light danced on the walls in caustic patterns. Kelvan had pegged one lamp to the rocks; the other was in his hand. Here, Prismer could better see the skipper. He was around twenty-five years old, on the border between juvenile and mature knyad. The darkest of his blue stripes ran from his forehead to the bridge of his nose.

'It's great, isn't it? I only found it today,' he said proudly. Above water, Kelvan's voice drawled at a slightly lower pitch. He sat at the edge of the tidal pool and snatched furtive glances at Prismer's face. 'These tunnels don't stretch very far west, so I figured you'd meet me outside.'

'I should let Illanu know I've found you.' Prismer pulled herself out of the water and activated the towaye. 'I'm with Kelvan. Listen, we are coming for you now.' Holding her breath, she waited.

'That's great. Thanks.' It was Illanu's voice, but her speech came out clipped. And something in the background sounded suspiciously like churning water.

Prismer ran a hand over her scalp. 'Illanu? You had better not have left the poolside.' But of course she had; the juvenile had answered her in Elementary. 'Enforcers are patrolling your tunnel exit,' shouted Prismer, not knowing if Illanu could even hear her. She waited for confirmation. When no reply came, Prismer smacked the device against her leg.

Kelvan leaned back and watched her, wearing an absurd grin.

'Unbelievable!' she said. 'I told the flotsamborns to stay put.'

'These things never go according to plan.'

Prismer buried her flat face in her hands. What else did she expect from an Ardedrian insurgent? Their lives were a series of crises and rash decisions.

'Relax, we'll find her,' crowed Kelvan.

'You sound so sure.'

'Ilu's showing initiative—that'll serve her well. Have a little faith.'

His cheerful tone irked Prismer. She might as well head home now. Kelvan and the juveniles seemed confident they could find each other without her help. And she was ready for all this excitement to end. The next time she got carried away with notions of playing the hero, she would remember this moment and let the embers of her idealism go cold.

She dipped her feet in the water. No, it couldn't end like this. 'What happens to Illanu after this is not my concern'—Prismer's voice wavered—'but I agreed to deliver her to you, and I never leave a job unfinished. I think I know what route she will take to look for us.'

'Great. I welcome your help,' said Kelvan, his demeanour infuriatingly mellow. 'I've only ever spoken to Ilu over the towaye. What's she like?'

Prismer sighed. 'A test of patience. It's just as well you're keen on challenges.'

They gathered their things, and Kelvan led Prismer back underwater, holding his lamp aloft.

'I'm anchored two leagues offshore,' he told her as they approached the vent exit. 'We're leaving in a Vistihlm Rider. The start-up is quick, but it's a bit loud for a stealth mission. And the take-offs can get rough.' He shrugged. 'It's all we could get at short notice.'

Though Prismer had little interest in watercraft, she asked him about sailing. It helped take her mind off the juveniles leaving the vent.

What vessel did he prefer for a mission like this?

An Express Rider, but he longed to own a Rindarian Cabin Cruiser.

How long had he been sailing for?

Twelve years.

Each prompt kept him talking for a while. Eventually, he came at her with a question of his own.

'So, Prismer, are you a regular smuggler for the Apideccan branch of the Front?'

'I'm not a smuggler at all.'

His mouth skewed in a smile. 'So that's why we haven't met before.'

The pair had not yet swum a quarter-league west when Kelvan caught Prismer by the arm and pointed to threads of light pricking between towering seafrond stems.

'Patrols. Do you think they are approaching?' asked Prismer, struggling to discern the lights' direction of movement.

Kelvan narrowed his eyes. 'No. They're going back to the docks now. Scouts cover the western half of the cliffs every hour; it leaves a fair gap between each pass over the vents,' he said. 'The patrols are mostly a preventative measure. They don't expect to find anyone.'

Just then, something moved at the edges of Prismer's vision. Murky shapes, only a few alkar away. Too large to be any of the creatures that lived in these waters: they had to be knyads. Her chest tightened. There was no point in hiding—she and Kelvan had been spotted.

One of the figures shouted in garbled Elementary, and she recognised the voice as Rosh's.

Prismer's alarm swiftly gave way to irritation. 'What do you think you are doing here?' she demanded. 'I told you to stay put.'

'Sorry if we scared you.' Illanu waved her arms and floated upright. She wore a pale blue aquaskin and had strapped her crutch to her back. Rosh came up behind her, carrying Illanu's rucksack. He had removed his shirt and swam wearing only his trousers. Tan patches covered his stringy back and ribs.

Illanu continued, 'After your earlier message was interrupted, we thought something had happened to you.'

Prismer pressed her fingers together over the place where her lips had been. 'You could have been spotted.'

'But they weren't,' said Kelvan unhelpfully.

Prismer swam up to get a better view of their surroundings, reluctant to believe the juveniles had managed to get here without being followed.

'We didn't want you to have to pass the enforcers again,' said Illanu. 'Rosh went ahead to look for them.'

Prismer drifted back down next to Rosh, who said, 'There was one, maybe a fifth of a league away, but ae was leaving. We didn't have to wait in the vent long.' Compared with the ringing intonation of Illanu's Elementary, he sounded congested. Generating underwater sounds could be challenging for knyads who had spent years at the surface. Elementary was spoken from a different part of the throat to Collective, through water rather than air. Prismer wondered how she would fare without the aid of the speech synthesiser.

'Here you go.' Rosh offered her the cord from the vent, neatly coiled. 'No evidence left behind.'

'Thank you,' she muttered, limply taking the coil from him. The pair looked overly pleased with themselves.

'Very thorough,' remarked Kelvan, turning to the juveniles. 'You've done your guide proud. Now, if you're ready, Ilu, we can leave for the watercraft.'

Illanu's cheeks paled. 'Already?'

'Your friends are welcome to accompany us a while longer,' he offered, looking to Rosh and Prismer.

Rosh gave a firm nod, no doubt wanting to extend his time with Illanu. Prismer agreed to follow them. She couldn't leave without Rosh; he would need help finding his way back to the city.

The group swam northeast, no longer parallel to the cliffs but further into the open water, until the debris-strewn ocean floor sunk into the darkness below them. They remained deep enough below the surface to avoid being seen by passing watercraft, of which there were very few this late into curfew. Behind Prismer, Rosh struggled to coordinate his long limbs in consistent forward thrusts. Illanu, by contrast, was transformed underwater. Uninhibited by the frailty of her legs, she moved with the streamlined grace of a permanent water-dweller. She would have easily kept pace with Kelvan if she weren't holding Rosh's hand.

Prismer looked behind them; the rippling moonlit cliffs would soon disappear from view. 'This is as far as I can go,' she told the others. 'We should part before I lose my sense of direction.'

'Yes, of course, you need time to make your way home,' said Illanu. Rosh caught up with her, and they hooked their arms. 'I've enjoyed everything about this segeind: the hike through the tunnels, Prismer's lesson on the Chambers, even sneaking past enforcers.' Her high voice quivered as she parted from him. 'I just wasn't thinking about the goodbyes.'

She looked directly into Prismer's eye, finding its centre. In that moment, Prismer understood how Illanu saw her: not as a broken, pitiful creature, but a person of worth. Maybe even a friend.

'This chance is yours to take, Ilu,' she said.

Bubbles escaped Prismer's gills as the juvenile suddenly threw her arms around her shoulders. She placed a hand on the little knyad's back.

'Thank you, Prismer,' said Illanu, looking up at her. 'I'll never forget this.'

Prismer pulled away and reached for the glassfolia brooch. 'Don't forget this, either.'

Illanu stilled Prismer's scaly hand as she struggled to unpin the brooch. 'Keep it. Please.'

Prismer was about to protest but, in her few hours of knowing Illanu, she had come to recognise that unyielding look on her face. 'Alright,' she said, tenderly brushing aside the pearlescent pink tendrils framing the juvenile's face. 'Stay out of trouble.'

Illanu blinked away invisible tears and gave a hiccoughing underwater laugh. 'I was going to say that to Rosh.'

'He'll be fine—provided he follows my lead on the way home.'

'You heard her,' said Illanu, returning to Rosh's side.

He handed over her rucksack. Then his impassive expression broke, and he shut his eyes tightly. 'Peers and moons, this is hard.'

She held him, resting her cheek against his, their difference in height negligible as they floated together.

Prismer let the pair have a moment alone and glided over to Kelvan, offering him the towaye. 'It is better that you keep this.'

'You sure you don't want to hold onto it? Contact the Front when you're ready to join?' he said with a half-grin.

She pressed it into his hand. 'I'm starting to think your sense of humour is what gets you through every mission. Keep it up.'

Kelvan nodded and swam over to the juveniles. 'Hey. Rosh, is it? We'll get news to you when we arrive at the base. Find a way for you two to keep in touch.' He pointed to each juvenile in turn.

'Thanks,' bleated Rosh, looking slightly less miserable. He squeezed Illanu's hand, and they drifted apart.

Then, without another word, the Ardedrian skipper and the fugitive turned from the cliffs and swam into the depths. Rosh's gaze stayed on the spot where they had disappeared. Prismer waited some alkar behind him. When he was ready, she led him away.

To the east of the cliffs lay Shillac Lagoon, a popular bathing site in the light phases. But even in the dark, some knyads were known to swim there before working hours. Prismer hoped that she, wearing her mask, and Rosh would be able to blend in with these recreational swimmers and dry off in time to join commuters heading towards the city.

Below her, Rosh crawled through the water. Prismer called down to him, 'Did you bring dry clothes along?'

'Ilu didn't exactly give me much warning that we were leaving tonight. I came unprepared.'

'We can work around that when we get to shore.' The worst of the journey was over. But it was too soon for Prismer to start yearning for a warm flask of redlint tea.

◦⟫═◦⟨◦⟩◦═⟪◦

Prismer and Rosh waited at the Shillac Train Terminal, shivering now that they had finally stopped moving. The knyad at the counter gave them a strange look. They must have seemed a bedraggled pair. Prismer's clothes were dry but rumpled from having been stuffed in her waterproof sling bag. She kept the hood of her fulver pulled over the straps of her mask, but she missed the warmth of her headscarf hugging the nape of her neck. None of the nearby clothing shops were open this early. Over his shoulders, Rosh wore the wrapped garment Prismer had bought from an informal trader at the beachfront. His trousers were still damp, and sea-water dripped from his short tendrils.

'Two single trips to the city, please. Sub-Orta,' said Prismer, dropping four punctured metal oblongs on the counter. The officer checked the subst tokens and fortunately accepted them. Neither Prismer nor Rosh had their mitters to process payments. They could have referenced their mitter codes, but such unusual transactions might draw the attention of anyone monitoring them. Prismer was not in the habit of travelling from the lagoon in the early hours of the segere. They collected their tickets and walked down the platform.

It would be another half-hour before the train left for the city. The railway line from Shillac ran several leagues into Apidecca, connecting with the tramline that served Gilstren and the Industrial Park.

Rosh crossed his arms tightly over his torso.

'You alright?' asked Prismer.

'I wi-will be'—he puffed out his cheeks, exhaling a cloud of vapour—'when we get on the train.'

Prismer did not suffer the cold as Rosh did, but the chilly air still seeped into her bones. Even the seawater had seemed warmer than this.

They passed the shining Praemor and Orta train carriages. The Sub-Orta carriage shared the elegant design of the others, though its paint was chipped and faded. To Prismer's relief, the doors had been unlocked. She and Rosh could wait inside.

They were so early that no other passengers had boarded the carriage yet. It was strange seeing such an empty interior. The trams Prismer usually used filled quickly, and she never expected to find a place to sit. She chose a seat at the back of the carriage. The stall was plainly furnished, but clean. Scouring marks on the walls suggested graffiti had been scrubbed away. Though Rosh had his pick of any stall in the carriage, he chose to sit opposite her.

Prismer indulged in the comforting thought of spending the segere in bed. The Charter's Exchange was over, the dignitaries would soon be leaving, and she would not need to make a presentation until well after the median.

'Prismer,' said Rosh. 'Back in the vent, when you got into the water, I noticed something...'

She tensed, bracing herself for a conversation about her deformities. She knew the sight of her face had disquieted Rosh, but had hoped the events of the segeind would overshadow his memory of it.

'The scar on your forearm,' he clarified, 'you had some tech embedded in that area. I'd like to take a look at it.'

She tucked her arm out of view. 'It's nothing, just an old injury.'

'Are you really going to turn down a free examination?' he asked with the persuasive manner of a mender.

She held out her left arm and rolled up the sleeve. Her skin dipped where a chunk of muscle was missing from between the bones of her forearm. It created a hollow where a narrow metal implant lay. Prismer had removed unnecessary accessories in the docking station of the implant, and the base appeared incomplete. She did not give much thought to her scars anymore; they were the least of her unsightly features.

'A synaptic implant,' said Rosh, looking up at her. 'You have nerve damage?'

'I'll tell you about it another time,' she replied.

'That explains why you were struggling with your brooch.'

'No. That was just because of these.' She held out her hands, twitching the dewclaws.

'That isn't another outcome of scumbling, is it?' Rosh almost looked as if he would rather she told him her thumbs had been hacked off. 'How can they expect you to do fine work?'

'Scumbling wouldn't be much of a punishment if it changed me for the better.'

Rosh let out a slow breath. 'I've covered neural interfacing at the Consortium. It would only take a simple prosthetic joint to simulate an opposable thumb.'

'Even if I could afford prostheses, I'm forbidden from pursuing normalising modifications. It undermines the purpose of scumbling.'

Rosh slumped in his seat and looked out the window. Suddenly his dark eyes widened, and he looked back at Prismer. 'Then maybe I can upgrade the synaptic connector in your arm? Don't worry about paying for it; I can find the parts.'

Prismer folded her hands in her lap and considered Rosh. He was serious. 'That is very generous of you,' she said, inclining her head at him.

The two of them said little after that. Prismer rested her mask against the window of the train. She must have fallen into a light sleep because she woke with a start when the train jerked away from the station.

# CHAPTER 12

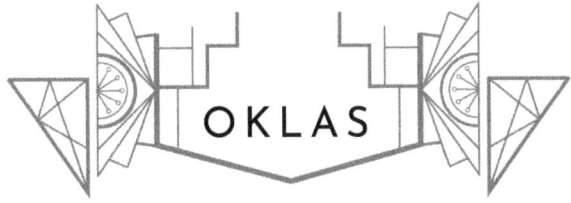

## OKLAS

ONE PHASE AFTER *the Charter's Exchange*

Passing knyads slowed at the sidelines of an arena to watch several combatants prancing back and forth in acrobatic jousts and parries. Dressed in sleek, steam-grey uniforms, the combatants sparred in pairs or groups as large as five. Others vaulted over obstacles in other parts of the arena. Patterned squares marked the floor like a giant game mat. The whole space was illuminated either by bright artificial lights or algae panels in the corners. Some knyads were unarmed, while others wielded weapons ranging from a simple staff to objects that could pass for stage props—the odd shapes testing the wielder's ingenuity.

Recreational Dahn had grown out of Edfahn, a form of combat developed in Rhestatyn. Despite its martial origins, the sport in its current state was low contact. The participants operated loosely as a team. Each session consisted of periods of conquest and defending existing territories. Oklas climbed from a pool of sponge chips and watched Udol, the knyad who had knocked him from the platform, advance to the Gleaming Pastures level. Perhaps Yvere was right about his centre of gravity being too high; he would have to work on grounding his stance. A shrill bell echoed, signalling the end of the class.

Dahn was among the few activities that reconciled Oklas's craving for mental stimulation with his repressed fondness for physical routine. It combined improvisation with sequences of movements wired into muscle memory through practice. Panting, Oklas returned to the bench where he kept his tog bag. Though his limbs were still warm from exertion, the air felt cool against the sweat at his temples. While drinking from his water flask, he noticed a stocky knyad with a ruddy complexion waving at him from the arena's curving border.

'Geshan,' spluttered Oklas, wiping the water from his chin with his sleeve.

His old friend wore a russet vest some shades brighter than his face. Geshan threw an arm around him; the bumps of his textured skin prickled through Oklas's uniform.

'Still playing your oversized table games?' asked Geshan, grinning.

'You should have been here two phases ago. I got all the way to the Citron Pearl level,' boasted Oklas.

'I don't know what that means, but you seem pleased about it.'

The pair started down the passage outlining the arena. The gymnasium floor plan consisted of four trapeziums, each five stories high, arranged around a central pool like the sharp-edged petals of a concrete flower. From the very top of the southern extension, it would be a fair walk to the lockers and bathrooms.

'Have you moved on to the fifty minah barbells yet?' asked Oklas.

Geshan shrugged. 'I was doing more reps with lighter weights today; it helps with recovery.'

'You have a high boredom threshold, my friend.'

'You can't build anything lasting if you don't stick to a routine,' retorted Geshan. 'I'm not gaining muscle as quickly as I did when I started, but my endurance is improving.'

'You may even be able to lift me one segment.'

'Oh please,' said Geshan tackling Oklas and grabbing him by the waist. He hoisted him up with ease. 'I've been able to do that since we met, leafweight.'

'You call this lifting?' gasped Oklas, his feet dangling above the ground. 'It's more like a hug. You haven't even raised me above your shoulders.'

With an unimpressed grunt, Geshan raised Oklas higher before setting him down. Oklas coughed, smoothing his grey uniform.

Geshan watched him with a grin. 'You're the engineering expert,' he said, folding his arms. 'How about you demonstrate leverage and lift me?'

After a few attempts of failing to so much as grip Geshan's solid back,

Oklas bent over, laughing breathlessly. 'We will reconvene when I find a suitable fulcrum for this exercise.'

'Maybe we could put some muscle on you if you trained with me instead of frolicking around that arena. Which reminds me, I've got something for you.' Geshan withdrew a sealed envelope from his tog bag. 'It's from one of your dancing partners. A peer, no less.'

'Ailynn?' Oklas spoke her name in a hopeful whisper. Geshan would surely tease him over that. He made a snatch for the letter, and Geshan gleefully slipped it behind his back.

'It looks like a romantic token. Shall I read it to you?'

Oklas barked a laugh and darted around his friend. 'When did she give this to you?'

'On her way to the waterfront,' replied Geshan, pivoting to remain facing him.

Oklas drew back, placing a languid hand on his hip and sighing in resignation. Satisfied that he had gotten the upper hand in their game, Geshan glanced at the letter. In a shot, Oklas pinched it from his friend's fingers.

'Hey!'

'If you were going to read it, you would have already. You know you'll be the first to hear if it's any good,' Oklas assured him, breaking the seal.

Written in a fine, angled script was Ailynn's mitter code. Excellent. He could contact her now, advise her about the next Charter's Exchange. A short note followed.

Geshan clapped. 'You're smirking.'

'It's an invitation for me to stay at the Kelabekian estate when I next pass that way,' said Oklas, folding the paper as they passed a pool at the centre of the gymnasium. Though modest in diameter, the pool was a tubular aquarium, almost as deep as the building was tall. Offshoots near the surface served as underwater meditation gardens featuring corals and seagrasses.

Geshan's keen yellow eyes were still on the letter in Oklas's hand as they walked. 'I got talking to Peer Kelabek on the ocean liner here,' he said. 'I had a feeling she would be your type.'

Oklas gave him a playful nudge. 'Thanks for putting in a word for me.' They proceeded down a flight of stairs, the first of several circling the aquarium on the way to the ground floor. 'But I don't get about as much as I did when I was an envoy to Emis,' he continued. 'I doubt I'll travel southwest any time soon.'

'Long-distance relationships have a certain allure. There may be something worth pursuing here.'

'I don't think I have the stamina for it anymore, not with everything the Assembly demands of me.'

'So resign, live a little. You prefer running the college anyway,' said Geshan as they reached another stairway.

Oklas gave an amused snort. He had considered ending his political career more than once, but he couldn't follow through. His job at the Assembly fed into his research at the college and his work with the Ardedrians. More than that, an apolitical life wasn't what Emis had wanted for him.

'What about you?' he asked Geshan. 'Surely a well-travelled merchant, an heir presumptive, has many opportunities to meet someone special?'

'I'm only seventh in line, and the governors will make sure I never manage the Sprijin estate. Besides, it's hard to make anything last when you're at sea half the time.'

'I think my excuse is better,' said Oklas, interlacing his fingers and stretching out his arms.

'This isn't about me,' insisted Geshan, pulling Oklas towards him. 'It's about the entertainment value of your romantic entanglements. You've been too sensible these past two years—I feel robbed.'

'It hasn't been that long since Bia?'

Geshan rolled his eyes. 'You have no sense of time. Actually, the knyad who sent you tumbling off that platform reminded me of Beatriz. They have the same strong jawline.'

'Udol's a quieter soul than Bia,' said Oklas, 'though just as competitive.'

'Too much for you, was ae?'

'No, but Apidecca wasn't enough for aer. I can't blame aer for leaving.' Oklas watched the swimmers effortlessly cross floor levels on the other side of the thick aquarium glass.

Geshan came down the steps behind him. 'Beatriz never was the grafting kind, but neither are you.'

Oklas's mouth tightened in a smile. It was true, not just for him and Bia but most knyads. They were communal beings incapable of producing young; there was no reason for pair bonding. It was a rare and precious thing for two friends to commit to each other completely. Though he found grafting ceremonies fascinating, Oklas couldn't see himself participating in one.

'Bia felt Apidecca makes us choose between different parts of ourselves. I'm starting to think ae was right,' said Oklas, recalling Teprill's warning about choosing between his roles. He looked to the aquarium floor below; he had never swum that deep. There was something oppressive about the contained space and the weight of the water above him. 'And yet,' he continued, 'I don't mind staying here. There are some parts of myself I keep returning to; things I recognise as "me".'

'Is Bia travelling these segs?' asked Geshan.

'Always. Ae is in the courier business with Diabra.' Oklas's brow furrowed. 'I couldn't expect aer to give that up, and I couldn't follow aer. When I decided to build the Emisrian College all those years ago, I didn't realise I was committing to something. It turns out I've made my home here.'

Geshan patted Oklas on the arm. 'You were bound to become boring eventually. You're not a juvenile anymore.'

'You would know something about advanced age,' said Oklas, affecting a stoop and putting on a feeble, croaky voice, 'having gotten there first.'

'See, this is why people want to knock you to the ground.' Geshan thumped him on the shoulder, overbalancing him. Chuckling, Oklas righted himself with some quick steps backwards.

The two continued down to the lockers and later emerged from the changing rooms clean and comfortably dressed. Oklas pulled a dark, weatherproof riding jacket over his pale yellow shirt. Together, he and Geshan left through the foyer, heading for the drop-off zone outside. The gymnasium lay in the lower part of the Lepotra District. Though still sunless, the sky was lighter than yesterday, and on the horizon was a faint glow: the promise of sunrise.

A rush of cold air stung Oklas's cheek. The wind direction was changing. He found his scrambler and helmet at the charging bay. Passing his mitter over the scanner, he confirmed his payment for the recharge and unlocked the vehicle. 'Need a lift?' he asked Geshan as he wheeled back the scrambler.

'On that zippy little two-wheeler of yours? With you driving?'

Oklas stroked the saddle of the slick, silver vehicle. 'Maybe "zippy" is just what you need in a crowded city with steep inclines? The *Moonsurge Simmer* handles them with unparalleled style.'

'Unparalleled?' repeated Geshan mockingly. 'You've never even tested its performance against a comparative series.'

'What can I say? I am committed to *Moonsurge* the way you are committed to wearing only shades of brown,' replied Oklas with a shrug.

Geshan frowned down at his shirt. 'I'll take my chances with the tram.'

'You remember I gave design input on the trams?'

'There's no escaping you.' Exasperated, Geshan threw his arms up. 'At least I know where to lodge my complaints.'

Oklas grinned, passing his mitter over the dashboard and flicking on the ignition switch.

'Oh, and Oklas,' said Geshan. 'I'll get you a crate of Mindalill wine on my way through the Dras Channel, yeah?'

'And candied inkroot, if you see any. I'll transfer the substants for them.' He pulled on his helmet. 'Safe travels at sea.' With the engine warmed up, Oklas let out the clutch, pulling back on the throttle. The smooth hum of the vehicle intensified. He pulled off, waving at Geshan as he soared up the road.

Much of the city was subterranean. It spread under rocky shelves in the depths of Long Shadow Gorge. But the most spectacular parts were above ground. The pre-dawn light tinted the white-walled villas blue. They covered the sides of the gorge in layers. Between the buildings, down narrow alleys, were strips of foliage. Trams ran in zigzags across levels, while cableways transported commuters between the surface and the High Street below.

The road was cobbled, which gave the scrambler some traction as Oklas wound it up and down hills. Along the pavements, frost-covered plants were coming out of hibernation. He drove down to the edge of Lepotra, where frozen waterfalls scaled the walls of the Crater Gardens. Downshifting, he slowed as he passed the Emisrian College.

Oklas looked over the roofs of the Traditional Quarter and watched the kites and wind instruments fluttering in the breeze. It was unclear how the tradition had started, but new kites often appeared during festivals linked to Adecai, especially the main holiday, Beyashisik. In their finery, the Eruds tried to set themselves up as gods, but no one was inclined to honour them with such rustic customs. You could not buy that kind of devotion.

Oklas turned the scrambler back up the hill and headed south. While he embraced the thrill-seeking image attached to scrambler riders, he usually rode at a leisurely pace. He did not want to miss out on the little details of city life around him. It was a joy to experience Apidecca at street level, a sentiment few of his fellow ministers shared. Most Praemor knyads travelled along private tram tracks and cableways, or flew over the city in fuel-hungry aerial propulsors. Admittedly, Oklas knew the Upper End far better than the Lower—business seldom required he travel there—but he was quickly learning routes to the best factories in the enigmatic Industrial Park.

Whenever he passed through the High Street, he liked to watch the pedestrians and guess at their stories. Since there were no true Apideccans, everyone had started life somewhere else. They had left behind what was familiar in search of something more, just as he had. Oklas hoped he was making it easier for them. He wondered how Illanu was adjusting to her new home. According to the Ardedrians, she had arrived safely at their next closest base, on an islet some leagues west of Apidecca. He would have to follow up with them soon.

Witalit Estate, his home, lay halfway up a hill. It was well into the segeind, but even in the median hours, there was little activity on the glistening streets of Ironglade Heights. Many of his neighbours spent only a few revolutions a year in Apidecca, living abroad in Praemor clans the rest of the time.

Oklas sometimes regretted not having moved to a compact apartment in the bustling Upper End, but the estate was closer to the college and gave him the space to display some of the items he had inherited from Emis.

He passed under the vine-covered archway on his way up to the sprawling front garden and lifted his visor to savour the brisk perfume of the stjarnflowers, which bloomed only in the long nights and would soon wilt.

He was glad to have his staff housed on the grounds; their cottages made Witalit seem less foreboding. At the top floor of the villa, on either side, were terraces that Oklas had installed. The western lookout offered a view of resilient, velvet-leaved bushes and the train tracks leading down to the harbour, while the eastern side overlooked the Traditional Quarter, the Emisrian College, and the dome of Apex Hall. Oklas had bought Witalit before starting work on the Emisrian. To some extent, the architectural style of his villa had informed that of the college. Both buildings were airy, bright, and thick-walled.

It was good to be home. Oklas looked forward to lounging on his favourite chair in the eastern wing with a warm glass of bira. After that, he would have to look at Antolat's amendments to the campus layout. The new term was fast approaching, and Oklas still hadn't decided where to accommodate the Environmental Sciences Department. It would be another late segeind. At least he might see the beginnings of the sun flushing the clouds with colour.

The solid front door creaked as Oklas, carrying his luggage from the scrambler, leaned a shoulder against its carved border to push it open. The foyer was quiet but gently lit with algae panels in the cosy orange hue he liked. Throughout the villa were studies, laboratories, and entertainment areas, all equipped for their respective purposes.

But the kitchen was one of his favourite rooms. Here, he would tinker with a prototype or conceptualise a new design while Furna, the cook, sped around him. The busy atmosphere helped him think, and he enjoyed the company. Furna didn't object to his presence in the kitchen, provided he remained in his corner of the table and did not work with chemical contaminants.

Oklas dropped his tog bag and files on the kitchen table. A savoury scent wafted towards him, and he noticed a plate of food on the other end of the table. Jellied lagoon eels garnished with fried sweetgrass and soft grains drizzled in kelsauce.

Strange. It was not like Furna to leave a meal to go cold when she knew he would be home late. There were always leftovers on the chilled shelves for him to warm in his own time. It couldn't have been there long; a trail of steam still rose from the plate. Oklas's stomach grumbled. He looked around and lifted the fork, letting it teeter between his fingers as he considered taking a bite. A dull bump came from the pantry. His staff were usually back in their cottages by now, but perhaps Furna was still here? She could have even made the meal for herself.

'Furn?' called Oklas.

The pantry door was open, and it was dark inside. Oklas walked to the entrance, stopping at the first of the cantilever stairs. He felt along the wall and took a step down. He didn't come into the pantry often enough to know where the light switch was. Apprehension clenched at his gut, and his appetite left him.

'Who is there?' he asked, his voice clear but faltering.

He took another step and waited, his ears straining for a sound. He put his foot out, about to take the fourth step when something grabbed his ankle. It dragged his leg into the gap between the stairs, and Oklas gasped. He was tipping forwards, plunging into the darkness. Metal clattered and his limbs struck wood in a continuous rumble until his chest hit the cold floor with a dull thump that forced the air from his lungs. Something made of glass shattered a few alkar away from him. There were other sounds too. Footsteps.

Oklas twisted around, heart hammering in his chest. He needed to get to his feet and draw breath to yell for help. There was no identifying the figures swooping down on him like nightmarish shades. Extending his arms, he pushed himself from the floor only to crumple in pain. He must have cracked a bone in the fall.

Arms reached from behind Oklas, hauling him up and restraining him. Voices echoed off the walls of the room. More than one attacker was here. Oklas kicked out at bodies he could not see, and his boot connected with something hard. A hand—covered in damp fabric—clamped over his nose and mouth. The chemical smell on it sent him thrashing. Streaks of light gave way to black as he felt his head sink to his chest.

# CHAPTER 13

## OKLAS

Awareness came to Oklas in rolling waves, pummelling him into himself, then drawing him further out. He could hear the steady hum of a vehicle—a city shuttle—in motion, and his body rocked against a seat. Each breath he took stung his chest, and his whole body ached. A dimly-lit cabin flashed into view, along with two figures. A third knyad was at his side, pulling at something from behind his head. The rough material that stretched over his cheeks slackened. He spat out the gag and searched the faces of his captors.

He had seen them all before, but the knyad opposite him stood out from the others—Seron.

The Furtim enforcer sat with her arms folded, surveying him critically. 'I didn't expect you to put up much of a fight. But your hysterical flailing almost dislocated Furto Etana's jaw.' She nodded to the stoic knyad at Oklas's side, who gave an indifferent grunt.

'Well, you did ambush me in my own home,' said Oklas shakily, looking down at his torn shirt and dust-covered trousers.

Seron laughed. 'You should have eaten your last meal. It would have drugged you without a fuss.'

'What do you mean by "my last meal"?' He winced. 'Are you going to kill me?'

Seron snorted, tilting her spiny head. 'If we were, do you think you'd still be talking?'

'Maybe you want to go about it creatively, for our sovereigns' entertainment?'

'Another time, perhaps.'

Oklas squirmed, and the chains of his cuffed wrists clinked. 'If Erud Teprill wanted to continue our discussion from the other segeind, she could have just summoned me.'

Lachesis, the Furtim enforcer next to Seron, looked on with interest. Oklas had not seen her at the Induction Ball; perhaps she was curious about what had transpired between him and her master.

'We've been investigating you, Sayve,' said Seron. 'Your case concluded today, but we already had enough incriminating evidence to arrest you at the ball. You can thank Her Grace for the reprieve. She didn't want to end the Charter's Exchange with messy internal affairs dragged out in front of the guests.'

Oklas opened his mouth wordlessly, and Seron surveyed him with a look of satisfaction. She continued, 'If you'd owned up to your involvement with the insurgents and given Her Grace names or the locations of bases, this could have played out differently.'

'How exactly did you come by this "evidence"?' asked Oklas evenly.

'We placed an agent at your college. An archivist.'

'Antolat?'

'That's the name you'd know him by. Can you guess what he found in your records?'

It couldn't be. Oklas had appointed Antolat personally. He doubled over, exhaling slowly.

Seron reposed in her seat, raising her chin. 'The plans for unregulated communication technology were damning enough. But your designs also depict components we've found exploded near captured insurgents. Now we know what these devices are and who the supplier is.'

Oklas straightened. 'Obviously, someone planted the plans on the premises. I demand a trial.'

'You've been found guilty of treason, Sayve.' Seron leaned forwards. 'There's no debating your way out of this.'

'So where are you taking me? To a labour commune?'

'That wouldn't be the best use of your talents. My masters have found a way for you to make it up to them right here in the city. But first, they need you to disappear from public life.'

Oklas scoffed. 'And how would they have me do that?'

'They outsource help,' said Seron, her green eyes glinting. 'The guild has erased individuals more infamous than you.'

Oklas's mocking smile collapsed. 'The guild,' he repeated weakly, his thoughts jumping to stories of resyncraft and punitive experiments. 'Is that where we're going? There will be questions from the Dras Channel, from my department.'

Seron ignored him, raising her hand in a gesture towards Furto Etana. Oklas scowled as Etana pulled the gag over his mouth once more.

There were no windows in the vehicle cabin, nothing to distract Oklas from the stony faces of his captors. When they did speak among themselves, they kept to banal off-duty subjects, seldom taking their eyes off him. Had Seron been referring to the Transmutation Guild? It was an urban legend, or so Oklas thought. He was used to revising what he knew to be true. Resyncraft was real. It wasn't hard to believe there might be a group of practitioners who pushed the limits of their abilities, even if the stories about them were wildly inconsistent. Oklas recalled an unsettling conversation with his mentor about it.

*Every society has its secrets*, Emis had said. *Uncover as many as you can, and no one can catch you off-guard.*

Oklas had failed to determine whether or not this guild of resyncrafters existed, let alone learn what they did. He supposed he would soon find out.

What felt like many unbearable hours passed before the vehicle slowed, tipping Oklas's shoulders forwards. He winced as the seatbelt pressed painfully against his chest.

The door slid open and Oklas stumbled into a dark void. Green lights dotted what looked like a black mountain rising before them. As his eyes adjusted to the darkness, Oklas realised the lights were windows in a building that stood many floors high. Parts of it appeared to have been carved into the mountain, while other extensions jutted from it. It reminded him of the Assembly Chambers, and was probably just as ancient.

But the starless landscape differed from even the deepest parts of the gorge. There was no hint of the sky, only rock—they were underground. A large stained glass window spread below the area where the building merged with the ceiling. It depicted a strange symbol: a star shape within an oval, surrounded by spiked motifs on either side.

A knyad in a white lab coat waited for them a few paces from the vehicle. Oklas certainly would have remembered such a person had they met before. Ae wore shoulder-length tendrils slicked back and fastened with a clip. Though ae appeared middle-aged, there was an unnatural tension in aer papery skin, as though it held back more decades than it showed. Ae had a slash of a mouth and an upturned, cartilaginous nose.

'Furto Seron, it is good to see you again. And so soon after your last visit.' Ae spoke in a light, conversational tone, but aer reedy voice was disconcertingly dry.

Seron brushed off the pleasantries with a curt nod. 'Are you ready to receive the patient?' she asked.

'Here, we are always prepared,' ae assured her. 'I see it is the young minister you have brought me. How marvellous.' Ae turned to Oklas. 'I am Master Raganys, andrid, one of the overseers here.'

'Careful what you say in front of this one,' Seron warned, 'and don't give him a tour of the place.'

'I will bear that in mind. It's a long drive back to the city. Perhaps you'd rather wait for us in the front rooms?'

'Furto Lachesis will remain here,' said Seron, indicating to the younger enforcer. 'We will return for Sayve this segeind. He'd better be ready by then; the Eruds don't require your perfectionism for this type of procedure.'

'Of course,' said Raganys. His gaze darted to Oklas's tensed shoulder, and he drew closer. 'May I look at that?'

Still gagged, Oklas could not answer him, but he stepped back instinctively. Raganys bent to inspect the injury, his head obscuring Oklas's view.

'Hold still.' Raganys pinched firmly between Oklas's sternum and right shoulder.

A dull bump sounded below his skin, and pain shot through his chest. Oklas bit down on the fabric between his teeth. He then raised his cuffed hands, carefully feeling where Raganys had realigned the bones of his clavicle.

Raganys batted Oklas's hands away. He then slipped what appeared to be a pen from his coat pocket. Leaning forwards, he stippled beads of clear liquid—a substance familiar to Oklas—along the injured area. A controlled vibration ran to the tips of Raganys's bony fingers. The liquid glowed teal, and he sent it sinking into Oklas's skin like water on a dry sponge. A menthol warmth tingled from the base of Oklas's throat to his ribs. The swelling receded. He tested the mobility of his shoulder, rolling it with ease. He had witnessed only a few superficial resyncraft healings on his travels, but had never experienced one first-hand. It was astonishingly effective.

Appraising the outcome with a look of pride, Raganys moved to Oklas's side and untied his gag. 'That's better. I like to converse with my patients.' He hailed Furto Lachesis with a wave of his hand. 'You may remove the handcuffs—we do not need them here.'

'I should escort him inside,' advised Lachesis, reluctantly dialling the code to release the lock.

'My security forces are up to the task,' the resyncrafter assured her, running a hand over his mitter.

From the black doors lumbered a bipedal creature, dipping its great head to cross the threshold. Its large limbs had a root-like texture and were knotted at the joints. As the creature drew nearer, Oklas noticed layers of bark sheathed its torso like armour. It had to be a convecorpra, a creature built from natural materials and animated by resyncraft. They featured predominantly in books on mythology rather than science.

At each convecorpra's core was living organic tissue, usually derived from a plant or insect. The assembled body needed to derive its essence from something. The creature's helmet-like head had a gap in the middle from which many yellow dots shone. If these served as its eyes, the convecorpra would have a panoramic view of its surroundings. It stopped just before Oklas, its loamy scent washing over him.

'The truncus is a more durable type of convecorpra, an update on the last,' Raganys told the Furtim enforcers. 'It will quickly subdue a captive at the slightest sign of resistance.'

Seron cast the creature a glare. 'Signal us on the mitter if there are any problems.' She stalked to one side, relaying instructions to Lachesis while Raganys led Oklas away.

They walked between rows of dark pillars towards the giant doors from which the truncus had emerged. A green slit from the interior appeared where one of the doors was left ajar, lighting a tangle of shapes and contorted creatures carved into the doorpost.

'How does your chest feel?' asked Raganys.

Oklas's tongue still felt dry from the gag when he answered, 'There's no stiffness, not even any inflammation. Does resyn heal all injuries so quickly?'

'There is much I could tell you about healing, but I think you will find my other talents more interesting.' Raganys held the giant black door open for Oklas. 'Come.'

Though remaining with the Furtim seemed more prudent, he followed Raganys inside. The resyncrafter's manner was *too* pleasant. Perhaps whatever darkness he harboured manifested itself in the creature at Oklas's heels. Despite its size, the truncus was so light-footed that Oklas jumped whenever its shadow fell over him.

The main hall did not extend very deep into the mountain. It intersected with three long corridors running parallel to the outer wall. Raganys led him down the second of these, their footsteps echoing through the cavernous building. The green lights seen from the front of the building were repeated throughout the interior, bright enough that they appeared almost white.

The highly polished tiles lining the corridor could have come from the same quarry as the black bricks outside. Oklas's haunted reflection stared at him from the glossy walls. Shadows veiled his eyes, and his tendrils lay flat against his head. The doors they passed were closed. With no obvious escape route in sight, Oklas decided he had to get the old resyncrafter talking. Perhaps he could learn something about the layout of the place.

'So this is the Transmutation Guild of legend?' he ventured.

'That is its most prevailing name,' said Raganys, still facing forwards. 'You have an interest in resyn, don't you?'

'I've encountered it, yes,' said Oklas, tugging at the collar of his creased shirt.

'You understate your experience,' said Raganys fondly. 'As a young engineer, you zone refined resyn crystals. And before that, I believe you even took a resyncraft aptitude test.'

Oklas frowned. Just how much did the old knyad know about him?

His confusion seemed to amuse Raganys, who continued. 'Not all resyncrafters are part of the guild, but we are a small community and word travels. We keep a record of every aspirant, even those who fail the test.'

Oklas's face flushed, and he pushed his shoulders back. 'I was merely curious about alternative uses for resyn.'

'I would expect as much from someone of your reputation. The commercial-grade resyn is good for little more than powering machines. Here, we have access to better than that.' He pointed emphatically. 'Gain an understanding of resyn, and you gain literacy skills in life's writing system. With that knowledge, you can bend more than metal components to your will.'

Intrigued, Oklas forgot the horror of where he was—if only for a moment. 'I always suspected resyn compliments natural processes, possibly even those that cause knyads to develop at sea.'

Raganys's sinewy face lit up. 'You think creatively for a non-crafter. Yes, we like to test the boundaries of the natural here.'

'How do you fund all this?' asked Oklas.

'Resyncraft has many practical, if somewhat mundane, applications. We've doubled the crop yield of dewberries by creating new variants that ripen even by the second-hand light of Axis. Though we do not rely solely on them, our wealthy patrons compensate us generously for our services. And the Erudean Pentarchy grants us additional resources, freeing us to pursue more...imaginative ends.'

'Like your convecorprae?' asked Oklas.

'They are more common than you may think,' said Raganys dismissively. 'We regularly construct simple convecorprae to work on inland mines. Unlike knyad workers, they do not tire, endure dry climates, and can carry loads up to fifteen times their own weight. Were resyn more abundant, convecorprae could easily replace the unclassified workforce. However, constructing the truncus poses a greater challenge; it is one of the more intricate convecorprae. Rigid plant cells were the obvious choice for the malleable anatomy. It may require further alterations, I still need to—' He closed his bony hand. 'Ah, but that would be revealing too much.' Though arrogant, it seemed Raganys was not so foolish as to hand a captive his warden's weak points.

Suddenly, a pair of knyads left one of the rooms up ahead. They were dressed differently from Raganys, not unlike ordinary menders, but Oklas assumed that they were also resyncrafters. They wheeled out a stretcher bearing a motionless body covered in a sheet. Oklas felt cold coming off the body as they passed. He could not help looking at it. The sheet was folded at the corner, exposing the upper part of the face.

No. It couldn't be a face. There were no signs of injury, but too much was missing.

A chill ran down Oklas's spine, and he backed into the truncus.

'Natural causes, not to worry,' whispered Raganys calmly. He studied Oklas as his associates continued down the corridor. 'Deceased knyads of this kind seldom have their bodies claimed by clan members. We learn much about their unique physiology during the post-mortems.'

'W-what?' uttered Oklas.

'Maskads,' clarified Raganys. 'They are knyads, only reduced to the essentials. In their forms, I see something of the simple aquatic creature from which we grow.'

'A knyad?' repeated Oklas, pivoting to watch the stretcher disappear into the distance. A noble design bound knyads together and yielded infinite variety. Their bodies detailed their stories, reflecting their coasts of origin and the forms they chose as tidelings. Adecai made them in Aer likeness. 'B-but,' Oklas stammered, 'aer face...it was so empty.' He turned back to Raganys. 'This is a violation.'

'Of what?' asked Raganys, lazily cracking the joints in his wrist. 'I see no innate virtue in knyadkind. But what I can see clearly is something primal and distorted within everyone, from the unclassified waif to the reigning Erud. I merely honour the ancient practice of bringing it to the fore. Scumbling is perhaps the most intuitive of resyncrafting techniques. It requires so little manipulation.'

Oklas had always assumed maskads hid their faces because they suffered from developmental defects or disease. Many considered them criminals and shunned them like they did the unclassified. To think they had once been whole. Oklas shook his head. 'You have no right to alter– to mutilate people.'

Raganys's smile broadened, baring long white teeth and his receding gum line. 'The rights of knyads brought to the Transmutation Guild are not determined by your General Assembly.' He hastened his walk down the passage. 'Scumbling accounts for only a fraction of what we do here, but it is the reason why the guild exists. For centuries we have remained independent of changing rulers and political regimens. Power struggles continually play out above ground, and always the vanquished are brought here.'

Pushed forwards by the truncus, Oklas hugged his sides, struggling to make sense of this. Every maskad he'd ever encountered had been processed here or in another cruel pit just like it. And he was about to end up like them.

He bolted, darting past the truncus and throwing an arm out to propel himself from the wall. Oklas had not yet run two lengths when ropes girded around his waist, jerking him back. No—not ropes, but roots. The truncus had extended its crusty arms, whip-like appendages distending from its hands like extra fingers.

'Where are you going, young minister?' asked Raganys, feigning disappointment. 'I thought we were getting along well.'

Oklas writhed helplessly in the grip of the roots. Why had he tried running? He didn't know his way around the guild. Even if he made it to the exit, Furto Lachesis would apprehend him. The truncus's body turned to the consistency of tar, sucking in Oklas's limbs and curling him against its abdomen. The sticky ooze clung to the tendrils at the back of his head. He was like an insect trapped in gum. 'I shouldn't be here,' cried Oklas, desperately searching the resyncrafter's glassy eyes for a trace of compassion.

'Unfortunately, you were on the wrong side of history this time,' said Raganys. He stroked his chin in contemplation. 'Perhaps "unfortunately" is not entirely accurate. There are benefits to scumbling. Research suggests maskads have excellent low-light vision and an enhanced immune system. Possibly even a higher tolerance for cold than whole knyads.'

'Curious to try it yourself, are you?' snapped Oklas.

'I can't overlook the disadvantages,' replied Raganys with a slight smile.

Slowly, the truncus released Oklas's legs, then his arms, and deposited him before the resyncrafter. Raganys turned his back on Oklas, walking a few paces ahead. He ran his hands over one of the black tiles on the wall. It bore a symbol, the same oval and star shape that Oklas had seen at the front of the building. Raganys pressed it, and a tiled door in the wall jutted out and slid open to reveal a tightly-coiled spiral staircase. The resyncrafter stepped inside.

Oklas's breathing sped up as the truncus jostled him onto the narrow stairway. The creature shouldn't have fit through the door, but its shoulders cracked and reformed, squeezing into the rectangular space.

Cold sweat dripped down Oklas's temples. In the tight, dark stairway, with the truncus at his back, his rushing thoughts drowned out his flimsy escape plans. The reality of what was about to happen loomed over him, immense as the truncus.

Raganys seemed to notice the change in his captive. 'That's a strong fear response. I'm not fond of small spaces myself. Don't worry, only a little further now.'

They came to a laboratory clad in more black tiles. The truncus pushed Oklas forwards and blocked the doorway. The corners were dark, but a pool of bright light at the centre of the ceiling poured over an adjustable chair and an array of tools and vials.

'Where are the others?' asked Oklas, finding his voice once more.

'Who?'

'Other resyncrafters.'

'They are occupied elsewhere. While my duties usually keep me from the simple art of scumbling, I couldn't pass up the opportunity to add a minister of the General Assembly to my portfolio.'

'I'm only a deputy. Sorry to disappoint you,' said Oklas flatly.

'A college director, then,' offered Raganys. 'You can put on the theatre robe laid out for you behind the curtain or simply remove your shirt—I will need access to your arms and torso.' The resyncrafter walked over to a row of cabinets and pulled one open.

Oklas walked over to the curtain, looking for a window or another door. The walls were solid, and the air vent above was too small for even a tideling to enter. A trolley loaded with equipment lay across his path. He snuck a sharp multi-tool from the tray up his sleeve—it would have to do. The air was dry and temperate, but he shuddered as he removed his ruined shirt. He tucked the blade between the folds of his theatre robes and made his approach as quietly as he could.

Raganys was putting on his gloves, his back to Oklas. He would have to get close for this to work. Oklas tightened his grip around the blade.

'You really should relax. You are in experienced hands,' said Raganys, turning to face him.

Energy spiked from deep within Oklas, sending his heart rate soaring.

'Release me!' he demanded, moving deliberately around the chair towards Raganys, the blade held aloft. 'The truncus, order it to move.'

Raganys laughed, raising his gloved palms and angling himself so Oklas could not see both him and the truncus at once. The resyncrafter stepped forwards but Oklas held his ground. He couldn't allow Raganys to drive him towards the door and the truncus—his only way out of here was with a blade held at the resyncrafter's throat. He closed in on Raganys, trying to keep his hands from shaking.

'Oklas, you're over-tired, like a tideling resisting the pull of sleep. But you needn't fret—I won't harm you.'

Oklas snorted. 'Only turn me into one of your abominations?'

'If you spoke to more maskads, you'd know that no physical transformation in itself makes you a monster,' said Raganys, 'but it can cause others to treat you like one.'

Guilt settled over Oklas. He didn't find maskads repulsive but, if he was honest, he didn't quite see them as people either. They existed in his mind as shades that haunted streets and dilapidated shacks around the city.

'It can't be helped,' continued Raganys. 'Mask-wearers represent a great deal in the collective imagination. People find it hard to connect with them; I suppose that is why some consider this a punishment.'

A root twisted the blade from Oklas's grasp. The truncus was upon him. He cursed himself for allowing Raganys to distract him.

'Think of it, rather, as a change in perspective,' said the resyncrafter as the truncus lifted Oklas off his feet, enveloping him.

Roots fanned over his mouth. 'Please. Don't,' implored Oklas. His voice was muffled, and he felt his limbs sink into the truncus's sticky arms and torso. Tears stung his eyes.

'Oklas, you are fighting for a life you have already lost,' said Raganys. From his top pocket he withdrew the pen he had used to heal Oklas earlier. He replaced the resyn cartridge with a full one, lifting the pen to Oklas's forehead. The familiar hot and cold sensation tingled where the pen tip scrawled on his skin. But the effect differed from last time. Instantly, all struggle left his body, even while his mind screamed on.

'That's better. Now, go to the chair and lie down so we can begin.'

The words reverberated through Oklas's chest. The truncus released him, and he slumped to his knees. Then his legs straightened. They were

moving, carrying him across the room. He was following Raganys's com-
mands as readily as one of the convecorprae.

'You may be relieved to learn that we won't need this,' said Raganys,
retrieving the blade from the truncus and examining it. 'Building a convecorpra requires the use of crude instruments. Not so with scumbling.'
He added it to the tray of tools and locked them in a cabinet.

Oklas lay back on the unfurled chair, his pulse slowing to its resting
state. He couldn't turn his head, but was able to move his eyes to the side,
where he saw a set of injections and teal vials.

Blinking slowly, he watched as Raganys put the pen tip to his face. The
resyncrafter began to draw symbols, starting at Oklas's lips, winding over
his cheeks and eyelids, and ending at his forehead. The tingling sensation
was more potent than before. It seeped deep below his skin, painlessly
making ligaments and bone pliable. There was a gentle tugging and pushing at the numbed centre of his face as Raganys, silhouetted against the
bright ceiling, made sculpting gestures. Oklas's mind still reeled at what
was happening, but he felt his resolve bleeding out. His fear grew dull and
remote. Whatever spell Raganys had cast over him, he could muster no
resistance against it.

'You worry I am controlling you, but we are partners in this process,'
said Raganys, drawing resyn from another vial with a fine needle.
'Remember how your true face emerged as a tideling? Its unmaking will
come just as easily when you show me the maskad already hidden in
your skin.' As the injection went into Oklas's limp arm, his blood burned,
flooding his body with the same unnatural thrumming that had started at
his face. A sound caught at the back of his throat, and he realised he could
not open his mouth. If only he could silence Raganys similarly.

'You have a striking facial structure underneath those distracting features,' remarked the resyncrafter. 'A pity the authorities insist on hiding
my work behind masks.'

Tendril vanes brushed Oklas's ears as they dropped away, their spiny
bases retreating into his scalp. Cold crept up his neck, then to the sides of
his head. He shivered.

Raganys's gaunt face came into view as he leaned over Oklas, his frown
lines deepening in concentration. 'This must feel like death to you, but
you will wake from it, maybe even find a kind of freedom on the other
side. A fresh start.'

Oklas's sight blurred—then blackened. Had he been blinded? He drew in a shallow breath, taking comfort in the familiar sensations of his insides. His ribs still expanded as his lungs filled, and his heart beat steadily in his chest even as his surface unravelled and reformed.

His life before his arrival at the guild seemed like a rapidly-fading dream. Oklas had not paid Geshan for the wine he had ordered. And there was a meeting in the segere—how would he find his way back to the Assembly Chambers? He had not finished the thought when sleep or something heavier than it overcame him.

# CHAPTER 14

## PRISMER

T HE MEDIAN BREAK had just ended and most of the ministers and
ambassadors were back in their offices or the auditoriums. Prismer
could once again move about the eighth floor corridor freely. The shelves
of her trolley were stacked with holographic display extenders, casting
platforms, and cables. She had only two meetings left to set up that segment, and the next one was not for another hour. It was not often that she
could slow down and study the ancient mosaics lining the corridors.

The high ceilings blazed with colourful arrangements of turquoise tiles
and molten orange glass, combining to form writhing plants. The contrast
was especially apparent now—at the beginning of the light phases—as
systems of sun tunnels flooded the higher floors of the Chambers with
daylight. The walls were made predominantly from natural stone, but the
colours of the embellishments changed on each floor. The neutral hues
of the ground level etchings gradually gave way to the warm earth tones
and greens of the middle floors, then to blues and purples. The Pentarchy
occupied the uppermost floor. While Prismer had never entered the
Eruds' Throne Room, she had walked the main corridor outside it. The
recessed ceilings were made of dark hardwood, and spangled with pearl
and metal polygons. White and gold-clad walls set the interiors apart
from others in the Chambers.

It suited Prismer that she was seldom required to deliver equipment
beyond the eleventh floor. She was desperate to avoid encounters with
those who frequented such opulent places. Not that she expected to meet

the Erud sovereigns in the public corridors—they used secret lifts and stairwells to their residences at the surface. She had not spoken with an Erud since Aurel had condemned her. It would surprise her if the Pentarchy spared her a thought anymore. The Erud Aurel she knew had recently retired and passed her title to a successor.

Of course, Prismer still had to interact with the courtiers from time to time. "The Ghoul of the Canal", they called her. But her reputation of being the resident maskad didn't assure her of ongoing employment at the Assembly. Even if the Eruds had forgotten her, she needed to prove to the courtiers that she could keep up with the other workers. She couldn't afford to lose this job.

Grinding and chiselling emanated from an open door up ahead. A stretch of tall glass panels in the wall overlooked several artisans at work. Prismer kept her head down and walked quickly past them, though part of her still longed to see what they were doing. There was evidence of restoration work on the floor below; a section of crumbling cornice had been replaced with genuine Apideccan sandstone and inlaid with gleaming leaf-coloured gems.

A tall figure left one of the rooms up ahead. It took Prismer a moment to recognise Dy Erla. She was not wearing her usual cultural attire, but a sleek tan suit with an indigo trim.

'Good median, Prismer,' said Dy Erla warmly. She frowned at the trolley. 'They have loaded you with an awful lot today. Do you need any help?'

'I can't let anyone catch you doing my work,' said Prismer, resting her elbow on the handle. 'Besides, I can manage.' She flexed a modest bicep under the maroon sleeve of her uniform. Although Prismer had gradually built up her strength working here, she could understand why Dy Erla might think her overburdened. Next to the retired soldier, she still looked scrawny.

'Thank you for setting up the display extenders in room thirty-four,' said Dy Erla, straightening. 'The view of the forest and lake from my contact's balcony in Rhestatyn was so life-like, I could almost hear the rustle of wind in the conifers.'

'How did you know I did it?' asked Prismer.

'The newer technicians aren't as meticulous as you.'

Prismer's chest lifted with satisfaction. She did not have the time to fine-tune every minister's presentation, but she made an effort for those who noticed it.

Dy Erla crossed her arms and continued, 'You're also the only one who can set the sound system to accommodate my preferences. Perhaps I should warn the others about my compromised hearing?'

Prismer believed her friend's combat stories about explosions and resulting injuries, but Dy Erla overstated her deafness. 'Should I tell them to "speak up" around you?' she asked teasingly. In the years before Dy Erla augmented her hearing with an implant and Prismer started speaking through a synthesiser, the minister had often implied she was too quiet.

Dy Erla laughed. 'I did give you a hard time, didn't I? At least you've always been clear. Some of the younger ministers could learn from you. They speak far too quickly.'

That reminded Prismer of something she had learned that segere, something odd. She ran a gloved hand over the metal handlebar of her trolley. 'You haven't heard from Minister Sayve recently, have you?' she asked.

'No,' answered Dy Erla, looking at her questioningly.

Prismer continued, 'It's just, I had set up a presentation for him in the fourth floor auditorium today. He didn't arrive.'

'It would hardly be the first engagement he's forgotten,' said Dy Erla, her nostrils flaring.

'I know, but I went to his office afterwards, and Domaćin said they haven't been able to reach his mitter since yesterday.'

Concern rippled across Dy Erla's brow, then dissipated. 'It is possible he has become preoccupied with something at the college. The next term will be starting soon.' She placed a hand on Prismer's shoulder. 'I will have a word with him.'

Prismer muffled a groan. It must have seemed to Dy Erla that she was complaining about Sayve. 'There's no need for you to confront him about it.'

'It's a matter of considering others,' stated Dy Erla, extending a hand for emphasis. 'You have better things to do than wait for him, and his staff have to manage his engagements—he should communicate with them at the very least.' There was no arguing with Dy when she was like this.

Prismer almost felt sorry for Sayve. He could be thoughtless, certainly. But he also treated those of lower strata as his equals. 'By all means, advocate for his staff,' she said, 'but don't bring me into it. I'll call on you to fend off one of the more difficult ministers. Sayve I can handle myself.' Prismer had not seen him since his satellite presentation, but if she could pull him aside, she would ask after Illanu.

Dy Erla inclined her head acceptingly, then narrowed her eyes as if targeting something escaping Prismer's mask. 'Have you heard whether our young friend has reached her destination?'

It often seemed to Prismer that Dy Erla could read the flow of her thoughts. That, or they shared similar concerns at this time. The Rhestian minister had remained deeply invested in Illanu's plight.

'She has,' said Prismer with the unsettling feeling that even the walls might absorb her answer. The news had come to her, not from Sayve but Rosh, who had taken to sending Prismer cryptic updates over her mitter.

Dy Erla's shoulders lowered. 'Are you sleeping any better now?'

'A little.'

Within two segments of Prismer's return from the coast, she had led Dy Erla on one of their secluded walks and recounted her mission in broad strokes. It had seemed enforcers would storm her room at any time. Had someone recognised her guiding the juveniles through the Industrial Park? Had she left any evidence at the cliffside or aroused suspicion at the train station? The possibilities looped in Prismer's mind. But there was also a chance that the mission had been a success. With each passing segment, it seemed more likely.

'Rosh says he has more to tell me. We're meeting at the market in Tramways Square next phase.'

'Didn't you say you would never leave home again after this?'

'A knyad can change her mind. Before that, I'll be at the Husk and Brewer, attending another gathering.'

Dy Erla's hooded eyes widened in thrilled disbelief. 'Two events in one segeind?'

'I'm catching up with some other maskads,' said Prismer, waving absently. 'It's not a regular get-together, just a reunion of sorts. We were counselled around the same time.' Prismer only hoped her progress would not inspire her friend to push her to meet more people. Time was still a valuable commodity, and she did not want hers spread too finely.

Just then, hurried footfalls echoed down the corridor. Prismer craned her neck to see who was coming towards them. The sound drew closer until a knyad, wearing a uniform matching Prismer's, rounded the bend. It was Moshe, a young technician who frequently partnered with her on set-up duty. Panting hard, he slowed down and glanced anxiously at Dy Erla. He was too new to know that, despite her formidable bearing, she was one of the kinder ministers.

Prismer approached him. 'Is there something wrong, Moshe?'

'I, uh,' he stammered at Dy Erla. 'Sorry to interrupt, Minister Rhestat. It's just that the castware'—he motioned to Prismer's loaded trolley—'we need it in Minister Graega's office now.'

Prismer flinched. 'Already?'

'He moved his meeting forwards by half an hour.'

Prismer lifted a small casting box from the trolley and thrust it into Moshe's hands. 'Run ahead with this and load the presentation. I'll follow with the rest.' Even if they rushed there, they wouldn't complete the set-up by the start of the meeting. She turned back to Dy Erla and sighed. 'I'd better go. Goodbye, Minister.'

'I can follow after you. It may help if I tell Minister Graega I held you up.'

'We'll be in room seventeen on the third floor, thanks,' called Prismer as she followed in Moshe's wake, pushing the trolley at a jog. She could not rely on Dy Erla to fight all her battles, but she would always welcome help dealing with disgruntled politicians.

# CHAPTER 15

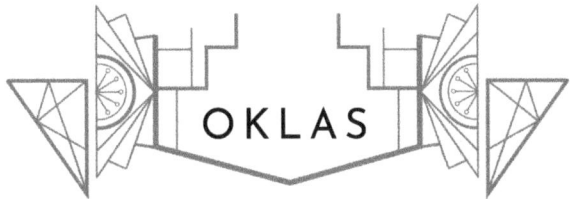

## OKLAS

THE FIRST THING Oklas could see was a smear of black and grey, which gradually turned into a brown haze as colour entered his vision. A sack covered his head, the course material scratching his skin. He tried to close his eyes, to surrender once more to blissful oblivion, but the stitching remained in view. Close by, familiar harsh voices sounded, and Oklas knew he was in the shuttle with the Furtim once more.

Images flashed in his mind. A silhouetted figure bore down on him. Oklas had been following instructions he could not remember: blindly putting on new clothes; going limp as a sea jelly; being carried by something wooden and scratchy. He was a passenger in his own body. Could he move at will now?

He flexed his fingers and relief flooded him. The resyncrafter's thrall had worn off. But there was something else, a heated tingling in his skin. It spread beyond his face and neck, all the way to his torso, arms, and legs. *Scumbling.* Had it really happened to him?

The hinge of Oklas's jaw slid open, but he had no sense of his tongue or teeth. The urge to rip the covering from his face seized him. But he could not do that here—alone and trapped with his captors. There would be other places to come to terms with this. *Stay calm*, he thought to himself. *Breathe.* He startled at the foreign sensation of air being drawn in at the sides of his face.

Stroking one hand over the other, he felt warmed metal press into his wrists. The skin brushing against the handcuffs was thick, almost scaly. There was something very wrong about the limited sensation in his thumbs—they felt like little more than hooked nails positioned low on his palms. How would he work with such an impediment? Would he even have a career to return to? Acid scraped at his empty gut as he slumped in his seat. What would become of his staff, of Emis's legacy? They couldn't take the college from him ...

His throat constricted in a silent sob.

The vehicle braked. Then the door slid open. Oklas could feign unconsciousness no longer. Hands pulled him out of the cabin. His feet hit the floor; the stone beneath his toes was worn smooth. Strange, he couldn't remember taking his boots off.

His legs wobbled and he dropped to one knee. The Furtim had no patience for his apparent weakness and dragged him along until he found his balance. A breeze, which smelled of salt, rust, and rubber, flapped his clothes. Was he back in the city? If he was, it was eerily quiet. He couldn't hear the distant whine of trams braking, or even jostling pedestrians. They had arrived during a curfew, but it couldn't have been the same one that had started during the ambush at Witalit. A full segment must have passed since then.

Oklas wondered where the Furtim were taking him. Was he to be left on a street corner? The metal grating of an outdoor stairway dug into his bare feet, and he began an ascent. Though his hands were cold and clammy, the rest of him felt feverishly warm. Each faltering step sent his heart racing. It was as if his body was fighting off an infection, rejecting the changes inflicted upon it.

'Move,' barked someone, prodding his back. He stuck out an elbow to support himself on the stairway railing.

Even with the sack covering his head, Oklas could make out more colours. A faint glow bathed the stairway in pink. The first rays of sunlight pricked through the stitching of his shroud. Were people watching this procession from nearby windows?

Keys jangled and a door creaked open. Oklas hesitated at the threshold. A hand gripped his shoulder and forced him forwards. A few paces in, a Furto pulled the sack from Oklas's head and shoved him into a chair. The room was dark but, from the gaps in the shutters, stripes of light slanted over the walls. The contrast irritated his eyes, but he couldn't blink the scene away. He raised his cuffed hands to shield himself from the too-bright light.

A mocking voice he recognised as Saron's sounded from across the room. 'They all turn out the same when Raganys is through with them.'

Oklas could make out the blurred edges of dark shapes stacked against the wall: furniture or boxes. There were figures too, but their faces were indistinct. Someone grabbed him by the wrist, unlocking and removing his handcuffs. He reached up to wipe his eyes, but his fingers found neither eyelids nor the bridge of his nose. In their place was a flat, rubbery surface. He jerked his hand away and tucked it with the other in his lap, afraid of looking too carefully at his overly long fingers.

'He's ready for you,' called one of the figures. Footsteps squeaked on the buffed concrete floor.

The newcomer drew up a chair opposite Oklas, who kept his head bowed. The edges of the chair legs gradually sharpened—his sight was improving. The visitor's polished shoes and pressed trousers were those of a bureaucrat, not an enforcer.

'Good median, Oklas,' said the other knyad in a brisk tone. 'I am your probation officer, Certus Nithan, andrid. My role is to help you adjust to your new circumstances.'

Oklas shrugged. He raised his head and stole a glimpse of Nithan, who was too busy sifting through the papers in his carry case to notice him. The officer was an unremarkable, middle-aged knyad with bags under his eyes and a large, bowed nose. His skin was a greenish-brown, ringed with bands in a lighter colour.

'I understand you will need time to recover from your procedure. We can go over the basics now, and I will return in the segere to give you a full debriefing.' He reached into his pockets, withdrawing a set of keys and holding them out.

Oklas watched the metal tags clink into a pile in his slack palms.

Nithan gestured around the room. 'This is your new home. Your essential items were delivered here this segere. As of now, the rest of your assets belong to the state.'

There was a static buzzing in Oklas's throat as a moan escaped him. Until now, he had not considered how he might speak. He touched the thin metal panel embedded in his skin at the base of his neck.

'Some important things to remember,' continued Nithan, ignoring

Oklas's attempted objection. 'As a maskad, you may not expose your face in public.' He presented Oklas with a tinted lens set in a stiff fabric, with straps for him to tie around his head. 'This is a standard-issue shroud, but any covering that completely obscures your eye and breathing slits will suffice. You may not disclose details of your experience at the Transmutation Guild. Failure to comply with these critical rules will result in your exile to a labour commune.'

Nithan withdrew a stack of pages from his file. 'The Erudean Pentarchy has assigned you to the Engineering Consortium as a resyn refiner, starting next phase. Since your new employers are accommodating you here, I advise you to accept the position.' He held out a thick file, almost bursting with stacks of paper, separated by dividers. 'We can sign the contracts tomorrow, but you may read through the documentation in your own time.'

Oklas could hardly see. How was he expected to read all of this? He opened his jaw to argue, but only a strangled sound and choppy syllables streamed from the announcer in his neck. Exasperated, he rubbed the lower part of his blank face and chin, finally whipping the file from Nithan's outstretched hand.

The bureaucrat snapped his carry case shut and got to his feet. 'If you still struggle to communicate by the segere, you can write down your queries or employ Elementary hand signals. Maybe use this time to reflect on anything you might know about Keanon Caswor. Furtim intelligence suggests you weren't close. Not enough for the Ardedrians to attempt to rescue you. If you can't provide his location, the names of his associates might earn you some compensation.' He paused, holding his carry case at his front. 'Good segment, Oklas.' With a quick nod, Nithan made for the exit.

'One more thing,' he said, turning to face Oklas before leaving. 'For the moment, the Pentarchy would rather you didn't go by your given name. You may choose a pseudonym for future interactions, preferably something discreet.'

Oklas was not sure how he felt about that. Anonymity made things easier for him, of course, but knowing the Eruds wished for him to disappear only made him want to run outside and shout his name for all to hear.

The Furtim, who had remained standing the whole time, stalked after

Nithan. The last to leave was Seron, who stood to the right of the doorway. Her expression appeared as a blur, but Oklas knew she was smiling. He knotted the muscles he could feel around his face, hoping they conveyed the glare he meant to send her way.

'Muteness suits you, Sayve,' she said cuttingly. With a click, the door closed on him.

Oklas looked at the papers in his hands—the words blurred and sharpened so erratically that he felt dizzy. Concentrating, he brought one into focus just long enough for the content to bore him. He didn't need a list of restrictions. He needed to see what had happened to him.

Alone—at last—he walked around the insula. He was in the living room, which opened onto a kitchen counter to the left of the front door. Very little light came through the shuttered window in the wall above the counter, but a sun tunnel at the back of the insula made up for it. Behind papery drywall, a bedroom adjoined the main living area. The edge of the sun tunnel protruded from the back corner, illuminating a bathroom smaller than some of the cupboards in Witalit. Here Oklas found what he was looking for: a narrow cabinet mounted on a wall with a mirror at its front.

He had seen enough at the Transmutation Guild to prepare him for the oddity of the creature staring back at him. And yet, he couldn't accept that this reflection was his. He recognised the planes of his face, his large forehead and prominent cheekbones. But his features—nose, mouth, the creases under his eyes—were gone. Levelled out.

In their place was a single, large eye. Perhaps the jagged black shape roving across his face was the pupil? The pattern rippling at its edges was not even the vibrant blue his eyes had been, but pale beige. The protective layer behaved like something between an eyelid and an iris. He tried closing the eye, and it narrowed to a scalloped shape. Maybe it was a cluster of ocelli, and it couldn't shut?

Oklas took a steadying breath. He now understood why it felt like the air was coming in at his cheeks. Two slits, resembling gills, opened on either side of his face. His ears flattened, new muscles at their bases allowing for an increased range of movement. Running his fingers along the gills and onto his bald head, he felt a few scaly ridges; they appeared slightly bluer than the rest of his slate-coloured skin.

*What have they done to you?*

An announcer in his throat implant engaged, reciting his thoughts: 'done /t/ ou.' It was a synthesiser. A neural interface received signals to speak, and the vibrations of the underlying larynx generated a tone of voice. The neat device would have fascinated Oklas were he not so dependent on it. He noticed a beaked node under the synthesiser—not an implant, he realised, but a part of him.

He was wearing a loose-fitting garment, like the fulvers he had seen on maskads. The fabric was damp with sweat. He pulled it off and looked down at his chest and arms, turning to glimpse himself in the mirror from the back. The scaly skin on his head and hands continued on his shoulders and the backs of his arms. His legs and torso, however, were virtually unchanged. At this point, anything familiar came as a comfort.

Oklas would not deny his vanity; his appearance had served him well in the past. But his face had been more than an instrument he used to charm people—it *was* him. What did it matter if he retained his proportions from the neck down? He couldn't approach anyone looking like this—couldn't make himself known. He finally understood why maskads seemed unable to better themselves, to integrate with society. Even if he regained his voice, he was missing something essential to all knyads.

For all his juvenile interest in resyncraft, Oklas had never encountered a mention of scumbling and had never realised resyn was the thing that blighted those retiring mask-wearers. The resyncrafters had successfully kept the cruellest of their techniques secret. And the Eruds ensured no one would listen to those who knew the truth about the guild.

Oklas turned away from the mirror, holding his upper arms and rocking. He would find a way to undo this wretched affliction, to reconstruct his face. His original form had to be there still, encoded in his genome. His rough nails dug into the fabric of his garment, and he released his grip, letting it drop to the floor.

Oklas returned his attention to the synthesiser in his neck. The noises he made sounded nothing like him, stilted and lacking inflection. He thought back to the maskads he had encountered, and how they spoke. Though there was a reverberating overtone in her delivery, the projectionist at the Chambers had a pleasant, husky voice.

There came a metallic buzz from the synthesiser as Oklas cleared his throat. He attempted a Drassian expletive worthy of his situation. After humming and grunting it a few times, a partial utterance reached his synthesiser in a crackly, '–ahst.' After a few more attempts, he was vocalising more consistently. Singing along to a well-known folk song seemed a good idea until he tried it. It took tremendous concentration to get only a few words in. At this rate, it would be revolutions before he could speak normally.

Groaning, he walked over to the windows overlooking the stairway and cracked open the drab shutters. It was piercingly bright, almost headache-inducing. Cupping his hands around his face, Oklas shielded his sensitive eye. He was on one of the higher floors of the block of insulae, facing north or east, judging by the sun's position. His focus adjusted to make out details in the distance.

It was not long before he recognised the hilly, narrow streets of Gilstren, surrounded by rock walls on all sides. Though located on a steep slope, the district still lay deep in the gorge. It was far enough below the surface that he could see only a sliver of sky cutting through the rocky ceiling. Letting the shutters fall closed, he retreated into welcoming darkness. Oklas already missed the trees and the view of the Traditional Quarter from Witalit Estate.

Surely that's where he would wake up when this nightmare ended? But if he were asleep, he was remarkably aware of his headache. And of how thirsty he was.

Oklas coughed. His throat felt dry and scratchy. He had not had anything to drink all segment. Rummaging through the boxes, he tossed aside an assortment of objects until he found a jug. He filled it and tilted his head over the kitchen sink, pouring the water into the slits in his cheeks. Immediately he bent over, retching and coughing. Rather than swallowing the liquid, he had inhaled it.

So the gill-like structures were no substitute for a mouth. Raganys could have at least adapted them to filter oxygen from water.

After coughing up the last droplets, Oklas rubbed his strained neck and chest—his hand ran over the beak, and it widened into a hungry maw. No, surely not. Before he could consider what he was about to do, he refilled the jug, threw his head back, and poured a trickle of water directly into the opening in his throat. He swallowed reflexively and shuddered. *Ugh.* Reluctantly, he gulped down the rest. Even though his stomach growled voraciously, he could not imagine wanting to eat like this.

The boxes he had hastily torn open in search of the jug lay strewn about the room. Oklas placed two of them on a heavyset table he recognised from his workshop and drew up a chair to start unpacking.

What the Furtim had left for him wasn't what he would have chosen to keep: practical clothes, toiletries, his least valuable furniture and appliances, and rudimentary tools. His smart suits, favourite books, and heirlooms from Emis were nowhere in sight. Laying his head on the table, he blocked out the light with his folded arms and sat still.

He had spread his possessions throughout an estate of fifteen rooms, his office at the Assembly Chambers, and a college campus. How much did he really expect to find in the poky insula?

Absently, Oklas activated the mitter at his arm. The interface had been wiped clean. Where were his contacts, his customisations? His old device must have been removed during his scumbling and replaced with a fresh one. He cursed. He had always meant to memorise the mitter codes of the people he knew. But, even if he had, what would he tell them? Which of them would stand by him now?

Reclining in his chair, Oklas felt a slippery textile brush his back. A riding jacket lay draped over the top rail. It was the one he had been wearing when the Furtim captured him. Reaching inside the front pocket, he withdrew a folded piece of paper. His heart grew heavy in his chest as he skimmed past the mitter code and read:

*To a dashing stranger,*

*Let me know when you next travel the Partesian Coast, and I will gladly host you in Kelabek.*

*Ailynn Nal*

Oklas's body quaked. He buried his blank face in his hands, but no tears wet his palms.

# CHAPTER 16

## PRISMER

A N ATTENDANT BEARING a tray of frothing bira tumblers stepped aside to let five masked customers pass by. The maskads continued down the aisle to the wooden ramp at the pub's exit. They were a peculiar group by most standards, but not unlike many of the Husk and Brewer's regulars. Also known as Huskhouse, the pub occupied a wonderfully crooked narrow building in the Dolna District. A stairway to the left branched out onto three incomplete floors set at different levels in the wall. Curtains were drawn around some tables, providing maskads with private spaces to eat unencumbered by their masks.

'Prismer,' called Gazda, the swarthy owner of the Husk and Brewer, 'don't wait another year to show that fancy mask of yours around here.'

Prismer held back from the group and turned to find him behind the counter. 'Your selection of steeping flowers alone will lure me back,' she assured him. Gazda thrust his shoulders back appreciatively.

Had it been a year since Prismer's last visit? She would have to return alone, with her sketches. It could become a revolution-end ritual. She passed the fountain made of barrel staves and started down the gravel path.

The Husk and Brewer lay between larger shops, at the end of an alley only wide enough for two to walk abreast. A wooden deck had been built above the gap, and the floorboards cast stripes of shadow and sunlight on the gravel. Strings of golden lights dotted the walls of the neighbouring buildings, guiding customers to the pub.

There were few safe havens for maskads in Apidecca, which could have been why the Husk and Brewer's scumbled patrons outnumbered their whole counterparts. If this scared off some knyads, it did not seem to trouble Gazda. He had found his niche and catered to the specific requirements of his patrons. The establishment offered everything from affordable drinks to specially-adapted eating utensils. No single maskad could spend a great deal there, but many of the three hundred or so in the city frequented the Husk and Brewer with some regularity.

The maskads Prismer knew waited where the alley opened onto the street. Taber stood to one side, facing the others. He wore his wooden mask with the vertical band painted in the ashy pink of his skin. Even before she heard his synth-speech, Prismer could tell he was deep in a discussion by the exaggerated movements of his head.

'And at the next meeting, Driminn will cover the subject of maskad-safe charities in the city. We're sharing a list of drop-off sites for food and clothing. You can find us in the workshop again.'

Gryta, a young maskad in a pale blue hooded jacket, groaned. 'I can't make that one—working late. Our shipments go off the next segere.'

'We can take notes for you,' offered Onella, slowly turning her stippled bronze mask from Gryta to Prismer. 'I know the Husk and Brewer is a fair walk from the Chambers, Prismer. Maybe we can find a venue closer to your side for our next social?'

Prismer replied with a resolute shake of her head. 'There are no good alternatives near the Upper End.' Once again, her privileged circumstances cleaved her from the others. She shook off the impression, reminding herself that the maskads before her had also known prosperity; a few were Praemor once. 'Don't worry,' she added, raising her chin, 'I'll spontaneously reappear from time to time.'

Nyék folded his arms, carnelian yellow hands tucked into his black sleeves. 'You, spontaneous?'

'When I'm prepared for it.'

'You're always welcome here, Prismer,' said Taber, fixing the upturned eyes of his mask on her. 'We have missed your unique perspectives.'

Prismer inclined her head, accepting the compliment. 'Thanks for having me.' Everyone had to put their energy into something; for Taber, it was service. He dotingly coordinated everyone in a manner that would make Dy Erla proud. It was no easy task; at least Driminn was there to support him. The problem with making a pattern out of people was that they presented many variables beyond your control. Prismer was grateful the mechanical components of her sculptures did not object to their places in her designs.

They parted and Prismer continued up the High Street, reflecting on her time with the other maskads. Compared with her adventure at the coast, a tram ride to the Lower End presented few obstacles. But an aversion to travel had never been the reason for her long absences from these gatherings. The situations in which most maskads found themselves were often dire, and she had no answers for their suffering. But, for today at least, it was good to see her companions prospering.

A monastery of Adecai devotees had taken pity on the homeless Onella and provided her with a room in return for help with chores. Gryta had started a new job at a shipping company. While the hours spent packing cargo were long, she finally earned regular wages. Then there was Nyék, a former forger. Many unclassifieds had gained entry into Apidecca using the false documents he had created. He was scumbled for his efforts, but past clients continually repaid him with jobs, food, and shelter. Each time Prismer saw him, he was staying in a different dwelling.

Something cold and wet lashed at Prismer's legs, pulling her attention back to her surroundings. She had walked into a muddy puddle left by a burst water pipe. At least she was not in uniform. The silt left a tea-coloured stain on the hem of her trousers. More knyads walked the pavements here; she had reached the High Street. The brakes of a tram whined, and the vehicle passed her on the economy lane tracks. She sprinted across the High Street, weaving her way between pedestrians and scramblers, to the next boarding post. The market was only a quarter-league away, but the tram would take her there quicker than her legs could. At the door, she presented her mitter for scanning. Above her, the trolley pole hummed on the overhead line. She found a space at the back and reached for a hanging strap.

She checked her mitter. Rosh still had not replied with the location of the Kuchari stall where they would meet. *Stop worrying*, she scolded herself. Anticipating problems at every turn was an exhausting way to live. Prismer had not always been this way. She had been nervous about her move to Apidecca, but she had embraced the excitement of it. For a short while, she lost herself in the unbroken *click-clack-clack* of flanged wheels against steel tracks and the rhythmic rocking of the tram.

◦◈═◦◉◦═◈◦

The market lay on the eastern side of the High Street, in a square on the corner of the tramline to Gilstren. It opened only during sun-up, on the middle and phase-end rest segments. A row of buildings, several storeys high with clean, undulating facades, lined the far side of the market. Strings of decorative paper shapes twisted around the iron trunks of dormant street lights. So far, Prismer had seen only two other maskads in the crowd. She preferred being in the Lower End, where she did not stand out so much.

All around were rich fabrics, spices, and elaborately-pleated pastries. Prismer drew aside to admire a craftsperson expertly shaping molten glass jewellery. She wondered how many years of training it took to achieve such skill? Hidden among the novelties were products of a more disturbing nature. "Easy-application" cybernetic implants sagged behind glass cabinets. Some looked like curled isopods, their many legs made of needles and spiny implements. Alongside them, colourful adverts claimed they enhanced aesthetics, symmetry, and muscle function. What would Rosh make of that?

Increasing her pace, Prismer left the lurid stall behind. Knyads passed her in a blur. She had gotten used to the cacophony of voices sounding above her in Apex Hall. But she was never in the midst of it all. This was too bright, too loud.

She stopped at a quiet corner and willed her surroundings to blacken, closing her optic pattern over her eye. She focused on the sound of her breath passing through the filters of her mask. Opening her eye again, she looked at the stall display to her right. On the shelves were rows of bottles containing bark, dried roots, insects, and ground-up shells or bone. Most of the substances were of no value to anyone but the superstitious, but she recognised a few useful herbs. They were the sort of ingredients that could be brewed into tonics to ease pain or enhance focus. She craned her neck, examining a jar of woody stalks with bead-like, iridescent teal flowers.

'Ah, the lure of the jaystrike,' rasped a shrewd voice from behind her.

Prismer whipped around to find the leathery face of the stall owner at the edge of her mask. The musty-clothed knyad looked at Prismer, aer pale eyes full of greedy intent. 'Nothing else keeps the emptiness of the hungry ghoul at bay—'

Prismer backed away. 'I don't want your poisons.'

The vendor followed her, undeterred. 'You buy only the best remedies from Geela Min. You will have no regrets.'

Prismer declined aer again and walked briskly from the stall. Jaystrike was nothing to indulge in.

The market was not quite as large as it had seemed. If she walked along the side of the grid layout, Prismer could check the stalls systematically. She finally recognised Rosh's tall frame and short, frizzy tendrils from the back. He waited in front of the Kuchari stall, looking surprisingly casual with a dark brown jacket slung over one shoulder. He also wore his powder grey Consortium overalls and trainers. Upon noticing Prismer, his mouth curved upwards. There was no trace of the moody, suspicious juvenile she had met only three phases prior. Their escapade at the coast had changed things between them. By the time Prismer had escorted him back to the city, he practically counted her as a harvestmate. She greeted him and looked at the punnets of ingredients in the trailer.

'I only ever order mine with rapha and roasted nuts,' said Rosh, holding out the bowl of sauce-saturated grains and purple vegetables, 'but if you like weird food, you can also add sides with spices or things like black mhizoa.'

'I'm not hungry,' replied Prismer.

'You sure? It's very—oh.' He stopped, outlining his face in the suggestion of a mask. 'You can't eat with that on, can you?'

'It's possible, but awkward,' she said, closing her collar around her neck. 'I ate before coming here.'

He nodded. 'Wise. You can never be too cautious with street food.' They continued down the walkway, passing a row of fine buildings on their left and more market stalls on the right. One of the shop fronts caught Rosh's attention. 'I'm just going in here to look at some of the mitter accessories.' He pointed to a glossy display behind the glass. 'Do you want to come?'

'I'll wait here.'

When Rosh insisted that she would like the offerings inside, Prismer had to point out the small sign on the door, featuring a mask with a black line dashed diagonally over it.

'Ah'—Rosh looked at it in surprise—'I didn't know they turn maskads away. Reluctantly, he said, 'I suppose I should boycott them?'

Prismer slowly tipped her head from side to side in contemplation. 'There's a lot of this towards the Upper End. They're only trying to keep their customers.'

Rosh chewed the inside of his thin cheek. 'Ilu used to make statements over things like this. Honestly, though, I don't think I'd be able to stay away for more than a revolution.' He gave an apologetic shrug. 'I'll go in later.'

They walked to a seating area near a decorative fountain, where three sheets of water spouted from horned shapes. Prismer sat, and the knyads at the table nearest to them moved on. Rosh started to share his news, careful not to mention inflammatory names or secret locations.

Describing his new association with the Ardedrians, Rosh confided, 'Signing up with the team was the only way to keep in touch with Ilu.' While he had not become an active member of the insurgent group, they now considered him an ally. Prismer wished to avoid becoming more deeply involved with the Ardedrians' affairs, but she needed to hear Rosh vouch for them. She had, after all, delivered his closest friend into their hands.

Rosh propped his bony elbow on the table and lowered his voice. 'I chat to Ilu at their base every few segs. They won't let me take a towaye off the premises, but it isn't far from my dormitory.' He idly traced the rim of his near-empty kahv flask and laughed. 'She's receiving combat training. You can imagine how much she's enjoying that.'

Prismer drew back in her seat. 'Militant for a group who denounce violence, aren't they?'

'It's mostly for self-defence,' Rosh assured her. 'They focus more on evading tactics. Ilu is keeping busy and meeting plenty of people. It doesn't take her long to make friends.' His wide-set eyes grew distant. 'Still, she keeps some a little closer than the rest.'

It was hard to move away from those you loved. Prismer still missed the harvestmates she had shared a dormitory with on Inclatia. 'I'm glad Ilu is alright,' she said.

Rosh shot her a half-grin. 'She sends you "hugs",' he said, folding his arms, 'but you'd probably prefer me to convey those verbally.'

'I think it's more comfortable for the both of us, don't you?'

At Rosh's look of relief, Prismer was almost tempted to hold her arms out wide—just to see what he would do.

One of Rosh's main reasons for meeting her here was to inspect the neural bridge in her forearm. He was still set on updating it. Any reservations she had about accepting favours vanished when she realised how much he was enjoying this. It was the same way she had felt when she made her first mask for a fellow scumbled knyad.

The neural bridge disconnected, and the tingling in Prismer's hands returned. Her fingers curled inwards. Rosh winced as he lifted the cybernetics and examined the scarred area below.

'They rebuilt this section with hard coral grafts,' said Prismer, running a gloved finger over the outer bone of her forearm.

'How did you get an injury like that?' asked Rosh, more fascinated than repulsed.

'My clan exported aquacultural produce. Everyone had a turn threshing pallisk stems or iodrem. During one seafrond reaping, I got stung by a cruttlefiend—tetchy little mollusc.'

'Their tentacle tips are lined with poisonous spurs,' said Rosh with a frown. 'By the look of it, you couldn't have received medical attention quickly.'

'The antivenom had to be rushed from Fentu Brise, the nearest city,' said Prismer with a shrug. 'I can't remember the wait—maybe because of the fever. They said my arm was so swollen that the skin split. The menders managed to save it, but they removed a lot of dead tissue.'

'You're lucky you only suffered minor nerve damage,' said Rosh, opening up a panel on the implant to look at the model number. 'I think I can create a better flow to the severed connections. When I'm done, the sensitivity in your fingertips should be the same as the right side.'

He measured the dimensions of her arm with a scanner he had checked out from the Consortium, and gushed over the quality and longevity of older technology. The implant was over twenty years old. But he insisted that, with regular maintenance, she need never replace it. 'You have ports for some slick accessories here, even a built-in microprojector,'

Rosh said, marvelling at the metal casing. 'Do you ever worry people will try to cut the cybernetics off you on the street?'

'I used to when I was new here,' admitted Prismer. Implant theft was rife in many cities, and Apidecca had a robust underground trade in stolen cybernetics. Prismer had known strangers to brush up against her in crowded streets, their deft hands slipping into her pockets or flicking to her arms in search of loose connections. She was prepared for them. 'I leave the most expensive components at the Chambers, but no one has tried to rob me in years. People don't expect to find much of value on maskads.'

Rosh grinned. 'Maybe they're afraid your tech carries a curse.'

'Maybe,' repeated Prismer with a humming laugh.

'Was the implant designed here?'

'No—Fentu Brise. They have decent facilities there. I asked the bio-mechanists to leave space for me to add other features, things that could improve my chances of being transferred to Apidecca. I used most of my savings on the microprojector.' With her good arm, Prismer reached for the device and activated it. A translucent General Assembly icon flickered above the table.

Rosh's hazel eyes narrowed. 'You didn't think your skills would get you here?'

'I wanted to believe I was more than my hardware,' said Prismer, switching it off. 'But I'm not sure my skills had much to do with my appointment. I was the only Orta applicant among unclassifieds, or so I have been told.' At first, she had blatantly disregarded the rumour. But the longer she stayed in Apidecca, the more likely it seemed that she had not truly earned her place there.

'Stratum-bias happens all the time,' said Rosh, tipping his empty flask back and forth.

Prismer looked down at her gloved hands folded on the table. The drone of footfalls and hundreds of overlapping conversations filled the silence between them.

Then Rosh spoke up. 'Ilu hated to think she was accepted into the Emisrian because of her mobility problems. The director is known for being a charitable sort. Of course, she could get in on her assessment scores alone—but if she didn't, it would be the one time her disability gave her an advantage.'

Prismer looked up to see him leaning back in his chair.

'You both got where you wanted to be,' he concluded, 'so why question it?'

Getting what they wanted had not done either of them much good: Prismer was now a maskad and Ilu a fugitive. Rather than pointing this out to Rosh, Prismer asked, 'Have Ilu's legs always been frail?'

'Since she was harvested off Maha,' said Rosh, his chin jutting solemnly. 'There were many factories along that coastline, producing things like fertilisers and pesticides. Some were shut down because of the pollution. Few tidelings wash ashore anymore, and those that do often have developmental defects.' He brightened. 'She's healthy otherwise. You saw her out-swimming all of us.'

Prismer made an affirming glottal sound.

Rosh turned aside and watched a pair of knyads sit a few tables away, holding hands. 'I used to be more interested in cybernetics than the people attached to them,' he said. 'To work with the best technology, you want to attract wealthy patients. I followed trends in implants and cellular treatments—things that can extend lifespans, make people faster, stronger, more attractive.' He shook his head.

'Then I met Ilu, who doesn't have access to any of that. Who never chooses the comfortable options in life. Peers, she's stubborn'—he laughed—'but she also knows what's important. She can't stop caring and then doing something about it. I still have a lot to learn from her.'

'We both do,' said Prismer, bobbing her head.

Rosh went on to describe the leg braces he was developing for Ilu, demonstratively running his hands over the table to make the principles into something tangible. Prismer rested the cool veneer of her chin in her palm and listened, an admiring smile stirring beneath her skin.

Rosh's mitter flashed—a third notification in the recent series he had been ignoring. He excused himself and put on the display visor connected to his device to check his messages in private. Turning back to Prismer, he said, 'I'm going to the Crater Gardens with some friends after this. Would you like to come along?'

'Only if I could spend all of tomorrow in recovery—which I can't,' replied Prismer.

'Actually, they're mostly Ilu's friends from college,' said Rosh, removing the visor. 'The one messaging me is Nusa, he shared classes with her. He says their second term has been delayed. You wouldn't know anything about that, being in the Assembly?'

'Minister Sayve's office there is closed, and I've heard talk that he's abroad,' said Prismer, tipping her head thoughtfully. 'But no official statements have been made. His college partners with an academy in the Dras Channel—he could be meeting the directors there.' The distance could explain Dy Erla's inability to reach Sayve's mitter. His departure had been abrupt, but it was not unusual for ministers to leave in haste when required by their home clans.

'Odd. Illanu said he didn't travel much these segs,' said Rosh. 'She said a lot of things about the director. It could get annoying.'

Somehow, Prismer could imagine half of the Emisrian's students being the same way. 'What about you?' she asked. 'Are you not smitten with any of your lecturers at the Consortium?'

His expression impassive, Rosh replied, 'Well, Master Rhea Verci does look very fetching in her stained lab coat with her goggles pressing into her frown lines.'

Prismer laughed, then—recovering her composure—continued, 'I'm sure Sayve has left someone in charge.'

'I told Nusa to enjoy the break,' said Rosh, getting up from the table. 'We don't get time off at the Consortium. I was even there today, catching up on my practicals.'

Just then, something behind Prismer caught Rosh's attention. He started shouting and waving, and Prismer traced his line of sight to the other side of the square. A figure in a pale tunic darted between knyads and stalls.

Prismer glimpsed goggles over the opaque fabric bandaging the stranger's head. Ae dipped aer covered face and strode purposefully towards the High Street. 'You didn't tell me you had other maskad friends,' she said, bemused.

'You'll always be the first, Prismer,' replied Rosh, his mouth twitching in a smile. 'He's someone I just met at the Consortium. His name is Koska, or is it Kota?' He rubbed his chin. 'Hm, it was on his badge. I tried to introduce myself to him, but he's even quieter than you—didn't say a word.'

Prismer watched the figure trudge on with the same hunched posture she had once worn like a heavy cloak. 'He seems new to this.'

Rosh looked to the edge of the market where his co-worker had disappeared into the crowd. 'Should I leave him alone?

'He may need some space,' agreed Prismer, pushing her chair back and standing, 'but not too much. Treat him as you would anyone else.'

'So, acknowledge him sometimes?'

'That should do it.'

Prismer and Rosh walked a short distance together, leaving the festive paper decorations and heady scents behind before parting at the High Street.

◦◈═◦◉◦═◈◦

Prismer wove her way through the backstreets west of the Upper End. Visiting the Traditional Quarter made for an indirect route home; she would have to circle around the Chambers to reach the staff quarters entrance on the eastern side. She could not tell why she had chosen to walk this street. Her feet had carried her here. Embedded in the cobbled path were decorative plates made of glazed ceramics. Inscribed on each plate was the name of a notable knyad and aer most significant contribution to the city. Most were clan leaders, cultural icons, engineers, or architects. Some of the plates were so old that they had worn smooth. Prismer had fancied seeing her name there, perhaps listed as the founder of an inspiring new district.

*Foolishness.* The city would continue to change, with or without her input. And it was past its prime. She contented herself with the more modest mark she had left two blocks away, on Oeillade Street. There, her moving sculptures could delight passers-by, and no one needed to know the artist was a maskad. Almost every narrow street of the Traditional Quarter had a character of its own; murals graced shop fronts, and platforms raised performers for all to see. Presently Prismer was walking up Founders Street—one of the oldest in the Traditional Quarter.

A *thud* sounded behind her. Something dark moved at the corner of her eyehole rim. She looked around—just the wind knocking a shop door against the wall. What did she expect to see? Nothing haunted these empty streets—except for her. A lone figure in a mask, dressed in a rumpled grey fulver—Prismer could see why she might make for an eerie sight. At least no one else was around to be frightened by her. The wind gusted in tunnels through this part of the city. She did not miss going this way unmasked, with the cold air battering her exposed cheeks and drying her eyes. Prismer tucked in the folds securing her headscarf at the back.

She stopped outside the shop she knew better than any other here. The gilded sign had tarnished since she had last passed this way, and the shop front was painted in a darker shade of green, but it was still the Viren & Stone she knew. Here, she had sourced her sculpting supplies—when she was not "borrowing" materials from the Assembly workshop.

Prismer could almost see her younger self walking through the entrance, wheeling a trolley bag to carry her purchases. She would have been in uniform after a median at the Assembly, her lengthened tendrils tied high at the back of her head.

It was dark inside Viren & Stone, but Prismer could see the interior layout. The carving stones used to be closer to the window. Now there were only jars of pastel-coloured paints in view. The shop door suddenly clinked open, and she jumped. It was Heykel, the shopkeeper. His stoop had deepened in the almost-fifteen years since she had seen him. But, from his jade green skin to the rounded tip of his nose, little else had changed. He even wore the same stiff apron.

'I closed the door early on account of the weather,' he told her, squinting, 'but you're welcome to have a look inside.'

'No.' Prismer's refusal was too ardent. She adjusted her synth-speech to a gentler monotone, hoping it would be enough to disguise her voice. 'No, thank you. I haven't come with any substants.'

'That's quite alright. Many people come in to browse or get away from the wind.'

Indecisiveness and shame held her in place.

'I don't turn anyone away,' he said softly, as if luring a stray animal closer.

He had always welcomed everyone into his shop—even maskads. Unlike Gazda, he did not even stand to profit from their visits. Prismer didn't want to be the reason he lost custom. But it seemed no one else was inside. She sometimes sent Moshe here to buy a block of carving stone for her to use on maquettes, but she missed the luxury of browsing. It could not do any harm to have a look.

Tentatively, Prismer followed Heykel over the threshold. She scanned the aisles and soon found the sculpting and moulding tools on the far wall. A set of fine jigsaws would help shape the fan blades she needed to complete *The Herald*. The right tools could compensate for the imprecise movements of her hands.

She would have to save up for these. Fidgeting with her long sleeves, she looked over to Heykel. Sure enough, he was watching her—not with the scrutiny of one who suspected a shoplifter, but with interest. He knew all his customers by their orders.

This place held too many memories. She had to leave.

As Prismer passed the counter on her way to the exit, Heykel pointed to her and said, 'Your scarf, I recognise the linear embroidery. Southeastern, isn't it?'

The old shopkeeper's memory was as keen as ever, and his attention to detail put even Prismer's to shame. When he last saw the scarf it had been looped around her neck, not tied over her head. Keeping her chin pointed downwards, she touched the white fabric that hung over her shoulder. 'It must have been imported,' she lied.

'A customer from the Fentu Brise area used to wear one just like it,' recalled Heykel. 'She also had an interest in sculpture. I haven't seen her in well over a decade. She just disappeared one segment.'

Prismer held her breath. Her impassive mask suddenly felt ineffective as a shield.

He continued, 'Such a bright talent. I was waiting to see her sculptures in the foyer of the Silversteam Trade Centre or the Assembly Chambers.'

She looked into his kindly face. The arrangement of his wrinkles signalled recognition, and she saw in his brown eyes the pity she dreaded.

Prismer tore her gaze from his, swallowing hard. Coming here was a mistake.

'I should go,' she said hurriedly. 'Goodbye, kyr.'

'Wait—'

She sped from the shop before she could hear the name he called. As Prismer passed poles and alleyways, a masked figure flanked her from a place of deep shade. It was her reflection, stalking her in the windows of shop fronts. She broke into a jog, the brush of her boots against sandstone drowning out the pounding of her heart. A knyad sweeping aer porch hastily retreated behind the door at Prismer's approach. She heard the door latch click as she passed. Only when she neared Clanfare Avenue, circling the Assembly Chambers, did Prismer stop to catch her breath.

# CHAPTER 17

## OKLAS

I F IT WAS not enough for the Eruds to imprison Oklas in this defective form and relegate him to a drudge's job at the Consortium, they now summoned him on his phase-end rest segment. They had arranged for their slimy nemertine, Certus Nithan, to accompany Oklas as he cleared his office at the Assembly Chambers. For segments, the probation officer had shadowed him at the Consortium. Oklas would never share the secret of Hidreth's safehouse, but, to appear cooperative, he had given Nithan Yvere and Tanuk's descriptions. They were already known insurgents and would forgive him for it. Gradually, he was earning some freedom. It seemed the probation officer had better uses for his time today; Nithan stayed only a short while before leaving Oklas with the office keys, which he would have to give to one of the guards on his way out.

Oklas looked into the box he had packed. It contained printed captures of him and Emis at his graduation ceremonies, some stationary, and his certificates. These things were of no value to anyone but him. Had he not come to fetch them, the Assembly would have discarded his keepsakes like rubbish. The state had already seized everything of importance.

The raised floor, basic furnishings, and Domaćin's heavy desk remained in place. But the office interior had been stripped of any character Oklas had contributed during his residence. It was blank and awaiting the next occupant.

When Oklas had inquired after his staff, the only assurance Nithan could offer was, *We have found no grounds for them to be penalised for their association with you.* Oklas prayed they would find other employment soon. Maybe they would return to work with his replacement, whoever ae was? Furna, Domaćin, Minister Kemia—they would all be better off working alongside someone who would not endanger them.

*No.* He would not regret the choices he had made, the things he'd done for Keanon. Balancing the boxes in one hand, Oklas closed the door behind him.

The place was quite empty on rest segments—no doubt that was why they had called him in at this time. Whether here or working in his corner of the Consortium, he was constantly ushered away from everyone. The cavernous corridors of the Chambers were still humid after two phases of sunlight at the surface. Even in Gilstren, the easterly breeze that rattled his window panes against their ill-fitting frames had died down. He looked forward to the coming dark phase—the first since his scumbling. It would be easier to blend in with ordinary knyads on the walk home, and in colder weather he might even welcome the smothering shroud over his face.

Perhaps it had been unwise of him to wear his good clothes that segment—sweat and exertion had crumpled his shirt. But Oklas refused to come here grovelling for scraps in the drab garment of a maskad, and he held up his obscured face with as much dignity as he could muster. His trousers matched the beige of his shroud and high-top shoes. He had only a couple of fulvers to choose from, but some of his tunics and oversized shirts covered him sufficiently. The shirt he was wearing now, was it blue or green? His new eye was seeing colours differently from his original pair. He left the buttons of his collar undone—they had vexed him enough already. What he would give for an opposable thumb …

Oklas's office was on the jade-tiled fifth floor, a fair distance from the exit. Passing a stairwell, he decided to stay on his path and head towards the lifts on the other side of the concourse. He was yet to make a mask for himself, but had some idea of what he wanted. It had to be comfortable and expressive, more a face than a helmet—that seemed to be what other maskads favoured. Not that he had met any of them since he had joined their ranks. But even if he found access to the right tools, Oklas doubted he could physically construct a mask any more than he could sew his clothes. Not without plenty of practice, and the thought of that exhausted him.

For the first few segments after his scumbling, he had avoided his stuffy insula as much as possible. Working at the Consortium was hardly much of a reprieve. He had endured his first phase there by acknowledging instructions with hand signals alone. Even his signing was often unclear, given the strange new proportions of his hands. How long did it take other maskads to get this right?

At work, Oklas adopted a standoffish demeanour. It was not a natural fit, but it guarded against unwanted conversations. A tall juvenile from another department had made a few attempts to speak with him before giving up. Oklas felt guilty over ignoring the trainee, but what else could he do? He was still struggling to form coherent sentences with his speech synthesiser.

He had started taking walks north of the Consortium each segeind, venturing into the Industrial Park and the Lower End before heading back to Gilstren ahead of curfew. Staying in constant motion couldn't fully distract him from his predicament, but the new sights and sounds sometimes sent his thoughts down more pleasant tracks. With each outing, he hoped to wear himself out so sleep would more quickly take him when he returned home.

It did not. Oklas had spent the previous segeind like many before: lying on a hard mattress and staring unblinkingly at the ceiling. He was starting to get some sense of his single eye. He had learned to distend the opaque beige pattern over the black contour at the centre of his face, dulling his sight. Still some light remained, and only when he shielded his windows was it dark enough for him to pretend he had eyelids to close. His eye strained to read material up close; he couldn't devour information like he used to.

He continued blearily down the corridor of the outer Chambers, reaching a wedge-shaped concourse that sliced through several floors. A magnificently detailed engraving on the wall stretched high above him. It was one of the more ancient artworks featuring the emblems of the first five clans: Teprill, Silvet, Aurel, Gorria, and Apidecca. Together these clans formed the first incarnation of the Pentarchy.

The emblems surrounded Apidecca's symbol—a coral sprig among sharp rocks. Alongside the coral was a more recent engraving of a ghijer, representing Clan Quental, the Praemor clan that had taken Apidecca's place in the Pentarchy. Oklas supposed they'd had no choice but to add the sixth oldest clan to their government or change the system to a Tessarchy.

He thought the proud ghijer, with its bared teeth and spiny hackles raised, seemed a poor symbol for the current Erud Quental. Built like a great aftill but less inquisitive than such beasts, Erud Quental exhibited little of the cunning the sovereigns were known for. There had to be something more to him. Perhaps his bluster had won him the title of "Erud"?

Above the Quental emblem were pillars embossed like a frame around two crescents—the larger of the two represented the planet, Axis, and the smaller one within it, the cousin moon. Oklas glowered up at Clan Teprill's emblem.

The scales of his back bristled with a sense of being watched, and he spun around. Behind a balustrade on the highest visible floor stood a pair of figures. Oklas could not see their faces, but he recognised Erud Teprill's cream gown and the charcoal grey cloak of Erud Silvet.

It had seemed strange to Oklas that he should be required to collect his belongings here when everything else had been delivered to his insula. Did the Eruds want to see evidence of the grim task Raganys had carried out? Or had Oklas's return to the Assembly Chambers been orchestrated only to humiliate him? He squared his shoulders. If the cowards wanted him here, they would have an audience with him, and this time he would make his feelings known. He needed no mastery over his speech for that.

He entered the nearest stairwell and began his ascent. Staggering onto the landing of the seventh floor, he searched for some sign of the Eruds, but he was alone. It irritated him to find his determination weakening. The cumbersome box, which seemed to increase in weight with each step he took, only drained him further. He had been too compliant, signing away his name and rights on the Eruds' ridiculous forms. Why not lash out at them now? It wasn't as if he had much more to lose.

But did he really want to be sent to a labour commune? He sighed. As satisfying as it would be to vent at the Eruds, they would have the Furtim tackling him to the ground before he was within ten paces of them.

Oklas felt a headache coming on. He slumped against the baluster overlooking the court. On the opposite wall, far above the Pentarchic emblems, was a small mural he had not noticed in all his years at the Assembly Chambers. It was a faded painting of a knyad with a pale bird in Aer hands. Aer indistinct face was wreathed in white, shining like the sun. Artists frequently depicted Adecai in this way.

The elders of Dras Sayve downplayed notions of any knyad god. So naturally, Oklas was drawn to the spiritual realm. He felt a strange connection to the figure, the idea that was Adecai. The Ardedrians were a diverse group, but many of them shared a common faith in Aer. Funny how both insurgents and the Pentarchy claimed the same entity as their own. The two versions of Adecai seemed wholly different from each other. One was compassionate and forgiving, the other stern and distant.

While Oklas had no relationship with Adecai, he believed, in his bones, that the best in every knyad reflected something of Aer nature. Maybe Adecai still saw something worthwhile in him. 'Looks like they would ra/ther for/get us both,' he told the mural in broken synth-speech, his disused voice crackling. 'Have not er/rased us complete/ly/ though, have they?' He gave a hoarse laugh. He was constantly surprised that the deliberate, artificial sounds came from him.

Maybe this would not be the segment he assaulted the Eruds with a stationery box. Oklas hoped the Ardedrians were safe. At least he had left them with the satellite as a parting gift. Whatever they did to undermine the authorities, it comforted him to think he could take some credit for it. He should have done more for them when he had the chance.

He got to his feet, queasiness rocking him, and started to return the way he came. He had lost his Praemor status, his inheritance. There was no returning to the life he knew. Emis was no longer there to rescue him. Oklas swayed and put down the box.

Grabbing the balustrade with one hand, he desperately loosened the fabric of the shroud around his neck with the other. A wave of nausea struck him, and he leaned over the side of the stairway, secretly hoping another of the Eruds was walking directly below. Oklas heaved and retched. He had consumed nothing all segment, and only bile came up. He wiped the maw in his throat and, gasping, leaned heavily against the inner wall. Black spots flickered before his eye, and a prickling numbness reached his fingers.

He had spent over a decade trying to keep promising juveniles from finding themselves alone and devalued. But he had only ever guessed what that might be like, and now that he was in that position, he didn't know what to do. Was there anything to him besides his old stratum and connections? Did he even stand a chance of rebuilding his life? He rested his hands on his knees and bent forwards, sending the blood to his head.

There came the pattering of footsteps, and from the quarter-turn of the stairwell below emerged a short, middle-aged knyad dressed in the maroon and grey of the General Assembly staff.

'So you're the one who just left a mess on the court floor,' ae chided, seemingly unbothered that he was a maskad.

Oklas looked into aer alert, round face and quickly straightened. It was Ognitta, the Chambers' steward and supervisor to all the staff on the premises. His stomach roiled again as he realised he would have to answer her.

'Sorry,' he said in an unconvincingly repentant monotone. It was better to say too little than too much. If he did not control his thoughts, he might vocalise them as he had accidentally done in front of his co-workers at the Consortium.

The steward picked up the box and ushered him on his way. 'Can't have you loitering here if you're going to be sick again. What business brings you to the Chambers, anyway?'

Oklas could picture a phrase, but no words came, and his voice vibrated uselessly against the synthesiser. He showed Ognitta the clearance tag Nithan had given him. It defined his reason for admission as a "delivery"—a plausible lie. Why else would a strange maskad be allowed to remove items from a minister's office? Listed alongside "andrid" was his new name.

Even though Oklas had chosen "Kosta" as an alias, seeing it written on his tag was strange. It was the name of a tideling in his dormitory on Dras Sayve, one of those harvested a few revolutions ahead of Oklas. The alias needed to be familiar enough that he would instinctively respond to it.

The stern set of Ognitta's mouth softened. 'Very well, Kosta,' she said gruffly. 'If you've collected your package, you should be on your way.'

Oklas was only too eager to leave the place, but he needed a moment to recover before he hauled his load back home. 'Fee/ling unwell. Please. May I sit some/where out-the-way be/fore I leave?' He formed each word slowly, haltingly. There was little chance that the steward would recognise him by his voice.

Ognitta heaved a relenting sigh. 'You can lie on a bench in the staff quarters for a short while.' She then held out a stout hand. 'If you're done with the keys, I'll be returning them to their proper place.'

He nodded and gave her the keys, hoping she would not take note of the office he had visited.

The architecture changed as Ognitta walked him down to the lower floors, away from the public areas. The walls were rougher and the corridors varied in shape, so they more closely resembled the caves around the Assembly Chambers. The space reminded Oklas of the inside of a shell, filled with the rushing sound of some unseen ocean. It felt wrong to remain quiet for this long in someone's company, but no amount of practice made his synth-speech sound any more conversational or appealing. Whenever he had felt stuck in the past, there had always been someone to fast-track his learning. He needed a teacher. Someone experienced with synthesisers and masks ...

Oklas suddenly spoke up, releasing a barrage of syllables from his synthesiser. 'There is some/one like me here. A projection/nist.'

The steward raised an eyebrow. 'You mean Prismer?'

'May I see her?' he ventured.

'That would depend,' said Ognitta, rubbing her chin. 'Do you know each other?'

Oklas almost said "yes", but the projectionist had never met Kosta. 'No,' he admitted. His concentration was lapsing, and his speech only deteriorated further. 'I think she may/be ay/ble to help me.'

The steward mumbled deliberatively. 'Hmm. I can't promise she'll agree to anything, but I can take you to her.'

◦◈═◦◉◦═◈◦

They were not far from the staff quarters. Ognitta showed him down a gloomy corridor. As he walked, Oklas rubbed his temples. He had not seen the projectionist since her return from the mission he had sent her on. Without Dy Erla acting as a go-between, he wasn't sure he could extract any further goodwill from Prismer. Now he was coming to her as a stranger in need. If she refused to see him, where else would he turn?

He was confident that, like the steward, Prismer wouldn't recognise him by his altered voice or plain clothes. Between his restless walks and his poor feeding habits, even his body had changed—he was growing skinny. Certainly the muscles of his arms and chest were wasting away.

They passed room after room, and voices sounded from behind almost every door. The staff were home. Oklas wondered how much further it was to Prismer's. He cast his thoughts for anything he could use to flatter the projectionist into agreeability but came up with nothing. When they used to work together, she discussed only his presentations, tensing when he good-naturedly teased her or gossiped. On her good segs, she commented on happenings within the Assembly. Prismer was thorough and obliging...something of an automaton. That was his impression of her, unkind though it was. But—in spite of her stiff manner—her speech sounded natural. That made her an ideal consultant.

The steward knocked at what Oklas supposed was Prismer's door. The delay that followed was long enough that he wondered if anyone was home—then a muffled reply came from inside.

Looking over her shoulder across the corridor, Ognitta met his gaze. 'Says she is on her way.'

First came a *bump*, then the grinding of something heavy, possibly furniture, being dragged over the floor. The door opened a crack, and a dishevelled knyad in a lopsided mask appeared.

Besides the mask, Oklas recognised very little of the projectionist from Apex Hall. Instead of her uniform, she wore a sleeveless black shirt, revealing green-tinged, speckled arms. A scarf was draped loosely over her head and gathered over one shoulder.

Prismer adjusted her mask and raised her arms to secure the straps at the back of her head. 'Sorry to keep you waiting, Ognitta. I wasn't'—she twisted the ends of the scarf over her exposed skin—'dressed for visitors.'

The steward waved off Prismer's apologies. 'I know you aren't on duty today, but there was something of an emergency upstairs. I have a maskad here, asking for you.'

'For me?' Prismer croaked as she peered past Ognitta, the eyegaps of her mask fixing on Oklas.

'He was making a delivery to the outer chambers,' continued Ognitta, placing a hand on her wide waist. 'Seems in a bad way, like he was about to faint.'

Prismer angled her body away from Oklas's side of the corridor, but he could still hear her when she whispered, 'Shouldn't he see a mender then?'

'As I remember it, you have a knack for blending herbal remedies. He's probably had a bit too much to drink. Give him something for mild intoxication and you can send him on his way.'

Prismer leaned forwards as if to protest, but Ognitta lifted her head, giving the projectionist a look Oklas could not see from the back. Prismer's shoulders slumped. 'I'll see what I can do,' she said dutifully.

The steward gave a swift nod. 'Call me if he gives you any trouble,' she told Prismer, tapping Oklas on the back as she passed him.

Oklas's reluctant host stood straight-backed, waiting for him. She drew aside to show him into her home, her movements becoming almost mechanical—just as they did when she grew flustered in meetings.

He entered her insula and a faint, woody scent greeted him. It reminded him of loam and dried leaves, and he realised he had smelled it before—when he drew near her in meetings. The scent clung to her uniform. He supposed it came from the strange pot plants and jars of herbs that occupied her shelves.

'You can leave your package here,' instructed Prismer, indicating towards a stool against the wall, and she closed the door behind Oklas.

He opened his jaw to thank her but made only an approving murmur.

Oklas put down the box and looked around the room. It was even smaller than his insula, but the thick walls, high ceiling, and historic location lent it a grandeur that his home lacked. Weak sunlight shone through a high window, and glowing brackets along the walls lit the corners. Clutter was an inevitable consequence of small living spaces, but Prismer had ordered hers admirably. For years there had always been someone to clean for Oklas, and he was only beginning to appreciate the work that went into it. At the back wall was another doorway and, to the right, an alcove with a kitchen counter. Prismer was in a corner covering something with a sheet. Beneath it, Oklas glimpsed a scaffolding of some sort.

Prismer returned to him, and he noticed, for the first time, that they stood at the same height. He supposed he was used to looking down on her, either seated at the projection booth or below stage level. He had always taken Prismer for someone slight, even emaciated, underneath that shapeless uniform, but her lean arms were well-muscled.

Inclining her paper-white mask, she considered him. 'Have we met before?'

Panic rose in Oklas. 'What?'

'At Maskad Support, perhaps?' she prompted.

Oklas froze, struggling to muster a response.

'Oh,' said Prismer, raising a hand to her mask, 'you haven't been, have you?'

'I am looking for oth/ther/ mask/ads. I learned at wo/work. Learned of you living-at-the Chame/bers.' The words spilt over one another, coming faster than he could think. He covered his throat. 'Sorry-my-synth/si/zer.'

Prismer shook her head and reached out as if to lay a hand on his shoulder before retracting her arm. She ushered him towards a huddle of furniture in the middle of the room. 'Would you like to take a seat, um ... ?'

'Forgive me, I am'—here he took special care to wipe *Oklas* from his mind—'Kosta.' He held up the clearance tag with his name and gender, then offered her his arm in greeting.

Prismer reciprocated, intertwining her forearm with his. Her calloused fingers gripped lightly below his elbow, and Oklas noticed she had filed her thick nails down to blunt stubs. He tried to obscure his own roughly-trimmed claws.

'Prismer,' she said, gesturing to her chest. 'Standard or gynid pronouns will do.' She then laid her hand on a padded bench. 'I'd recommend this spot—you can lie down if you like. The others are all covered in tools and alabaster shavings.'

Oklas studied the mismatched dracca accent chairs opposite him. One was covered with a pile of books, drafting implements, and carved symbols.

'Thank you, Prism, I mean Pri—ugh.' He sat down and resigned himself to mangling her name. 'Pir.'

'It's no trouble,' she said acceptingly, stepping aside.

He looked up to see she was removing her mask. After years of knowing Prismer only by her white and green outer shell, it seemed indecent to look upon her like this. Her dark eye turned on him just as he was raising a hand to block her from view.

She yanked the scarf back over her bowed head and buried her face in her hands. 'I'm so sorry.'

'No,' said Oklas, shaking his head as he struggled to summon more words.

'I'm too used to being seen by other maskads,' said Prismer, 'I shouldn't have assumed—'

'You should-be-com/fo/table in your own home,' said Oklas, cringing as he offered the empty platitude. Just then, he thought of a way to ease her embarrassment—he only hoped it would not turn out to be a mistake. 'I wan/ted to ta-take mine off too, may I?'

She nodded and lowered her hands, revealing a deep red eye pattern, like a garnet set in pale stone. It was like staring at the reflection Oklas was coming to know in his mirror, but with marked differences. Where his face was broad at the top and narrow at the chin, Prismer's was long and angular, ending in a smoothly-curved jaw. Speckles mottled her scalp, as they did the rest of her skin. Maybe scumbling had altered his perception, but Oklas did not find her monstrous. It was hard to discern age in a maskad, but he doubted she could be much older than him.

He raised his goggles and said, 'It has been a...rough me/dian.' The self-deprecating remark almost sounded like the person he had been, and his heart sang—until he remembered he wasn't supposed to sound like himself in front of her.

Prismer watched him as he pulled the shroud from his head. He searched her unfathomable face and posture for any sign that she recognised him. Though he could not easily read her, he felt her presence more keenly now; through the slight movements of her patterned eye or the breath drawn in at her gills.

Finally, Prismer spoke. 'You look fine, just a bit dehydrated.'

It seemed she saw no trace of the minister she knew; this came as a relief, but it also stung.

'I'm going to make you a tonic,' she said, clasping her hands together, 'I'll be right back.'

Oklas watched her pluck herbs from a tiered rack, gather a few items from her counter, and disappear behind the back room door. He slumped back, tapping his fingers on the bench arm. The covered structures along the wall intrigued him, and...was that a map on the table?

# CHAPTER 18

## PRISMER

I T WOULD HAVE been easier to make the tonic at the kitchen counter, where Prismer kept her ingredients, but she needed a moment alone to steel herself. She placed a heating rod in the ceramic pot she had filled with water and then laid out a mortar, pestle, and jars of dried leaves on her chest of drawers.

Being around strangers never got any easier. Already she had done something inappropriate around her unexpected guest. Even so, Kosta had taken her unmasking well—maybe it had been a good thing, permitting the maskad to lower his guard.

Her heart was a sticky thing, reflexively picking up on the suffering of others. But that was not the same thing as kindness. Prismer wasn't kind. Removing herself from someone in need soon numbed her conscience. Admittedly it was taking longer than usual for her to stop caring about Illanu and Rosh.

She crushed the leaves into a paste. What was Adecai doing? First, sending her the juveniles, and now a maskad? She added a sprig of balsamenth to the simmering leaf brew, leaving it to soften, and reflected on what she knew about Kosta. He wore the plain covering all maskads received after scumbling, and he still struggled to speak. He couldn't have been this way for long. His clearance tag indicated he was making a delivery on behalf of the Consortium. Strange that they should schedule it on a rest segment, but they were hardly the only employers to take advantage of scumbled staff. He had to be Rosh's new co-worker, the maskad who had left the market in such a hurry.

Waiting for the liquid to thicken, Prismer fetched her embroidered fulver and pulled it over her head. The long sleeves lapped at her knuckles reassuringly. She removed the heating rod and stirred the brew. Returning the scarf to its wrapped design on her head, she peeked through a slit between the door and the wall, only to see Kosta examining *The Herald*.

'Oh, no.' She muffled her synthesiser with a cold hand. She had covered the sculpture with a sheet—was that not an obvious enough indication that she didn't want anyone looking at it?

Prismer poured the still-cooling tonic into a pitcher, then took it to Kosta in the living room. His large eye remained fixed on the sculpture.

'The wings. They are de/signed to change in-the-wind?' he asked, his synth-speech settling into a casual tone.

Prismer set the pitcher on a table and picked up the discarded sheet. 'I wasn't ready to show it to anyone,' she said, slipping between Kosta and the sculpture. 'It's a messy first attempt.'

Kosta raised his hands in an apology.

Prismer draped the sheet loosely over the top of *The Herald*'s wings. 'I don't mind showing some of my work to you. But please ask next time.'

'I will,' he promised, pulling his gaze from her map. 'Is this your studio?'

With a nosy guest on the loose, Prismer was glad to have her other things stored in the cave behind the bedroom wall. 'It is my workspace and my home,' she answered. 'I suppose it's a bit impractical.'

Kosta looked up at her with a mischievous glint in his white-gold eye. 'Anything worth doing is.'

Prismer began searching through the three-dimensional designs stored on her mitter. 'I have been making smaller ones for some time, simple systems of cogs, joints, and blades. I started with abstract shapes, things based on sea life.' From her cybernetics, she displayed one of her earlier creations as a near-opaque form. It was a reel of a red bristler, its spiny, radially-symmetric body swaying rhythmically.

Kosta's eye glittered with interest. 'I have seen this be/fore. Kites. Tradi/shi/nal Quarter.' He walked around the hologram, viewing it from different angles. 'Have never seen you put/ting them up.'

'Someone does it for me,' said Prismer. If people learned a maskad had crafted some of the structures, they would vandalise them in no time. It was why she paid Moshe to hoist hers up on the line.

'Yours stand out,' said Kosta, making comical gestures as he tried to describe her work. 'The spines, the bear/ings, the creepy shapes.'

Was he making fun of her? She folded her arms. 'I'm still working up to more complex figures. Not everyone has a background in engineering.'

'You mis/under/stand. I wasn't fault-finding.' He gave a good-natured chuckle; the sound struck Prismer as familiar. Perhaps it only stood out because it was a striking departure from Kosta's otherwise-stilted speech. 'Gran/ted, they-are weird,' he added, 'but wonderful/ly intri/cate.'

Prismer uncrossed her arms, dropping them to her sides. 'You mean, you like them?'

'Yes. And now I-have-the pleasure of mee/ting the-artist.' He gave a little bow.

'Th-thanks.' She stepped back, rubbing her upper arm. 'It makes for a nice change from setting up presentations.' By now, the tonic she had brought Kosta had cooled to a gel-like consistency. She lifted the pitcher to him. 'Here, you should drink this.'

'It has an in/tresting smell,' he said politely, his gills tightening shut. 'What-is in-it?'

'It's a nutrient concentrate,' said Prismer, leading him back to the table in the middle of the room. She dropped to the edge of a dracca chair. 'You haven't been eating properly, have you?'

'Is-it that obv/ious?' he said, pulling at his loose-fitting shirt as he returned to the bench opposite her.

'It's the biggest challenge next to talking.'

He looked dejectedly at the pitcher. 'Food does/ent hold the ap/peal it used to.'

Prismer walked over to her counter and returned to the bench, offering him a syringe. She pulled down her collar and indicated he should do the same, then demonstrated how to place the wide nozzle at the beaked opening of his oesophagus. Kosta accepted the syringe from her.

'It helps to think of it as just another eating utensil,' said Prismer, 'like a prong or a knife. When you start eating solids, you can use a pair of feeding tongs.'

Kosta groaned. 'You can chew with/out teeth?'

'The inner part of your beak crushes the food.'

Much hacking and spluttering came from Kosta as the tonic slid down to his stomach. But he wasn't choking, so Prismer didn't intervene. He kept going until the barrel of the syringe was empty. 'That was'—he swallowed the last of it—'not awful. Actually. It went better than usual.' When he spoke slowly and deliberately, his words didn't overlap or break.

'It'll take effect shortly,' said Prismer, praying it would be so. When Kosta recovered, he could leave. Part of her desperately wanted to return to lying flat on her stomach with a reed pen in hand, drawing. Before Kosta's arrival, she had been copying her sketches onto a larger map of the coastal tunnels. 'I know you were feeling unwell, but is that the only reason you asked Ognitta to bring you here?'

'I need your advice,' he said fluidly, motioning to some invisible thread connecting them, 'on eating, talking, everything.'

She baulked at the prospect. 'I'm not a good teacher.'

'You've just taught me some/thing now,' he said, tipping the empty syringe.

'A group of maskads meet at Kaldrend's workshop after hours,' said Prismer, taking the syringe from him. 'They can help you. I'll give you Taber's mitter code; he's one of the counsellors.'

While Kosta entered Taber's details into his mitter, Prismer walked over to her bookshelf. She came back and presented him with a blue handbook. It had a sturdy cover, plainly embellished with linear designs. Years of constant use had frayed the page corners. 'Someone at Maskad Support gave this to me. It's a more practical guide to your anatomy than anything the guild would have left you.'

Kosta flinched at the mention of the guild.

Prismer continued, 'You will find information on speaking through the synthesiser. The chapters on dress codes and preparing food are also helpful. And at the back is a list of maskad-safe venues in the city, though it's a bit outdated.'

Kosta accepted the handbook. 'Will you not need it?'

'Keep it. I've memorised the important parts.'

'Thank you,' he said, flicking through the pages. 'If I go to this group, wi-will you come with me?'

Prismer looked away from him, folding her hands. 'I don't know. I'm quite busy most segments.'

'Of course,' he said, disappointment entering his voice. 'It can't be easy wor/king here. At the-whims-of so many self-important poli/ticians.'

'They aren't all bad.' Guilt settled over Prismer. Her busyness was of her own making. But she was not about to rush into commitments with strangers. 'I can give you a few tips on speaking now, if you like,' she said, leaning into her chair.

There were some synthesiser-engaging exercises Prismer remembered, and she gave Kosta simple phrases and rhymes to repeat. She was almost envious of how quickly he brushed off mistakes that would have mortified her—it had to make learning with others more enjoyable. Teaching in itself was a new challenge for Prismer. It was hard to explain the workings of something that had become instinctive.

They made fair progress in their half-hour lesson, but Kosta asked many questions, and Prismer found she could not answer some of them without due consideration. She spread her gills in a yawn and arched her back.

Even her student's enthusiasm was starting to flag. Kosta flopped back on the bench. 'It sounds better. But still too slow.'

'Speed and varied tones come later,' said Prismer, poised in her seat. 'Rushing it will only garble your words.'

Kosta turned his doleful optic pattern on her. 'How long did-it-take you? To speak?'

'I can't remember. A few revolutions, maybe,' replied Prismer. Making comparisons was never helpful. Kosta had to find his own technique, to accept, as she had, that he might never sound like he did before. 'I think that's enough practising for today.'

'For today,' he agreed. 'You know, I sometimes spent entire segeinds talking?'

'I can believe that.'

Kosta was surprisingly candid about the things he missed. He craved conversation in a way that Prismer never had. There was still much she didn't know about his past, but the support group had taught her it was best not to press for details of a maskad's life before aer scumbling. She was content to leave that emotionally messy process to the counsellors.

'You'll find your voice again,' she said, standing to stretch her legs. 'But the speech pathways in your brain are still associated with your mouth.

You can't redirect them to the neural interface of your synthesiser in a phase.'

'Ah, repetition over time,' said Kosta ruefully. 'And here I hoped someone as crea/tive as you could help me bypass tired learning methods.'

'Sometimes there are no shortcuts,' Prismer shot back, briefly entertaining the idea of drugging him with a sleeping vapour and leaving him in the corridor. She took a deep breath, hoping to spare herself the trouble of dragging his unconscious body outside.

'Keep sounds in your throat,' she told him, grabbing at the air as if to pull some unseen floating words down into the synthesiser at her neck. 'Don't send them above your jaw. And don't think of too many ways to say something.'

A laugh bubbled from his chest. 'And you say you make-for-a poor tea/cher.' Kosta turned onto his side and propped himself up on his elbow. 'I think part of me has been hol/ding back. Trying not to learn any of this.'

'Why?'

'Be/cause...because that would make it all real. Lasting.' Kosta's head dipped. He took a shuddering breath and wiped at his gills.

'Oh,' said Prismer weakly. She looked around her room, digging her fingers into the cuffs covering her palms. He was crying, and there was no one to call on here. She knew how to alleviate physical discomfort, but not this kind of pain. Leaning over from the other end of the bench, she lightly touched him on the shoulder.

Eventually, Kosta's breathing eased. 'Thank you,' he said hoarsely and sat up. He looked brighter for the intense release of emotion. The light patterns of his face converged towards the table where Prismer's mask lay. 'So, this support group,' he said, clearing his throat, 'is that where you got the mask you are wear/ring?'

'I uh, I made it,' she replied, taken aback by the sudden change. He had seemed so broken only moments before. 'It's not my best, but I've grown rather fond of it.'

'You must have made others then. How much do you charge?' he asked, looking around eagerly as if expecting a mask to materialise out of nowhere.

'Only the cost of the materials,' she said, picking up her own. 'My early designs were hand-molded, but I mostly use xylemfibre technology now.'

At the mention of "technology", Kosta's ears pricked up. 'Tell me more.'

Prismer found herself talking without interruption for what seemed like a long time, but if Kosta was losing interest, he did not show it. 'Then I sculpt the mask around the dimensions of your head on a casting platform,' she said, framing her face with her hands in a demonstration. 'The xylemfibre labs grow the finished design into shape.'

He stood up. 'Will you measure me for one now?'

The counter stool provided an ideal spot for Prismer to seat Kosta and scan his face from different angles. She had expected him to fidget, but he complied with her as she raised her arm with the scanner and supported the back of his head with her other hand. His eye contracted, becoming more gold than black as the sheet of light travelled over it. One of the main goals of scumbling was to dull a knyad's individuality, so Prismer made a point of appreciating the things that distinguished one maskad from another. Kosta made for an engaging subject—his skin was almost grey, darkening to a bluer hue at the back of his head. Even when he held still, his optic pattern was bright and curious, alive with movement.

'Do all maskads cover up with false faces?' he asked, pulling her back into the moment.

'False faces?'

'Masks with eyes, noses…mouths.'

'Most do.'

'Surely a riding helmet or a veil would look less distinct/ly maskad-like?'

'You can try to pose as a regular knyad, but it won't fool anyone,' mused Prismer. 'People don't cover their faces completely if they don't have to. Besides, I feel better wearing an expression. If you let something of yourself show through, you find a way out of your mind.' She tapped at her temple.

Kosta rearranged himself into a more casual pose on the stool. 'Maybe I should have my face animated as a holo/gram. Display it in a visor.'

Prismer made a disapproving static noise. 'A plain mask is enough to blend into a crowd.'

'Did I say I wanted to blend in?'

'Some wear a display with simple icons to express themselves. It can be effective, but I wouldn't try recreating a whole face.'

'Why?'

'The closer a hologram comes to reality, the more you notice its life-lessness,' she replied, filling the sink with water from her tank.

Kosta leaned onto the counter. 'Progress is being made all the time. Isn't it worth investigating?'

'Trying to recapture what you were can become an obsession,' said Prismer quietly, fetching the syringe and pitcher from the living room table. 'Sometimes it's best to let go of the past.'

Kosta's shoulders sank.

Prismer continued, 'I can always customise your mask.'

'Don't tempt me with all the options—I can be painfully indecisive,' he said, popping into a standing position. 'I trust you with the details.'

'I'll let you know when the mask is ready,' said Prismer.

Kosta looked at his box next to the wall. He probably needed to leave soon. 'You know,' he said, 'I feel well enough to run back to the Consor/tium. What did you put in that tonic?'

'Nothing that would exceed your natural energy levels,' replied Prismer. 'I'll show you to the exit on Clanfare Avenue—can't have you getting lost down here.'

The pair of them covered their faces and made for the door.

Kosta was bending to collect his box when he jumped back with a start.

'What's wrong now?' asked Prismer.

He gulped, pointing at a fuzzy speck with six legs and tiny pincers. It was a spindlemite, picking its way through a broken web.

Prismer held out her hands. 'Leave her be. She catches the midges coming from the canal.'

'People don't always appreciate that about them,' remarked Kosta, his voice slightly higher than before. 'It's the sudden, skittering move-ments—they're unnerving.'

Prismer swept the web aside, careful not to disturb the creature. She presented the box to Kosta. 'People can learn to look past that.'

Rather than taking him back up to the ground floor of the Chambers, Prismer led Kosta to the staff gateway at the back of the building. Leaning against the metal bars of the security gate, she watched him walk the avenue until he disappeared around the curve of the ramparts.

# CHAPTER 19

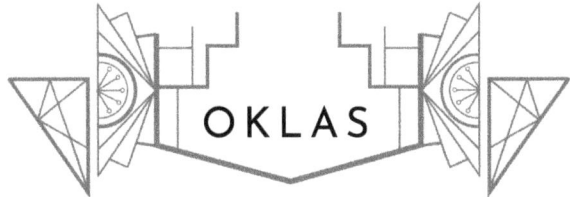

## OKLAS

Like many Praemor cities, Apidecca fractionally distilled crude resyn on an industrial scale. The Engineering Consortium received an allotment of the condensed liquid and tasked their new maskad employee with converting it into elemental resyn. Oklas then gathered the spongy pieces and packed them into casks where they would be melted and grown into crystals—the rechargeable material used to power high-end technology such as mitters and cybernetics. Every segment at the Consortium passed the same way. Process resyn. Weigh and pack. Repeat.

Oklas hadn't studied resyn engineering only to enter into this mind-numbing routine. Not after being raised on Emis's stories about the endless possibilities resyn held.

There were no windows in the laboratory in which he worked. He remembered the space from his time as a trainee—it was here that he first learned how to process resyn. Wired into his muscles was the memory of taking precise liquid measurements. But scumbling had impaired his fine motor skills, making him more accident-prone. He wondered how Prismer, balancing a pen between her fingers, had managed to complete the detailed drawings he had seen on her table. They must have taken her an age to finish.

'Kosta,' called someone from across the laboratory.

Oklas's head shot up. Levent, the lead engineer, was approaching his workstation.

'Are you still on the third batch?' asked Levent, his pointed nose wrinkling as he examined Oklas's scale, filled only halfway with spongy resyn.

'Yes, kyr.'

'The zone-refining team needs to start melting it by the fifth-median, and we have another order coming through straight after.'

'I can understand the urgency.'

'Then act on it. This is a working lab, not a rehabilitation centre.'

Oklas's fingers twitched, and he stifled a retort. Though his coordination was poor, the flow of his speech had drastically improved. Prismer's tips on using the synthesiser yielded results.

Levent left in a huff. His criticism was harsh, perhaps unfairly so. But he had a point; Oklas was holding everyone back. Without explanation, the resyn refinery engineers had been saddled with training a feeble maskad.

Oklas had encountered some of his new co-workers during his time as Kemia's deputy, but they didn't recognise him. The masters here, some of whom had known Oklas since he was a trainee, hadn't even acknowledged him since his scumbling. He assumed the Pentarchy had informed the Consortium directors of his true identity. Although, if his salary was anything to go on, they did not know his worth. The Pentarchy had probably compensated them for their silence on the matter and for tolerating his impediments.

The median break arrived, but Oklas stayed at his station. He would have to skip his regular walk through the neon-lit streets. The Engineering Consortium lay in the shadow of the Whistling Gallery, a half-league from the Assembly Chambers, behind the shop fronts on the eastern side of the High Street. It was a commercial district, backing onto light industrial areas.

As a trainee, Oklas had spent his free time following the roads branching off the Consortium and getting lost. In doing so, he discovered delightful eateries, the ironmongery, and antique shops he wasn't even looking for. But it was no longer safe for him to get lost, and some of his favourite venues wouldn't allow him through their doors now. He no longer ate in public, avoiding even the Consortium canteen. But there were promising developments, too. Already the tips from the maskad handbook had helped him feed more regularly, albeit alone.

Oklas refocused on the burette and beaker before him. Around him, the laboratory whirred and hummed. Machinery clanged rhythmically in the distance. Sometimes the ambient drone helped him pretend he was back at the Emisrian College, surrounded by friends and fellow researchers.

In reality, he worked in a corner with a glass divider around his workstation. The other engineers on the floor did not interact with him. He missed collaborating—it sharpened his mind—but nothing reminded him of his situation like the wary expressions people shot him whenever they passed by.

He scooped out another batch of spongy resyn, packing it into a cask. Strange how the substance he was handling, something seemingly harmless, had utterly ruined him. It remained colourless and opaque at his touch. He would only ever be able to process resyn as a chemical compound. In the hands of a resyncrafter, it was so much more. Some considered their intuitive command of the substance "magic", and maybe it was. It seemed a crime that Raganys, twisted as he was, should be blessed with such a talent.

Had Prismer also been changed by him, or some other wretched resyncrafter at the guild? And how long had she been this way? In the phase since he had visited the projectionist, Oklas questioned things he hadn't in all his years of knowing her.

Through the tinted glass divider in front of his desk, Oklas noticed a lanky juvenile entering the department. He was the only knyad in the Consortium to have approached Oklas socially—though Oklas had done nothing to encourage it. The trainee caught sight of him and strode in his direction. He stopped on the other side of the divider. 'Hello, kyr,' he said, wearing a mild expression, 'it's me, Rosh. We met outside the canteen last phase.'

'Yes,' said Oklas, fixing his head forwards as he continued to work. He could more easily speak now, but that did not mean he was in the mood for it.

'Master Nirube from biomechanics sent me to fetch the casks of elemental resyn.'

'You can take the first two over there,' said Oklas, pointing to his left. 'If you wait for the reducing agent to do its work, the third should be ready soon.'

Oklas returned to his equipment, pouring the reducing agent into the burette. It only took a minor miscalculation to ruin a beaker of condensed resyn.

His wrist shook as the beaker hovered under the burette, and he supported it with his other hand.

'Can I help you?' offered the trainee.

Oklas turned the tap of the burette, releasing a few drops of the clear liquid. His wrists shook harder still and knocked over the container of reducing agent. Time slowed as Oklas swiped at it, trying to keep it from spilling into the beaker. The beaker fell instead, and glass caked in powdery resyn shattered over the floor. He buried his covered face in his hands.

'What's going on over there?' called Levent, his tone brusque.

Oklas heard the trainee—Rosh—reply, 'It's my fault, kyr. I was moving the elemental resyn from the beaker to the last cask, but I lost my grip.'

Levent's skin darkened to an irritable orange. 'Another setback, as if this wretch wasn't taking long enough as it is,' he seethed. 'This is an expensive substance, juve. I'll have the value deducted from your wages.'

'Yes, kyr,' said Rosh.

Levent turned to Oklas. 'Pull yourself together. I want you here early tomorrow to make up time.' He spun around, returning to the central workbench.

Oklas sat upright and sighed before retrieving another beaker. He did not look at Rosh as he said, 'You needn't have taken the blame.'

'I thought I could afford to,' replied the young biomechanist as he left with the two remaining casks.

◦⟨◇⟩═◦⟨◉⟩◦═⟨◇⟩◦

The tram to Gilstren rattled along, jarring Oklas's legs as he stood, gripping a hanging strap. He watched the rocky columns of the Whistling Gallery disappear behind tall buildings that grew progressively dingy. Kemia needed to fit these economy trams with better suspension. The Lower End loomed ahead, and the tram turned a corner, leaving the High Street behind. Towering places of business gave way to factories and insulae only three or four stories high. The tram strained as the incline increased. At the edge of Gilstren, the tramline ended. Oklas disembarked and started his walk home. There were cableways to the highest buildings, but spending his substants on those seemed a waste when he was not exactly in a hurry to reach his insula. He missed the convenience of riding a scrambler, and briefly wondered who had come into possession of his Moonsurge.

The golden lights lining the streets of Gilstren were growing dimmer as the dark phase wore on. Their soft glow brushed the unlit canvas lanterns that rustled between poles. The pavements bustled with knyads on their way home from work, shopping, or seeking entertainment before curfew. Oklas noticed their numbers thinning as he walked up the cobbled, hilly paths. People branched off into grey buildings and down alleys until no one was immediately ahead of him. A shadow crept up his ankles. Turning around, he noticed a vine hanging from a balcony in the street behind him. It swung lazily in the breeze, its shadow lengthened by an artificial spotlight. A waste skip stood before the entrance to an alley. *No one is hiding there*, he thought. He continued on his way, walking a little faster.

A shadow darkened Oklas's feet again, shaped not like a vine but a head and shoulders. He quickened his pace, and the knyad behind him did the same, but neither of them broke into a run. His pursuer kept a few lengths between them. Other knyads crossed Oklas's path, but the stranger continued to follow him, taking every turn he made. Aer footsteps whispered over the cobbles. Oklas scanned the shops, hoping to find one that hadn't yet closed for the segeind. He needed to find someone who would shelter him. The goggles he wore blocked the edges of his vision; he couldn't study the silhouetted figure at his back without turning his head to look at aer.

Then his pursuer called out, 'Why the hurry, Director? Do you have somewhere to be?'

That raspy voice could only belong to one person. Oklas came to a standstill, keeping his back to the Ardedrian agent. 'I'm no longer the director of anything.'

'To Keanon you are,' said Yvere, her tone devoid of her usual scathing playfulness. She drew alongside Oklas, pulling her scarf below her chin. Even under the harsh security spotlight, her sharp features were more temperate than he had ever seen them. She kept her burnt-orange hood pulled up and disguised her wiry frame under almost as many layers as Oklas wore. Over her left shoulder were bundled thick tendril fibres. They came in cool blond, with the lower layers in a deeper shade of crimson than the braids she had sported previously. 'You didn't think Keanon would go off you just because you no longer have fine suits to wear to his parties?'

'They took me,' began Oklas, his throat tightening. Then he recalled Seron mentioning "captured insurgents". 'Wh-what about the rest of our group?' he asked. 'Are you all safe?'

Yvere nodded. 'We haven't lost anyone this past revolution, at least no one you know. Hidreth's cover remains intact, and everyone else has kept a low profile. We shut down communications for two segments after you disappeared—to monitor our network's security.'

Oklas shook his head incredulously. 'You thought I was going to talk?'

Yvere shrugged. 'It was a precaution. We didn't know what they would find in your possession.'

'If keeping secrets is your priority, removing me from their custody would have worked just as well.' It was a spiteful thing to say, but Oklas was too tired to pretend he didn't feel let down by his friends.

Yvere frowned, lowering her gaze to the street. 'Word reaches us fast, but the Furtim carry out their assignments even faster. We failed to intercept them en route to the Transmutation Guild.'

'Wait,' interrupted Oklas, 'you know about the guild?'

'There are enough maskads in our ranks to give us some idea of the place, but we still haven't located it,' she said, her thin eyebrows knotting tighter. 'We could only wait for you to resurface. I've been searching for reports of new maskads. My tip-off came from someone at the Consortium.'

'Thanks for your concern,' said Oklas dryly. 'As you can see, I am thriving.' He straightened the collar of his drab Consortium overalls and turned on his heel.

He had not taken two steps from Yvere when she called after him, 'Keanon has a proposition for you.'

'He has his communication network, and I have nothing more to contribute—the Pentarchy made sure of that.'

'Oh stop playing the victim,' she bit back, striding ahead of him and blocking his path, 'you knew the risks when you joined.'

He laughed sourly. 'It's good to hear you yell at me again.'

'Then you'll be glad to know there's plenty more whe—'

Close by, something clattered. Yvere's hand darted towards her holster.

She eased, realising the sound had come from a closing shop door; the loose pane of glass still vibrated in its frame. Yvere looked around to check no one was overhearing them. 'Let's continue our chat in the alley, shall we?'

Oklas followed her behind a flower shop. The dank smell of rotting plant material wafted from the compost bin at the alley entrance.

'Listen,' said Yvere, 'I don't take my responsibilities lightly. We do everything in our power to protect the information of our supporters. It's not our fault that you trusted the wrong person.'

The last part stung, and Oklas swayed, letting the truth of it seep in. He had always considered himself an excellent judge of character, but perhaps he really didn't know people as well as he thought. 'I interviewed Antolat, selected him myself,' he said, slumping against the sandstone wall, sickened afresh by the betrayal.

'Don't get hit up about it,' said Yvere, her tone blunt but not unkind. 'A professional infiltrator won't apply for a position at their target organisation—it's too desperate. They curate their skill sets to attract talent scouts and wait for the right offer. Antolat needed you to think you hired him.'

Yvere pulled a thin pipe from her pocket, packed the bowl, and ignited it with the flint lighter on her multitool. She had to be on edge if she was smoking again. 'Since your arrest, there has been an increase in casting assaults on our network,' she said, placing the mouthpiece between her teeth and taking a long drag. 'So far, we've kept ahead of them. You couldn't have kept much of our collaboration on record.'

'I left most of my notes with your casters,' said Oklas. 'They will keep adapting the system as needed.' He had worked extensively with the Ardedrian engineers and trusted their collective proficiency. 'Antolat could only have found the designs for the early towayes. It was enough for them to link me to you.'

Yvere lowered her pipe and exhaled the smoke. 'Why did you hold onto them?'

'I am somewhat sentimental about these things,' said Oklas with a cough. 'If I hadn't gifted them the evidence to persecute me, they would have planted something in my rooms. I was in their way.' He coughed again. Whatever she was smoking, it irritated his gills. Even the fabric covering Oklas's face did little to filter the peppery, tar-like scent.

Yvere lazily waved away the cloud. 'You aren't the first to be burned in the game of politics.'

Oklas scratched at his neck and adjusted the shroud. Sometimes it felt so airless that he found himself gasping. He began pacing, focusing on his breathing, trying not to give in to panic.

Yvere stood watching him, her tendrils a feathery frame around her pointed chin. 'Keanon asked me to track you tonight. He said you could do with some friends.'

'Is that what he wants to be?' asked Oklas through a laugh. 'Someone who imparts canid training tips over drinks?'

Yvere rolled her eyes. 'He wants to provide you with a lab.'

'What?'

'Someone has to break it to you, Oklas,' said Yvere, dropping her pipe to her side, 'your greatest asset was not your pretty face, but your mind. You still have plenty to offer.'

Oklas placed his hands on his hips. 'Keanon will want me to join full-time, of course.'

'I don't know,' said Yvere, looking into the glowing ash of the pipe bowl. 'He said he'd understand if you wanted to leave the Ardedrians behind. But if you think you still have some inventions left in you, he'd like to hear about them.'

'Where is this lab?'

'At our permanent base. I'll tell you how to get there, but you can't write down the directions. Not with that probation officer investigating you. I've seen him in your insula while you're at work.'

'I knew it,' said Oklas bitterly. At least Yvere had confirmed that the notes on his workbench hadn't rearranged themselves. He was beginning to think he was going mad.

Yvere leaned in closer and spoke in a low voice. 'Look, I need to go soon. Are you familiar with the southern end of the Industrial Park?'

She went on to describe a sequence of landmarks. Oklas placed each of them in his mind.

Before leaving, Yvere dug his side with her elbow. 'I was impressed you noticed me following you earlier,' she said, as if congratulating a tideling for walking on land. 'You'll want to keep up that kind of vigilance when you visit the base.'

Within moments, she was a flash of orange staining the shadows, moving swiftly down the street. Oklas exhaled and pulled his shroud tighter around his neck, then made his way up a path of steps to his insula block.

# CHAPTER 20

## PRISMER

I T HAD ONLY been two phases since Prismer had agreed to make Kosta a mask, and already she had cultivated the three-dimensional xylemfibre structure. On dark segments, the Assembly Chambers tended to be quiet, and with constant downpours flooding parts of the High Street, there had been little else to occupy her after work. Kosta had provided enthusiastic feedback on the designs she sent him, and he was familiar enough with the castingware she used to make some specific suggestions. She could not take offence. Deciding on a new face would always be a deeply personal process for any maskad. And, while slightly fussy, Kosta was an amiable customer.

Early that segere, Prismer had collected Kosta's finished mask from a xylemfibre lab in the Industrial Park. Provided he liked it, all that was left for her to do was paint and seal it.

Gilstren lay a short walk to the south of the lab and across the tramline. Prismer followed Kosta's directions to an insula block halfway up the suburb. It was built just in front of a sheer rock wall. She climbed slowly up a metallic outdoor stairway to the fourth floor, taking care not to slip on the wet steps. Each insula's façade was a replica of the next: a shallow-set window followed by a door and a smaller window. Exposed brickwork separated the floors and insulae, and cerulean light emanated from algae panels positioned above each door. Rainwater dripped from the gratings above, trickling down Prismer's neck. She shivered.

A deck protruded from the top floor. It was likely a solar charging station for the occupants; they were common in poorer areas. Each dwelling in Apidecca paid for a daily energy quota from the city power grid. The allocation available to Praemor suburbs was far higher than in places like Gilstren. If residents' requirements exceeded this quota, they had to make their own arrangements and stock up on rechargeable fulmenum cells.

The floor vibrated, and Prismer noticed a scrappy juvenile run inside aer insula at her approach. Only a few insulae displayed numbers. Some were covered in etchings and fading paint. Black and orange packaging stickers—cut up and arranged in spirals—decorated the door to the juvenile's insula. Prismer looked back to find the juvenile peering at her. A pet pegwing sat on aer shoulder, grooming the leathery folds of its wings.

'Next door over,' the juvenile called out to Prismer, raising aer upturned nose.

Prismer knocked on the rusty door. She had a feeling she was in the right area. There came the metallic scraping of a latch, and the door creaked as it was pulled open by a shrouded figure wearing goggles.

'Prismer, you ma—'

Kosta's voice gave way to static as an excited squeal sounded from Prismer's side. He turned just in time to see the juvenile nipping back into aer insula.

'I met your neighbour,' said Prismer, still looking at the spot where the juvenile had been moments before. 'Ae seems very young to live in the city on aer own.'

'Ae stays with a few others—all fresh from the docks,' said Kosta, his synthesiser whirring back to life. 'You'd think they had never seen a maskad before.'

Prismer knew something of what that was like. 'What do you think they will make of two?'

'An invasion of the ghouls?' he suggested breezily. 'At least, they used to scream something to that effect whenever I passed. I think they're losing their fear.' Kosta placed his hand on the metal doorframe only to snap back from it. 'Foznits, it's cold. Come in, Pir. Come in.'

It didn't surprise Prismer that Kosta was freezing in the doorway; he wore only a fulver over what appeared to be his sleepwear. Though his fleece pants, printed with looping shapes, did look comfortable. He ushered Prismer inside with a flick of his white sleeve and closed the door behind them.

His home extended deeper than she would have guessed from the outside. Very little floor space was left uncovered by boxes or piled objects. There were few cupboards and no shelves.

'Um, this is it—my insula,' said Kosta, waving towards the dimly-lit room. Under the warm indoor lights, his fulver appeared more yellow than white. 'I have not yet found a place for everything, and even when I do, I doubt it'll look much tidier.'

'All you need is a proper storage system,' said Prismer setting the wrapped xylemfibre mask down on the kitchen counter. 'It takes time—adjusting. But your speaking is coming along.'

'I have a good teacher,' he said, taking a bow and twirling a hand at her, 'one who enunciates like a clan peer.'

'I do not,' said Prismer, vigorously unbuttoning the weatherproof coat she wore over her green fulver. 'Though my accent used to be more...regional. Maybe I am spending too much time around crusty orators in the Assembly.'

'Now I have to hear what you sounded like before.'

Prismer squirmed out of her coat. 'On Inclatia, the sounds are rounder,' she said, drawing out her words in a clear, melodic tone.

Kosta stroked his chin. 'It has something of the flow you hear from planet-side Praemor merchants.'

'Well, we have traded with Rhestatyn for decades.' Prismer surveyed the room, looking for a place to hang her coat.

'Here, let me take that for you,' Kosta offered.

Prismer handed him her wet coat and pulled the ruffled hem of her fulver over her trousers. Kosta draped the coat over a stack of his hastily-folded clothes, piled atop boxes and machines. Pairs of shoes lined the walls, almost double the number Prismer owned. A solid workbench and a chunky couch took up much of the space. Both were of a size more suited to one of the auditoriums at the Chambers than an insula.

'The clans have so many different dialects,' said Kosta, removing his goggles and shroud. 'I hope we never lose that variety.'

Prismer followed suit and slid off her mask, relieved that he had been the first to show his face this time. 'Clans continue to meet and influence one another. There's little you can protect from change.'

He rubbed the side of his head. 'Would you like anything to drink: water, kahv, gel?'

'Warm water, please.'

He gave her a strange look, his optic pattern quirking to one side.

'It goes down easier than when it's cold,' she explained.

'Huh. I suppose it would.'

Prismer sat on a chrome barstool and watched him fetch his new pitchers, their spouts specially adapted for maskads. The outer metal was glazed dark red with pale green leaf patterns.

'I got them from the pub you told me about, the Hull Brewery, was it?'

'The Husk and Brewer.'

'I thought I should get two. I don't expect I'll be entertaining much, but I'm always losing things.'

It took a while for him to prepare their drinks as he turned a simple task into quite a process. He insisted Prismer should try the flavoured water. She looked on, intrigued, as Kosta darted around the kitchen. He wanted everything, from the temperature to the steeping time, just right. He had a lot of opinions about food for someone who lacked a nose and mouth. 'Try breathing in the steam before drinking,' he suggested, his slanted eye bending imploringly. 'You will detect a citromoss flavour.'

How was it that, recently scumbled, he could already convey subtle emotion with only the shifting patterns around his eye? Prismer didn't think she could have expressed herself any better when she had a face. 'I can't smell the moss,' she admitted.

Kosta's proud posture buckled.

She raised her pitcher at him. 'But it's refreshing, and I feel warmer.'

The ceiling lights flickered, and both of them looked up.

'I don't dim them just for the sake of atmosphere,' said Kosta. 'My solar cells aren't running on a full charge.' Outside, raindrops began to click against the metal and glass. 'I may have docked them at the deck rather late.'

Prismer spluttered in surprise and set her pitcher down. 'Will you have enough power until sun-up?'

'Only a few more segments to go. At least the building is warmed by the communal generator.' He tipped the spout of his pitcher into the opening in his neck and gulped. Leaving the kitchen, he continued, 'I suppose you're used to looking after yourself at the Chambers. Actually, I was surprised to find someone like you working there.'

Prismer slipped from the stool and followed him. 'Employing a maskad makes the General Assembly seem merciful,' she said.

'No, I didn't mean it like that. Those snobs are lucky to have you.' Kosta picked a path between the workbench and piled objects. He sat at the far corner of the chunky couch and tucked his legs in. 'You just seem a bit overqualified for the role.'

Prismer gave a dry laugh and sat on the other side, straight-backed. 'What makes you think I have an education?'

'There's your clear enunciation, for a start,' answered Kosta, his eye twinkling. 'Then there are all those books and sculptures in your room.'

'Hobbies,' said Prismer dismissively, pushing herself to the deep back-rest, her boots overlapping the edge of her seat. 'After completing my foundational schooling, I worked in aquaculture, same as everyone else on Inclatia.'

'And how did a farmer come to work in a city like Apidecca?'

'Back home, I received training as a technician. That's what got me here.'

Kosta locked his eye on hers. 'But you didn't come here to continue working in a trade, did you?'

Prismer stilled, deliberating how to answer him. 'No. I wanted to study spatial planning. Of course, I soon learned how prohibitively expensive that would be.'

'Some of these places offer grants.'

Prismer snickered. 'I applied at the Institute of Developers, not the Emisrian. They don't run on philanthropy.' She raised the pitcher to her throat. Swallowing, she cradled her drink in her mottled hands. 'Imagine being plucked from an uncategorised clan and brought to prominence? It makes for a heartening story, doesn't it?'

Kosta murmured in agreement and drew his knees up to his chest.

Prismer continued matter-of-factly, 'But life doesn't always follow the stories we prefer. When you feel stuck, you do desperate, foolish things.'

'The kinds of things that get you scumbled?' asked Kosta.

'Yes,' said Prismer quietly. Outside, rain rapped against the window. She got up, staying Kosta with her hand as he made to follow her. 'But that's enough about me,' she said. 'You will find this more interesting, I'm sure.'

She fetched her parcel from the counter and presented it to him.

'For me?' he asked delightedly, pressing his blue-tinged hands to his chest.

'I've seen you glancing at it since I arrived.'

Hands trembling, he carefully folded back the brown wrapping paper. Kosta raised the mask until it was level with his dark head and examined every deget of it.

The unpainted base was the colour of bark, smooth but with a slight grain on the outside. The stylised face Prismer had crafted matched the planes of Kosta's head. Wide eyeholes were set in a darkened lens that crossed the face in a band, allowing for improved—albeit tinted—peripheral vision. A straight, refined nose protruded only slightly from the front. The lips were raised but not rendered in any detail. On either side were air filters.

Prismer tucked away a loose fold of her headscarf. 'You'll find the xylemfibre more breathable than alternative materials.'

Kosta touched the nose and mouth of the mask, his other hand reaching for his cheek.

'If you like it, I can proceed with colouring it.'

'Thank you, it is—' The words caught in his throat. For a moment, Prismer thought she had upset him. Then he laughed and put on the mask. 'It's perfect. Now I must go somewhere to show it off.' He stood up, modelling it for her. Though dressed only in sleepwear, Kosta looked like he belonged on stage. Perhaps he had been a performer.

'Very dramatic,' said Prismer approvingly, 'and it's not even gilded yet.'

'What colour would you recommend?'

She looked at her lap, considering his question. 'I am better with form than colour, but you should take inspiration from your natural complexion.' Her head bobbed up. 'The gold in your optic pattern contrasts well with your skin.'

'Gold?' repeated Kosta, laughingly. 'More like muddy brown.'

Maybe the star at the centre of his face was more beige than gold. But that made it no less striking.

Prismer stroked her scarf. 'I didn't take you for someone who would have trouble accepting compliments.'

'Oh, I had my share of admirers,' said Kosta, the horizontal curve of his eye downcast, 'but there's not much to be said for what the resyncrafter has left of me.'

'It doesn't matter to everyone,' said Prismer, thinking of Ilu and Dy Erla, whole knyads who could look past her otherness.

'It matters enough that we have to hide.'

Something inside Prismer's chest twisted painfully at his observation. 'Well, I am only a scumbled worker,' she said, her voice rough, 'what do I know about what most people like?' She turned from him, wiping her gills and sniffing. After all this time, she thought she was past feeling this way.

'Oh, Pir,' said Kosta, placing a hand on her shoulder. 'I'm sorry. It's only my vanity—I didn't mean to burden you or any other maskad with it.'

'Stupid of me really,'—she pulled the scarf off her head and bunched it up—'pretending this isn't so bad.'

'I look up to you, Prismer. You've adapted, moved on with your life,' he said, the patterns of his face lifting. It was almost a smile. Prismer tried to mirror the expression, knowing her own optic pattern would remain stubbornly static.

She sighed. 'I can't give you permission to be comfortable in your skin, Kosta; I am not sure I'm even comfortable in mine. But I have thought about it, and I will take you to the support group.'

'Really? That's great!' He sprung upright. 'You know I wouldn't have gone alone.'

'I know.'

The rain eased, and dull vibrations sounded through the walls as Kosta's neighbours walked the platform outside.

'Is it part of the regulations, wearing a hood or scarf with the mask?' he asked.

'No,' replied Prismer, 'why would you think that?'

'Only I notice you usually keep yours on all the time.'

She touched her head, remembering she had taken off her scarf on impulse. She tensed, whirling around to look for it. Kosta fetched it from her side and offered it to her.

'I feel the cold,' she said dismissively, though the warmth around her gills suggested otherwise.

Kosta tilted his head at her, his eye questioning. 'There's nothing to be ashamed of,' he said, 'you have a perfectly normal cranium, no lumps or dips.'

'It's just…I used to wear my tendrils with long fibres. I sometimes miss the weight of them on my head.' Prismer ran her fingers over the soft, stretchy fabric. The texture provided grip and was neither slippery nor coarse. 'When I left Inclatia, my harvestmate gifted me a collection of scarves. After I was scumbled, I started experimenting with them. I've worn them every segment since.'

'I understand.' Kosta returned to his seat next to her. 'Wearing them makes you feel more like yourself.'

'Something like that,' she said, arranging the fabric over her head in a series of practised folds and twists. 'Sometimes I just need something to keep my hands busy.'

'And those busy hands of yours have also given me a means of expression,' he said, looking fondly at his mask before returning it to Prismer. He fetched a pouch from the high table before them. Taking Prismer by the hand, he turned her palm upwards and pressed several subst tokens into it.

Her hand dipped under the weight of them. Too many metal tags with punctured centres. She tried to return the surplus to Kosta, but he pulled away as if she were offering him a spindlemite. 'No, you don't,' he said. 'I already think you are undercharging me.'

She kept her hand open and raised. Kosta folded her fingers over the tokens. 'Please, keep them,' he insisted.

'That's very generous of you,' she replied, finally accepting the payment. 'Thank you.' She decided she would pay for their drinks next time they went to Huskhouse.

'I'm still getting a good deal,' said Kosta, draping a languid arm over the back of the couch. 'What would you charge if this were a sculpture for a foyer in the Upper End?'

'I don't know,' said Prismer, shoving the substants deep into the side pocket of her fulver. She thought back to what she used to charge for her commissions. 'For something of comparable detail: three thousand?'

'Oh, Pir,' said Kosta, shaking his head despairingly, 'I've seen things that belong in a waste skip sell for twice that price.'

'You'll have to introduce me to the buyers.'

'You're already rather well-positioned at the Chambers, lots of people with substants to throw around pass through there.'

'I'll have to find an attractive knyad—someone persuasive—to pose as the sculptor. Ae could sell my work and split the profit with me,' said Prismer, wrapping Kosta's mask.

'A pity I'm only partially qualified for that,' said Kosta wryly. 'I haven't quite recovered my persuasive speech.'

Prismer narrowed her eye at the crafty engineer. 'You must surely have some substant-making schemes of your own?'

He stroked his chin thoughtfully. 'There are contraptions I'd like to make, though I can't find the motivation to work on them. Do you ever get bored halfway through a project?'

'I wouldn't say "bored",' said Prismer, 'but I have a hard time knowing when something is finished.'

Kosta got up to fetch a folder from underneath a pile of papers on his table. He looked from the folder to Prismer and back again, before tucking it under his arm. 'An old contact of mine has been in touch. He has a venue I can use as a workshop.'

'He is standing by you even now?' she asked.

'I am very fortunate, I know,' he said, flipping through the folder. 'I have so many ideas, but I don't have enough resources to work on all of them. I worry I'll put everything into the wrong one.'

Prismer watched the pages of Kosta's folder turn and glimpsed slanted handwriting, too deftly penned to have been written by someone lacking a working thumb. It had to be something he had kept from his old life. 'The right project is the one you complete,' she said. 'You give it value by bringing it into reality.'

'Where others can value it,' finished Kosta, his face brightening.

For a moment, it seemed to Prismer that he was about to show her the folder's contents. Then he hesitated, and put it away. Though curious about his ideas, she didn't press for him to share them. She was also protective of her innermost thoughts.

When the time came for Prismer to leave, Kosta got up to fetch her raincoat, which was now only damp to the touch. 'Are you sure you don't want to stay for a meal? Or wait until the rain ends?' he asked.

'If I return home early, I can paint your mask and add the finish tomorrow.'

'Just seeing it at this stage has made me feel better.' He gestured to the parcel in her hands.

'You can wear it to the support group.' Prismer collected her own mask and buckled it over her headscarf. 'You'll be popular with the others,' she said, following Kosta to the door. 'Had I known you were this chatty, I may not have been so quick to teach you how to use your synthesiser.'

'Think of the entertainment you would have missed out on tonight.' Kosta opened the door for her and almost followed her outside when he realised he was not wearing his mask. Saying his goodbyes, he withdrew into his home and waved. Prismer waved back and slowly walked down the platform. The rain clouds had passed, and a few stars blinked far above.

# CHAPTER 21

## OKLAS

A RUSTY, LASER-CUT sign depicting a wreath of fruits and nuts appeared up ahead, and Oklas took another turn to the right. Yvere's directions led him into a part of the Industrial Park he had never been to before. She had warned him against writing anything down, but the icons he had scrawled on the paper in his hand would hardly make sense to anyone but him.

A rocky roof jutted from the side of the gorge, blocking sections of the sky from view. The ambient light of a misty sunrise illuminated Oklas's way, marking one revolution since he had started this strange new existence. He felt more confident entering this light phase than his last: he had mastered his speech synthesiser and now wore a polished mask. The final colour closely resembled his skin, graded from steel blue at the top to a warm grey at the chin. The serrated beige filigree Prismer had added made for a nice touch. It covered his temples, tracing the area where his tendril-line had begun. Though the mask was comfortable, far better than his shroud, Oklas often needed to go to the Consortium washroom to remove it. Especially in those moments when it seemed everything was closing in on him.

The way forwards was clear, due in no small part to the assistance of his guide. Indeed, Prismer navigated maskad life the same way she charted subterranean routes to the sea, with a reassuring steadiness. Though Oklas messaged her most segments, he had not told her where he was going after work today. He did not need to hide his association with the Ardedrians from her; she wouldn't report the people she had aided to the authorities. But if Oklas invited Prismer to the base, if she were to meet Keanon and Yvere, his worlds would collide. She would learn who he was. He wasn't ready to let go of the only friend he had who simply knew him as Kosta.

Fortunately, their conversations tended to stay in the present—when they weren't veering towards what could be. But Prismer was starting to confide in him, and it turned out that her contained world was not altogether dreary. Oklas had to restrain himself from prompting her with too many questions, or he would owe her transparency in return.

He neared a factory shopfront branded with the sparkling emblem of a cleaning franchise, *Dissolutions*. They supplied businesses with waste dehydrators and offered some of the best polymatter-dissolving processes in the city. If Yvere's directions proved correct, this branch was also a front for the Ardedrians' Apideccan base.

Before entering, Oklas turned to check for anyone following him. He had done his part to appear inconspicuous. In a washroom at the Consortium, he had changed from his uniform into a black hooded shirt with grey trousers.

Behind the front desk, a stout knyad with a visor over aer sunken eyes was jotting calculations down on a holographic writing pad. A badge on aer lapel identified aer as "Administrator Emek, gynid". The administrator's eyes darted around the lit visor; she seemed to look through Oklas when he entered the foyer. He did not recognise her as one of the Ardedrians from Keanon's clandestine meetings, and he gripped the crumpled list of landmarks tighter against his satchel. What if he was in the wrong place?

Without looking at Oklas, she said, 'If you're here about the charity feeding scheme in the Lower End, we've already arranged two drop-offs for tomorrow.' He drew back, confused, before he recalled that Dissolutions redistributed recently-expired food items. She must have thought he had come to beg.

Oklas looked around and, in the forthcoming tone he had recently recovered, he said, 'Either this place has unusually fragrant products, or you have excellent taste in perfume.' The administrator met his mask with a dead-eyed stare, and he cringed inwardly. His attempt at flattery would have worked better if he could flash a smile or wink at her. If she did not understand the code he was about to share, he would have to move on.

He cleared his throat. 'I won't hold you up after what must have been a demanding shift. Tieben sent me to inspect the rising damp in your basement.'

Administrator Emek's heavy-lidded eyes widened, and she removed her visor. 'Hold out your arms,' she instructed, fetching a baton. Oklas complied and she hovered the baton over his chest, then moved it around his limbs and back, scanning him for trackers. 'All clear,' she announced, 'I'll show you through.'

She called for a younger knyad to take her place at the desk and led Oklas down wooden steps to a storeroom full of vats, vacuums, and hydraulic parts. They reached the back of the room and Oklas looked around, searching for a doorway. There had to be more to this building.

The administrator stalled and withdrew a familiar device from her pocket—a towaye. Within seconds of her signalling whoever was on the other side, the tiled floor began to fold in on itself.

'In there, Director.' She indicated to the gaping rift in the middle of the basement.

Oklas peered over the edge. A large platform stopped several alkar below floor level. Surrounded by metal bars and mesh, it looked like a cage.

'Careful boarding the lift. The ladder's missing a rung,' said the administrator.

Oklas climbed down the ladder, and when he reached the platform, the motor above whirred to life and the suspension ropes rolled into place. He stumbled towards the bars for balance as the platform shuddered below his feet. The artificial lights of the basement disappeared behind the floor folding over him. Mesh shadows, cast by other lights, roved over him as the platform lowered into a cylindrical chasm under the building. He tore up the directions and dropped the pieces through gaps in the bars, sending them fluttering down the dark shaft. At the edge of his vision, rocks protruded from sections of the curving wall. He counted two—no, three—levels before the lift reached the ground.

Oklas fiddled with the latch on the lift gate, struggling to grasp it with only his clawed forefingers. When he opened it, he entered a partitioned space. A haphazard arrangement of white room dividers—just short enough that he could see over them—stretched like a maze of boards to the other side of the room. Banging and rumbling echoed from the floor above. A light at the highest floor shone through transparent sections of the floors below, reaching the bottom where Oklas now stood. It was too bright to be artificial; there had to be an opening at street level.

Before he rounded the corner of the divider, Oklas heard low voices on the other side, one raspy and the other deep. Standing at an oval table were Keanon and Yvere, dressed in the dull browns and greys they wore when they wanted to blend in. Yvere was focused on what appeared to be diagrams spread out on the table, while Keanon had his back to the lift and Oklas. Under the table, Keanon's canid lay on her side. Nesta raised her head, her ears rotating to pick up new sounds.

The gate clicked shut again and the lift ground upwards. Yvere raised her head, her bright braids tumbling over her shoulder, and Keanon turned around. Oklas was wearing a mask neither had ever seen, but recognition lit their faces.

The swarthy Ardedrian leader ambled over to Oklas. 'It is good to have you here, my friend.' Markedly absent from Keanon's greeting was his usual boisterous clap on Oklas's back or his full-bodied laugh. He embraced his long-time ally with restraint, as if Oklas was something brittle—or already broken.

Nesta trotted over and pressed her neck against Oklas' leg, leaning into his reach as he scratched her head. To her, at least, he was just the same.

'Glad you could take the time to meet us here.' Oklas gripped Keanon's arm in greeting as Nesta scampered towards the lift shaft, checking for other surprise visitors.

'I am hardly overwhelmed with invitations at the moment,' said Oklas setting his bag on the table.

'What they did to you ... '—Keanon's calloused fingers squeezed into a fist—'I am so sorry. We weren't there when you needed us.' The tension in his arm released as he placed a gentle, great hand on Oklas's shoulder. 'I wasn't there.'

'You would love to take full responsibility for all my misfortunes.' He mirrored Keanon's greeting, placing a hand on the Casworian's shoulder. 'But as much as I don't want to believe I brought this upon myself, there's no fun in blaming you. I'd rather we were united in our blame of the Pentarchy.'

'Aye, Director,' said Keanon, his craggy face breaking into the grin

Oklas had been waiting for. He pulled Okas into a tight embrace, only to suddenly release him. 'I can feel your ribs through your clothes. We must do something about that.'

'If you couldn't put muscle on me before, I doubt it'll work now that I am feeding through a tube.'

Yvere stalked by wearing her pointed smile. 'I told you they hadn't wrung all the humour from him.'

'At least let me get you a flask of kahv,' said Keanon.

He took Oklas on a quick tour of the bottom floor and explained that they used the base as a hideout where Ardedrians could find food and shelter between missions. On the highest floor were bunk beds and a washroom. The second floor primarily stored cargo due to be shipped to bases on nearby islets.

'The storage area currently extends to the bottom floor,' said Keanon, 'but if we organise our goods on the second floor more efficiently, we need not overflow into this space.'

Oklas supposed the move was the cause of the noises above them.

'We will leave some items on this level,' continued Keanon, gesturing to a cabinet of wires and spare parts, 'the kinds of things that might be useful to an engineer.'

Oklas was too taken with the overall impression of the room to focus on anything in particular. Already he could visualise a furnished laboratory where there was only a heap of rubbish, and a thrill engulfed him. He sensed Keanon watching him eagerly, searching for a reaction. Oklas was used to relying on his expressions in these situations. A tweak to his brow and a grateful smile could diffuse a mood through an entire room and change how his words landed. But his body was another instrument he could use. 'This is perfect,' he said, allowing fluidity into his limbs and opening his posture with a tilt of his spine. 'Thank you for keeping me in mind, going through all this trouble.'

Keanon rocked on his feet appreciatively.

'So how did you come by this lair?' asked Oklas.

'I am the beneficiary of two decades of planning and hard labour undertaken by my predecessors,' said Keanon as he folded back some of the dividers and showed Oklas through to the other half of the floor. It was a circular room with a rectangular alcove extending from the wall opposite the lift. 'Initially, this was nothing more than a ditch below the basement, but we knew there were natural caves further down,' he explained. 'Our sponsors have gradually been buying the factories on this block. We needed to ensure no one would report us when we excavated the space further. There's only so much you can do to smother the sound of construction.'

Through the semi-transparent ceiling, Oklas saw knyads on the next floor collecting sacks of food from the lift. 'You know, Keanon,' he said, 'these past few phases, I've had more time to think than I would ever want.' At the alcove, he turned to survey the maze of dividers and crates. 'I always valued the work of the Ardedrian Front, but only now do I have some sense of the difficulties you face. The Pentarchy tries to belittle this group—they don't want people to believe you present a genuine challenge to their rule. Eventually, you'll have to show everyone what you stand for. Are you ready for that?'

Keanon folded his arms. 'It never ends well when power is seized rather than relinquished. There will come a time to act quickly, but it is not now. We must focus on winning over most knyads, rather than fighting the Eruds.'

'And are you gaining a following outside of Apidecca?' As much as Keanon emphasised patience, Oklas needed assurance that the Front was moving towards its goals. That all he had been through would be worth it in the end.

'We are trying to ally ourselves with other insurgent factions. We enter into discussions with them and seek common goals. Many have merged into the Ardedrian front, but others differ too drastically from us in approach.'

'Too hasty?' guessed Oklas, leaning against the archway to the alcove.

'You could say that. There is a radical group operating in the Iridium Gulf area—they assassinated the peer of a Praemor clan north of Caswor.'

'What did they hope to achieve?'

'It's a violent statement. The peer was seen as a puppet of Apidecca, someone who lived extravagantly and did not represent the concerns of his poorer neighbours.'

'Sadly, that is the role of clan peer as the Pentarchy created it,' said Oklas. 'There are proactive peers, those who want better for everyone in their regions.' For a moment, Ailynn flashed in his mind.

A muscle twitched in Keanon's jaw. 'Frustration is growing among the unclassifieds, who have neither peers nor ambassadors advocating for them. They feel locked in poverty. Many are looking for ways to effect change. We are trying to reach out to them before more radical groups do.'

'The Ardedrians have the most far-reaching presence, and you have been active for many years. I'd say you stand a good chance.'

'Maybe so. Our diplomacy doesn't stir people as violence does, but we have outlasted groups who appeal only to their anger. Conditions are changing, and we may soon find more allies. There is talk of discontent even among the Praemor.'

'It's difficult to identify the forces at work there,' said Yvere, creeping up on them from behind a screen, a rucksack slung over her shoulder. 'We have a presence in only a few Praemor clans, but we have heard whispers of Ukohn the Conspirator being sheltered by powerful allies.'

Ukhon Bekleme had been field marshal of the enforcers when Oklas had just started acting as Emis's envoy. Oklas remembered his mentor commenting that Bekleme took too active an interest in the changing currents of politics to be content with security concerns alone. His strategies in managing the enforcer divisions proved highly effective, and the Eruds had come to rely on his advice. By the time the Furtim uncovered evidence of him plotting against the Erudean Pentarchy, Bekleme had already fled the city.

'The Pentarchy still searches for him,' said Oklas, pacing in front of the alcove archway. 'I'd be surprised if he was not spending his exile productively.' Having a betrayal so close to home, within the ranks of their security forces, had shaken the Eruds and made them more paranoid. Certainly in the years that followed, they seemed to have come down harder on perceived threats, however minor. They no longer appointed a field marshal, only a board of generals, so no single enforcer held too much power.

'There is much beyond our control, both here and abroad,' said Keanon. 'Let us concentrate on what we can do now.'

'Like the errands I have to run before segere,' said Yvere, wrapping her distinctive braids under a grey band. 'Hope the accommodations are to Your Highness's liking.' She gave Oklas an exaggerated bow.

'Only if you are on catering duty.'

Keanon saw Yvere off to the lift, but Oklas could not hear the whispered exchange between them. He strayed over to a dauntingly empty workbench pushed against the wall. No notes or stationary were strewn across it, and no charts lined the walls. He needed to put up some pictures for inspiration. What would he create now that he had the time? His mind responded with morbid suggestions of Raganys's convecorprae. As much as the Transmutation Guild enflamed his curiosity about resyncraft, thinking about it only made him feel ill.

From a box labelled "miscellaneous" on the oval table, he picked up a model of Knyadrea. The solid metal orb fitted in his palm. With the press of a button at the south pole, it was covered with a hologram of the ocean. The blue-green glow bulged at the planet-side of the moon, while more noticeable fluctuations in the tides shimmered on the far side.

The Ardedrians had their towayes, and the specialists to develop them further without Oklas's help. He had never set out to manufacture utilitarian devices, but that was largely how he had spent his career at the Assembly. Launching his first satellite had reinvigorated him, spurring him to flout more of Apidecca's restrictions. He yearned to take a chance on a bizarre idea, like landing an automaton with a camera feed on Dryadene—maybe even visiting the cousin moon in person.

He sighed, putting down the bauble. The Ardedrians were no more likely than the General Assembly to fund such expeditions. Perhaps he could begin with miniaturising cameras and sending lightweight drones into Praemor clans to obtain the information Yvere could not. Whatever he learned from the process could eventually be extrapolated and applied to space exploration, informing things like his choice of materials.

Booted footsteps thudded against the concrete floor, bringing Oklas back to himself.

'Sorry that took a while,' said Keanon, wheeling a chair to the oval table and gesturing for Oklas to take a seat. With the uncomfortable countenance of a tideling confessing to having broken a window, Keanon remained standing in front of him. Not for the first time that segeind Keanon stared at Oklas, looking perhaps for some trace of his friend under the impassive outer shell. It was safe to remove the mask here, but Oklas could not bring himself to do it. It was different from unmasking around Prismer, who was the same as him.

Keanon spoke. 'Given your change in circumstances, I'm sure you have questions about our ongoing collaboration.'

So they were going to negotiate. Shielded by his mask, Oklas felt prepared for that. 'I question everything, Keanon,' he said, crossing one leg over the other as he leaned back in his chair.

Keanon smiled and sat beside him. 'In agreeing to use our facilities you are not obliged to join us full time, to leave your job and home.'

'Yvere is right about something: I'm not suited to a life on the run. Just don't tell her I admitted to it.'

'We need all kinds to make up the Ardedrian Front.'

'Even maskads?' asked Oklas, inclining his head.

Keanon's dark brow furrowed in a sorrowful expression. 'We do not see scumbled or whole in our ranks, only people.'

Oklas should have expected such goodwill from Keanon, but he didn't know what to do with it and remained silent, kicking back his swivel chair.

'If you were to change your mind about staying with us,' said Keanon cautiously, 'you might find a better life away from Apidecca. Many maskads have moved to our islet settlements. We'd show you the same dignity we do all knyads.'

Oklas pressed his fingers together; his stubby dewclaw thumbs did not meet. 'Ah, but would I have the dignity of my own living quarters?'

'It is a bit like a dormitory full of rowdy harvestmates,' said Keanon, his beady eyes alight. 'You have to join the canteen queue early if you want a decent meal, and sometimes your belongings go missing.' His gruff voice softened. 'But you'd never be lonely.'

'You know how to make an offer tempting,' said Oklas with a sigh. He could not deny the part of himself that longed to re-join society. To be surrounded by movement and diversions was its own kind of bliss. 'No, I am not yet ready to leave. As much as Apidecca hurts me, I am still beguiled by this city.'

'I understand,' said Keanon.

'It's not that I don't appreciate all of this,' said Oklas, with a sweeping gesture to the walls of the would-be laboratory around them, 'but what are your expectations exactly?'

Keanon inhaled through his nose, his broad shoulders hunching and releasing. 'Come when you are inspired to work on something.'

'So you don't need me to put in a certain number of hours per phase?'

'Oklas, we are not going to exploit your situation or put pressure on you,' said Keanon, a shard of hurt caught in his deep voice. 'The base is active—here for you to use however often you can come. It'll be like old times.'

*Only the roles of sponsor and beneficiary have switched*, thought Oklas. 'This is recompense enough,' he said evenly. 'Now, what are the Ardedri-ans hoping to gain from this arrangement?'

'When you think of a project, you need only come to me to approve it and allocate a budget. If an invention proves to be especially useful, we may ask for your permission to replicate it...as we did with the towayes.'

An ironic edge entered Oklas's voice. 'So you would be happy if I built a frosted-cream maker?'

Keanon let out a thunderous laugh. 'Hidreth would be your best friend if you did,' he said, clapping his knee. 'Obviously we may find some inventions more valuable than others. I can give you some indication of what we're looking for.'

Keanon wouldn't admit it, but the Ardedrians' resources gave them control over Oklas, who could only barter away his scraps of freedom. Looking through Nithan's notes, Oklas had recently learned that no ter-ritory on Knyadrea allowed maskads to patent their inventions. Still, the Ardedrians had not abandoned him at his lowest point. For that, they had earned his loyalty.

'Will the Front recognise anything I contribute as my intellectual property?' he asked.

Keanon gave a firm nod. 'Of course.'

Negotiations continued for a while longer. Keanon was hard-pressed to mention a figure when Oklas inquired about the budget for a single project. He continued to whittle away at the Ardedrian leader until he gave an answer. Oklas had to bury his disappointment. Forty-five thou-sand substants must have seemed a large amount to Keanon, who had lived a hard life and knew how to go without. But compared with the resources Oklas was used to having at his disposal, it was pitiful, not even enough to cover one of the more modest projects he had thought of. He would need to think carefully about how he would use it.

The lift, which had been moving between the top and middle floors for some time, rattled to a stop behind them.

'Ah, that might be your assistant arriving,' said Keanon, standing up.

'Assistant?'

'Given the state of your hands, we sought someone from within our ranks to help you perform tasks that require some...dexterity.'

Oklas could not help but feel slightly offended by Keanon's estimation of his motor skills. He looked at his spindly fingers. His palms sometimes cramped after hours of compensating for his withered thumbs. He supposed Keanon had a point.

'I'm not interrupting anything, am I?' asked the visitor in a youthful, slightly nasal tone familiar to Oklas, whose stomach dropped.

'Not at all,' said Keanon.

Rosh took a step back at the sight of Oklas's mask—the same mask "Kosta" had worn at the Consortium for the past two segments.

'We selected your assistant from within our ranks,' Keanon told Oklas, beckoning Rosh over with a wave of his brindle arm. 'Rosh, allow me to introduce you to Director Sa—'

'Kosta, he can call me Kosta,' Oklas interjected, his head snapping to Keanon. He got up from his swivel chair and placed a firm hand on the Ardedrian leader's upper back. 'Can I have a word?'

'Excuse us,' said Keanon as Oklas whisked him behind a row of dividers in front of the alcove.

Desperately willing it to be so, Oklas asked, 'You haven't told him my name?'

Keanon cupped the back of his thick neck, avoiding the hollow stare of Oklas's mask.

'Grike.' Seething, Oklas turned away from him with his hands on his hips. 'So I take it my identity is common knowledge to the whole of the Ardedrian front?' he asked, the hurriedly-generated words almost overlapping.

'It is known only to the few stationed here,' Keanon assured him in a hushed tone. 'Rosh is very knowledgeable, and he is a friend of your former student, Illanu.'

'Did you know he works with me at the Consortium?'

'Give the juve a chance,' said Keanon, rounding the corner of a divider on his way back to Rosh and adding more loudly, 'Now I must be going.' Oklas followed to see Rosh almost knocked off-balance by Keanon's farewell arm grip. The juvenile was only a little shorter than him, but half his breadth. Keanon whistled for Nesta, and the canid came bounding after him from the other side of the room. 'I will leave you two to get acquainted,' he said as he headed towards the lift.

Oklas rummaged irritably through the miscellaneous box, keeping his back to Rosh as the lift trundled up its shaft. He angled his head to one side and noticed the juvenile rooted in place, watching him. 'As you can see, I have not yet started work on anything,' said Oklas, 'so there is no need for you to stay.'

Rosh walked over to him and leaned on the opposite side of the oval table. 'So it was you at the Consortium this whole time'—his thin lips tugged into a smile –'Director Sayve.'

'Not what you expected?' said Oklas, pushing aside the distracting box and presenting himself to Rosh.

The juvenile looked him up and down. 'I didn't know this had happened to you. I only wanted the chance to ask why no one at the Emisrian has seen you in a revolution.'

'I see...well, you have your answer now.' It was tempting to ask about the college, but Oklas held back. He was not sure he wanted to know what was happening there yet. Wagging a long finger at Rosh, he added, 'I'd rather you didn't get into the habit of calling me anything but Kosta. Understand?'

'I wouldn't be here if I couldn't keep a secret,' said Rosh with a shrug. 'For what it's worth, I don't care that you're a maskad. It was a maskad that saved my best friend.'

Oklas laughed, exasperated. 'Of course, you know Prismer too.' Another complication.

'And you know each other from the Assembly, don't you?'

'As far as she's concerned, Oklas and Kosta are two different people. I'd like to keep it that way.'

Rosh opened his mouth, as if to ask a question. Then, thinking better of it, he simply said, 'Yes, kyr.'

'Good.'

Oklas had once been a friend to juveniles, a favourite among his students. But he hadn't given Rosh a reason to see him as anything but a grumpy, bitter maskad. He ran a hand over his sparsely-scaled head. 'I have to protect my anonymity, Rosh. It's one of the few assets I have left.'

'I understand.'

'And I would be grateful for your assistance. I hope the Front compensates you well for it.'

'Ilu told me you were one of the Consortium's most promising graduates,' said Rosh, mischief dimpling his chin. 'I thought I'd see if that was true. And it's not every seg that I get to work with someone famous.'

'Not everyone would want to work with a wreck like me,' said Oklas, looking up from the table brightly. 'I'm glad you're keeping an open mind. My knowledge only has any value if it is passed to others.'

Rosh grinned. 'Ilu used to quote you on that.'

Another hour passed as Oklas and Rosh talked. The juvenile explained that he was from an unclassified clan, Temas. He was confident—bordering on cocky—but quick to accept correction. Oklas liked him already. Rosh didn't see Prismer frequently, but he agreed not to tell her about Kosta or the lab.

The dash home in time for curfew left Oklas puffed, but he didn't regret spending extra time at the base getting to know the young biomechanist. He even learned things about Illanu he had never known, like the fact that she wrote poetry or was unbeatable in the game of viginti. Somehow, knowing his former student was safe and content lessened his losses. After segments of constant change, collaborating with the Ardedrians once more brought him a sense of normalcy.

# CHAPTER 22

## PRISMER

GUSTS OF WIND scattered dust and paper packets, pocketing them in corners and crevices of the Dolna District. The dark blue hood of Kosta's fulver blew down, and he tugged it back over his head. Though she knew nothing of trends, Prismer had helped him select the garment for his first meeting with the other maskads.

He glanced at her as they continued up the High Street. 'I thought Taber was planning on keeping us there until segere, blocking the door like that.'

Prismer hummed a laugh. 'He was in good spirits today—Taber never feels as accomplished as when he has collected another outlier.'

'"Collected" is a strong word. I doubt I'll come consistently.'

'Good. Leave them wanting more.'

Kosta skipped over a raised flagstone. 'So that's why they were so surprised to see you.' The static expression on his grey mask warmed with his tone of voice.

'Yes,' said Prismer, 'surprised.' It was the first time she had brought anyone along to the support group, let alone someone as outgoing as Kosta. His presence at the meeting had allowed her to pull back. Kosta had a way of making people feel they had known him for years. She would have never guessed the near-mute maskad who had stumbled into her home mere phases ago could so deftly snatch the attention of a room. He must have spoken to every attendee, instinctively adjusting his bearing and style of conversation to suit each of them. Every exchange rose and spiralled like a complex piece of music as he flitted from topic to topic, or slowed to listen and give a measured response. It was both impressive and a little exhausting to watch.

'I did not expect so many of the maskads to be former merchants or entertainers,' confessed Kosta as he and Prismer dodged a knot of passengers disembarking from a tram.

'What type of knyads did you think were scumbled?'

'Quiet, serious types,' he teased, nudging her shoulder as they walked. 'I should have guessed they wouldn't all be unclassifieds.'

'A few are unclassified, but most are from more powerful clans. There's not much point in erasing someone if ae is already invisible.' Prismer hugged herself against the cool breeze. 'For some of us, it's a fall; for others, it's only a step-down.'

Kosta tipped his head forwards but said nothing. For all his affability during the meeting, he was still a mystery to Prismer. She had not even learned his clan of origin, not that there was anything wrong with that. He would open up when he was ready, as she had. Of course, when she did speak, Prismer struggled to be anything but candid.

'Can I say something?' She looked to Kosta at her side. 'I was actually quite scared of going today.'

He exhaled a laugh. 'Not as scared as I was. First impressions are so important.'

'You didn't need me there to introduce you,' she said, bumping her shoulder into his—a bit harder than intended. He stumbled, and she caught him by his sleeve, pulling him back and steadying him with a gloved hand on his chest. Stepping back from Kosta, she shoved both hands deep into her pockets. 'The thing is, I've been this way for so long now, and I never did go out much. The less I try, the harder it becomes.'

Kosta spun around, walking backwards to face her. 'Then let's go somewhere now, keep you in practice.'

Prismer looked around jerkily, half-expecting to find he was addressing someone else. 'Now?'

'There are still two hours before curfew.'

'Where will we go?' she asked, stroking the section of her scarf draped over her sternum.

Kosta tapped his mask on the forehead. 'See if you can guess before we get there.'

The sandstone-clad buildings grew more elegant towards the Upper End, with pillars, stonework, and embellishments. But when Kosta turned to the right, ahead of the Traditional Quarter, Prismer became surer of their destination.

They climbed the side of the gorge just west of the High Street, and the buildings gave way to solid rock. The thick walls closed off the wind from this section, though it wailed faintly from high above, and the sun-filled tunnel grew warm. They followed a procession of other knyads down a pathway and eventually came to a row of arches almost as tall as the buildings they had left behind. Tomorrow was phase-end, and the area was bustling with knyads looking for ways to unwind.

'You had me worried,' said Prismer. 'For a moment, I thought you were leading me deeper into the city.'

'To some overcrowded, dingy club?' proposed Kosta teasingly. 'No, the mindless percussion does little to foster quality conversations. I have something else in mind.'

'The Crater Gardens?'

He nodded. 'Maskads are allowed, aren't they?'

'I've been a few times. Just stay away from the popular places.'

The Crater Gardens consisted of a giant hole in the gorge, a league in diameter with high walls and overhanging ledges that offered shade throughout the light phases. A river running through the Lepotra District fed into a belt of waterfalls which cascaded into deep plunge pools. Several springs bubbled from underground. The best sections of the gardens were cordoned off for the exclusive use of Praemor knyads, but the rest was open to the general public.

Prismer squinted through the lens of her mask at the brightness of the sky, taking in the painterly streaks of high cloud. The sun—which had not yet reached its highest point—washed the western wall in golden light. Shadows tinted the opposite side indigo. Many knyads congregated in the warmer half of the crater.

'Come, I know of a place we can stop at,' said Prismer, taking Kosta by the forearm and leading him away.

Staying on the shaded eastern side, she led him past a series of smaller pools swelling at intervals along one of the lower streams. She stopped at a pool set back from the others, partially sunlit and only chest deep. There was no one nearby.

'You seem to know your way around for someone who claims to be indoorsy,' said Kosta, taking off his shoes.

'I go on adventures, just seldom with company.' Prismer picked up her boots. A springy lichen grew at the rim of the pool and she walked over it, testing its texture beneath her toes. 'I usually bring notes with me here. It helps to throw off enforcers if you stay out of the way and look busy.'

She rolled up her trousers, letting her feet dangle over the edge on the sunny side of the pool. The water was already quite warm, likely geothermally heated.

'Are you going to swim?' asked Kosta.

'Not today.'

'But you've come all this way.'

'If you had warned me we were coming here, I could have put on an aquaskin.'

'You don't need one.'

Kosta pulled off his fulver and, still wearing his trousers and mask, leapt into the sunny side of the pool, causing water to splash over Prismer.

'Kosta,' she growled, making a disapproving clicking with her gills.

He bobbed to the surface, lifting his chin and pushing the water back from the peak of his forehead. Prismer removed the glassfolia brooch that secured the knot in her scarf. Water dripped down her arm as she scrunched the damp material.

'You may as well come in now.'

'I'm not walking all the way home in drenched trousers, thank you very much.'

'Come in—you can dry off in the sun.' Kosta showed her to a rock next to the pool. Some knyads passed by, and Prismer reached for his shoulder, dunking him neck-deep into the water.

'What was that for?'

'You're not covered up—they'll arrest you for indecency.'

'I'm wearing the mask.'

'And what about your arms and torso?'

'What, I must now cover up my few remaining good features?' he said, spreading his arms out.

Though not endowed with considerable upper body strength, Kosta was, truthfully, rather well-proportioned. Prismer had never seen his grey-blue skin in the sunlight before, never noticed the scar-like threads of beige—the same shade as his optic pattern—standing out from his dark shoulders.

'It draws attention,' she said, looking at her hands as she folded them in her lap.

'Blasted legislation,' muttered Kosta as he floated on his back. 'You should swap your fulver for mine. It's drier.' He pointed to his discarded garment draped over a rock.

While her trousers were not too wet, the top of Prismer's green fulver was sopping.

'Thank you, but you'll need it when you get out. I have another idea.'

Looking around to check for passing knyads, Prismer removed her headscarf and peeled off the cold fulver clinging to her back. She was not keen to display her scaly, mottled skin or the uneven musculature she had developed from years of favouring her right side, and wasted no time in unfurling her scarf and wrapping it like a shawl around her shoulders.

Kosta hauled himself out of the water. 'May as well show what skin you can before they make more rules about it. Some sun will do you good.'

'It'll only make my markings stand out even more,' she said, rubbing her head. 'If my complexion darkened to your storm-cloud hue, I might also want to show it off. Almost everyone on Inclatia is speckled. But this is excessive.' She held out her arm to show him her unevenly-spotted skin.

'I've always envied knyads with clan markings: spots, stripes, patches,' he said, wiping his arms down with his fulver before pulling it on. 'It says something about the environment that shaped you.'

Knowing that a flush of colour was creeping around her gills, Prismer fumbled with her glassfolia brooch as she tried to pin the scarf in place.

'Superb detailing,' said Kosta, drawing close for a better look at the brooch.

'A friend gave it to me before she left the city,' said Prismer nonchalantly. He didn't need to know about the circumstances of her friend's departure. Prismer's dealings with the Ardedrian Front were a thing of the past.

'It reminds me of the plants growing in the waterfall over there.'

'Those are vittas glacies—ice ribbons. They grow in rivers around the Nebbian Continent, freezing over during the dark phases and reviving when the sun returns.'

Kosta raised his brow.

'Of course, you didn't need to know all that.' She faltered, placing a hand at her temple to shield the eyeholes of her mask from him.

'Don't apologise,' he said with a laugh. 'I just didn't realise you were a keen botanist. Where did you learn that?'

Prismer wound her scarf around her wrists. 'It started with the produce we grew on Inclatia, but I wanted to learn about other herbs too. One of our clan elders, Caja, was a mender. She had such knowledge of plants. Some said her remedies were the work of an undiscovered resyncrafter. While my harvestmates played, I would sneak into her bungalow and help grind the ingredients for her tonics. She explained all the properties of her herbs. I learned quickly that way. She taught me more than any book could.'

'How wise you were to spend time with her,' said Kosta, his voice suddenly laced with regret. 'You get used to having a mentor to call on for segments, years even. Then suddenly they are gone.'

Prismer waited for him to say more, to share something about the person he had lost, but he only heaved a sigh and looked at her expectantly.

'There was still so much I hadn't learned from Elder Caja when I left for Apidecca,' she admitted. 'I didn't value traditional practices as I should have; I thought the city would offer me more. In hindsight, I should have stayed.'

'Are you still in touch with your clan elders or your harvestmates?'

'No.' There were things Prismer was also not ready to talk about.

Kosta looked to the crater's edge, where terraced buildings backed onto the cliffs. Prismer followed his gaze. 'Some of the first residences in Apidecca were built in Lepotra,' she said.

'It's the view.' He pointed to a row of buildings, larger than the rest. 'Properties in the streets overlooking the pools are still the most sought-after.'

'On one of my walks here, I spotted the border of the Traditional Quarter.' Prismer got up, looking between trees and bushes for any sign of it. 'I remember seeing the back of the Emisrian. Maybe I was viewing it from another angle?'

'Ah, yes, the Traditional Quarter would be on the other side of the wall, a little lower down the slope,' said Kosta, following her. He stood on tiptoe, scanning the crater's rim, and pointed in another direction.

'Further back, over there, you can see the central dome of the Assembly Chambers, rising to the surface.'

Prismer gave a soft laugh. 'Apex Hall. I sometimes forget all this beauty is only a short distance above me.'

'Have you ever been to Apidecca's surface?'

'A couple of times, when I arrived here,' said Prismer through a sigh. 'I won't forget the view. Can you imagine living in Lepotra, looking down on the whole city every segment?'

'Yes. My work used to take me through the suburb regularly.'

'What's it like?'

'Palatial buildings, water features, lush gardens,' said Kosta, lowering himself onto a spongey patch of lichen, 'typical extravagances of the Praemor stratum.' Submerging his feet in the pool, he lazily trod water.

'I remember seeing reels of those places back on Inclatia,' said Prismer. 'I thought all of Apidecca was whitewashed walls and villas built into the mountainside. Looking at buildings by architects like Viraj Balint made me want to come here.'

Kosta's head raised at the name.

Prismer sat beside him. 'You know Balint?'

'I-I encountered him once. You'd be surprised where deliveries have taken me,' he replied. 'Balint is renowned for combining aesthetics with energy efficiency. He refers to ancient building techniques but isn't afraid to innovate.' Kosta pushed himself back, lifting his legs from the water. 'Of course, you wanted to study architecture, didn't you?'

'Spatial planning,' Prismer corrected him. 'The buildings here are so grand; I couldn't improve upon them. But I would've liked to establish blended districts with recreational areas like this, to bring knyads of different strata together.'

'Noble goals.'

'Goals that were never within my reach.' Prismer lay on the soft flakes of lichen. 'I wanted to leave a mark on this city, but it marked me instead.'

Kosta watched her from a seated position, his legs crossed. 'I know this is a bit personal, but when were you scumbled?'

She blinked halfway, her vision darkening. 'Fourteen years ago.'

'You couldn't have been more than a juvenile.'

'Juveniles are perhaps the best at making rash decisions.'

'Whatever you did, I'm sure you weren't in the wrong,' said Kosta. 'It seems every maskad I met today was punished for making a stand.'

Prismer looked at the sky. 'Then it makes sense that I never fitted in with the others.'

'What do you mean?'

It was strange, bringing up her past again, only a revolution after recounting it to Rosh and Illanu. Prismer put the details of her crimes plainly to Kosta, but she felt something she hadn't when speaking to the juveniles—a faint concern for what he would think.

Kosta interlaced his fingers and listened. He went very still. When she finished speaking, he quietly said, 'If circumstances were different, you wouldn't have had to steal.'

'I didn't have to,' she said with a shrug. 'The Assembly met all my basic needs. But I kept wanting more.'

'Wanting to reach your potential isn't the same thing as greed, Prismer.' Conviction steadied his voice. 'All things considered, I think you're very...well-adjusted.'

Prismer barked a laugh. 'Hardly.' Rubbing her arms, as if shedding the subject, she said, 'I've been talking too much. Why don't you tell me something about yourself?'

Kosta lay down, folding his arms behind his head. 'I recently learned to whistle through my gills.'

Prismer gave an annoyed huff, her eye drifting to the mist sweeping beneath the high clouds. Perhaps he thought these deflections made him seem mysterious. 'What's it like, becoming a maskad as an adult?' she asked.

Kosta was quiet for long enough that she thought he wouldn't answer her. Then he spoke. 'Parts of you feel too solid to bend to the change. Maybe some things have to break before they can reset?' He rolled onto his side and propped himself on his arm. 'There is a lot I want to say, Pir. When the time comes, it's not the support group I'm going to share it with.'

'I look forward to hearing it,' she said sleepily, raising her arm and supporting her neck with her hand.

In the quiet of the garden, she was content to have someone next to her, listening to the squawks of predes and pegwings roosting in the rocks above, or the bubbling of the stream. The two of them dozed there and, for once, Prismer allowed herself to lose track of time. Still, she was grateful when an enforcer passed their way, ordering them to move on. Had ae not, she could have stayed there well into curfew.

# CHAPTER 23

## OKLAS

IT WAS OKLAS'S third visit to the Ardedrian base in a phase, and he was pleased with the progress they had made in turning the cave into something resembling a laboratory. The Ardedrians who stayed on the higher floors moved only the items he and Keanon had set aside for storage. They made for a considerate team, leaving everything else untouched. There was nothing more infuriating than returning to a workspace only to find his half-finished projects and tools cleared away. Items were still misplaced, but Oklas had only himself to blame for that. Rosh had taken it upon himself to devise an organising system for him. The juvenile had clustered equipment into the cabinets lining the curving walls.

In addition to the furniture Oklas had seen on his last visit, two narrow workbenches now hugged the wall of the alcove. Keanon had delivered whatever equipment he could quickly obtain; the laboratory was now fitted out with a fume hood, a distillation column, and an adapter hub. Oklas would not necessarily need them. But until he decided what projects he might focus on, he was loath to decline anything.

Together he and Rosh had sifted through boxes of spare parts, salvaging hardware and tools that were of use to them. They left the items they didn't need in a pile between the lift shaft and the washroom behind it. Rosh dumped another box of rubbish there and returned to the oval table. His normally-ochre skin flushed a warmer shade of brown. 'When I signed up for this, I didn't think heavy labour was going to be involved,' he complained, wiping the dust from his dark trousers.

Oklas huffed through the filters of his mask and pushed a plate towards Rosh. 'The biscuits will surely make it worth the effort.'

'Ta,' said Rosh, grabbing a still-warm biscuit and collapsing on the chair opposite Oklas.

It was thoughtful of Keanon to bring them Yvere's expertly-baked goods. The biscuits had been Oklas's favourites: crunchy and spiced on the outside, with sugared fruit on the inside. But they were too fiddly for him to eat now. The crumbs stuck to his throat and fell down his shirt.

'You've done well. It's...tidy,' said Oklas, looking mournfully around the empty laboratory. For a moment, the clinical space was disquietingly reminiscent of Raganys's cold theatre. Oklas had kept some of the dividing screens to partition the floor space. The laboratory was small compared with the lecture halls of the Emisrian or the airy rooms in Ironglade Heights. So why did he feel swallowed by the place? Perhaps he was becoming too used to hiding like a pegwing in his tiny insula.

Still chewing his biscuit, Rosh shot him a concerned look from across the table.

Oklas straightened. 'I will miss the oddities strewn about. It can be very stimulating to have some randomness in a workplace.'

'I don't know how you concentrate.'

Oklas was coming to appreciate his opinionated new assistant. Imagining scenarios in which he might need discarded items, Oklas had consistently returned to the rubbish pile to retrieve various gadgets. This continued until Rosh, tired of seeing his sorting undone, took the cruel but necessary measure of banning him from the area.

Oklas raised the drawing board from the oval table and activated a pocket-sized portable projector. A list appeared before him. With a pen linked to the laboratory's casting system, he crossed off the items they had already collected. They both knew what was coming next. Oklas needed to focus on a single project; he could not afford to blow his limited budget on novelties. Once he decided what he wanted to make, he could ask Keanon to bring him specific items related to the purpose.

Oklas shortlisted some of the ideas he and Rosh generated. Working with the changed anatomy of his hand, he wrote from his shoulder instead of his wrist and enlarged his lettering. After an hour, the initial flurry of prospective inventions began to ebb. Oklas sauntered to the workbench. He opened a compartment in the diffuser and added a drop of brunia oil to it.

Rosh wrinkled his nose.

'You'd prefer me to leave the diffuser off?'

'It's not the diffuser. But the essential oil, is it really so…essential?'

'It's meant to energise you,' said Oklas, clicking the lid shut, 'and it disguises the smell of mildew.'

Rosh cupped his face in his hands, his elbows on the table. 'How about camouflage technology? Something like the Furtim's uniforms?'

The juvenile seemed to have espionage on his mind today. All the technology he proposed fell under the categories of evasion or infiltration.

'I suppose we have the resources for that. I'll add it to "maybe",' said Oklas, returning to the lit drawing board. His difficulty came not in generating ideas but in settling on one. He yearned to investigate resyn-powered technology further, but it would be costly. And the Ardedrians were more concerned with pragmatism than breaking new ground. He deactivated the notepad hologram. 'I'll review these tomorrow.'

'You don't want to do any of them, do you?' asked Rosh as he put down his pen.

'It's not that your ideas aren't any good,' said Oklas, folding the drawing board closed. 'They're very realistic. The Ardedrians would fund any one of them. I also appreciated your feedback, though your assessment of my deep-sea drone was a bit harsh.'

'It's extravagant and doesn't meet any of our immediate needs,' said Rosh with a shrug. 'But Keanon would probably welcome something that can scout the harbour. You have enough materials to construct simple marine drones.'

It seemed the Ardedrians had enlisted the astute juvenile just to curb Oklas's imagination. 'You're frighteningly good at implementation,' he observed.

'I'm productive,' said Rosh, sliding his hand over the hinge of the drawing board. 'If you don't like the drone idea, we could choose something else on the list.'

'Nothing stands out yet. I fear my creativity is spent.'

'The notepad looked full. Just walk away from it for a while.'

Oklas made a tent of his fingers and swivelled his chair towards the roughly-excavated wall. Sunlight streamed in from the top floor. 'You should go outside, Rosh. Enjoy the rest of your mid-phase break.'

'It's too hot up there today,' said the juvenile. 'I'd rather organise the stuff we shoved in those crates last time.' He pointed to a bulky chest under the closest workbench.

Oklas gave him the go-ahead, and Rosh went to fetch the empty cabinet drawers. Together, they gripped either end of the chest and carried it to the table. Oklas's lower back protested. He shifted the weight onto his knees as they tipped out the contents.

Immediately, Rosh took charge of the task ahead. 'We can organise them by category. Circuit boards and solder can go in the top drawer. Screwdrivers, pliers, and wire strippers are in the middle, along with trays of small general-purpose bits. Lesser-used items at the bottom.'

Oklas doubted he would keep to Rosh's elaborate sorting system, but he went along with the juvenile's suggestions, secretly smiling at the sight of Rosh in his element. He started gathering the tiny components for the middle drawer. It was the sort of task that frustrated Oklas at the Consortium, but here, without the pressure of time constraints, it was surprisingly therapeutic.

Absently separating bolts and rings, Oklas confided, 'I worry I won't be able to give Keanon what I have in the past.'

Rosh's hands hovered above a tray of solder. 'I don't think he expects you to.'

'I didn't practice as an engineer for long after graduating from the Consortium,' continued Oklas, not looking up from his work. 'Much of my success came from assembling teams of specialists to fill the gaps in my knowledge. I'm on my own this time.'

'No, you aren't,' said Rosh, 'you just have a different team.'

Oklas nodded appreciatively. 'If this were your business, what strategy would you employ?'

'Just pick one "good enough" idea. Set up a system that works for everyone and sit back while it reaps a profit.'

'Profit? The Ardedrians rely on sponsors and informal trade. Even if they do make something from my inventions, how much do you think will come back to me?'

'They want to offer you more, as much as they can spare.'

'I worry by the time they take to power'—*if they ever do,* thought

Oklas—'they will have forgotten how to dream.' He turned around and lifted his mask to rub away the ache at his temples. Rosh dropped his gaze back to his sealed circuit boards, waiting silently. They had a comfortable understanding concerning the mask. Sometimes Oklas just needed a private moment to be free of the thing. He lowered it back over his face. 'I...I want to do something more experimental. Something that doesn't guarantee results.'

'A lot of your ideas involve resyn,' said Rosh, waving a moisture barrier bag at him. 'I'm sure they'd find that useful.'

Oklas shook his head. 'It would cost too much to equip the lab as a resyn refinery.'

'You don't have to process it here. Keanon can probably source purified resyn.'

'He already has, but not in the quantities I'd like. It'll only arrive next revolution.'

'And it'll be here, in the lab?'

'Yes,' said Oklas, amused by the sudden buoyancy in Rosh's voice. 'Eager to work with it, are you?'

'It is the cleanest power source. The crystals can hold a charge for decades,' said Rosh, vigorously stacking the sealed circuit boards in an empty cabinet drawer. 'Only qualified biomechanists have access to it in their work. I use the standard fulmenum cells in my thermoelectric units.'

'It is a remarkable substance,' said Oklas, adding his last bolts to the tray. A cramp was starting in his palm.

Rosh blinked at him. 'You specialised in resyn engineering, didn't you?'

'I never completed the program. Emis redirected me into a political career. As his envoy, I travelled extensively and gained experience as a diplomat. After he passed...well, I became too busy to pick up my studies again.' He looked into the distance, through the rays of sunlight and past the cave wall. 'The applications of resyn in technology only offer a glimpse of its true nature. It was always the mysticism surrounding it that captivated me.'

'Even now? After they...' Rosh drifted, raising his eyebrows and gestured at his face.

Oklas ignored him. 'Imagine being able to combine resyncraft with technology? We could alter organic matter to interact optimally with implants. Of course, it would have to be governed by a code of ethics.'

The juvenile folded his arms, unimpressed. 'And what do cults know about ethics?' he scoffed. 'Apparently there is even some bunk aptitude test for resyncraft.'

'I know, I failed it twice.'

Rosh pursed his lips disapprovingly.

'I had to be sure about it,' added Oklas, flexing his fingers to ease the cramp in his palm.

'You're better off dabbling in politics than'—Rosh let his voice take on a comically spooky tone—'dark magic.' He fluttered his fingers for effect.

Oklas chuckled, shaking his head. No more was said about the subject his assistant was so morally opposed to. 'I notice you untangled the cables for me. Keanon said you spent the last curfew here.'

'It's better than the trainee dormitory at the Consortium,' said Rosh, pulling a sensor from the pile on the table.

'Do they still have the faded orange curtains?'

'They're some other awful colour now. The air vents rattle there. It keeps me up sometimes.'

'I imagine the other trainees are mostly Orta or Praemor,' said Oklas, remembering that Rosh was from an unclassified clan. 'Have you had any trouble with them?'

'There was some bullying in my first year,' he replied, placing the sensor in a drawer. 'It's gotten better now that I am a senior.'

Oklas stretched his legs and walked to Rosh's side of the table. 'How were you placed at the Consortium anyway?'

'A generous peer came to Temas and selected some of us to be educated at her clan. My foundation phase test results were the highest in the class. The Consortium scouted me from there.'

'What happened to the others?'

'My harvestmates are mostly studying engineering or mending at Orta institutions. They're doing well.' Rosh bit his lip as he rolled a servo over in his hands. 'Today, my friends from the Emisrian found out they've lost their places at the college. It's closing.'

The news came like a blow to Oklas's chest. He rested a hand on the back of Rosh's chair. 'Do they have somewhere to transfer to?'

'They are reaching out to former lecturers to accredit their education.

There is a rumour...that you fled to Dras Sayve after committing some kind of misconduct.' He paused, putting the servo away. 'If people keep asking after you, the Pentarchy may have to give them an explanation.'

Oklas drew back. 'They won't share the truth—it would only strengthen the reputation of the Ardedrians.'

'I guess knowing what happened to you won't make a difference to my friends anyway,' said Rosh solemnly, pushing away the drawer.

'Rosh, I—'

What did he want to tell Rosh? Oklas knew his students were resourceful; they did not need him. But they had overcome enough obstacles to get here, and he hated presenting them with more. At the opposite end of the laboratory, the lift shuddered to a halt, and Keanon's knyads started collecting the crates of rubbish left outside the washroom. Oklas gently gripped Rosh's shoulder and went to speak with them. He watched the lift travel up the shaft and returned to the oval table. Rosh had finished packing the drawers.

Oklas drew up a chair next to his assistant. 'If you have any projects of your own, you're welcome to bring them here,' he offered.

Rosh leaned back, eyeing Oklas from the side. 'Could I use one of your resyn crystals in a cybernetic implant I'm upgrading?'

'You only need one?'

'It's for Prismer.'

'Her left arm?' Oklas recalled her telling him about her accident in one of their mitter conversations, though he had not seen the scar beneath her implant.

'You'd think they would have better protective gear for aquaculture labourers,' said Rosh dryly. 'Ilu wouldn't have made it to the coast without her. I wanted to thank her.'

'By all means, take whatever you need,' said Oklas, gesturing at the hardware they had sorted.

Rosh gave a tentative smile. 'She uh, told me she went somewhere with you recently.'

'We've been to a few places about town: the gardens, support group, and she showed me to a place called the Husk and Brewer. A friendly establishment. I've never seen so many maskads in one place before.' He laughed. 'I almost felt normal there.'

Rosh narrowed his eyes in an interrogating look.

'And no,' said Oklas, 'I still haven't told her we know each other from the Assembly.' Idly picking up the tiny projector from the table, he continued, 'I could always count on Prismer to solve a problem. Whether it was finding an adapter for my casting platform or editing my presentations.' He set the device down again. 'But we never mixed socially.'

The corner of Rosh's mouth lifted. 'She doesn't let people get close easily.'

'In fairness to her, it is hard to connect with anyone from behind a mask,' said Oklas, tapping his own.

Rosh fetched one of the full drawers. 'You know,' he said, pausing alongside Oklas, 'a lot of people are afraid of maskads, but a Praemor politician can also be pretty intimidating. Maybe neither of you really knew the other before.'

'Is your wise counsel part of your service here, or will you charge me extra?'

'I don't think even Oklas Sayve could afford me,' said Rosh on his way to the cabinet, 'but for a friend, it's free.'

Oklas watched him leave, then packed the projector away with his other equipment.

# CHAPTER 24

## PRISMER

POLITICIANS FILLED THE first four floors of Apex Hall in a swathe, and more filed in through the doorways at the fifth and sixth floors. Prismer's hands were clammy as she refolded her headscarf for the third time that median. The complete Erudean Pentarchy would be present for the quarterly meeting of the General Assembly, viewing proceedings from their pre-eminent gallery. On such occasions, it was not uncommon for their representative to make an announcement. Sure enough, one of Erud Teprill's courtiers came to Prismer and relayed the Erud speaker's requirements. To accommodate her time onstage, the last two presentations of the meeting were to be rescheduled. Ae then uploaded a single secured presentation onto the casting box. Erud Teprill would signal its unlocking with her mitter. Only then could Prismer display the contents. She supposed she should be grateful it was not a complex task. Whenever the Pentarchy was present, technical errors seemed more commonplace.

The domed ceiling had turned a glassy black, though the sky was not yet dark. Above, gears creaked and the great aperture panels twisted closed, shutting out the intensifying drizzle. Red algae panels softly lit the aisles, fading into the background as bright, artificial lights came on at the stage. The meeting was about to begin.

The routine presentations dragged on. Aside from skipping a slide on a public infrastructure report and cycling back to find the right one, Prismer managed to keep her proficiency from falling apart. She wondered where Dy Erla was in the audience, and whether Minister Sayve had returned from the Dras Channel.

The last diagram before the interlude flickered above the stage, and Prismer settled back into her seat. The only aspect of this job that challenged her was performing it in front of scores of influential knyads, many of whom—if they spared her a thought—believed she was good for nothing more than this. It was to be expected, given what she was.

*If you alone hold your abilities in esteem, how can you be sure your detractors are in the wrong? Who is the deluded one here?* whispered her inner voice.

But it wasn't just Prismer anymore. Kosta too seemed to think she had more to offer. Perhaps she had already wasted too many years confined to a projection booth in Apex Hall. Her expedition to the coast had revived a restlessness in her. But she was not ready to believe Kosta, not entirely. It would mean letting go of tools she had developed to protect herself.

Shuffling activity marked the end of the first half of the meeting, as courtiers and assistants ran to the stage and began their preparations. It did not take long for Prismer, together with two technicians, to make adjustments to the sound and lighting. The interval was for the sake of ceremony, allowing a droning anticipation to fill the hall. The arrival of the Erud speaker was to be set apart from mundane affairs. Onstage, courtiers assembled an elevated podium gilded in platinum, and raised banners featuring the Pentarchy's symbol: a crest made of five differently-patterned fragments united at the centre by a coronet. The knot in Prismer's stomach, which she had managed to ignore during the earlier part of the median, tightened. If experience was anything to go on, the Erud speaker would likely bear some dire news. The policy changes she communicated were usually advantageous to no one but the Praemor.

Something about the set-up struck Prismer as strange. Erud Teprill shared the stage with no one. But tonight, several politicians congregated at floor level as assistants arranged chairs in a row behind the podium. Prismer noticed all the ministers were from the Research, Education, and Communications departments. Minister Kemia looked especially grim, and her deputy was markedly absent.

Erud Teprill would not weave her way through the gathering to climb to the front of the stage. She would come down from the gallery via a private stairwell. Prismer looked to the back corner of the stage, a slight tremor vibrating the hand she held poised above the console.

A pale figure emerged from the back corner of the stage. Prismer set the automated spotlight to track Erud Teprill's billowing progress to the podium. Every knyad in the room, from the ministers to Prismer in the projection booth, stood to attention. White tendrils fanned out from behind Erud Teprill's radiant crown. It was the beautifully menacing halo of a disdainful deity. The Erud's gown was the pale gold and sienna of Clan Teprill, and her high collar spread into sections resembling fierce flames. A Furto flanked her on either side, their edges shimmering like mirages in the warm hues of the stage background. Briefly, Prismer wondered whether the Erud had always carried herself as if she expected her surroundings to reshape at her bidding. How did someone, having been raised in a Pentarchic clan, go about setting aerself apart as an Erud?

The pale sovereign ascended the podium, and the procession of politicians climbed the stairs and lined up behind her, standing before the row of chairs. 'You may be seated,' came Erud Teprill's crystalline voice. Prismer noticed that the Eruds' courtiers had put out one chair too many. It was not like them to be imprecise. Stranger still, the empty chair was not on the far end, but between Ministers Kemia and Dhara. Neither one of them moved to fill the gap.

Erud Teprill began her announcement as she did her others, reiterating her commitment to Apidecca and thanking those gathered for managing commonplace operations. She considered it an honour to present the Erudean Pentarchy's decisions to the General Assembly. Prismer tried to imagine what it was like to look over the crowd in Apex Hall from a gilded podium. Did Erud Teprill feel as confident as she sounded? Did she believe to her core that Adecai had set her above them all? Or did it feel like their awe and respect could evaporate at any moment?

Prismer refocused on what Erud Teprill was saying. 'As of next phase, we welcome the new Deputy Minister of Research and Development, Skep Benzun.' There was a collective murmur, followed by delayed clapping. *The new deputy?* Prismer hardly noticed Benzun making his way onto the stage. By the time she had silenced her internal flurry of questions, the solemn young knyad had already occupied the seat next to Kemia.

Erud Teprill proceeded to describe Benzun's many accomplishments and the contributions he was sure to make to the field. But she failed to address a subject that had been the source of gossip in the Chambers for some phases—the absence of Benzun's predecessor, Oklas Sayve. Minister Kemia's expression was hard to discern, but the lines in her cheeks had deepened under the stage lights. By contrast, Erud Teprill was glowing—enjoying the mounting suspense in the room.

'The ministers behind me have collaborated on several occasions in service to this city and others abroad,' said the Erud, her voice as light as her sheer cape sleeves. 'All have made contributions in fields concerned with innovation, improving the health of Knyadrea's oceans, and the prosperity of our civilisation.'

Prismer straightened her back, bracing herself for whatever would follow.

When Erud Teprill spoke again, cold ire spiked her tone. 'Unfortunately, there are also those within our system of governance in whom we have misplaced our trust.' With that, she signalled the release of the locked presentation, and a capture flickered into view. It took Prismer a moment to process what she was seeing. The capture featured Oklas Sayve at a social event, surrounded by some of those now onstage. A few ministers bowed their heads, and Minister Dhara wriggled in her seat. Erud Teprill continued, 'I regret to inform you all that Minister Benzun's predecessor, Oklas Sayve, was arrested last revolution following investigations linking him to a known terrorist organisation.'

Prismer gripped the edge of the console as Erud Teprill elaborated on the details of Sayve's wrongdoings, dismantling him piece by piece. Within minutes, she had cast him as a betrayer and schemer who had used his position to plot against those he served. *Poor wretch*, thought Prismer. Dy Erla had worried his dealings with the Ardedrians would eventually become known. But how? Prismer's gut churned as she considered whether this was related to Ilu's escape. No—if it were, she and Rosh would have also been arrested by now.

Erud Teprill's serene face loomed large on two screens displayed on either side of the stage, shrinking the capture of Sayve into insignificance. 'Given his high profile in Apideccan society and his influence over younger generations, we deemed it necessary to close the Emisrian College of Innovation. Enforcers will continue investigating his former staff and students.' She surveyed the crowd, raising her graceful neck. 'But simply removing Oklas Sayve from office would not contain the spread of his dangerous ideology. Therefore, the decision was made to reclassify him under the maskad substratum.'

Inside the projection booth, Prismer crumpled. Had she been standing, her legs might have buckled under her.

'There have been only two other ministers in Apidecca's history to which this punishment has applied,' continued Erud Teprill. 'Relegating someone to this lesser mode of being is not a decision we take lightly. The Initiator is said to have made all knyads in Aer image: with hands eager to create and souls shining from our faces. But when a soul is as tainted as Sayve's, little else about him can be worthy of wholeness.'

The rest of Erud Teprill's words grew faint. Prismer went cold. She hunched over, unable to look at the capture of Minister Sayve any longer. The image depicted him in his element, enthralling those around him. Prismer could hear the breezy sound of his laughter even now—she had heard it only recently on a walk around the Crater Gardens. She couldn't breathe fast enough. It felt like her chest was about to burst. Sinking to the dark floor of the booth, Prismer pretended to adjust the cables beneath the console. For a moment, she was alone. She saw it now, the way the light hit Kosta's brow, the familiarity of the facial planes she had carved into his mask.

*It can't be easy working here*, he had told her in her living room, *being at the whims of so many self-important politicians.*

He had been one of them.

Prismer returned to her seat and trained her mask on the stage. This whole time she had been keeping the company of a minister. Feelings she could not name flooded her like the incoming tide, leaving her nauseous. But, until the meeting was over, she could not leave the booth. The Erud's words continued to rise and fall, and Prismer tried to focus on what she was saying.

'...manage the decay within dank corners of our city, but how much more rapidly will it spread from the heights of society? The Apideccan enforcers continue to protect our city with rousing dedication and unmatched efficiency. May these revelations serve as a reminder that both Praemor ministers and unclassified immigrants stand equal before the law.'

The sleights against Sayve began to pierce Prismer's defences. She knew the Pentarchy was biased against him, and she could not judge Sayve when she was a willing accomplice in some of his illegal activities. But what if Teprill wasn't entirely wrong about him? Had Prismer just been another component in his schemes?

'Sayve is being monitored, and his location will remain undisclosed,' said Erud Teprill. 'But rest assured that he is no longer in the position to cause further harm. It is our hope that, in his current state, he will be more receptive to rehabilitation. There are still many uses for those of his kind.'

Erud Teprill's deliberate gaze fell on the projection booth. Every instinct urged Prismer to look away from her. Instead she jutted out her chin, holding her masked face high. Now was not the time to shrink back and allow the Erud to demonstrate her mastery over maskads. On the screens, a smile flitted over Erud Teprill's lips.

The announcement came to an end, and Erud Teprill disappeared. All around, knyads dissolved into the aisles in a haze of rustling cloaks and whispers. Dazed, Prismer packed away the equipment. She stacked some items incorrectly, and the sound cones did not fit on the trolley. A figure loomed at her side, and she turned around to face Dy Erla. Apex Hall was almost empty now, the Pentarchy had departed, and only a few politicians lingered at the exits, too caught up in hushed gossip to pay the minister and the projectionist any heed.

'Minister Rhestat,' croaked Prismer, her dry throat closing on itself, 'I'm so sorry about today's news—about your colleague.'

'It came as a shock to us all,' replied Dy Erla, eying Prismer with a look that suggested they could not be too open in their support for Minister Sayve. 'Right now, it is you I am concerned over. You seem...out of sorts.'

In her conversations with Dy Erla, Prismer had not mentioned her encounters with Kosta. He had been her secret. She was glad of it now. 'It's nothing,' she said offhandedly, 'I'm just tired. I should probably lie down after this.'

'It was unfair of the Erud Speaker to single you out as the only maskad present,' said Dy Erla with a sympathetic frown. 'I'd understand if you felt uncomfortable with the whole of the Assembly's attention on you.'

After all that Prismer had learned, Erud Teprill's belittling comments about maskads were the least of her troubles, but she latched onto it as an excuse for her appearing shaken. 'It shouldn't have affected me. I was being unprofessional,' she said, looking the trolley over and reordering the sound cones and display extenders.

Dy Erla offered her help, interpreting Prismer's reluctance to talk as cause for a change of subject. 'I started to suspect Sayve was in trouble when Witalit Estate was repossessed. That building, and his college, had personal value to him. He wouldn't abandon them.'

Prismer remembered Dy Erla had been searching for her former colleague and wondered whether their paths had crossed since his scumbling. 'Have you had any success tracking him down?' she asked.

'I don't know where they have placed him,' said Dy Erla. 'I don't suppose you have met any recently-scumbled knyads at the support group?'

'No, not at Maskad Support,' said Prismer, pleased that the synthesiser disguised her evasive tone. 'If you will excuse me, Minister, I should return this to storage.' With a polite dip of her head, she wheeled the loaded trolley around.

'Prismer,' said Dy Erla gently, resting a hand on her back, 'are you going to be alright?'

'I will be,' she said, turning to look at Dy Erla from the corner of her eye gap. 'I'll explain more later.'

In some ways, telling Dy Erla about Kosta would ease the burden Prismer felt. But that was not her secret to share, and she needed time alone. Dy Erla was kind to her, but they weren't equal; it was plain as their difference in height. Nor were Oklas and her the same; the Pentarchy had only cut him down to her level.

Breaking into a run, Prismer pushed the trolley along, her gloved hands tensing around the handlebars. She threw her whole weight into pushing it up a ramp at speed. The muscles of her arms, her legs, and her back strained. She panted, heading down to the basement. From a side corridor, Ognitta yelled something about Prismer scuffing the floors with her boots. Prismer apologised, probably too quietly for the supervisor to hear, and slowed only a little.

Putting everything in its proper place in storage was a routine she knew well, and she performed it quickly today. Packing away items on the shelves, she bent and straightened her knees until they ached. Touching the cheek of her mask, she felt the forceful exhale of air coming from the filters at the side. She pushed herself to perform every task faster, hoping her heart would beat too quickly to feel, its sound drumming her noisy thoughts into silence.

On her way to the staff quarters, she ran again. Unencumbered by her load, Prismer's surroundings became a blur. The door to her insula streaked at her side, and she skidded to a stop. Once inside her room, she pulled out her drawers, searching them for something to take the edge off her nerves and clear her mind. Her fingers grasped the bulbous base of a familiar bottle. She pulled out the beroli extract, and noted with relief that it had not yet expired. Shakily, Prismer drew the dark liquid from the bottle with a dropper. Like a warming sap, it slid down her throat. It would not take effect instantly, but even knowing she had ingested it steadied the jitter in her hands.

Prismer had designed Kosta's mask while sitting here at the kitchen counter. She could still feel the weight of it in her hands, could trace the planes of the face she imagined beneath her fingers. She tried to picture it, but all she could see were blue irises flashing tauntingly at her from behind the eye gaps. The light that had been in Sayve's eyes was still there beneath Kosta's skin. But Prismer would never again admire the choreography of his elastic expressions.

'Stop it,' she scolded herself out loud. She had hardly taken the time to lament her own disfiguration, let alone his. Besides, she could not let herself think of him in that way.

Her skin itched with sweat. It was as if Erud Teprill's revelations had scurried up Prismer's sleeves and burrowed into her flesh. She fetched freshly laundered clothes from the basket in her room and headed back down the corridor to the staff showers.

# CHAPTER 25

## PRISMER

THE STAFF QUARTERS housed communal washrooms, showers, and laundry facilities. In each of these settings, Prismer used a designated cubicle or space. Ognitta wasn't one for making special accommodations, but it was a measure she took to allay the fears of the other staff. Some believed sharing facilities with a maskad would contaminate them. Prismer didn't object to the special treatment, though she sometimes wished they'd allow her to use the laundry machines instead of a scrubbing board.

Shower cubicles lined the wall of a chamber—the one at the end of the row was Prismer's. Sliding the curtain closed behind her, she removed her mask, putting it in the waterproof bag she had hung on a hook. She then began shedding the stale layers of her uniform. Her gills widened in a gasp as lashes of icy water hit her shoulders. It would not become much warmer, but at least the steam piped into the chamber made the air pleasantly humid. Holding herself, Prismer raised the lever with her free hand, increasing the flow and allowing the cold to envelop her. Each numbing splash brought her further clarity. Or maybe it was the beroli extract doing its work.

She caked her hands in a soapy lather, wiping it over her sinewy shoulders and down her arms. Scumbling had thickened and hardened her pale green skin, but the texture of it no longer alarmed her. Maybe protective armour was a necessary adaptation for someone like her. She studied the scales of her arms and the knotted edges of the scar beneath her cybernetics. Then there were the speckles marring her body—those at least had always been there. Seeing past the peculiar form of a maskad was an acquired skill. Prismer could find redeeming, even striking qualities in others of her kind. Folds of tough skin and ropey discolouration did not have to be ugly. The jagged edges of optic patterns could be quite mesmerising. And yet, nothing could match the profound beauty of emotion lighting even the plainest of faces.

Breathing in deeply, she opened her palms and closed her optic pattern over her eye. The revelations of the median meeting had rocked the Assembly. It was understandable that she, like everyone else, was in shock. But what was this ache in her chest? Prismer allowed herself to feel the pain, to make sense of it. She opened her eye again. A burning sensation rose to her jaw, and her hands balled into fists. Underneath her sorrow was something less decent: scalding anger at Kosta's deception, at her own ignorance. She could think of many reasons why he hadn't told her who he was, but none of them fully extinguished the feeling. What was she to do with it?

Sprays pattered and clicked against the ceramic tiles as Prismer finished rinsing herself. She stopped the flow of water and leaned against the wall, dripping. She missed Minister Sayve's presence in Apex Hall. Without him, the meetings were crushingly austere. She would also miss what she had with Kosta. In his presence, she laughed more easily. It lifted her spirits in a way that no tonic could. Knowing Sayve and Kosta were the same person, she felt she had lost them both.

After Prismer had helped him adjust to maskad life, Sayve shouldn't have needed anything more from her. So why did he continue to seek her company under the guise of Kosta? She did not possess the education, the social connections, or the charm to hold the interest of someone like him. Oklas Sayve belonged to no one; over the years, she had watched him move on from enough exquisite partners to know he never would.

Prismer grabbed her towel and dried herself. Even as a tideling, she knew she preferred a solitary lifestyle. She hadn't shared a room with anyone since parting from her harvestmates. Scumbling sealed her decision, changing her in ways that repelled most knyads. Had it never happened, would she have eventually sought out someone to inconvenience her? Strangely, the things she did for Dy Erla, Illanu, and now Kosta, she did willingly. Her regular outings with her maskad companion weren't as tiring as expected; she actually felt better for them. He had almost lulled her into sharing the parts of herself she had buried the deepest. Almost.

She had still confided in him more than she should have. Inside, she was no different from any other knyad; her transformation had not relieved her of that old longing to be understood. Now fully awake, she saw her revolution with the golden-eyed maskad for what it was: a fading dream.

◦◈═◦◉◦═◈◦

Dressed in a plain white fulver, Prismer left the showers. It was still early. If she returned to her insula now, the segeind would stretch on for an unbearably long time. She glanced again at the message draft hovering above her wrist, reading, "Kosta, can I meet you outside the Crater Gardens now?" Taking a deep breath, she sent it. A reply came before she reached street level: Kosta would see her there.

The earlier rains had left the ground damp but not saturated with puddles. As the High Street fell into deeper shadow, the clubs of the Upper End stirred to life. Music pounded the walls and pavement, reverberating in Prismer's chest as she passed. She reached the entrance to the gardens and saw Kosta waiting for her. Until she heard otherwise from him, "Kosta" is who he would remain. Prismer clung to the slight possibility that the maskad up ahead was someone ordinary like her. But looking at him now, she could not help seeing something of the deputy minister in Kosta's light-footed stance, in the way he swayed back and forth like a reed in a gentle current, his head turning to take in the activities around him. His gaze landed on Prismer, and he reached her in a few quick strides.

Kosta invited a hug, and Prismer's fingers flexed at her side. She caught his arm, lowering it in a more cordial greeting. He adjusted his posture, breezing through the awkwardness.

The cautious grip of Kosta's clawed fingers did not feel like the buoyant arm-grasps the minister gave. But Prismer recognised the blue hue of his skin, even if it was a little duller than before. A couple of beige flecks splintered the dark background of his wrist, discolouration caused by scumbling. He tilted his head curiously at her, watching her studying his hand. She quickly released it.

'So this is what it is like to arrive early,' he said cheerfully. Indeed, it was the first time he had reached one of their meeting places before Prismer. 'I should try it more often, if only for the people-watching.'

'Thank you for coming on such short notice,' she said in a too-formal voice.

'I knew you had a spontaneous streak, how could I not encourage it?' He led her through the arches to the gardens beyond. 'I was about to catch the tram home, but I'm glad you stopped me. Look at the colours in the sky.'

Prismer had hardly noticed the pool of rosy light above them. Layered pink gauze reached towards one or two bright stars, while more voluminous clouds lined in gold drifted at lower levels. Kosta raised a hand in a sweeping gesture, following the contours. 'All this will have faded by tomorrow segeind.'

She nodded. 'That's the nature of special things—they don't last.'

'Is something wrong?' he asked, concern plucking at his voice.

'It's, uh—' Until now, Prismer had thought she was holding up well. Trust Kosta to pick up on her discomfort. He had a frightening sensitivity to the slightest shifts in a person. 'It was a long median,' she finished. 'Let's go for a walk.' She didn't know how to go about this. A part of her had come here to rage at him. But now that he was next to her, her anger dissipated. Kosta had lost so much more than even she had and still, he considered others.

There were fewer knyads in the Crater Gardens than on their last visit, though some still gathered in clearings or on the sunny eastern side to admire the sky. Prismer and Kosta followed their familiar path up to a place where the buildings of Lepotra, now cast in the shade of the gorge, peeked over the crater's edge. Artificial lights blinked from some of their windows.

They stopped at a rocky outcrop. Above them, pegwings skittered from their roosting holes. Prismer perched on a rock, the low rays of sunlight warming her back. Opposite her, Kosta remained standing with his hands behind his back. There was something expectant about his upright posture; he was waiting for her to speak.

She looked to the Praemor district above and said, 'You lived there once, didn't you?'

He went rigid, stepping back into the shadow of a pillar. Hesitantly, he followed Prismer's gaze. 'Yes,' he said softly, 'yes I did.'

The admission, a grain of truth, brought Prismer some consolation, but she couldn't wait for him to decide how much more he would share. 'Of course, you can't see the Crater Gardens from Ironglade Heights,' she added, indicating to the part of Lepotra that curved out of sight, 'but I'd imagine it has a lovely view of the city...and your college.'

The maskad she had come to know as Kosta exhaled a whimper, as if struck in the abdomen. He bowed his head. The ruse had ended.

As still as the rocks around her, Prismer watched him.

The maskad took a deep breath and lifted his chin. Just like that, it was no longer Kosta but Minister Sayve looking back at her from behind the mask. 'I've wanted to tell you for so long. How did—'

'I didn't figure it out,' said Prismer abruptly, brushing one hand over the other in her lap, 'but I should have. The Assembly made an announcement today—about the crimes of Oklas Sayve.'

'Crimes?' He gave a hollow laugh.

'And his sentencing.'

'Of course, they have done everyone a favour by removing me from society.' He started pacing agitatedly. 'Just how much did they disclose? Did they mention their plans for the Emisrian College?'

White-hot energy flashed through Prismer and she sprang from the rock, thrusting her fists at her sides. 'I did not come here to report facts to you,' she fumed. 'I am not a member of your staff anymore!'

The skin of Sayve's neck and arms paled. 'It's not like that, Pir.'

'It's Prismer,' she said stiffly, walking further into the shadows.

He followed her, seeking her face. 'I must know what they will publicise about me. I ask this of you as a friend.'

'Are we friends?' she asked, her throat tautening. 'I'm not sure I've had a friend since I left my clan.'

'What about Dy Erla?'

'Dy?' scoffed Prismer. 'She only helps me out of pity or some misplaced sense of duty. I can't do anything for her without her repaying me.' How churlish, how ungrateful she sounded, but she couldn't hold back the tide of emotion now that it had burst forth. 'I suppose I was glad to help someone else for a change. When Ognitta brought you to my rooms that segment, I felt useful. It's all I can hope to be.'

'Useful? Prismer, there is so much more to you than that.'

'No. Please don't say that.' Prismer stopped Sayve with her palms raised. She continued, her voice low and hoarse, 'It may not seem like it, but I am easily moved by kind words, even when I know they are only lies.' Sayve took a step back, stricken. It had to be said, but why did it hurt Prismer to see him like this? Raggedly dressed in his loose-fitting overalls, there was no trace of his usual flashiness.

'Forgive me,' she said, rubbing her mask, 'I chose a bad time to confront you about this. You'd think after all my years of watching politicians, I would've learned when to say something and how to say it. But I don't have your different settings.' She sank to her knees and lowered her head. 'I sometimes wish I did.'

'Prismer, you don't want to be like I was. Please, look at me,' said Sayve, kneeling in front of her. She stared into the depths of the mask she had made. He spread his hands out helplessly. 'This is all there is now. If anyone has seen the real Oklas Sayve recently, it's you.'

He meant it; she could hear it in his voice, which was rawer than she had ever known it to be. She sighed. 'You came to me because you didn't have another maskad to turn to.'

He nodded. 'I know it must seem like I used you.'

'You did.'

'To some extent,' he allowed. 'I planned on telling you who I was. I know that doesn't help now.'

They sat in the angled rays of sunlight. Around them, dappled shadows washed over the floor. After a while, Sayve stood up and placed a hand on his chest. 'What would you ask of me?'

'I—' The question caught Prismer off guard. She was still reeling from the events of the segment. 'I can't think of anything now.'

'You don't have to trust me; don't even have to see me again if you don't want to. But if you'd like to discuss this more, I'll be at the Husk and Brewer's after work tomorrow.'

She looked up at his mask. 'I'll be there too.'

In silence, they walked back the way they came. When they reached the High Street, Prismer turned to Sayve and said, 'During the announcement, they didn't mention "Kosta" or the Consortium. I don't think they plan on sharing it.'

He inclined his head at her. 'Thank you for letting me know. Goodbye, Prismer.' Slowly, he backed away before taking a path to Gilstren.

Prismer looked up at the street-side buildings. Above them rose the turreted exterior of the Assembly Chambers. *She did want to see Sayve again.* But she would never again set up a presentation for him in Apex Hall. Where could they go from here?

Prismer always looked for solutions from within, not because she thought she was always right—she had outgrown that—but because she could see into no one else's mind but her own. 'Please help me to be as honest as he thinks I am,' she whispered, surprised that, for once, she was turning to Adecai before herself. She needed the knyad god to grant her the hope she could not muster. 'Please don't let me pull away as I always do.'

Sayve wanted to talk, and she owed him some secrets of her own. They might drive him from her but maybe it was better if that happened now, before they grew any closer. It was already too late for her to separate from him painlessly.

# CHAPTER 26

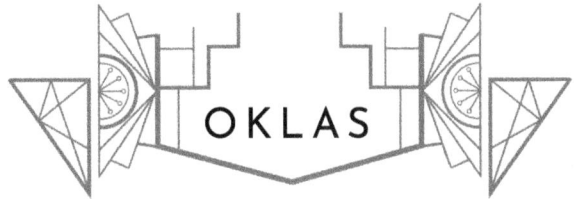

## OKLAS

OKLAS HAD BOOKED a table on the highest floating floor in the Husk and Brewer. He drew out Prismer's chair and pulled the curtain around their table, blocking them from view so they could unmask. He hadn't noticed the curtains on his last visit: it was doubtful they could do much to muffle a conversation to those outside. At least theirs was the only table on the small platform.

Oklas unbuckled his mask, removing the first barrier between them, and Prismer followed suit. She demurely took to her seat, then shrugged off the weatherproof coat he had seen her in last dark phase; beneath it, she wore her embroidered grey fulver. By candlelight, her dark red head-scarf matched the colour of her optic pattern. In Prismer's eye, Oklas saw the highly reflective surface of a leaf-stained river. The movements over her face were difficult to read, but as compelling as cloud formations or abstract art. The more he studied her appearance, the more he came to accept his own.

Heart skipping faster, Oklas passed his mask from one hand to the other. 'It's not especially private here, but I couldn't think of many alternatives.'

'It's perfect,' she assured him in a low voice, some of the mechanical rigidity in her posture easing. 'Now please, sit.'

Relieved, he obeyed and dropped onto his chair in a rumpled heap of blue fabric. He could count on Prismer to be direct when he did not know what he was doing. He had not expected he would be this nervous seeing her again. Before coming here, he had changed from his overalls into his best tunic. Prismer didn't pay much attention to fancy clothes, but he wanted to put in some effort. Despite their history, it felt like this was his chance to introduce himself to her properly. Whether or not this would be their last meeting was for her to decide.

'Thank you for coming, Pir,' he began. Remembering the nickname had angered her, he covered his eye with his hand. 'Sorry, *Prismer*.'

'I've had some time to think about it, and I'll allow "Pir",' she said, sweeping the scarf over her shoulder like a thick plait. She twisted it back into a coil at the side of her head. 'I'm just not sure what to call you. I only ever knew you as Minister Sayve.'

He shuddered at the formality of his old title and protruded his chin in a would-be smile. 'Oklas is fine.'

'Alright—Oklas,' she said, squeezing her eye almost shut. The edges of her optic pattern fizzed with mischief. Oklas couldn't help but chuckle. At that moment, she reminded him of a tideling repeating an offensive word she had just learned.

A bell rang behind the curtain, announcing the presence of their waiter, a fellow maskad. Oklas felt a swell of appreciation for Gazda, who went out of his way to employ those who needed jobs most. The tall maskad took their orders: for Prismer, redlint tea, and for Oklas, a flask of kahv—with a shot of bitters—to ease the flow of his synth-speech.

His companion rested her elbow on the table. 'Should I keep calling you "Kosta" when people are around?'

'I trust it to your discretion,' he replied. 'After the news breaks, my co-workers at the Consortium will no doubt figure out who I am. Hopefully no one else will.'

'The Eruds hide behind their enigma, but ministers?' Prismer shook her head. 'It's like no part of your life is truly yours.'

'It had its benefits. I didn't look for fame, but some part of me must have wanted it because when the spotlight came, I never tried to hide from it.'

'You'll still have some anonymity under your new name—the Assembly will make sure of it—but after tomorrow, there is not a city in Knyadrea that won't hear what happened to Oklas Sayve.'

'It will be the last time I dishonour my home clan.' He gave a rueful laugh. 'There are so many people I will never see again. So many friends who will never hear my side of the story.'

Prismer leaned forwards. 'Anyone who knows you well won't believe the Assembly's version of events.'

'You know how many guises I wore in politics. I'm not sure those I care about—or even I—can easily tell them apart anymore.' He reached up, reflexively pushing phantom tendrils back from his forehead; his fingers met only skin. 'There is one peer in particular...I worry she will think—' Oklas stopped himself. It seemed inappropriate to mention Kelabek here.

'Who is she?'

'Someone I met at the Induction Ball. Nothing had started between us, but maybe that is why I still think of her occasionally. She is a mirage, all the possibilities just beyond my reach.'

On the other side of the curtain, a bell rang. The waiter served them their drinks in pump flasks—the simple designs appealed to the inventor in Oklas. Pressing the button in the lid of the flask siphoned the liquid through a funnel connected to a tube which fed into a maskad's beak. The cheaper pitchers he had bought offered a quicker way of feeding, but they did not look this sophisticated. He missed the sharp flavour of kahv on his tongue, though his gills could pick up rich, invigorating scents he had not noticed before.

'Something has been bothering me,' said Prismer, stirring cold water with the steeped redlint flowers in her flask. 'You were arrested shortly after Ilu's escape. I keep wondering if there was some evidence I had left behind, some detail I'd forgotten that traced them back to you.'

'It wasn't your fault,' said Oklas firmly. 'Teprill had all this planned before you even met with Illanu.' He swallowed his spiked kahv. 'Evidence of my collaboration with the Ardedrians was unearthed from my records at the college. I was careless.'

As she listened, Prismer's tea trickled from the glass mixing rod she held onto the cuff of her sleeve. She made a tutting sound and put it down. 'I'm sorry if I was a bit terse with you after the announcement,' she said. 'It was a lot to take in.'

'I should have told you who I was from the start—here.' Oklas dampened a serviette and offered to dab her sleeve. Steam wafted from Prismer's flask, and a spicy, wooded fragrance filled the air.

'To think,' she said, 'I was telling someone who has sent satellites into orbit about putting up kites in the Traditional Quarter.'

'I enjoyed learning about them,' said Oklas, patting the fabric dry, a sienna stain absorbed into the tissue.

'I am glad *you* did—I'm still getting over the embarrassment of it.' Prismer withdrew her gloved hand and tucked the damp part of her sleeve under her fingers.

'If anyone should be embarrassed, it's me. Thankfully I have very little shame. Maybe you wouldn't either if you mixed bitters with your redlint.' He held the flask aloft. The front of Prismer's gills puckered, hinting at what may have once been a dimpled smile. A veiled image of her features popped into Oklas's mind, only to disappear before he could specify the shape of her nose or mouth.

Swiftly siphoning the last of his kahv, he removed the tube from his beak and said, 'I want to apologise that you had to find out about me the way you did. And for all the times I caused you problems at the Assembly.'

'You don't need my forgiveness,' she said, setting down her flask. 'It really isn't worth that much.'

'I disagree on both counts.'

He was coming to know the obstinate set of her chin. Her eye roved over her face in a circle, and she sighed. 'Of course I forgive you.'

A weight lifted from Oklas's shoulders. 'I do hope we can keep up these outings. It's not often that I find someone who has the patience to listen to me, let alone give thoughtful responses.'

Prismer rocked the glass rod up and down between her fingers, the red patterns of her face suddenly downcast. 'Please don't think too highly of me, Oklas. It only makes this harder.'

'Prismer, if this is about your stealing from the Chambers, I already told you it doesn't matter.'

'There is more to it than that. You don't know what I was like.'

'Then tell me.' Oklas sat back in his chair, his open palms coaxing her into speaking. Whatever the nature of her secrets, he would hear her.

Prismer cleared a space on the table before her, as if about to roll out one of her maps. 'I used to buy materials for my commissions from Viren & Stone in the Traditional Quarter,' she said, eying Oklas. 'A maskad begged outside the shop every segment. People called him Tatters, for the frayed clothes he wore. I never learned his real name. Now, I should tell you what I believed about maskads at the time because it impacted everything else. I was raised on cautionary tales about twisted, faceless creatures. But, until I arrived in Apidecca, I had never seen a maskad. They weren't the ghouls I'd expected, but I noticed people still didn't want to be near them. My co-workers told me this was because maskads carried a disfiguring disease. It made sense, so I believed them.

'On windy segs, Heykel used to invite Tatters inside the shop. It angered me; I couldn't understand how he wasn't afraid of being infected or why he put his customers at risk. I never said anything to him, but Heykel knew how I felt by the glares I shot him, or the way I held my breath when I passed Tatters.'

Prismer's usually straight posture folded inwards. Ruby threads tangled around her narrowed eye. 'I never asked Tatters about his condition. My assumptions were all I needed.'

Her stories about maskads differed from those Oklas had heard, but he understood what it was to be frightened of the unknown, fascinated by it. So many unspoken terrors consolidated in the hollow eyes of a mask.

'It's not a simple—' His counterargument died in his throat. Prismer did not want him to absolve her of guilt or console her. But Oklas could offer better than that. 'You know, developing tidelings take on the colours and textures of the seabeds around them. From the start, our environment shapes who we are. We don't always see it, but we are similarly influenced by what the people around us believe.' He reached for her hand, his fingertips brushing her gloves. 'You are not alone in battling your own prejudices.'

Her fingers curled instinctively over the edge of her mask; it lay at the table's centre, flashing yellow in the candlelight. 'If I had taken up that battle sooner, perhaps I wouldn't have made so many mistakes. I did something awful, something I'll never forget.'

Haltingly, she began to recount her story. Soon she was so fully inhabiting it that Oklas lost any inclination to interrupt her with questions. A scene unfolded before him.

The Traditional Quarter of fifteen years ago was much the same as it was today; shopfronts and even fashions changed little there. From the painted doorway of a quaint shop emerged a juvenile with dark, watchful eyes. She wore the maroon uniform of a General Assembly technician.

Prismer described her past self distantly, as if she were a younger harvest-mate confined to this moment.

Encumbered by a case of carving stone, the young Prismer's progress down the cobbled street was slower than usual. She had neglected to bring along a trolley that segment and had tucked the case under her arm, the base resting uncomfortably on her right hip.

Through the corner of her eye, she spied her likeness in the window-pane of a shop. A bundle of feathery tendrils beat her back in a rustling tempo that matched her stride, but her attention snagged on something lurking a few paces behind her. She recognised Maskad Tatters by his umber robes and the shroud he wore over his face, grotesquely cinched at the neck. Suppressing a surge of fear, she assured herself that the maskad had no reason to follow her from the shop. Nevertheless, she quickened her pace. Behind her, flapping fabric suggested the maskad was also walking faster. A glance at the windows showed the creature close behind her, his hollow gaze fixed on her. Everything inside Prismer demanded she run, and she took heed.

Hurtling down the congested street, she took care to dodge passing knyads. She kept up her urgent pace for another block, her footfalls pounding the cobbles—but the foul creature was closing in on her, following the path she had whittled between pedestrians. Glimpsing her pursuer from over her shoulder, Prismer considered dropping her load. Better to let him steal the case of alabaster than rip the cybernetics from—

The thought was interrupted by a dull *thud* as she smacked into something wooden. A hard edge dug into her chest and elbow, throwing her off-balance. The street whipped around her, and she found herself sprawled on the ground next to an aftill cart. Flipping onto her side, she kicked against cobbles to back away from the approaching maskad.

'Stay away from me!' her voice broke in a terrified cry, ricocheting off the surrounding whitewashed walls. Every knyad in the street was watching them. Maskad Tatters froze as if impaled. A storm of sound and movement followed. Arms reached for the fallen juvenile, helping her up, while an enforcer escorted the maskad away.

'I had almost reached home when Heykel called me on my mitter,' said the person sitting opposite Oklas, the Prismer he knew. 'An enforcer had dropped off something of mine: the keys to the Assembly storeroom.

Heykel had seen them fall from my pocket as I left Viren & Stone, and Tatters offered to run after me and return them.' There was a slight twitch around Prismer's gills as she added, 'Of course, the enforcer thought he had stolen the keys. Tatters told aer they belonged to the shop, hoping Heykel could clear things up.'

'And did he?' asked Oklas.

'The enforcers didn't believe his story. I went to the High Street station to explain what had happened. Tatters still had to spend a revolution in a labour commune up the coast. Too many people had seen the "assault". It even made the news—only as an ancillary article, mind you.'

The low thrumming of many speech synthesisers drifted up from the floors below. Oklas grasped for a way to show Prismer he understood the gravity of what she had shared. 'It was a misunderstanding,' he said artlessly. 'At least you tried to correct it.'

'Not the way you would have,' said Prismer. 'I was afraid to defend him too adamantly in case it hurt my career aspirations. I told myself no one cared for the truth anyway.'

'What happened was bigger than you, Prismer; bigger than anyone there.' Oklas's fingers straddled her side of the table. 'Witnesses would have reported what they thought they saw. The authorities use incidents like that to maintain the public's fear of maskads. If they had released Tatters, it would've brought too much into question.'

Prismer shook her head. 'I knew I had disappointed Heykel that segment. I never apologised to him or Tatters. Unable to face them, I stopped going to Viren & Stone and started taking more materials from the Chambers' workshop. It all went wrong from there. For a long time, I believed Adecai intended that I take that path. That Ae wanted me scumbled.'

'I hope you don't entertain such thoughts anymore,' said Oklas firmly.

'I don't,' replied Prismer, folding her arms. 'My choices led me here, not fate. I had become so obsessed with my work, I hadn't even tried making friends in the city. When my life fell apart, I couldn't expect anyone to care. I'd closed myself off from everyone long before I became a maskad.'

Oklas considered her from the other side of the small table. 'It doesn't have to stay that way. You have to forgive yourself.'

'I think Adecai has forgiven me, which is, perhaps, even better.' Her eye widened in a faraway look, while the rest of her face remained inscrutable. 'Ae sent me Dy Erla when I had no one else. She always has a way of knowing what I need. I trust her.'

Oklas fidgeted, tapping his boot against the leg of his chair. He had leveraged that trust when he asked Dy Erla to go to Prismer with his request. 'I can finally thank you for what you did for Illanu,' he said. 'You can't be all bad, Prismer. Not everyone would risk themselves for a stranger like that.' Among the red daubs that made up Prismer's optic pattern, Oklas searched for her core. He sensed her doing the same with him.

She lowered her gaze. 'I didn't leave Apidecca when I should have. I thought if I could stop someone from sharing my fate...well, it wouldn't make up for anything, but—'

'You rescued my student,' concluded Oklas, 'after I had endangered her.'

'Your students are old enough to make their own decisions, to adopt your politics if they choose. You only ever opened them up to possibilities.' Prismer's ears flattened against her head as she added, 'You should never have been scumbled.'

'Because of my philanthropy?' Oklas gave a dry laugh, then swallowed hard. 'I also gained from running the college. It offered a welcome reprieve from the tediousness of the Assembly. Yes, I drew most of my students from the unclassified stratum, but they were all young, bright, enthusiastic. Not one among them was a maskad. I excluded those who are as I am now because ... '—his synthesiser cut off as he considered his words—'because I found them off-putting.'

Not long ago, he wouldn't have admitted to such a thing. It was too candid. But he could not hurt Prismer with the truth; it was her preferred language, and he wanted to honour that. 'We always worked so well together, you and I,' he said. 'If I had been a better person, I would have tried to learn more about you.' He lifted Prismer's mask from the table and studied it. 'I wouldn't have let this come between us.' Gently, he set it down in front of her. The worried tangle around Prismer's ruby eye dissolved, and her jaw unclenched. Oklas could not be sure if she had meant to speak—they were interrupted by a shout from somewhere near the pub entrance. He got up and pulled back the curtain. Some maskads jostled for the exit. Above the modulated voices, Gazda called for everyone to remain calm.

Oklas looked back to see Prismer standing in her coat and putting on her mask.

'What's going on?' he asked as she shoved his mask into his hands.

'Cover up,' she urged, just loud enough for him to hear above the commotion, 'it's a raid.'

Oklas hurried over to the window at their level and slid it fully open. A cold rush of air prickled the sides of his head.

Behind him, Prismer hissed, 'Okl-Kosta, what are you—'

Oklas hopped off the window ledge and onto the deck of a neighbouring property. He motioned for her to follow. She tore her gaze from the lower floors and leapt after him. There was a rumble of furniture inside the pub, and new voices barked instructions. Oklas closed the window behind them.

The buildings lining the street blinked in and out of view, keeping time with the flashing lights of parked scramblers below. Oklas avoided the edge of the deck, where he would be in view of any enforcers waiting outside the Husk and Brewer.

'This way,' said Prismer as she gripped a pillar and launched herself onto the balcony of a neighbouring shop. Unable to offer a viable alternative to this, Oklas trailed her, clearing the two-alkar gap between the buildings. He had not thought this far ahead. The patchwork architecture of the Dolna District—of the entire Lower End, for that matter—was a mystery to him. The balcony they had landed on turned out to be a continuous platform that ran along the front of the building. The metal floor thudded lightly under their boots as they passed rows of shops. Oklas searched their surroundings for a route to street level. He hoped it wouldn't come to clambering over dormers, quoins, and jutting belt courses.

Prismer caught him peering over the handrail. 'Come on,' she whispered, 'I think I know of a way down.'

'Where?'

She placed a finger over the lips of her mask and held her other hand over his throat. 'Some of the shop owners live here, above their premises. We must try not to wake them.'

They reached the end of the block, but the platform did not open onto a stairway as Oklas had hoped it would. Prismer tapped him on the shoulder, and he turned around. At the side of the building, the platform extended over an alley, forming a bridge to a neighbouring building. A gate blocked their path to the bridge and the cylindrical structure beyond it. Locked in the cylinder of metal vines was a spiral staircase.

Prismer tried pulling and pushing the bridge gate open, but it didn't budge. She swung her leg over the handrail, her boot finding a quoin at the corner of the building.

Little of the night sky was visible here, and there were no street lights in the dark alley but, lifting his mask, Oklas saw the pavement far below quite clearly. 'Prismer, is this part of the plan?'

'It is now. Just stay quiet—I need to concentrate.'

Gripping the mesh-covered sides of the bridge, she started to side-step her way across. There was just enough space for her feet on the outer edge of the platform. Prismer leaned over to reach for the wrought iron bars of the cylindrical cage. They were mere degets beyond her reach.

'It's too far,' said Oklas. 'We'll have to think of another—'

She jumped, her arms outstretched. Clawing at the metal shapes, she pulled herself up and found her footing on a serpentine branch. She looped the elbow of her cybernetically-altered arm through the bars and wove her other wrist through a metal vine, securing herself to the side of the cylinder. Feral energy charged Prismer's practised scrambling. It animated her limbs in a way Oklas had not seen at the Chambers. Here, she was as graceful as any dancer.

From inside the building, more searchlights appeared. The enforcers knew someone had fled the Husk and Brewer. Oklas followed Prismer's route to the edge of the spiral staircase, breathing slowly and focusing on each step.

'Come,' said Prismer urgently, holding out her good arm.

Balancing precariously on the ledge outside the bridge, Oklas had no space to gain momentum ahead of a jump. 'I don't know if I can make it.'

'You should have thought of that before you climbed out the window back at the pub.' She raised her mask to meet his. 'I won't let you fall.' As if to emphasise her promise, she extended her arm further.

Oklas gripped her hand and propelled himself from the railing. Prismer swung him against the cage, and his fingers flexed, snapping closed around one of the curling vines. He quickly entwined his limbs with whatever ornamentation was in reach.

'Well done,' said Prismer breathlessly as she started scaling the side of the cage. Oklas tried not to think of the enforcers as he followed her route to the other side of the sheathed staircase.

The climb down was even more thrilling than Oklas's Dahn sessions at the gymnasium, though he could have done without being chased. He had expected to struggle swinging from bar to bar. For phases he had watched his muscles atrophy, but the grip strength of his altered hands was actually better than before. The thicker skin of his palms prevented him from slipping, and he felt only a little strain in the joints of his long fingers as they supported his weight. Prismer matched his pace, never moving more than a few alkar ahead of him. She always leaned to her right, as if she didn't trust her cybernetics on the other side not to let her down. The pair continued the rest of the way to the ground.

Oklas's legs wobbled as he hit the floor, but there was no time to recover. Voices came from the platform high above and flashlights passed over the alley. Prismer rounded a corner and entered the street, and Oklas sprinted after her. They quietly strode away, blending into the light pedestrian traffic of the Dolna District. Prismer continued to check for signs of enforcers until the back streets connected to the more populated High Street. Lost in a crowd of unclassified and Orta workers—and several other maskads—they passed oddly-constructed shacks protruding from dim rows of buildings. A few knyads gathered under the light of street-side algae panels.

They stopped in a quiet pocket in the Lower End, panting. In a sudden release of nervous energy, Oklas burst out laughing. Within moments, Prismer was laughing too.

'Poor Gazda,' she said, between gulps of air. 'We will need to transfer him our substants tomorrow.'

'Is the Husk and Brewer raided often?' asked Oklas.

'In the dark phases—yes. All the regulars are used to it. The enforcers search you for stolen goods or illegal substances. Usually, nothing happens if you comply.'

'Why didn't you tell me?'

'I was trying to when you started running. After that, we had to do things the hard way.'

Oklas remembered the enforcers pursuing them from inside the building. It must have looked like they had something to hide. 'It was a fun way to end the segment,' he said. 'You are as good a guide as Dy Erla says.'

Prismer glowed at the compliment.

Together they slowly made their way towards the Lower End tram terminal. Oklas drew closer to Prismer, and cupped his hand over the side of his synthesiser.

'Since we've been confessing things...I think it's only fair that you know I am working with the Ardedrians again.'

Prismer walked on, looking at the glistening wet flagstone pavement as Oklas explained that his workshop in the Industrial Park was actually a laboratory, and that the friend who had provided it was none other than the Ardedrian leader, Keanon Caswor. He even brought up Rosh's involvement.

'I thought Rosh had been evasive recently,' said Prismer, tucking the ruffled fabric of her scarf under the buckles of her mask.

'He'll be relieved that you now know who I am; it bothered him that you didn't.'

Prismer hummed approvingly, then asked, 'You're still on probation, aren't you? Don't you worry the Assembly is monitoring you, that you might draw them to the base?'

'I know I have a poor record with precautions, but Keanon and Yvere don't. They are looking out for me.'

Prismer halted him with a raised hand. 'It's better if I don't know much more. I can't be part of this.'

'I understand if you'd rather we didn't see each other after this. If you felt safer.'

'No, I didn't mean—' She faltered as a tram pulled up. They hurried to join the queue at the terminal. Prismer turned her back to the knyads in front of them and lowered her voice. 'I won't come and meet your "friends" or visit your laboratory. But whether I like it or not, I am involved because you and Rosh are. Perhaps you can tell me about your research? I always looked forward to your presentations.'

'There isn't much to tell,' he admitted.

'Maybe not yet.'

They boarded the tram and shuffled past the other passengers. At the back, they held onto the hanging straps and Oklas told Prismer of his vision for Knyadrea: of space exploration and his quest for the resources that would enable it, of his desire to better understand resyn and solve the problem of its scarcity. Prismer listened intently, occasionally stopping him and commenting on details that interested her or asking a question he had not considered. Not once did she point out the ridiculousness of his goals.

All too soon, they reached the Gilstren station, and Oklas disembarked.

# CHAPTER 27

## PRISMER

S EVERAL KNYADS LEFT the tram ahead of Prismer as she gathered her groceries. She walked to the exit and looked over a dark sea of faces outlined by neon lights. There was not a mask in sight at the Upper End Tram Terminal. Something brushed against her shoulder. She pivoted on the spot, and a familiar mask spun into view. Oklas leaned against the side of the tram with one leg crossed over the other, languidly brandishing a roll of informaprint.

'Kosta,' she said, clutching his arm. It was the name she would always associate with her friend. But "Oklas" was also coming more naturally to her, gradually replacing "Minister Sayve" in her mind. It had been almost a phase since, from the window of another tram, Prismer had watched him disappear behind a row of buildings verging the Gilstren station.

He had dressed more smartly that segeind, looking more the urbane minister than the underpaid engineer. Tonight, he wore a dark jacket over his Consortium overalls, with a rucksack slung over his shoulder. Prismer was also in uniform, though she had quickly pulled her weatherproof coat over it before heading out to buy ingredients for their segeind meal. Other commuters parted around them, and the pair moved on. Unfurling the informaprint, Oklas pointed near the bottom edge of the page.

'Take a look—I'd like to hear what you think.'

Prismer accepted the paper. After a median of Minister Albryn addressing her as though she were no more alive than the machines she operated, it was refreshing to have someone ask for her opinion. Of course, she would have preferred Oklas to ask her for feedback on something less provocative than an article entitled "Disgraced Minister Still at Large?". She missed the simplicity of advising him to reduce the number of images in his presentations. It had been a difficult phase for him as he dealt with the aftermath of his ousting being made public, which was why she had invited him to her home after work.

Prismer folded away the informaprint as she and Oklas passed through the congested terminal gates. The dim green light of algae panels, highlighting the edges of figures, didn't easily distinguish maskad from knyad. People drew closer to Prismer than they did in daylight. Someone did a double-take in her direction and startled at the sight of a frozen mask where ae expected to see a face.

The pair of maskads continued down Clanfare Avenue, which curved outside the Assembly Chambers' moat. Prismer glanced again at the informaprint, which turned out to be a Shell-to-Ear publication. It looked much like the other media reports on Oklas's crimes. At least he was not making headlines anymore; that honour went to a merchants' conference at the Silversteam Trade Centre. Only four segments ago, news agencies released the bare facts of Sayve's arrest and conviction. Most publications gave bloated retrospectives on Oklas's irregular political career, but the Shell-to-Ear skirted closer to reality. The article claimed Sayve was still working in the city at an undisclosed Upper End facility.

The Shell-to-Ear was one of only a few circulating publications unapproved by the authorities. While controversial, it did not drastically depart from the Pentarchy's narratives, so it endured, albeit with a small print run. Prismer supported the crinkled paper between her fingers. Above the text was a portrait of Oklas Sayve, the Exhibitionist, someone far removed from the overall-clad maskad at her side. His smile came across as smarmy in the capture, a pity because Prismer knew it to be genuine by the way it touched his eyes.

She looked up to see Oklas staring at his portrait on the page in her hands. He snorted. 'I'm tired of seeing my face everywhere except in the mirror.'

Prismer loosely rolled the informaprint. 'Has anyone come asking after you at the Consortium?'

'No,' he replied, 'the directors have taken measures to contain the spread of rumours. No one is allowed to give interviews about the recent appointment of a maskad.'

'And outside of the Consortium, will you be safe?' asked Prismer. Only yesterday Oklas had told her over the mitter that he had come home to find a pane in his window shattered.

'I'll be fine,' said Oklas, burrowing his hands into his jacket pockets. 'Nothing was taken from my insula. I don't have anything anyone would want to steal. It could have been one of the neighbours prying.'

Prismer gave an unconvinced nod and slowed to match his more casual gait. 'Do you think your neighbours suspect anything?'

He shrugged. 'Maybe. There must be hundreds of maskads in this city; any one of us could be Oklas Sayve. Someone is probably fed up with him about the delayed tram upgrades and chose to vent their frustrations on my window.'

'You know you are welcome to stay as long as you need.'

'Thank you, Prismer, but it'll probably look less suspicious if I return as soon as the glazier has repaired the window. I ought to check on her work sooner rather than later; she's already overcharging me.'

As they walked, the rows of buildings diverged from Clanfare Avenue so that each new property was set further back from the moat than the last. The Chambers rose many stories high, blocking out the moonlight. The unassuming gate to the staff quarters was in sight. Together, Prismer and Oklas crossed the moat bridge.

Pressing her key into the indentation of the security gate, Prismer held her mitter under the scanner. It buzzed open, and she smuggled Oklas through. Mercifully, the corridors were clear, but even if none of her co-workers saw "Kosta" with her tonight, she still had to contend with her supervisor. Ognitta needed to grant permission to any visitors staying after curfew. It reminded Prismer of the dormitory rules for tidelings, and her face flushed beneath her mask. Her supervisor had been a little too delighted to learn that she had kept in touch with Kosta after their chance meeting; it was unlikely that Ognitta would object to his stay. But Prismer wasn't sure she was ready for the knowing looks and rampant assumptions. Ognitta's hand-carved door lay ahead, only a few steps away from the street-level gate. Checking to ensure Oklas was behind her, Prismer lifted the weighty door knocker.

Swiftly, Prismer and Oklas passed the storeroom on their way to her insula.

'Ognitta definitely knows,' he observed.

'If she does, it worked in your favour,' said Prismer, unlocking her door and showing him in. 'She was fond of you before.'

'I knew she was a decent sort.' Oklas flopped on her bench and removed his mask.

'Yes. She was the first to speak to me again after my scumbling.'

'It must have been difficult for you, returning to work in the same place—all the staff knowing what happened.'

Prismer dropped her groceries on the kitchen counter and took off her mask. She couldn't quite recall how she had felt at the time. It was a desiccated pain, something that she had stored away. When acquaintances hurried from her in the corridors, part of her wanted to follow them—to flee her own body.

'I think the hardest part of this is feeling the same inside. Forgetting why people look at you differently.'

'I've had that a lot recently.' Oklas rubbed his hands over his face, following the direction of his gills. He got up and helped her unpack. 'Levent has been astoundingly patient with me. I think realising who I am has embarrassed him. I hate that we can't discuss it openly.' Every quirk of his optic pattern or twitch in his wrist spoke of the irritation Oklas had been suppressing all phase. 'Honestly, I preferred it when I was just a delinquent maskad to him.'

Prismer had used her voice more this past revolution than the whole year prior, but she still could not think of how to respond. 'Give it time,' she said, knowing it sounded too simple. She quickly returned to organising the food on the counter: pickled butterbulbs, trays of shelled grains, clam-drupes, and several differently-coloured vegetables. Cost and nutrition affected Prismer's choice of foods more than presentation or flavour. Oklas accepted her bland cooking, but she knew he was only being polite. His tastes were far more refined than hers.

'I daresay I will miss the attention when it all blows over,' he said, drifting beside the counter. The slight pout around his chin suggested he was feeling ignored. He arched his back in a stretch and continued, 'What are the ministers saying about me?'

'Just because I am in the position to overhear idle gossip, you think I participate in it?' asked Prismer incredulously.

He drew back, evaluating her with his cycloptic gaze. His posture slackened as he realised she was teasing him.

Prismer laughed. 'Word is you eloped with a renowned dance chore-ographer before the Pentarchy could catch you. But Ambassador Begiral insisted he saw a maskad, who is definitely you, busking outside the Trade Centre.' That earned her a chuckle from Oklas, and she felt ridiculously pleased with herself.

'I wonder what instrument the ambassador thinks I play?' he mused, placing his hand on his chin as he looked at the algae panel in the ceiling.

Watching him, Prismer's gills twitched. There were cruel mutterings in the Assembly too. Some said Oklas should have seen this coming. Others expressed glee that the Eruds had put him in his proper place. Those sen-timents she would not relay to him.

'What about you, Pir?' he asked. 'Did you have any guesses as to what had become of Oklas Sayve?'

She paused in front of her small pantry cupboard, the jar in her hand hovering above the second shelf. 'I liked to think he sailed into the rising sun, looking for adventures somewhere better.'

The edges of Oklas's face tautened, and his brow raised. He was beam-ing at her. 'I like it. Of course, I'd have to find someone to run the Emis-rian for me while I'm gone—someone responsible.'

'Of course.'

He went quiet for a moment—folding his arms over the counter—then asked, 'Where would you sail off to?'

She closed the cupboard. 'I don't know if I could leave Apidecca now. It's safe here. No other city has so large a maskad community.'

Oklas's face blanked, and Prismer worried her answer had disap-pointed him. Why did the truth often feel like a poison, rather than the tonic she knew it to be?

He laid a hand on her shoulder. 'You seem tired.'

'I will rest after I've fetched a spare mattress and prepared our food.'

'Leave the cooking to me—come.' He returned to the living room bench and patted the spot next to him.

Against her better judgement, Prismer followed him. Maybe she was allowed to stop and enjoy herself even while things were imperfect. She sat down, noting that someday she would buy a softer couch, something long enough to recline on. 'The Assembly is dull without you,' she told Oklas, surprising even herself with the confession. 'The presentations all run on time with fewer interruptions, and I don't have to call your office for the latest changes to your schedule.'

'At least you're seeing more of me after hours,' he said, tugging at her headscarf and loosening the knot. Prismer gave his hand a reproving tap, then sighed and leaned over until their shoulders touched. Oklas rested his head against hers. It was comfortingly warm.

They sat like that for some time before he drew back and said, 'You don't like the predictable life nearly as much as you think you do.'

'And you can look after yourself rather well when you have to.'

'No, no. Please take pity on this hapless wanderer.' Laughing, he raised his hands defensively. 'That reminds me, I brought something I'd like you to keep for me—if you don't mind.'

'Let's see it, then.'

Oklas fetched his rucksack from the table and opened it. 'I have been keeping these stacked in boxes in my insula. After last segeind, I'd feel better knowing they were here.'

He passed her a thick folder filled with loose pages. Tucked between the partitions were handwritten letters and unframed captures of a polished city with snow-capped mountains. Only when she came upon captures of Emis Rindar and a bright-faced juvenile did Prismer realise the significance of the contents.

'These are all I have left from my old life,' explained Oklas, picking up one of the letters. 'I've scanned them all onto my mitter, but they have no place in Kosta's insula. If anyone were to break in and find them—'

'Oh. I don't know, Oklas,' said Prismer, clasping her hands together. 'It's a big responsibility.'

'I trust you.'

'What if my insula flooded?'

'What if mine were to go up in flames?' he countered before adding gently, 'Anything can happen, but the staff quarters are secure, and you look after your belongings far better than I do mine.'

'Alright,' she relented. 'I think I know of a place to put them.'

Prismer led him through to her bedroom. The warm light from the brackets neutralised the blue of her walls. Oklas looked from Prismer's laundry basket to the few blankets and clothes overlapping her bedframe, then to the jars of herbs on her side table. Prismer opened her narrow wardrobe. On the top shelf was a row of her journals and maps. She pushed them across to make space for Oklas's folder. Was this really all they had left him with? She supposed he might keep some of his belongings at the Industrial Park base, but they could be lost or damaged if the Ardedrians needed to clear the laboratory at short notice.

Since Oklas had told her about his search for a new project, Prismer couldn't stop thinking about a particular phenomenon she had always wanted to research. Her lack of scientific training made it difficult to discern whether it was even worth considering. If Oklas had already decided on something, she could forget about it.

'Have you settled on a project at the lab yet?' she asked him, twisting the key in the wardrobe lock.

'No,' he replied with a meandering glance in her direction. 'I have some in reserve, but I'll only use them if I can't come up with...' His eye narrowed. 'You've thought of something, haven't you?'

Years of serving Minister Sayve had taught Prismer how to facilitate his agile mind as it darted to unexpected places; she hoped he would bear with her now. As it turned out, presenting other people's ideas wasn't nearly as stressful as sharing her own. 'Don't get too excited. Either everyone has already thought of it, or it's something altogether impossible.'

'That's what your employers would have you believe,' said Oklas sadly. 'Never doubt the value of your insights.'

She saw something of the patient, encouraging teacher in him, and it calmed her. 'Um. Last phase, you mentioned resyn shortages,' Prismer began, 'how we cannot predict where we may find the next reservoir because we don't know what process causes the formation of resyn.' She took a deep breath. 'I was wondering, has anyone ever taken soil samples from the deposits?'

'We understand the stratigraphy of the underground basins,' said Oklas. 'They usually rest on layers of clay or impermeable rock.'

'Have any fungi been found in the soil above the basins?'

Oklas's eye widened. 'I haven't come across such research. We understand resyn as a naturally-occurring chemical element, but you think there's a connection to organic matter?'

Prismer sat on the edge of her bed and nodded. 'Elder Caja knew her plants and fungi. She understood resyn too—though she couldn't often access it. She always said it was not a mineral fuel but a living substance. I remember her comparing it to the mycorrhizae that connect the root systems of trees in a forest. Like a forest, a resyn basin acts like a single, giant organism.' Prismer pointed to her back wall, where the caves began. 'I've seen strange colours in the rocks verging the empty basin under the Chambers. A fungus in the soil may have produced the resyn.'

Oklas began pacing her room, invigorated. 'Now that's an intriguing hypothesis. We can cultivate fungi.'

'Yes,' said Prismer, standing up, 'I could fetch you some samples to study.'

'If we find a way to produce resyn in a controlled environment,' said Oklas, 'we could eventually encourage the emergence of new resyn basins.'

It was good to see the visionary in him reemerge. Prismer had forgotten how to dream on that scale. But she could start with the options available to her. 'The Apideccan basin is dormant, but perhaps the samples can show us why that is?'

'We will also need samples from other basins, especially active ones.'

'But there isn't another basin anywhere on this coastline.'

'Don't worry,' said Oklas, 'I'll make a plan. I have my sponsors' backing.' He came back to himself with a laugh and embraced Prismer, catching her off-guard. 'Once again, I am in your debt, Pir. It is deeply unfair that after having so much at my disposal for so long, I now have nothing to offer you.'

'You've done more than you know.' She brushed his shoulder and pulled back to face him. 'We have a saying on Inclatia: "Those who gather around a bonfire never grow cold". For the longest time, I chose to grow cold, to feel nothing at all, but I didn't see what it was costing me. Before you sent Dy Erla to me, I'd almost forgotten what it was like to care about anything. You and Ilu gave me a purpose—made me feel whole.'

Oklas took her hands in his. 'We won't let you drift that far again. It does hurt to care, but please, for your own sake, don't stop.'

A short while later, ambient instrumental music played through a sound cone connected to Prismer's mitter. She had not shared her favourite music channels with anyone in years. Oklas proved his emerging talent for cooking with a stir-fried meal. He then washed their bowls and feeding tongs, and Prismer packed them away.

Perhaps she had been wrong to think Adecai concerned Aerself only with those who lived in villas and temples under vast skies. It seemed knyads felt their creator's presence most keenly in the forgotten depths of this world. There was a change in the wind, a promise of better things to come, and Prismer was a part of it.

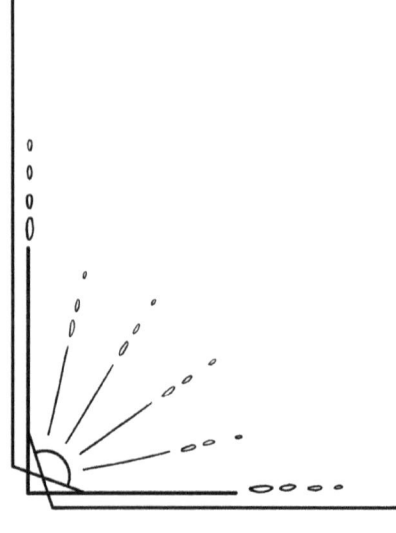

# APPENDIX

# I. THE ORIGINS OF KNYADKIND

Knyadrea is named after the sentient species inhabiting the moon, knyads. The exact nature of their origins is a mystery. On certain shorelines, they arrive with the tide in the form of fist-sized polyps, resembling corals. They rapidly develop, assuming a complex bipedal form within a few revolutions. Some believe divine intervention to be the source of their development. Others believe an undiscovered natural process in the deepest regions of the sea triggers genetic modification in ordinary corals. Knyads have little control over their populations, as they cannot sexually reproduce.

# II. LIFE CYCLES

## TIDELING POLYP

0–3 revolutions. An embryonic state. Polyps are gathered by trained carers and taken to underwater nurseries at sheltered parts of the coast. Here, they can filter feed and grow. Often their adult colouring is influenced by sea conditions from this period of their lives.

## TIDELING

3 revolutions–5 years old. When mobile and alert, tidelings start learning to speak in a simple underwater dialect and understand the land-based language, "Collective". The harvesting ceremony marks their official departure from the water and usually occurs within their first year. Upon harvesting, they are physically at a pre-adolescent stage of development. In their first 4 to 5 years on land, tidelings' markings and features frequently change as they settle into their bodies. They may also start exhibiting features that could be described as masculine or feminine, though they lack distinct secondary sexual characteristics. While it seems they can exert some influence over their development, it is unclear how much control they have over their final appearance. Tidelings are accommodated in dormitories with those of a similar age (their harvestmates) where, in most developed clans, they receive a foundational education.

JUVENILE

>5–25 years old. At 5 years old, they have reached their adult height, though their brains continue to develop for another two decades. As such, younger juveniles often express themselves in an emotionally raw way. They spend the next 20 years maturing: learning life skills, acquiring specialised knowledge, and gaining career experience.

ADULT

>25 years old onwards. The average life expectancy of a knyad in a developed clan is 120 years old.

## III. GENDER IN KNYADS

At harvesting, a tideling's gender is not clear and they all use standard pronouns. As they grow, many come to identify as either male (andrid) or female (gynid) and will likely adopt the matching pronouns. When meeting a stranger, it is considered polite to refer to aer using standard pronouns, which signify the personhood of all knyads. Introductions are often accompanied by a knyad's preferred pronouns.

AE, AER, AERSELF

>standard pronouns.

HE, HIM, HIMSELF

>andrid pronouns.

SHE, HER, HERSELF

>gynid pronouns.

## IV. SOCIAL STRATIFICATION

A worldwide social stratification system heavily favours ancient clans who have harvested tidelings from their waters for many generations. These clans are usually wealthy and powerful. All knyads are given first and sometimes second names. Clan names become important in cities where knyads from different places congregate.

PENTARCHY

The first 5 clans. From each of these, a sovereign or Erud is selected. Collectively, the Eruds govern the whole of Knyadrea as the "Erudean Pentarchy".

PRAEMOR

Established, influential clans, many of whom emerged soon after the Pentarchy. The term also includes Pentarchic clans (all Pentarchic clans are Praemor but not all Praemor clans belong to the Pentarchy).

ORTA

Developing clans that often provide the Praemor with services or raw materials. Many were founded by the Praemor.

UNCLASSIFIED

Relatively new tideling harvesting sites, not formally recognised as clans by the Erudean Pentarchy. Many lack sponsorship and usually have few resources to offer besides physical labour.

# V. UNITS OF TIME

SEGMENT

A period of 24 hours. The sun's position in the sky does not noticeably change over this period (unless you are in a sunrise or sunset segment).

PHASE

A 6 segment period.

REVOLUTION

A period of 5 phases, the time it takes for Knyadrea to orbit Planet Axis. In this period, every part of Knyadrea experiences one lunar day and one lunar night.

A YEAR

14 revolutions.

In summary, there are 6 segments in a phase, 5 phases in a revolution, and 14 revolutions in a year.

TODAY

This segment of a lunar day.

TONIGHT

This segment of a lunar night.

LIGHT CONDITIONS IN APIDECCA THROUGHOUT THE REVOLUTION:

An ancient equatorial city, Apidecca sets a standard time that is used across the moon. The first segment of a new revolution signals the start of the lunar day. The 2nd phase is light. The sun begins to set by the middle of the 3rd phase. The lunar night begins and the 4th phase is dark. By the end of the 5th and last phase of the revolution, the city begins to transition into dawn.

SEGERE

Equivalent of 1 am - 9am (1st - 9th segere)

MEDIAN

Equivalent of 10am - 3pm (1st - 6th median)

SEGEIND

Equivalent of 4pm - 12am (1st - 9th segeind)

EXAMPLE OF STATING THE TIME

4th median (4th hour of the median period, the equivalent of 1pm).

# VI. UNITS OF MEASUREMENT

DEGET

A small unit of length based on the average knyad's distal phalanx.

ALKAR

The length of the average knyad's forearm.

LENGTH
5.7 alkar, the height of the average knyad.

LEAGUE
2500 lengths, applicable to land and sea.

MINAH
The equivalent of 500 grams.

MILLITRU
Mililitre.

LITRU
Litre.

## VII. ANIMALS AND PLANTS

AFTILL
Bulky but gentle herbivore with impressive, ornamental horns. A
beast of burden.

BEROLI
Herb with calming properties.

BALSAMENTH
Refreshing herb that can ease nausea.

CANID
Small to medium omnivore with a long snout and cloven hooves.
Easily domesticated and trained.

CRUTTLEFIEND
Mollusc with toxic spurs.

CÚTALPUR
a large tree with furry, silver leaves.

GHIJER
Fierce carnivore with a patterned coat.

GLASSFOLIA
Plant with lacy, transparent leaves.

ICE RIBBONS
The common name for "vittas glacies". Aquatic plants that grow in waterfalls.

IODREM
Edible aquatic plant.

JAYSTRIKE
Woody-stemmed plant with small, teal flowers. Narcotic properties.

LAGOON EEL
Long-bodied fish found in freshwater and saltwater estuaries. A delicacy.

LAMINIRI FROND
Edible aquatic plant.

PALLISK
Edible aquatic plant.

PEGWING
Tiny, cave-dwelling omnivore with leathery wings. Often kept as a pet.

POKMATI
Dainty, one-eyed cephalopod.

PREDE
Cliff-dwelling seabird.

RED BRISTLER
Invertebrate with a radial body pattern.

REDLINT
Bush with fine leaves that makes a sharp, floral tea.

SPINDLEMITE
Insect with six legs and pincers.

SPINY BRIMMER
Salt-water fish with silvery scales and pronounced spines.

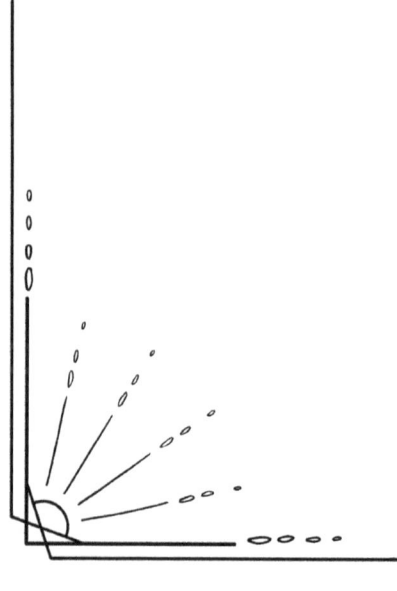

# GLOSSARY

## A

ADECAI
  The most widely-recognised deity on Knyadrea.

ANDRID
  Denotes someone who identifies as male.

ANNOUNCER
  Microphone.

AQUASKIN
  Form-fitting swimwear.

ARDEDRIAN FRONT
  An insurgent group.

AUTOMATON
  A mobile mechanical entity with a system that supports castware.
  Designed to perform mundane tasks.

## B

BIRA
  A light alcoholic beverage

## C

CASTER
  Those who write and edit the casting language systems that run
  technology.

CASTING PLATFORM
  Any device that can support castware.

COLLECTIVE
  Land-based language spoken across Knyadrea.

### Convecorpra

A creature that is similar in function to an automaton but made of natural materials and powered by resyncraft.

### Cybernetic implants

Prostheses that restore some functionality to damaged limbs or organs. Some also have cosmetic applications.

## D

### Dahn

A sport that is part obstacle course, part puzzle. Some of the manoeuvres are derived from the Rhestian martial art, Edfhan.

## E

### Elementary

A basic language system of sounds and hand signals. Used almost exclusively underwater.

### Enforcers

Militarised units operating as city law enforcement.

### Erudean Pentarchy

A ruling council of five sovereigns, known as Eruds, who are selected from the Pentarchic clans.

## F

### Fulver

A tunic often worn by maskads, covering the neck, arms, and hips. The term is derived from "full cover".

### Furtim

A small, elite special operations team who guard the Erudean Pentarchy. Selected from the Enforcer ranks, each Furto gives up aer clan name and is hence known as Furto (First Name). They work closely with the Eruds to whom they are assigned.

## G

GENERAL ASSEMBLY

A gathering of politicians from around the moon who operate in Apidecca and other major cities. They consist of ambassadors and ministers from Praemor and a few upper-Orta clans. Ambassadors represent their peers and governors before the Eruds. Ministers implement the Erudean Pentarchy's policies, running Apidecca and other major cities around the moon.

GYNID

Denotes someone who identifies as female.

## H

HARVEST

When tidelings first leave the water to live on land.

HARVESTMATE

Knyads raised alongside one another.

HOLOGRAM

A projected 2-D or 3-D display of captures (still images) and reels.

## J

JUVENILE

A knyad between 5 and 25 years old.

## K

KAHV

An energising hot drink brewed from a bean.

KNYAD

The semi-aquatic sentient beings inhabiting Knyadrea.

KYR

Sir or Madam.

# M

Maskad
Social outcasts who must wear masks in public. Presumed to suffer from deformities. A secretive subclass of knyad.

Mitter (Transmittal Inset)
A universal identifier and a miniature casting platform essential to city life. Equipped with the ability to connect to some devices.

# O

Optic pattern
A ring-shaped protective membrane. It expands or contracts to control the amount of light reaching the cycloptic pupil at the centre of a maskad's face.

Orta
The working and middle classes.

# P

Peer
A title conferred on those who were discovered as polyps under special environmental conditions. Some take an active role in running their clans, working alongside local governors. Others are merely figureheads. Though regional leaders manage their clan's affairs, they still come under the authority of the Erudean Pentarchy.

Phase
6 segments (see Appendix, Units of Time).

Polymatter
A non-biodegradable substance that is used in moderation. Production was severely restricted after it was discovered that polymatter pollution at sea negatively impacted knyad populations.

Polyp
The coral-like embryonic form of a knyad.

Praemor
The upperclass.

PROJECTOR
Hologram generators.

PUMP FLASK
An eating utensil used by maskads, along with feeding tongs and pitchers.

## R

RESYN
A naturally-occurring substance found in subterranean deposits on Knyadrea. Though lauded as a clean fuel, it is uncommon. It is believed to have supernatural properties.

RESYNCRAFT
Knyads gifted with the ability to access the supernatural properties of resyn.

REVOLUTION
5 phases (see Appendix, Units of Time).

## S

SCUMBLING
A transformative resyncraft technique that reduces a knyad's facial features to a large cycloptic eye and breathing slits. The digestive system, hand structure, and skin are also altered.

SEGMENT OR SEG
A 24 hour period.

SOUND CONE
An apparatus that converts electrical impulses into sound.

SPEECH SYNTHESISER
An implant mostly used by maskads to speak. The neural interface works with vocalisations from the larynx, to help the user form words in a voice that sounds like aer own.

SUBSTANTS OR SUBST TOKENS
The currency of the Pentarchy. Some Praemor clans have their own currency, but substants are the most widely used currency across the moon.

STANDARD
Universal pronouns (ae, aer) that apply to all knyads. Some use these exclusively.

STRATUM
A social class in knyad society (see Appendix, Social Stratification).

SYNTH-SPEECH
Artificially-generated speech.

## T

TENDRILS
Thread-like structures that grow from a knyad's head. As with feathers, barbs extend from a central shaft, only the shaft is thinner and more flexible than most quills. They naturally do not grow to a length beyond 10 degets (see Appendix, Units of Measurement).

TIDELING
A knyad between 3 revolutions and 5 years old.

TOWAYE
Two-way communicator used by the Ardedrians.

TRUNCUS
Large, root-based convecorpora.

## U

UNCLASSIFIED
The underclass.

## V

VISOR
A headset that overlays the user's natural environment with an interface connected to aer mitter.

## X

XYLEMFIBRE
A genetically-modified, woody substance that has largely replaced polymatter. In a laboratory, its growth is directed to follow castware instructions. This way, it can rapidly create a variety of 3-D forms.

## COLLOQUIALISMS

BACA
> A term of endearment often but not always applied to someone younger than the speaker. The meaning, "bead" could be an exaggeration of the smallness of tideling polyps.

BLARNE-HEADED
> Determined in an admirable but exasperating way. A Blarne is a resilient but obstinate creature known for surviving falls and impacts to the skull.

FLOT
> Derived from "flotsam-born". An insult often hurled at misbehaving tidelings or juveniles.

FOZNIT
> An expression of discomfort, usually caused by cold. Also a name for shrimp-like creatures that swarm under the ice in the northern reaches of the moon.

GRIKE
> An expletive.

LEAVE THE SHALLOWS
> Taking a risk.

PEERS AND MOONS
> An irreverent expression often uttered in shock or disbelief.

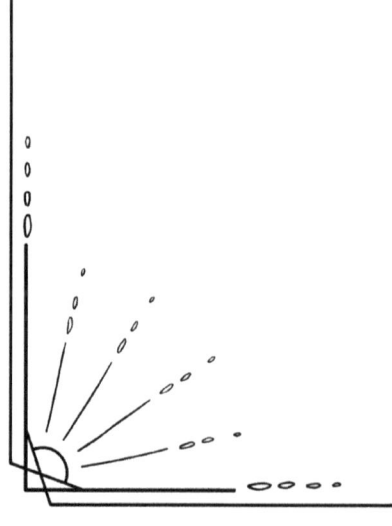

# ACKNOWLEDGEMENTS

Though this is an indie title, I could not have taken *Far Removed* from concept to publication without a team. My characters acted as a constant reminder that we are not meant to be isolated, even when we think it is what we want.

Jonathan Oliver, my copy editor, brought clarity to a draft that had spent years percolating first in my mind, then in a Word document. The chapters are all better structured for his professional touch. Proofreader Laura Soppelsa refined my prose and helped me make my writing style more consistent and distinct. Though I am an illustrator by profession, formatting a book is a different kind of art. I am glad to have employed the specialised skills of Phillip Gessert, my typesetter. Reluctant to go near social media while drafting, I dared to set up an online presence at the editing stage, and I'm so glad I did. There are many indie clans within the wider writing community, and I am grateful to Lydia Russell and Chesney Infalt for providing a way in. At present, I am producing an audiobook with the help of Kevin Stillwell at Lantern Audio. Narrators Amy Jensen and Christopher Tester deliver soulful and dynamic readings of Prismer's and Oklas's POV chapters.

I must also thank the people who brought me to the point of attempting this project. To my parents and brother: who would have thought my early obsession with picture books would lead us here? You cultivate certainty in me and care for me in tangible ways when my work and creative pursuits become all-consuming. I love you. Lee-Anne, my dear friend, your wit and warmth made some difficult years more tolerable, and you introduced me to the best of the Internet. People need to read your stories. Several special teachers did wonders for my confidence. Mr Coleman, I hope this novel is worth the 17-year wait. I don't want to mislead anyone into thinking this odd work of fiction contains any religious doctrine, but my faith will have left an impression on the themes of *Far*

*Removed*. If there is anything good and worthy in this story, I must credit this to my God, who gives me life and hope.

To you, dear reader, thank you for taking a chance on an unknown writer and an incomplete duology. I am currently drafting the second half of this story and will strive to deliver it to you within the next couple of years. In the meantime, you can check my website for more information about my novelette, *The Tidelings of Dras Sayve*, a prequel to *Far Removed*. Your reviews are greatly appreciated as they help extend a book's reach.

# ABOUT THE AUTHOR

Mountains, sea and urban sprawl: these are as much a part of imaginary worlds as the place where Coe Lansdell lives, at the tip of Africa. Her dogs ensure she is exercised daily. Encounters with birdlife and fynbos on weekends are essential to her creativity. For best results, she should be left to soak in a rock pool at least once a month. Most days, she can be found in her home office, wearing her headphones to drown out the howling southeasterly wind. A textbook illustrator of over a decade, she conceptualised every design in this book. She also works with traditional media, such as acrylics, watercolours and fineliners.

Author Website: https://cblansdell.com

Milton Keynes UK
Ingram Content Group UK Ltd.
UKHW011929070923
428268UK00017B/224/J

9 780639 770390